THEY CAME TOGETHER TO SOLVE A DEADLY MYSTERY—
AND STOP AN INVINCIBLE ENEMY . . .

INDIANA JONES—Whether slogging through steaming jungles, investigating ancient ruins, or chasing grave robbers, the world-renowned archaeologist and adventurer has faced death many times. But he's never confronted anything quite so bizarre as the deadly "aircraft" terrorizing the skies.

WILLARD CROMWELL—The portly, hard-drinking former RFC fighter pilot is known for his quick wit and command of languages. Armed to the teeth, he vows to protect Indy anywhere he goes—from back alleys to the Tibetan mountains.

GALE PARKER—The red-haired Ph.D. just happens to be the daughter of an English witch and is herself an expert in the black arts. Beautiful and daring, she has only one slight problem: taking orders from Indy.

TARKIZ BELEM—A former professional wrestler and bodyguard, the huge, swarthy man was as alert as a cat and eager to work any kind of deal. This time, however, has he sold Indy out?

RENE FOULOIS—The famed WWI fighter-pilot ace had a dozen passports and his own personal arsenal. The darling of the international social set, he would find this mission "most amusing."

The Indiana Jones series
Ask your bookseller for the books you have missed

INDIANA JONES AND THE PERIL AT DELPHI
INDIANA JONES AND THE DANCE OF THE GIANTS
INDIANA JONES AND THE SEVEN VEILS
INDIANA JONES AND THE GENESIS DELUGE
INDIANA JONES AND THE UNICORN'S LEGACY
INDIANA JONES AND THE INTERIOR WORLD
INDIANA JONES AND THE SKY PIRATES

and the

SKY PIRATES

Martin Caidin

BANTAM BOOKS
NEW YORK • TORONTO • LONDON • SYDNEY • AUCKLAND

INDIANA JONES AND THE SKY PIRATES
A Bantam Book / December 1993

Cover art by Drew Struzan.

For information address: Bantam Books.

ISBN 0-553-56192-8

Published simultaneously in the United States and Canada

Bantam Books are published by Bantam Books, a division of Bantam Doubleday Dell Publishing Group, Inc. Its trademark, consisting of the words "Bantam Books" and the portrayal of a rooster, is Registered in U.S. Patent and Trademark Office and in other countries. Marca Registrada. Bantam Books, 1540 Broadway, New York, New York 10036.

PRINTED IN THE UNITED STATES OF AMERICA

RAD 0 9 8 7 6 5 4 3 2 1

™

and the

SKY PIRATES

1

They watched the first train go by, laboring upslope, its wide stack spewing thick black smoke and glowing embers. It was a rolling fortress consisting of, first, an armored car built of inches-thick steel pierced with slits for machine guns, with a revolving turret on top mounted with a 57mm rapid-fire cannon. Then came the roaring locomotive, and trailing that two flatcars built up with metal barricades and sandbags, behind which eight men manning machine guns scanned the heavy growth to each side of the train.

It was a killer train ready for anything, an advance scout meant to assure the safe passage of the second train a thousand yards behind, maintaining the same speed along the southwestern coastal flank of South Africa. The second train held within an armored car a thick safe, triple-locked, bolted to the floor and wrapped with chains. Within the safe was a single bag, triple-lined with waterproof sealskin and thick leather. A bag holding more than a billion dollars of diamonds. Almost a hundred incredible stones, huge, perfectly formed, their destination fortresslike shops within a walled enclave of Amsterdam.

Diamonds were normally shipped directly from Cape Town. At least that's what the mine owners had everyone believe. But they might depart from Port Elizabeth or East London, or farther up the southeastern coast from the ports of Durban or Maputo. Troops of heavily armed soldiers always accompanied such shipments—again, so everyone was led to believe. Often the shipment was "rumored" to be gold, and attacking well-armed gold shipments was an exercise in futility, if not stupidity, because of the defending firepower as well as the bulk and weight of the gold.

The name of the game in diamond shipments was subterfuge. One man could carry on his person a greater value in diamonds than several railcars jammed with gold bars, and Christian Vlotman, the Afrikaner charged with the safe passage of such bounty, always moved in mysterious and deceptive ways.

It was he who had sent the two trains rumbling northward toward Alexander Bay, edging the border of Namibia, what had been in earlier times South-West Africa. Alexander Bay lay at the spillage of the Oranje River. Vlotman had had a deep bay entrance dug long before this moment, and waiting for his train would be a powerful, heavily armed cruiser that would continue the shipment to Amsterdam.

The warship captain would have a long wait, one that would not be rewarded.

As the lead train, its armed guards with trigger fingers at the ready for the slightest interference, came about a turn and began crossing a trestle spanning a rocky riverbed several hundred feet below, a man nestled between boulders on a nearby steep slope twisted a T-handle in his hand. Two hundred pounds of dynamite, wrapped with cables about the thick wooden beams of the trestle, vanished in a blaze of violent light and a massive concussion. Thick beams splintered, tearing away from one another, and even before the glare of the explosion faded away, the trestle began its collapse from the explosion and the weight of the heavy train above. Thunder boomed down the riverbed and rolled between the flanks of the hills, and in a terrible slow-motion sunder the train twisted, rotating and shaking madly. Thin screams sounded above the growing roar of the downward-plunging trestle, pursued by the cars of the train now on their sides, still rolling, spilling bodies haphazardly in the fall.

The earth shook from the blast, shook again from the roiling shock waves, and seemed to heave painfully as the locomotive and the massive armored car smashed against the boulders below. Smoke and dust spewed upward, and then new blasts tore between the hills as the steam boilers exploded.

Well behind the catastrophic eruptions the ground rose and fell, moving the steel rails beneath the second train like writhing spaghetti. The train held, the shock waves passed through, but there was no mistaking the disaster that had taken the forward guard train. Immediately, the engineers slammed on the brakes, sending sparks showering away from steel wheels sliding along steel rails. The chief engineer tugged on the cord that blasted a steam-driven shriek to warn everyone aboard the train that disaster had struck and danger was immediately nearby. Moments later the train stood still, the engine puffing in subdued energy.

Then the guards looking down the tracks behind them saw the trap closing, as a series of fiery blasts ripped apart the railbed over which they had just traveled. Now the train was caught. It could not go forward where there had been a trestle. It could not retreat, for its tracks were gone. It lay pinioned like some ancient dinosaur, its deadly spikes in the form of machine guns and other weapons. But like even the greatest predator it was frozen by its own mass. The guards waited for the attack they knew was imminent.

No bullets; no mortar shells. No bombs. Instead, white smoke poured down from the high ridges inland of the railway. There was nothing to be seen at which they could shoot. Just . . . *smoke?* It made no sense as the smoke, heavier than air, rolled and flowed down the ridges to envelop the entire train.

Men breathed in the smoke that was not smoke. They gasped and struggled, hands clutching at their throats and chests, as the phosgene gas spilled into their noses and mouths and savaged their lungs. The cloying sweetness of new-mown hay was everywhere; the sweet fragrance of choking death as the gas spasmed muscles and nerves. Men fell, convulsed, and died.

Phosgene poison gas in its persistent form dissipates in less than thirty minutes. But the men atop the ridges had no time to waste. Colonel Hans Stumpf spoke calmly but sharply to the men awaiting his commands; each man received the colonel's orders by radio through an earpiece clamped to his head.

"Move out—*now,*" snapped Stumpf. The men rushed from concealment, protected by bodysuit armor they no longer needed, wearing gas masks to fend off any inhalation of residual phosgene. They scrambled down the embankment in well-rehearsed and perfectly executed moves.

Small packages of nitro blew open the heavy doors to the armored car. Inside, submachine guns at the ready, they found eight men in the twisted death agony of asphyxiation. They dragged one body aside, set explosive charges about the safe, and retreated outside. Again a handle was twisted and the muffled roar of an explosion sounded within the armored car. They went back inside immediately, ignoring the smoke boiling out the opened door.

The safe door lay hanging by a single hinge. One man removed a steel box, pried open the cover. Inside, wrapped in velvet bags, lay their quarry. Dazzling, an emperor's ransom and much more in huge diamonds of various shapes and colors. The man kneeling by the safe with a fortune before him seemed transfixed. Not by the diamonds, but by a single cube, three inches on each side, and engraved with strange symbols. A cube of burnished copper-bronze. Quickly he and another man placed the diamonds and the cube in sealed flotation bags. The leader gestured to one man, and the three men started down the hillside. At the water's edge Colonel Stumpf waited for them. He gestured at the flotation bag. "It is all there?" he asked, his usual hard tone pitched higher by concern.

The men removed their gas masks. "Yes, sir. It is all here. Everything from the safe."

"And the, ah, special item?"

A gloved hand patted the bag. "It is here, too."

The colonel managed a trace of a smile, then his lips tightened. "Excellent. Berlin will be pleased. Proceed."

They moved quickly to a large rubber raft concealed in a cove. "It is getting dark," Stumpf remarked aloud, scanning the sky. "Have the men finish with the train. I want everyone aboard their rafts ready to move in twenty minutes."

Along the railroad the men remaining with the train set new explosive and incendiary charges. Everything happened with practiced efficiency, and soon they joined their comrades along the shoreline. Night was falling quickly as Colonel Stumpf scanned the open sea with binoculars.

"Ah!" he called aloud. "I see the blinker light. Move out! Everyone, *move!*"

Four rubber rafts pushed the two miles across the sea to where they saw the dim silhouette of a submarine conning tower. Remaining low in the water, the submarine swallowed the killing team. Stumpf was the last to slip through the waiting hatch. He stopped, turned to look at the train barely visible in the gloom of early night, and jammed his thumb down on a radio transmitter. Huge chunks of train and bodies ripped upward from a series of powerful explosions. In moments the dry brush along the radio line was also ablaze. Stumpf nodded with self-satisfaction, and tossed the transmitter into the water to sink along with the rafts that had been stabbed with knives and were also sinking into dark water. Moments later the submarine was gone.

The rescue train appeared two hours later. Its crew stared in disbelief at the horrifying devastation that greeted them.

The next morning . . .

Seventy-four miles west-southwest of Cape Dernburg, beneath a sky gray with rain squalls, the submarine rose to just beneath the surface. A high radio antenna rose below a balloon released from the conning tower. Two hundred feet high the balloon stopped, tugging at the antenna, holding it taut as a homing signal beamed outward.

A lookout called to Colonel Stumpf. "The aircraft, sir! On the port beam. Very low over the horizon and he is coming directly to us!"

Stumpf brought binoculars to his eyes. They were taking no chances. This would be the Rohrbach Romar of Deutsches Aero Lloyd or they would shoot it to pieces with machine guns and continue their voyage submerged.

The big flying boat engines throbbed unmistakably, the

sound of heavy propellers slightly out of synchronization. It circled the submarine in a low, wide turn, confirming by coded radio signal its identification. Colonel Stumpf turned to the sub captain. "The smoke, sir, if you please?" he requested.

The captain nodded and called out to crewmen on the deck. "Smoke! Two grenades! *Schnell!*"

Two men pulled grenade pins and placed the grenades on the sub deck. Flame hissed and thick smoke boiled out, marking wind drift and velocity. The flying boat turned in the distance for its landing run into the wind. Colonel Stumpf looked with pride at the great high-wing monoplane, so perfect for this mission. Its rugged hull was flat on both fuselage sides above the contoured bottom, and its wings spanned more than a hundred and twenty feet from tip to tip. Three powerful BMW VLuz engines throbbed with a physical force. Those four-bladed wooden propellers, massive and thick, churned a heavy blow all about them. Stumpf knew that von Moreau was flying. He was the best, and to handle this forty-thousand-pound monster on the open sea demanded the highest skill. The Romar settled onto the water, skimming along as it felt gingerly for the surface, then lowering deeper as von Moreau came back on the power. The Romar taxied close to the submarine; close but safe. Deckhands lowered a raft into the water and held it by securing lines.

Three of the men from the attack forces came to the deck, one carrying the flotation bag. Stumpf motioned them to wait for him in the raft. He turned to the captain. "Thank you, Captain Loerzer. Your timing, everything, was splendid." The two men shook hands. Loerzer smiled. "When I think of what this will do for our new Germany . . ." He shook his head, almost overcome with emotion.

Stumpf offered a quick salute and climbed into the raft.

"Go," he snapped. The men paddled steadily, powerfully, to the waiting Romar and climbed aboard as Stumpf turned back to the raft and fired several pistol shots to assure it would sink.

He recognized von Moreau looking back from the cockpit. "Hello, Erhard!" Stumpf shouted. "Waste no time, my friend!"

Von Moreau waved back as he nodded. Moments later deep thunder rolled across the darkened ocean surface. Flares from the submarine arced high overhead, their reflection providing von Moreau with the visibility he required. Well before the flares, drifting beneath their small parachutes, hissed into the sea, the great Rohrbach flying boat was in the air and climbing steadily. Von Moreau leveled off at seven hundred feet and swung into a turn that would keep the airplane at least one hundred miles off the coastline of South Africa. No one would expect a flying boat here at night, and certainly they would never expect a flying machine of any kind to be flying southward, a hundred miles out to sea from Cape Town. Only later would they begin the long journey eastward and then to the northeast.

Stumpf went forward to the flight deck. "How is the fuel situation?" he half shouted to be heard above the engine thunder.

"Excellent!" von Moreau replied. "Without full passengers and with no cargo, the extra tanks will give us a range of more than two thousand miles. We will meet the ship on time, but with plenty of reserve."

Stumpf squeezed his friend's shoulder. "Thank you. Now, I will get some sleep. Call me if anything unusual comes up."

Seventeen hours later . . . "The ship is approximately five miles ahead of us," copilot Franz Gottler said to

Flugkapitän Erhard von Moreau. "Bearing three five two degrees. I have already made contact and the ship is steering into the wind as our marker."

Von Moreau nodded. He stifled a yawn, having been at the controls for most of the past twenty-eight hours. Now he forced himself to again be alert, eased the Romar slightly left of his heading, and gently began to come back on the three engine throttles beneath his right hand. The huge flying boat began its descent, settled perfectly to the ocean where long gentle swells promised a good surface, and threw back a perfect bow wave and water plume as the hull went into the sea. Von Moreau taxied close to the merchant vessel, the airplane fended off from the ship by two lifeboats staffed with sailors working long rubber-tipped poles. A hose snaked down and Romar crewmen quickly started refilling the tanks and the oil reservoirs. Other men passed along sealed containers of hot food and several kegs of dark beer. Finally a note was transferred to von Moreau from the ship's captain.

> "Take off as soon as you are fueled and ready. The moment you are airborne we will file a position report as having recorded the passage overhead of Aero Lloyd Flight 977 on its scheduled commercial run from Lake Victoria, with your machine on time for its run. Congratulations on your visit to the south. All hell has broken loose down there among the dogs. *Hals und Beinbruch!*"

Von Moreau smiled. *Break your neck and a leg.* The captain must have been a pilot to know the final words of airmen just before they took off on their combat missions. He leaned from the cockpit window, saw the captain, and waved. Several minutes later they pushed back from the ship, taxied into takeoff position to accelerate into the wind, and thundered into the air toward the darkening sky. Now von Moreau went for greater altitude. The fewer people who had a close look at the Rohrbach as it closed the distance to Germany, the better. He climbed to fourteen thousand feet, near the limit for the heavy flying boat. He nodded to Gottler in the right seat. "You fly. I will sleep for a while. Wake me for *anything* unusual."

"Yes, sir."

In moments von Moreau was fast asleep. The flying boat thundered northward.

Fourteen hours later, Flugkapitän Erhard von Moreau nodded in satisfaction and tapped the chart of the Mediterranean Sea on his lap. He glanced at his copilot. "We are exactly on schedule," he said with obvious pleasure. "A remarkable flight! Who would have imagined us crossing in the night over Uganda, up through the Sudan and across all of Libya, so smoothly, without a hitch to our progress."

Gottler smiled in return. "I see only water now, sir. What is our exact position?"

Von Moreau held up the chart. "See here? The Libyan coast? When we crossed over El Agheila we were then over Golfo Di Sidra, that took us over the open stretch of the Mediterranean, and right *now,*" he tapped the chart, "we are, um, here. Thirty-five degrees north latitude and eighteen degrees west longitude. Sicily and Italy are dead ahead, and if we hold our present course we will fly over the Strait of Messina, here, then over Livorno and right on home."

Von Moreau had held up the chart for his copilot to see more clearly. Now, his eyes still raised where he folded the chart, he saw clearly through the thick windshield. He lowered the chart slowly, staring into the sky, a look of amazement on his face.

"Franz! Look carefully. Almost dead ahead, thirty degrees above the horizon." Sunlight reflected off something in the sky, a flash of light.

"Sir, it looks like . . . like a zeppelin! But it is *huge*!" Gottler strained to see. "It is very high, Captain, and the reflection is so bright that I—"

"Hold our course and altitude," von Moreau snapped. "I'll use the glasses." He reached down to his right side, to the pouch holding his flight gear, and his hand brought forth powerful binoculars. He adjusted the focus and swore beneath his breath.

"Mein Gott . . ."

"Sir, what is it?" Gottler called to him.

"It has a torpedo shape. I judge it is at least fifteen hundred feet long, but . . ." He was talking now as much to himself as to his copilot. "But that would be at least *twice* as large, or larger, than the biggest zeppelin we have ever built! At first I thought maybe we were seeing the Graf Zeppelin. It has been crossing the Atlantic for more than two years now."

"Captain, we're at fourteen thousand—"

"Yes, yes, *I know*. Whatever that thing is, it is at least at twice our altitude, and the zeppelins do *not* fly that high! Besides—here," he interrupted himself. "I have the controls, Franz. *You* tell me what you see."

Gottler held the binoculars to his eyes. "It is as big as you say, sir. But . . . that is not a fabric covering, like the Graf. That vessel, sir, is metal-covered from stem to stern. And it is thick through the body."

"What else!" von Moreau demanded, wanting desperately to either have confirmation of what he had already seen—or be told his eyes were playing tricks on him.

"Engines, sir. I mean," Gottler stuttered with his disbelief, "*no* engines. I see no signs of engines, and that's impossible. Look, it is tracking at an angle across our flight path. Even though it is much higher, it is flying an intercept course. But how . . . how can it do that without engines?" He lowered the glasses, and studied von Moreau. "Sir, I don't understand—"

"To the devil with understanding! Write down what you see, every detail, understand? Take notes!"

Von Moreau leaned to his right and half turned to look back into the radio compartment. "Stryker!" he shouted to his radioman. "Can you make shortwave contact with Hamburg? Try it at once!"

He turned back to Gottler. "Well? What else?"

"I cannot believe this, Captain, but even at this distance I can see that the vessel has accelerated. It is definitely moving faster, and—Captain! There are several shapes descending from the vessel! Can you see them, sir? They are shining like lights in the sun and . . . I have never seen anything like them. Look, Captain! Their shape! Like . . . like *crescents*. Look how fast they move! And . . . this is incredible, sir! No engines, no propellers!"

Von Moreau grabbed for the binoculars. "Take over," he snapped to Gottler. "Hold course, hold altitude. Stryker! What about that contact with Hamburg?"

Radioman Albert Stryker hurried forward to the cockpit. "Sir, something is blocking all transmissions from and to this aircraft. I can get only static. It is deliberate interference."

"Did you try the alternate systems?"

"Sir, I have tried every frequency we have. Nothing is getting through." Stryker was looking through the windscreen now; he had caught sight of three gleaming crescent-shaped objects curving down from high altitude directly toward them. His mouth gaped.

"What . . . what are those—"

"Back to your radios, Stryker," von Moreau ordered. "Keep trying, anything, everything, but get through."

"Yes, sir. I'll do everything I can." Stryker rushed back to his radio equipment.

"I have never seen anything like this before," von Moreau said to his copilot. "It is amazing. A monstrous torpedo shape, now these crescents that race through the sky—they must be doing four or five hundred miles per hour." He shook his head. "*Something* propels them. But *what*? And where are they from? Who are they? What do they want?" Questions burst from him without answers.

Stryker ran headlong back into the cockpit. "Captain, sir! Those things out there . . ." He pointed with a shaking hand to a gleaming crescent shape that hurtled past them with tremendous speed, curving around effortlessly, magically. The other two machines had taken up position, each off a wingtip of the Romar flying boat.

"They are in contact with us, Captain."

Von Moreau stared at Stryker. "What language, man?"

"Ours, Captain. *German*."

"What do they say, Stryker!"

Stryker swallowed before speaking. "Sir, they order us to land immediately on the sea below, or be destroyed."

Von Moreau ran the insanity of the moment through his mind. The huge shape above. Obviously a flying mother ship of some kind, an airborne aircraft carrier. Impossible in shape and size and performance, but there it was, nevertheless. And now these even more incredible crescents, gleaming, impossibly swift and with no visible means of propulsion. So far advanced over their powerful Romar that they might as well have been in a rowboat. He had no doubt that the threat of destruction was real.

"Tell them we will comply," von Moreau said. Gottler stared at him disbelievingly.

"I cannot do that, sir," Stryker said. "Their orders were for us to begin our descent *immediately*. They also said there was no way for me to return the communication."

Von Moreau had no doubts. Instinct born of flying combat experience, years of controlling great airliners, what he was seeing of such incredible performance: All came together in unquestioned intuition. His right hand began easing back on the throttles to reduce power, the nose lowered, and they were on their way to a landing at sea in the middle of the Mediterranean.

They could not call anyone on their radios, but von Moreau knew they were being tracked on charts in Hamburg and in Berlin, and when they did not make landfall over Catania in Sicily, which lay directly beneath their projected flight path, the alert would be sounded. "Stryker, keep sending out an emergency signal with our position. Send on every frequency we have. I know; the radios are jammed somehow. But something *may* happen. Changing altitude may make a difference. Whatever; do your best."

"Yes, sir."

Von Moreau concentrated on their descent, preparing for the landing. Gottler peered ahead. "There is a low cloud layer moving in from the west, sir," he reported. "There may be fog very soon on the surface."

"I hope so," von Moreau said sourly. "I do not like *any* of this. I feel like a rat in a trap."

"Yes, sir."

Now they were on the water, holding the nose of the flying boat pointed into an increasing wind that pushed the clouds toward them and sent the first wisps of fog swirling about the flying boat. But there was just enough light and visibility for them to see the monstrous vessel that had been far above them also descending, moving directly toward them.

"You know, Franz, when we get out of this madness—*if* we get out of it—and we tell people what we are seeing and what has been happening, nobody, absolutely nobody, will believe a word we say."

"I'm sure, Captain, we don't need to worry. Not with what we are carrying, sir. They won't stop at anything to find us. Berlin won't waste a moment."

Von Moreau studied the dismal weather closing in, the huge shape growing ever larger. "Except that no one knows where we are, and that what we are looking at cannot possibly exist. Other than that, my fine young friend, we haven't a thing to worry about, do we?"

Franz Gottler didn't attempt a reply.

2

He's aged. Good Lord, the years have been heavy on the old man. I never thought I'd see him in a wheelchair. Unless, of course—Professor Henry Jones smiled to himself—*he had a rocket tied to the back of it and went flaming about these hallowed halls.*

Jones feigned a casual acceptance of the approaching presence of Dr. Pencroft. Even in the wheelchair and at the age of seventy, Pencroft still carried with him his aura of authority and domination. He had been Chairman of the Department of Archeology of the University of London for more years than most people could remember, and now, with the years amassing against him, his hair a white shock above eyes gleaming behind thick glasses, he left no doubt that he remained in control of his office. The spectacles seemed to narrow his face even more than the constriction of parchmentlike skin. One expected a frail voice to accompany the body; whoever thought so was taken aback by Pencroft's strength and energy when he spoke. There was never hesitation, never a question of his experience and authority.

Professor Henry Jones—who much preferred his nickname Indiana—held old man Pencroft in great admiration. For his part, Pencroft treated Jones with a dichotomy of approach, seemingly intolerant of Jones for being so much younger and for committing the unforgivable sin of being an American, an interloper from the colonies, as it were. It was all facade, for he much appreciated Jones's enthusiasm and knowledge, his almost reckless willingness to pursue any goal set for him, as Pencroft so long ago had been guilty of the same hard drive. More than once Pencroft had intervened against the bludgeon of university authority as it sought to remove Jones from its staff and send him back across the ocean "where he belonged, along with the crudities and crass manners of the Americans." Outlander Professor Jones might be in ancient and hallowed halls, but he was an outlander with a brilliant mind and an incredible intuition for finding whatever he sought in the secrets of the past. Pencroft would never admit that he thoroughly enjoyed acting as buffer for Jones; it was like watching himself decades past.

Pencroft's manservant stopped the wheelchair precisely six feet from Professor Jones. For long moments neither man spoke. This was Pencroft's way, to take his time when approaching a situation different from any other in the past. Gather his thoughts, consider what was afoot, and speak not a word until he knew what he would say, not just at this moment, but in the exchanges to follow. And certainly, from what Pencroft had been told in a very private conversation, *different* held a meaning he'd never before encountered.

Indeed, Pencroft didn't believe a word of it. Sheer nonsense and balderdash. Frightened men and ghosts and goblins; that sort of rubbish. He'd been flabbergasted when the people from Number 10 Downing Street had come to meet with him, and the more those people talked the more grew his own amazement. Not at their outlandish tale, but that the highest levels of government would even bother with such rot. And he'd told them so in no uncertain terms. Representatives of the Prime Minister or not, he almost accused them of being sodden drunks.

They took it all in stride, which itself was a critical clue for the wily old Pencroft. It was immediately obvious to him that they had already gone through the very thoughts he was experiencing as they spun their outlandish tale. So they were quite serious, after all, and if they'd stepped down from their bureaucratic heights to visit Professor Pencroft, they must be desperate indeed.

Which had finally brought him to seek out Professor Jones. More precisely, Indiana Jones, that ridiculous name the man had attached to himself. He knew that Jones's closest friends had shortened his name to Indy, but Pencroft couldn't quite lower himself to do so. He pushed aside the peripheral nonsense in his head.

"What are you doing now?" he demanded suddenly of Jones. The moment he'd uttered the words he regretted the slip. Jones had too much fun with the thrust-and-parry.

"Unless I am sadly mistaken, sir," Jones cut back, "I am occupying a space in this hallway, as you are. It's a rather bleak place to meet, I would say."

"The devil you say!" Pencroft snapped. He tipped his head to one side. "Listen to me, you troublemaker," he went on with a touch of gnarly affection. "Come to my office. Ten minutes from now and not a moment later."

"I have a class," Indiana Jones said quietly, aware that Pencroft knew his schedule.

"You have *a* class, but you lack class," Pencroft jibed. "Ten minutes." The smile faded. Pencroft coughed with pain, swallowed, and his hand gestured weakly. "I am quite serious, Indiana."

That did it. When Pencroft used that name in public he

was bloody well serious. Jones nodded. "I'll get a substitute," he said. "I'll be there."

"I've already arranged for a substitute," Pencroft went on, pleased with even this diminutive one-upmanship. He waved to his servant to continue on to his office. Jones watched him as they turned down a secondary hallway.

Pencroft's obvious discomfort intrigued Jones. It wasn't like him. In fact, if he didn't know better he might have judged that the old gaffer had been rattled by—by whatever it was that called for breaking into his teaching schedule. In this emporium of education you shot your dog before you interfered with schedules. Something very big was up; that much was clear. But Pencroft hadn't given him so much as a hint. Well, he'd find out soon enough.

Jones went quickly to his own office and strode briskly through the outer waiting room where his secretary, Frances Smythe, held up a stack of telephone messages. He waved them away. "No calls. Nothing, understand?"

The dark-haired woman shook her head. "No, I do not understand. Elucidate, please."

"You sound irritable, Fran."

"I'm confused. By you," she retorted. "I know, I know. Pencroft's office in a few minutes. They called here looking for you. All very mysterious, the way they had the substitute teacher already set up for your class. Care for a cup of tea while you tell me what is going on?"

"I'll take coffee. Lukewarm. No time for a hot mug. Besides," Jones sighed, "I haven't so much as a nudge as to what's going on."

The coffee mug was in his hands almost at once. He never understood how she could do that, have his coffee ready at whatever temperature he requested. He checked to see that he had his glasses with him.

"I do wish you'd get something more appealing than

those black wire rims," Frances sighed. "You look like a mongoose when you wear them in your class."

"It keeps the beautiful young ladies at a proper distance," Jones laughed. He glanced at his watch. "Here." He handed her the coffee mug. "Time to march."

"Good luck."

He stopped in his tracks. "What?"

She was flustered. "Indiana," she said softly, her tone so personal it was intimate. "The last time you were called in by Pencroft in this manner, well, you know, it was that trip to the Amazon, and—"

"Let it drop," Jones said brusquely. He didn't need reminders of the stunning young woman to whom he'd been married only a short time. *My God,* he mused as he walked along the hallway to Pencroft's office. *It's been four years since Deirdre was killed and it still hurts like it was yesterday. . . .*

He put aside everything but what he would hear from Pencroft as he entered the old man's outer office. "Go right in," Sally Strickland told him. Obviously even the secretary here was on edge about something. She hadn't bothered to smile or offer her usual friendly greeting. He stayed with the mood, nodded, and went into Pencroft's office.

"Close the door," Pencroft said unnecessarily. Indy edged the door shut with the heel of his shoe. The old man was testy for a reason, and it seemed to be a signal to Indy: *Watch it; exercise care.* He turned to take measure of the third man in the room.

If there was one word to describe the stranger, Indiana Jones had it immediately: *severity.* Whoever, whatever he was, this man was a true professional. Demeanor, self-confidence, piercing eyes, the cut of the suit, the catlike relaxation while the man remained fully alert, mentally and physically . . . it was all there, and he had even managed to rattle Pencroft's cage of self-assurance.

"Professor Henry Jones," Pencroft said stiffly, "this is Mr. Thomas Treadwell. Mr. Treadwell—"

Treadwell came to his feet in a single gliding motion, right hand extended to grasp Indy's. Once again, Indy was filled with the strength and presence of this man. He spent a few precious seconds absorbing all that he had noticed by removing his glasses from his shirt pocket and cleaning the lenses with his handkerchief.

"Treadwell, is it?" Indy said casually. "Is that your real name, Mr., um . . ." He let it hang.

"It's real enough," Treadwell said. Indy knew from his tone that he had all the proper cards and papers, identification to choke a horse if necessary, to "prove" he was Treadwell.

"Well, I see we've got a cat-and-mouse situation here," Indy said to both men. Then he directed his gaze to Pencroft. "Do I find out where our visitor is from?"

Pencroft nodded. He had only a scratch of information himself and he didn't like it. You could feel and smell *security* in the room. Anyone who regarded Pencroft as simply a doddering old professor was making a mistake of grand proportions. Long before his permanency at the university he had served the British army well, rising to the rank of brigadier through a half-dozen wars, large and small, before retiring from enough wounds to kill several men. Like Indiana Jones he knew when a professional was at hand.

"I won't play any games with you, Professor Jones," Treadwell answered. "I'm military intelligence. Not Scotland Yard, as I'm sure you already deduced on your own. You have certain body language that speaks aloud."

Indy smiled and nodded, waiting.

"For the record, I'm required to impose the highest

level of secrecy on what you're going to be told," Treadwell continued. "I know that you're an American citizen, and I won't go through the formal blather of papers and all that. Your word will suffice for us."

"Wait, wait," Pencroft interrupted. "I'll be hanged if I'll sit here with a parched throat." He pressed a desk buzzer. "Sally, tea. *And* brandy. A good measure of both."

They waited until the tea was poured and mixed with brandy and Pencroft's secretary had departed. Suddenly a radio blared from the outer office. Indy lifted an eyebrow toward Pencroft, and the old man smiled. No one would hear their conversation with the racket outside.

"First," began Treadwell, "I don't expect you to believe what I'm about to tell you."

Twenty minutes later Indy knew the other man was right.

Treadwell related a story more fantastic than anything Indy had ever heard. And he had trailed Indian spirits in South America, crawled through the tomb passageways of the pyramids, faced voodoo doctors and shamans who performed feats all science would consider not incredible, but impossible. He had seen the ghosts of ancient giants at Stonehenge, trod the thin vaporous lines that seemed to separate this world from other dimensions. He had—well, *pay attention,* he commanded himself harshly.

Treadwell gave the details of the ambush and hijacking in South Africa, the use of poison gas, the performance of a paramilitary team that left all the signs of professionals trained to the *nth* degree. A billion dollars' worth of diamonds was the estimate, but Indy's interest flared when Treadwell mentioned an ancient object with some form of symbols engraved on its surface—an object that could not have been created by any terrestrial energy or people if its historical dating were correct. Indy suspended further contemplation as Treadwell went on.

"We know this operation was German. Not only was there a certain Teutonic efficiency involved," Treadwell explained, "but we do keep tabs on how Germany is transforming itself from a beaten nation into a new power. Officially, that part is nonsense, of course, because our leaders still believe in the goodness of men, including the Germans, which," he interjected, "I do *not.* They are too busy beating their plowshares into weapons. They have created an entire new secret service organization. We know that Hermann Göring has been making the rounds of industry. There are all the signs of rearmament."

"The diamonds," Indy broke in. "I imagine this is part of their program to finance a new military force."

Treadwell nodded. "But that's not the way it worked out, Professor Jones." Something in his tone told Indy he'd soon find out why he'd been called in here with all this secrecy mumbo jumbo.

Pencroft gestured. "How did you *confirm* the Germans in all this?"

"Aside from keeping tabs on certain individuals," Treadwell said quickly, "we keep an ongoing record of Germany's movements within, to, and from Africa. They are unabashedly making their move to control most or all of that continent, just as they are doing through their Condor airlines and other groups in South America. I do not wish to get off the track, so to speak, but the more I can impress upon you that we *know* what Germany is doing, the better you may comprehend what follows.

"We know that a certain German airline captain, von Moreau, was flying a Rohrbach commercial flying boat on its regular run between Germany and South Africa. We, ah, obtained the passenger manifest without the knowledge of Aero Lloyd—"

"Skullduggery, is it now," Pencroft offered with a smile.

"Yes, sir. My point is that we checked on a number of the passengers listed on that manifest. They were not on the flying boat. Their names, reservations, passport numbers, everything was in order, except that they never made the flight. Obviously, it was a covert operation of some kind. Also, we worked with the South Africans who went over the wrecked trains. Their chemists, working with us, have identified the type of explosives right down to the factory, the chemical plant, where they were produced. No one else we know of has that very particular chemical substance. Enough small debris was remaining for absolute confirmation."

"There was something else I'd heard about," Indy said carefully.

"You heard about this affair? Before now, I mean?" Treadwell asked sharply.

"Not exactly," Indy said. "But there might be a connection."

"Please, Professor, if you would—?" Treadwell pressed.

"It's no secret between this university," Indy said, "and our associates at the Archeology Division of the South African university, that some sort of incredible find *may* have been discovered deep in one of the diamond mines. They're very sticky about security when it comes to those mines, but what was found was so bizarre that even the mining company people had no choice but to make what they thought were discreet inquiries as to the nature of what they had in their possession. I must alert you to the fact that none of this might have even a grain of truth to it, but in our business, Mr. Treadwell, you never overlook any kind of a lead."

"What, ah, was the nature of this find, Professor Jones?"

"A cube, with markings of a type never seen before."

Pencroft broke in, looking aggrieved. "I hadn't heard any of this, Indiana. You must keep me better informed."

"It may be nothing but balderdash, sir," Indy responded, using one of Pencroft's favorite expressions. "The cube supposedly came from a section of the mine being dug for the first time. It is deep. *Very* deep. The engineers estimate the surrounding quartz is anywhere from a hundred thousand to perhaps several million years old.

"And what," Indy went on softly, "is a cube with cuneiform markings doing in a diamond vein, while mankind was still climbing down from the trees?"

"You're that certain of the age?" Treadwell asked.

"No way!" Indy retorted. "All this is still unconfirmed. Normally it would be discarded as so much errant nonsense. But that cube, if it exists, could be only a thousand years old. Or, as some people in Rome seem to think, *two* thousand years old."

Treadwell showed his confusion. "Rome? Two thousand years old?"

"About the same time as Christ," Pencroft said, a touch of glee in his voice. "You remember him, don't you, Mr. Treadwell? Jehoshua, Jesus, the Savior, by those names and others. As for Rome, I'm certain you know where the Vatican is located."

"That's why," Indy added, "even the slightest thread, the most tenuous possibility that the cube exists, that it *is* a cube, that it *may* have cuneiform inscriptions, that it *might* be two thousand years old, or that *perhaps* it has some connection with Christ, apparently has the highest levels of the Vatican almost frantic with desire to gain possession of this object. *If* it exists, with all the ifs, ands, or buts that I've mentioned to you."

Treadwell sank back in his seat. Finally he looked up, first at Pencroft and then back to Indy. "What you have just told me makes what I still haven't related to you even more incredible."

"This isn't a suspense show," Indy said, impatience in his voice. "Get on with it."

"Yes, yes," Pencroft pushed. "I'm out of tea and brandy and at my age that's more important to me than this conversation that seems to have no end to it." Indy knew the old man was in pain but was concealing it beneath sudden brusqueness.

Treadwell took a deep breath. "The flying boat, that Rohrbach with the diamonds aboard and perhaps this mysterious cube as well, *never made it to Germany.*"

That brought up both Indy and Pencroft, fully attentive. "Don't tell me that someone hijacked the German airliner!" Pencroft said, on the edge of bursting out into laughter.

"What happened?" Indy asked quietly.

"We were *told* what happened," Treadwell said, hesitating.

"Speak up, man!" Pencroft shouted.

"There is one man we talked with," Treadwell said slowly and carefully, "who apparently was a member of the Rohrbach crew. The *only* survivor of an attack on that airplane. He told us they had flown the night through to cross Africa. The pilot kept the airplane high, at fourteen thousand feet, which is about the limit for a Rohrbach with a heavy fuel load. He also spoke about the cold at altitude, and some of the crew having headaches from the lack of oxygen."

"Yes, yes," Pencroft prompted. "Then what?"

"There was a great deal of excitement in the cockpit. He saw the radioman—he remembered him as Stryker, and we've confirmed that, by the way—anyway, Stryker was upset about his radios not working, and then after some more excitement in the cockpit, while they were over what was apparently the center of the Mediterranean, von Moreau started his descent to land on the water."

"You haven't said why he'd do that," Indy said critically. "I don't want this to be a guessing game about engine problems or fuel or whatever. Why did the pilot start down?"

"The crewman—"

"Wait a moment," Pencroft interrupted. "You said one survivor. How'd you get this bloke?"

"A French airliner, flying low over the sea to stay beneath clouds at night, saw a fire beneath them. They didn't know what it was. It could have been a crashed airplane or a ship of some kind. They fired off a radio distress call right away. We were fortunate enough in having a British vessel nearby, and it went promptly to where the French had reported the fire. They found some wreckage in the water, and their searchlights picked out one man clinging to a section of wood. He was injured rather badly. Broken bones, burns, shock. The moment they had attended to him as best they could, the purser asked him if there might be any other survivors, lifeboats; anything. He said no."

"Go on. What *did* he say?" Indy demanded.

Treadwell took a deep breath. "He said they were forced down by some huge vessel in the sky, gleaming, silvery. That it was perhaps a thousand yards in length, very fast—"

"That couldn't be a dirigible," Pencroft murmured. "Nothing of that size—" Indy gestured to Pencroft to let Treadwell continue.

"A lot of what he said seemed to be babbling, and of course he was suffering from his pain and his injuries. But the purser said he was quite adamant about this vessel and its size, that it was very fast, and that several of the crew were amazed to notice that it didn't have any engines."

"That's one hell of a sausage balloon you're describing," Indy said, openly disbelieving.

"*I'm* not describing. I am telling you what we heard from this one man. There's more."

"Go on, go on," Pencroft prodded.

"A number of silvery, or golden, the man wasn't sure, craft separated from the huge ship. They were shaped like scimitars, he said. Or perhaps crescents, or boomerangs. Whatever they were they moved with tremendous speed, whirling about the Rohrbach like it was stuck in mud." Treadwell paused. "And those didn't have any engines, either."

"Why did the airliner land?" Indy asked.

"Apparently there was a radio message from the larger ship telling them to land, or be destroyed. Then the scimitar ships took up close formation with the Rohrbach. They landed on the sea, the bigger vessel came down very low, and what appeared to be humanlike figures lowered from the vessel to the flying boat. They shot up the wings, first, then opened fire on the crew. The two pilots were killed immediately. That's all this man knew. He was hit, and tumbled from the Rohrbach into the water. He had on an inflatable vest, but didn't use it right away. Moments later, he said, the flying boat was burning and then it exploded. He was burned in the explosion, and just managed to get his vest inflated before he passed out."

"What happened with this great machine and the scimitars that fly about without engines?"

"We don't know."

"You're certain this isn't all a fairy tale?" Indy jabbed at Treadwell.

"Professor Jones, there are thirty-two dead men in South Africa, two destroyed trains, and a railway trestle blown to smithereens. The South Africans are frantic with the loss of what they say was a billion dollars worth of gems. A Rohrbach flying boat is destroyed, or if not destroyed, most certainly it and its crew are missing. We have an eyewitness with incredible stories of what he claims to have seen, and you have not heard the hysteria within Germany about the entire affair. And your rumor from South Africa *did* reach the Vatican; the Pope and *his* inner circle are in a dither about the artifact."

"Can I talk with this survivor?" Indy asked aloud.

"*I'd* like to talk to him as well," Treadwell answered, his tone showing clear disappointment. "Unfortunately, he did not live very long. Right now our people in Germany are using their special contacts to determine his identification, if that's still possible. You may imagine the tight security the Germans have thrown up about all this. They're fairly frothing at the mouth."

"There's a point you haven't gone into," Indy said.

"Which is, sir?"

"*Who* were the people in that flying whatchamacallit, or whatever it was? And in those scimitar-shaped machines as well?"

"We don't have the first clue, Professor Jones."

"You realize," Pencroft broke in, "that the machines you have described to us don't exist? That nothing of those descriptions exists, or has been made, by any country known to us?"

"Yes, sir."

An uneasy silence fell between them. Pencroft used the moment to have more tea and brandy brought in by his secretary. Then it was time to get to what Indiana would call the nitty-gritty.

"A few questions, please," Pencroft said abruptly, to bring events back to the fore.

"Of course," Treadwell acknowledged.

"You didn't come to this institution by accident."

"No, sir."

"I suggest you came here specifically to seek out and in some manner enlist the services of Professor Jones?"

"Yes, sir."

"Who sent you?"

Treadwell took a deep breath. "M.I. Two."

Pencroft's brows rose with confirmation of so high a level in the British government. He exchanged glances with Indy, then turned back to Treadwell.

"So now," Pencroft said slowly, "you pursue the services of our good archeology professor."

"Yes, sir."

"That," Indy interjected, "makes as much sense as your sky devils, or sky pirates, or whatever they are—if they even exist. People who've been blasted, burned, shocked, and dumped into the sea are capable of seeing *anything*. But we'll let that go for the moment. Mr. Treadwell, I'm on sabbatical leave from Princeton University—"

"Where you are a professor of Medieval Literature and Studies," Treadwell finished for him.

"You're up on your homework," Indy said with a nod. "Which means your office at least knows how to look up people's names and titles in a university staff telephone book. But to continue. I am now teaching Celtic Archeology. This isn't my first relationship here."

"We threw him out once before," Pencroft chuckled. "He'll tell you he became fed up with overstuffed, overbearing academic versions of our everlasting Colonel Blimp and left here of his own volition. Frankly, he's really quite insufferable, he breaks rules, he dashes off on wild goose chases, but," Pencroft said seriously, "he often manages to return with the golden eggs laid by the geese. Like bringing us the Omphalos of Delphi, for which we had searched for decades, believing it was always linked somehow with Stonehenge. We were right, but getting nowhere. Our misfit colonist here," he nodded at Indy, "did the impossible, broke all the rules, but succeeded in what we thought was really quite impossible."

Treadwell didn't miss a beat. "And Professor Jones has a pattern."

"Oh?" Indy said.

"Yes, sir. He's subject to a disease the Americans call cabin fever. He can take just so much of academia and then he fairly bursts with the urge to get out in the field and rummage about antiquities, whether in deserts or mountain regions or jungles. I apologize, sir," he said to Indy directly, "if there is any seeming lack of consideration for the loss of your wife some years ago. None was intended."

"None was taken," Indy replied coolly. "I point out to you that my remaining time here is limited. I plan to return to Princeton or perhaps some other university that is involved in field missions."

"I don't believe you'll be doing that," Treadwell said.

"You fascinate me, Mr. Treadwell. Very few people have ever judged my future with such conviction."

Treadwell laughed. "No such control was intimated, sir. To use a favorite expression from your side of the ocean, Professor Jones, I believe we have an offer for you that you simply cannot refuse."

He leaned forward in his seat, and the other two men in the room knew he was coming down to the heart of the matter.

"We desire that Professor Jones undertake to learn the identity of the unknown aerial vehicles we have discussed. To find out whatever is possible about them, identify their source. We are convinced there is more to this affair than the ravings of an airliner crewman in shock. For reasons that will be readily apparent, we also desire that Professor

Jones continue a very public association with the University of London, so that he will arouse no special interest, no matter where he may go in the world for his, ah, archeological digs. He would, of course, be working for us, but completely *sub rosa.*"

"Do you have any concept of the financial burden you're talking about?" Pencroft broke in. "The university board of governors would never approve of—"

"No one outside this room is to know of our relationship," Treadwell said, a bit too sharply. He was all business now. "The only exceptions would be those Professor Jones at his own discretion chooses to inform. As for the costs, all will be taken care of. It won't cost this establishment so much as a tuppence."

"That's different," Pencroft said with open wonder.

"You said there was a gift," Indy reminded Treadwell. "You apparently have something very special up your sleeve."

"Oh, I do," Treadwell smiled. "It's the offer you can't refuse. There will be other teams on this mission, of course—men with other skills and connections. But if you are the first to find that cube, or whatever is the artifact rumored to have been with the diamonds—it's yours to keep."

"You mean it is *ours*!" Pencroft burst out.

"That is your affair, sir. My point is that the Crown will relinquish all claim to the object." Treadwell had almost a Cheshire cat smile on his face. "Professor Jones cannot turn his back on something that might have a direct relationship with Christ. That is strictly an unfounded supposition about the cube, of course, and I am out of my depth as to what else it might be. But I do not need to know more. My interest is specific and unambiguous."

Treadwell rose to his feet to face Indy. "Your answer, sir?"

Indy extended his hand. Treadwell took it firmly to end the questions. "Done," Indy said.

Treadwell turned to Pencroft. "Is there anything you wish to add or to ask, Professor?"

Pencroft pondered the issue. Then he shook his head slowly. "The entire affair seems quite mad, Mr. Treadwell. My interest, however, also lies in that area you described as an offer that could not be refused. Such a find is beyond all monetary consideration. I also am agreed."

"Thank you, sir."

Treadwell opened his briefcase and handed a sealed packet to Indy. "Everything you need is in there, including protected telephone numbers and a schedule of times you can reach me."

Indy took the packet. "I'm not sure if I should thank you for all this," he said.

Treadwell didn't smile. "Only time will tell, sir."

Suddenly, Pencroft began to cough harshly. He pulled forth a handkerchief with shaking hands and brought it to his mouth. Treadwell and Indy glanced at one another; by trading nods, they agreed to wait until the old man could catch his breath. Finally Pencroft dabbed at his watery eyes and took a deep lungful of air.

"You two," he wagged an accusing finger at them, "sound like a bunch of old women at a tea and crumpets party, the way you are gaggling at each other. Get out of my sight and let this school get back to its function of illuminating young minds!"

Treadwell and Indy left the room together. Without another word between them they went their separate ways in the corridor, Treadwell departing the university through the main entrance, Indy returning to his office. He waited fifteen minutes, finished the coffee Frances Smythe had waiting for him, closed his briefcase, and started for the exit.

Smythe stopped him with a piercing look. "It must have been quite a session for you not to say a word to me," she said with a touch of criticism to her voice.

Damn, she's right, Indy thought. *Saying nothing is worse than any kind of story.* He turned to her. "Some sort of government nonsense," he said airily.

"Like I'm hearing right now," she countered.

"You're too smart for your own good," he chided her in a compliment she couldn't miss.

"I'll ignore the poisoned blessings." She smiled. "You have forgotten, Professor, to give me whatever story it is you wish people to hear that will explain your continued absence from your classes."

He started to offer a spurious tale, stopped, started again, and thought better of story-telling to this woman. "Make up what sounds best," he directed her, "and leave a memo on my desk as to what it is I'm supposed to be doing."

"You *are* devious," she remarked.

"Enough, Sherlock. Just kindly attend to whatever fabrication passes through that lovely brain of yours."

"Ta-ta!" she called as he left.

Twenty minutes later he slipped into the Wild Boar Pub. Indy stood at the bar, ordered an ale, picked up his mug, and wandered slowly toward a back door. With no one paying attention to him, he slipped through the door to climb a narrow winding stairs to the private room that was his destination.

Thomas Treadwell greeted him with a wave of his own half-finished mug of ale. Indy slipped into an easy chair. "I really hate doing this to the old man, you know," he said abruptly.

"It's necessary," came the immediate response. "The whole purpose of that meeting at the university was to keep Pencroft involved in a position of authority, but not to let him know *too* much. At his age he could easily slip and give away the game. Besides, right now he feels completely justified in springing you free of your duties."

"I know," Indy sighed. "Do we bring him up to snuff before any more meetings?"

Treadwell shook his head. "We can't risk it. Professor Pencroft not only *appears* to be the soul of innocence, he *is,* and that's what we need from him."

Indy laughed without humor. "He'd kill me with his own two hands if he knew I was partly responsible for that blamed cube."

"You're being too hard on yourself. That was a masterful job you did with your cuneiform markings. Good Lord, Indy, that artifact is as real as anything from the past I've ever seen."

"I know, I know," Indy broke in. "When does the real word get out?"

"All in good time. Right now whoever it was that forced down the flying boat, the whole bloody lot you already know about, is still convinced the artifact is, or may be, real. That means they'll try to unlock its secrets. Failing that, as only you and I know they will, they'll try to move it to a high-paying buyer. So long as that pattern is followed, Indy, it remains our very best opportunity to start identifying people."

Indy raised an eyebrow. "That's your problem, Thomas. All that cloak-and-dagger dashing about isn't my game."

"But you're very good at it. Your background suits the situation perfectly, you know. And we *do* need somebody willing to become a target for this gang, whoever they are. You'll have to keep on the alert, just like any M.I. operative."

"I'll ignore your lumping me with spies and assassins, if you don't mind," Indy retorted. Then, in a more serious tone, "Do we have anything more on those saucer things?

I'm not even certain as to how to describe them. I've heard saucers, discs, crescents, a whole porridge of names."

"Tell me, Indy, what do you think of them?"

"Assuming that they're real and they perform as we've been told?"

"Yes."

"Well, all I can say is that they're really remarkable."

"Do I detect a note of subtle evasion there, Indy?"

"Not at all. Listen, Thomas, not being fully informed doesn't justify drawing conclusions based on a *lack* of data. You can go dead wrong in a hurry that way."

"I'd like you to remember the name of an American you'll be meeting up with soon," Treadwell said abruptly.

"What's that got to do with those machines?"

"More than you may think. The name is Harry Henshaw. He's a colonel in your military flying force. Brilliant man, really. He's in technical intelligence. That means he's everything from a test pilot to an investigator of anything and everything that flies. He's part of our team. Hands across the sea, that sort of thing. And right now he is turning heaven and earth upside down trying to find anything and everything in the present, and in the past, that may relate to disc shapes in flight."

"What's his opinion?"

"The things are real. They fly as we've heard. Blistering speed and all that."

Treadwell went infuriatingly silent. "*And?*" Indy pressed. "Are they, in his opinion, *ours*, or," he looked upward, "theirs? Whoever and whatever they may be."

"Too early for conclusions, but he leans to a huge leap forward in aerodynamics, not something flitting about in space."

"Why?"

"You'd better find out from Henshaw directly. By the

by, he's given me a message for you. One with which I concur completely, I might add."

"Sounds serious."

"It *is,*" Treadwell said. "Henshaw said for you to watch your step and to keep your eyes open. No matter how smart we think we've been, the people we're trying to identify know more about us than I like."

Indy's eyes narrowed. "How?"

"Henshaw suspects—no; he's convinced there's a traitor in our little group. Which means as well, Indy, that you would be wise not to let your own people know too much of what we've discussed."

"My people are fine," Indy said defensively.

"I hope so." Treadwell was unruffled by Indy's sudden change in mood. "I dearly hope so. But I'll tell you this much from my own experience. You will *always* be surprised in this game."

3

Willard Cromwell lifted the bourbon bottle in a slow, deliberate motion to his lips, neatly surrounding the mouth of the bottle with his own, and took a long, gurgling swallow. He brought down the bottle slowly, smacked his lips, belched, and with the ease of long practice replaced the cork. His powerful hand banged the bottle on the table of the living room in the isolated farmhouse Indy had rented for a month. They felt they were in the middle of nowhere, the fields and farmhouse nestled along the banks of the Maquoketa River in eastern Iowa. But for the moment his companions seemed fascinated with Cromwell's every move.

Cromwell had flown as a squadron commander in Britain's Royal Flying Corps against the best of the Kaiser's sharpshooters in their Albatross and Fokker and Rumpler machines. Flying the wicked-handling Sopwith Camel, he'd twisted and whirled through enough battles to send sixteen of Germany's finest spinning earthward, giving up their lives for the Fatherland in the Great War raging across the continent. Then some snot-nosed young replacement, terrified by his first taste of combat and watching his comrades burning to death as their planes whirled crazily earthward, had panicked in the midst of battle and flown wildly through a huge dogfight. Cromwell saw him coming, knew he stood no danger from another Sopwith, but could hardly have imagined that the fear-frozen young man would in desperation have squeezed the triggers of his Vickers machine guns. And kept down the trigger handles, spewing fragments of death in all directions, friend or foe notwithstanding. What the Germans could not do, a spindling youth in terror managed quite well, placing three of his bullets into the legs and one arm of Willard Cromwell.

He made it back to his home field only moments before he passed out from loss of blood. Four months in hospital, every single day of that time cursing the unknown blithering idiot who'd brought him down. Cromwell didn't know if that madman survived the battle. "Bloody good luck if he didn't, because I'd like to finish him off with my bare hands," he snarled at his visiting fellow pilots.

Cromwell earned good-natured laughter for his toothy profanity, but he accepted the laughter along with the whiskey smuggled into hospital to him. Then he could walk again, a bit stiffly, and he had a magnificent long burn scar on his arm from the incendiary bullet that had nearly done him in. He insisted on returning to the fight, but fighters were out. "You're rather scrunged up, you know," his squadron commander told him. "A bit sticky trying to match the young men in maneuvering, eh? But I'm with you, Willard. I'm posting you to the navy."

Cromwell nearly choked. "You're putting *me* aboard a bloody ship?" he howled. He smashed his cane across the other man's desk, scattering papers and personal items throughout the office. "Never!"

"Come off it," his commander said affably. "No warships or ground duty for you, old man. You're being given command of a flying boat. It's an important job, Captain. You may not shoot down many aeroplanes, but see what you can do with a few of the Hun submarines, would you?"

Off to Coastal Command, to special training for the cumbersome huge machines. Not one to wallow—like his seaplane bomber in the air—in his own rotten luck, he applied himself to what could be either a lump of an assignment or, he judged well, a rare opportunity. No need to hone his piloting; he was one of the best. But now he learned the idiosyncracies of heavy machines and the special touch they required. He spent his ground time with the mechanics and became as adept as any man with a wrench and wiring. He learned to repair and rebuild and in the process he became the equal of any aeronautical engineer.

All this, of course, to "see what he could do with a few of the Hun submarines." Most attacks against German U-boats were made in a careful, level approach for bomb dropping, which had the unfortunate result of providing the German gunners on the sub deck with an excellent steady target for their weapons. The casualties were horrific. Willard Cromwell considered all aspects of the situation, and at the conclusion of his survey, Madman Cromwell came into being.

He modified his own flying boat. With mechanics and his own flight crew working together, they strengthened the struts and wires and rigging of their machine, fine-tuned their engines for extra power, and stole stove lids from wherever they could be found to surround their crew positions with armor plating. Then they mounted a long-barreled 37mm recoilless cannon in the nose gunner position, doubled the number of machine guns on the flying boat, and went hunting.

No one had ever attacked a submarine before with a

screaming plunge in an aircraft infamous for its plodding gait and painfully clumsy response. Infamous the other machines were; not this wide-winged bird. As Cromwell dove against his target, the forward gunner pumped heavy shells against the submarine, supported by three men hammering away with machine guns. Cromwell aimed to drop his bombs right into the conning tower of his target if at all possible, and the only way to do that was to go right down to the deck in a steep dive so that the bombs would follow a properly curving ballistic arc and explode *inside* the submarine.

He sank two submarines, fought off several more, saved ships and lives, and met his comeuppance once again through no direct action of the enemy. Attacking a German sub on the surface in his usual brash dive, his bow gunner pumping shells at the enemy machine gun crews on deck, he was short of his aiming point for the conning tower. One bomb struck the flat deck and bounced wildly back into the air to smash into the tail of Cromwell's flying boat. By the good graces of the angels who look after such madmen, the bomb fuse failed to trigger, but the heavy bomb ripped through the airplane's structure, severing the controls to the tail surfaces. Cromwell and crew tore past the submarine just as his first bomb exploded within the U-boat. The explosion not only ripped outward from the submarine hull, but also struck the flying boat like a giant hand slapping a mosquito. Into the water they crashed. The airplane shed pieces in a rapid but steady progression, each structural collapse easing the shock of deceleration.

When the moment ended, the submarine was sinking in a spume of steam, smoke and spreading oil, and Cromwell and crew in life jackets were clambering onto a section of the hull still floating as a somewhat leaky lifeboat.

A British destroyer raced to their aid and hauled everyone from the sea.

Cromwell ended up in another hospital, this time with a broken shoulder, minor burns, and many lacerations about his body that produced scars he would spend years displaying to awed friends. In the years that followed, Cromwell added to his already distinguished abilities by becoming expert in weapons and demolition. Judged by his superiors to be the recipient of a charmed life, he was sent on missions to trouble spots where British control slipped into disrepute and no small danger. He was as adept in learning languages as he was blessed with an extraordinary memory, and he became as much at home in dark alleys and back streets as he was in the cockpit of any flying machine.

By now, with the war years well behind him, Cromwell was a portly man of large stature and a huge handlebar mustache, assuming the appearance of the typical "Colonel Blimp" of colonial England. And it was all appearance, for Cromwell beneath his outer flab was massively muscled, adroit, and flexible, and a dangerous man indeed with weapons of any kind, as well as with his powerful hands. He had spent two years in Turkey training with their professional wrestlers, a field exalted and held in honor for multiple generations. They taught him well, soaking his hands and much of his skin in stinging brine so they became tough and as hard as boards.

This was the man Indiana Jones had selected as his "shotgun," able to perform duties as a mechanic or weaponeer, a pilot or a skulker among the alleys of almost any city in the world. He was lethal in hand-to-hand combat and yet, strangely, well steeped in academic lore, master of a dozen languages and with a memory that forgot nothing. Those people who thought they knew Indiana Jones well found it hard to comprehend his friendship with the hard-drinking, unpredictable Cromwell. But Indy had chosen very well indeed. Cromwell was worth a dozen men.

And at this moment, in this remote farmhouse, amid wide fields in every direction, Cromwell was thick with whiskey and impatience. He brought shudders to the others in the room with another gut-wrenching belch. "When in the blazes is Indy getting back here!" he thundered, a question they all knew to be rhetorical. Indy would return from Chicago when he had accomplished the needs of his trip, and he had insisted on going it alone. Something very special and secretive had them on edge. Even the powerful and tough Ford Trimotor hidden alongside the biggest barn nearby seemed chained to the ground. They wanted to *do* something. Waiting scraped against their nerves, and they would have been surprised to know that this was precisely the situation Indy had carefully maneuvered. His team had to be able to function in perfect harmony, whether in action or in stop-motion, waiting as they were now without knowing the reasons why. If there was to be friction or a falling out, this was the time to reveal the problem and remove the fault at once.

"Most men who drink as much as you do," observed Gale Parker, watching Cromwell with mixed distaste and admiration, "would have passed out long ago. Instead, you just seem to get as nervous as a cat trying to get out of a cage. How do you do it?"

Cromwell blinked at her. The fiery redhead, quite beautiful in a most rugged fashion, had caught him unawares. Women usually expressed some empty-headed prattling criticism. But not this one. They knew little of her. Even her accent defied identification, but Cromwell, adept at many languages, recognized Parker's linguistic flexibility with her first words. She was feminine, but imbued with a strength he recognized and respected: a physical strength as well as some inner force. He saw quickly that in many ways she paralleled Indy's own style. She had long been a loner; Cromwell knew the look in the eyes, and he respected any woman strong enough to maintain her presence of self in a world where she was surrounded by men who regarded women as intruders in "their" world.

What Cromwell could not determine, but was so well known to Indy, was that her appearance as an American, or at least someone from eastern or northern Europe, had been carefully manufactured and nurtured. Gale Parker was the name she adopted when she decided that she wished neither her Mediterranean background nor her real name, Mirna Abi Khalil, to signal that much information about her. Her father was Muslim, but Gale, at the time still a youngster known to her friends as Mirna Abi, spent her formative years with her mother, Sybil Saunders, in England's New Forest. The elder Saunders was a bona fide witch of the Wicca religion, and was the senior of an unbroken line of witches and covens going back fourteen hundred years. Born in 1899, as was Indy, Gale had devoted her entire life to intense discipline in academics and skills in the field, living off the land and learning to "read" the signs of wildlife, as well as recognizing the artifacts of her mother's native land stretching six thousand years into the past.

She tripled up on her academics, took strange herbs from her mother that let her rest fully on four hours of sleep every night, and earned her doctorate in ancient cultures by the time she was but twenty-four years old. Living in the New Forest, trained by masters of ancient traditions, she was intensely athletic, but in the real world rather than in field and track competitions. Mountain climbing, swimming, hunter tracking, acrobatics, even expertise in jujitsu learned from an elderly Japanese who had adopted his own lifestyle to that of the Britons, all these had created a brilliant versatility in one so young.

It was on one of her trips into deep forest that she met Indiana Jones as he moved through ancient ruins in the thick woods. The encounter was one of instant competition between wills. This strange American fascinated her, for he knew as much of the Celtic past as she herself. When she learned he was a professor her admiration lessened rather than increased and she took no steps to hide her feelings. To her professors were stodgy, closeted behind ivy-festooned walls, and experts at talking rather than doing. Yet here he was in the thickets and, like her, living off the land.

An unexpected fight for life changed them both. Walking together through thick woods, Gale stopped Indy with a sudden touch on his arm. She had frozen in place; he did the same. Immediately she had her powerful bow in her hands, arrow strung, ready to draw and shoot. At that moment a huge wild boar erupted from nearby bushes, charging directly at them. Gale had the bow back fully and in one swift motion fired. The arrow went straight and true, burying the notched head deep into the animal's shoulder. The boar went to a knee, but was up, enraged, still able to run at them with a limping gait. The wound would not protect them against the fierce tusks. Gale had already snatched another arrow from her quiver and was ready to shoot. Too late! The animal charged her directly. Suddenly she felt herself lifted through the air and hurled to the side.

"That tree!" Jones shouted. "Shoot from there!" She saw the wisdom of his move. She would be out of range from the tusks and she could still release her arrows. But even as she clambered to the safety of a branch she was ready to come down again. Indy had no weapon she could see and now the enraged animal was turning on him. It was her turn to be amazed as she watched Indy pulling open his jacket; a moment later a huge bullwhip was in his hand and whistling through the air. A crack like a pistol shot sounded as the whip end lashed across the eyes of the boar. It screamed in sudden pain, blood spurting as though a knife blade had sliced open its tough hide. It spun swiftly, charging again. Indy had time for one more slashing strike with the whip. He aimed at a foreleg. The whip whirled about the leg and Indy ran to the animal's side, jerking with all his strength on the handle.

"Shoot!" he yelled as the animal tripped and for a moment fell over onto its side, its vulnerable belly exposed. Gale sent an arrow deep into the animal, then another and another. The boar thrashed about madly. Gale found Indy seated calmly by her side on the tree branch.

"We'll just wait until it dies," he told her.

She stared at him in amazement. She'd never seen anything like that whip or the incredible speed and power he wielded against the beast. "Where . . . where did you ever learn . . . I mean, how did you *do* that?"

He held the whip handle easily. "I've had this since I was a kid. I learned to use it against snakes, mainly. When it was serious, that is." He hefted the handle again. "It'll slice a rattler or a copperhead in two just like a bowie knife." He offered a crooked grin. "You're no slouch with that Robin Hood outfit of yours, either. You saved both of us a nasty time when you fired that first arrow."

"There wasn't time to think," she said quietly.

"That's the rule in moments like these. *Don't* think. *Acta non verba.*"

"Deeds, not words," she replied in translation from the Latin. "Whoever you are, you surprise me. An American, which is obvious, with a bullwhip and using an ancient tongue."

Again that lopsided grin. "We'll try languages later. In

the meantime, I hope you're as good a cook as you are a bowman."

"*Woman,*" she emphasized.

He scanned her from head to toe. "What's obvious doesn't need explanation."

She was amazed. She blushed. She slipped down from the tree, wary of the animal still twitching. In a moment he was beside her. "Take your choice—whatever your name is."

"Parker. Gale Parker."

He extended his hand. "Jones. Indiana Jones. You want to do the honors with dinner or gather firewood?"

"I'll cut, you gather."

Over the fire, dining on fresh meat, they talked well into the night. That first encounter sealed an unspoken relationship. Instant friendship, but with a mixture of exasperation, wit, brilliance, and a shared distaste for the social world. He marveled at her deep instinctual knowledge of ancient arts and cultures, her comfortable depth with the black arts of gypsies, and she had him wondering with her admitted research into the paranormal. But she was as good a scientist in the ancient worlds as she was a woodsman. Indy was more than familiar with the spirits and gods of cultures throughout the world, but he had never encountered such depth on a personal level.

In the years following their initial encounter in the deep woods, they kept in touch. They had worked together on several research projects, and she had, somewhat dubiously at first, even joined him with studies at the University of London.

And then had come that unexpected call. A special project, he called it. It meant fast travel, it promised danger, it was extraordinarily important. "That's all I can tell you now. You'll learn the rest later. But I want you as part of my inner group. No reservations. Yes or no?"

She sighed. She knew she couldn't turn him down.

Now she was waiting, bemused by what she didn't know, in an isolated farmhouse in a place called Iowa, waiting for Indy to return from Chicago or wherever to join his, well, *unusual* was a gentle term for this oddball mixture Indy had gathered about him.

And as complex and impressive as was Willard Cromwell, she had never met anyone quite like Tarkiz Belem. Except that on the moment of her first meeting with the swarthy Kurd, one word leaped into her mind: *Danger.*

Tarkiz Belem was one of the most amoral human beings she had ever met. His connection with Indiana Jones confused her, for Tarkiz seemed his opposite in intelligence, compassion, wit, and just about everything else Indy represented. Yet Jones had personally sought out the swarthy Kurd—*if* that were true—for their special mission.

No one, Indy knew, was better qualified in the scummiest of dives and back rooms of the Middle East and the Mediterranean border lands than Tarkiz. He was at home in every language of those lands, from high political office to the dregs of the gutter. He seemed to have critical contacts at every level of those countries, including even roving Bedouin bands. And yet, he could also gain entry to the Vatican if that were his wish.

"He's got something on everybody," Indy had explained to Gale, "and no one knows better than you that in that part of the world there's no better passport. If Tarkiz were to be assassinated, there'd be an explosion of scandals from the information he's placed in different bank vaults to be released on confirmation of his death. So it behooves the people he deals with to play ball with him, to meet whatever it is he wants. The man is greedy and grasping beyond belief, but he's also smart enough to know that you make deals that work both ways. It pays people well to do his bidding. He takes good care of them as well."

"You said he was smart," Gale said, irritated that Indy would even use that word in the same sentence with the name of Tarkiz Belem.

Indy grinned at her. "Okay, so he's got the intelligence of a goat. But it's a very shrewd goat."

"And he smells like one," Gale murmured.

Indy laughed. "So true! But think of it this way, Gale. Even if you can't see him, you'll always know when he's coming."

She couldn't help her smile. Indy never held a cup that was half empty; it was never less than half full.

"Is he really a Kurd? I mean, he could be from the original Iraqi clan, or Turkish, or Indian or Afghanistan. How can you tell? The man has more than one passport and—"

"Fourteen," Indy broke in. "Look, no one can survive the way he does in the places he goes. He's multilingual. He's as tough as nails. He grew up in gutters and back alleys and learned to survive by his wits. You seem to resent his lack of formal education, but he's got the best qualifications in the world for digging up information where no one else could even get the right time of day."

"He's a criminal, isn't he?" she pressed.

"No doubt about it. Officially, he's wanted in at least five countries for a list of crimes longer than your arm. But every time he's arrested, the charges are dismissed and he's back on the streets in an hour. He buys his freedom with money, blackmail, contacts; anything and everything. The word is that for years he was a professional assassin."

Gale shuddered. "No doubt. Women and children, too."

"If that's the job, I'd have to agree with you. What's

crazy about this man," Indy continued, "is that he has his own code of ethics and he sticks to it like glue. I can't fault him for that. He's the product of an environment where skullduggery and killing are as normal as coffee and apple pie are to me back home. From where I sit, it's his religion that keeps me a bit on edge about him."

"His *religion*?" Gale sputtered.

"Gold. He's religious to the point of paranoia to the Great God of Gold. Not just money. I mean the metal. Gold in any form. Jewelry, ingots, coins; whatever."

"I wonder," Gale said darkly, "how many gold *teeth* he has in his hoard."

Indy didn't laugh. "No doubt, a bunch."

"Aren't you afraid that someone else will offer him more money than you're paying him?"

Indy caught her by surprise. "Oh, I'm not paying him in coin of the realm. No money, I mean."

"Then—?"

"There's an old saying, Gale. It says that every man has his price. It's not true that anyone can be bought if the payment is high enough. The reality is that everyone has a price—*or a reason.* Even to someone like Belem, there's something that transcends money. Or gold, for that matter."

"And you know that reason?"

He smiled at her by way of answer. She knew when to quit. Quickly she changed the subject. She directed her gaze to the fifth member of their group. "Our Frenchman. He seems the exact opposite to Belem."

Indy glanced at Rene Foulois. "Oh, he is. Decidedly. He can gain entrance to places just about impossible to the rest of us. Kings, emperors, presidents, dictators, just about anyone and anywhere."

"I don't know very much about him."

"He's a pilot. A master aviator. So is Cromwell. And having two pilots, each equally skilled, is insurance."

She never did learn his true background. Foulois had been a famed fighter pilot in the Great War, responsible for more than forty kills of German aircraft. That made him an ace eight times over, a sensational hero in France. It didn't hurt that he was tall and slender, with a whipline of a mustache, and that he was skilled in the social and diplomatic graces. He was the darling of the international social and diplomatic set. The Foulois family owned huge vineyards; their superb wines went to every corner of the world. Wealth is always a welcome passport, and Foulois was daring, brave, a national hero, wealthy, brilliant, and charming, openly granted "welcome passports" by a dozen governments.

It was all cover, but the cover was *real.* Which served perfectly to conceal Foulois's position as a special secret agent of the French Foreign Legion, which made all the world his assignment. By long-standing agreement with the national police of many countries, the legion's undercover arm had a "reach" into almost anywhere in the world. The group spread its tendrils everywhere, operating under the legal and profitable International Wine Consortium, Ltd., with offices in Bordeaux as their headquarters.

To Foulois, the Jones Project, as the special operation became known in high circles, was an amusing diversion from social and diplomatic functions. At heart, Foulois remained the quintessential fighter pilot, seeking action that would keep alive within him the flame of combat and the exhilaration of risk.

He also thought the entire affair was utterly ridiculous. Foulois had been assigned to Indiana Jones by none other then Henri DuFour, head of the French Secret Service. When he described to Foulois the crescent-shaped machines and their huge mother ship, Foulois reacted with disdain. He simply did not believe a word of it, no matter what any eyewitness so claimed.

Yet he accepted his subordinate position without hesitation. DuFour had put the case convincingly. "It does not matter what we believe about these fantastic machines, Rene. What matters is that the war with Germany has been over only twelve years and we are faced with a Hun who is already rearming with a frantic pace. You are aware of the training program in Russia for the Germans? For their navigators and pilots especially? Good; then you know how serious this may be. We must find out the specifics of what the Hun is doing. That is your task. You will work for this American fellow, and you will proceed as if you believe everything."

Foulois nodded. "It promises great sport. I understand they will modify one of their Ford aeroplanes. The trimotored machine. I look forward to flying it."

In the meantime, isolated in the lonely farmhouse, chafing at the bit, they all wondered what Jones could possibly be doing in Chicago that was so important to keep them on edge all this time.

They would simply have to wait.

4

The burly man wearing a heavy windbreaker and a seaman's cap snugged to his head walked briskly, with the sign of a slight limp, through the Chicago bus terminal. Anyone who saw the man would remember those salient points; the clothing, the cap, the aura of strength, and that slight odd walk tipping him to one side as he threaded through the crowds.

Outside the terminal he stood close to the building, watching lines of people disappearing within a slowly advancing stream of taxicabs. Soon the crowd had thinned, and he turned to walk along the line of taxis. He seemed casual or nonchalant in his movement, but his eyes moved carefully from one cab to the next until he saw the yellow-and-red markings of the vehicle for which he'd been searching. The seaman stopped, cupped a cigarette lighter between his hands, and pressed a button. No flame appeared, but a tiny bright light flashed rapidly. Almost at once the cab's headlights flicked on and off two times. The seaman slipped the "lighter" back into a pocket, walked to the cab, and climbed inside. The moment the door closed the driver pulled out into traffic.

"Nice evening, sir," the driver said, studying his passenger through the rearview mirror.

"Except that the kitchen's too crowded," came the answer.

"More saucers than cups, I'd say."

"You prefer your tea hot or cold, sir?"

The passenger smiled to himself. "I like my coffee black."

That was the confirming line for Professor Henry Jones to make to the driver. Now he had his final line to accept *from* the driver.

"As I do. Pour it into the saucer to cool it off quickly."

"Excellent," said Jones.

"Treadwell does overdo this back-and-forth a bit, doesn't he?" The driver laughed.

"Depends," Indy said noncommittally. "You know his routines. I hardly know the man. I didn't get your name," he added quickly.

"I didn't give it. Suppose you tell me what it is and we can dispense with all this secret palaver."

"Colonel Harry Henshaw, United States Army. Fighter pilot, test pilot, technical intelligence, experimental projects."

"Professor Henry Jones. Professor of Medieval Lit and Studies from dear old Princeton," the driver said. "How come they don't call you Hoosier instead of Indy?"

Indy laughed. No question now that this *was* the army officer Treadwell had set up for this meet. "Most people can't spell Hoosier, I guess."

Henshaw chuckled, then cut off his mirth as if with a switch. "Your plans still on for the train tomorrow night?"

Indy accepted the change in tone and attitude. They were down to business. There was another confirmation that at this moment all was well: He hadn't told the driver —Henshaw—where he wanted to go, but Henshaw was making a direct line to The Nest nightclub that was Indy's destination.

"It is," Indy said brusquely.

"I'm supposed to ask you some questions," Henshaw said.

"Ask away."

"You've got a lot of people hanging on the fence, Professor, and—"

"Indy. No Professor."

"Okay. Like I said, there's a lot of fence-hanging going on. Like what was so hot about that train cargo down in South Africa."

"Treadwell didn't explain?"

"No, sir. My instructions were to hear it from you directly."

"Colonel, let's start by your telling me what you've heard," Indy directed.

"Something about an artifact. The grapevine, which, by the way, is so hot the wires are glowing, has it that the artifact is either from an ancient civilization or," Henshaw hesitated, "I know this sounds crazy, but it may be extraterrestrial."

In the gloom of the cab's rear seat, Indy smiled. The plan he and Treadwell had put together well before this moment was working. Treadwell was a long-experienced investigator of both military intelligence matters *and* criminal activities. He believed firmly that it's easier to pass off a big lie than a small one, and when you combine skillful deception with the greed of others you can get people to believe almost anything you want them to believe.

Indy recalled what Treadwell had told him: "When there's a chance you may lose something very valuable, or it may be taken by force, you can't always defend yourself properly. So the trick is to put a tracer in with your valuables. In many cases you can't use chemicals or a radio signal. Distances, time, other complications; that sort of thing. So you want to trigger an action in the people who've done you dirty, and that way *they* become the tracer."

Treadwell had also told Indy it was important for his cab driver—a.k.a. Colonel Harry Henshaw, U.S. Army—to be told the truth, that the artifact in the South African robbery had been engineered in concept by Treadwell. With Indy's unique talents in archeological mysteries, together they had masterminded a fake artifact that *seemed* to be of such extraordinary rarity that it was almost beyond price.

"Harry's a strange sort of duck," Treadwell had explained, "but the man is absolutely brilliant. Unique, too, in the way he works. He's like a, well, a walking encyclopedia of thousands of bits and pieces of information that he brings together to make sense out of things that baffle the rest of us. Tell him the truth about the artifact, but, please, Indy, do so when you two are very much alone and your conversation is secure."

Indy looked about him. Obviously the taxi in which he was riding didn't belong to any cab company. It had to be government property, used for just such "unusual transportation" as of this moment. And since Henshaw would be a very tight member of the group trying to find out what Indy was after, those incredible discs or cresents or saucers, or whatever they were, well, Treadwell was right. Get Henshaw started as soon as possible in his own special investigative way.

"Harry, is this cab secure?" Indy asked the man at the wheel.

"Secure? Indy, this thing is armored. So is all the glass. You could empty a Thompson submachine gun at this cab and the bullets would bounce off."

"I don't mean that," Indy said quickly. "Any recording equipment? Mikes, radios?"

"No, sir. She's clean."

"Harry, Treadwell wants you brought into the picture about that artifact."

The cab swerved suddenly; Henshaw was *that* taken by surprise. "I . . . I'm glad to hear that," he said. "I'd be a liar if I said I wasn't, well, hanging on the edge to know about it."

"Don't bother looking at the stars, Harry."

"What do you mean?"

"You know what the expression 'red herring' means?"

"Yes. A false lead. Something you plant to mislead other people."

"Well, that cube's a red herring."

The colonel kept his silence for a while. "You're certain of that, Indy? I mean, we've been hearing such wild stories—"

"You're supposed to hear them," Indy broke in. "That's been the plan from the beginning. Of course, you do *not* repeat this to anyone else. Treadwell's convinced there's a leak somewhere in his organization, so he's playing everything close to the vest. But it was his decision you be informed as to what's going on. If Treadwell is right, that cube could give us some good leads."

Henshaw laughed humorlessly. "You know something? I was hoping, you know, a wild sort of hope, I guess, that it really *was* from, uh," he gestured with one hand, upward, "from out there."

"Not this time, Harry." Indy studied the scene outside the cab. "We're almost there. I want you to let me off about two blocks away. Around a corner so no one at the club sees me coming from this cab."

"Got it. You want a backup?"

"No. This is a solo job. You know where our group is staying, right?"

"We'd had the place screened and covered before you landed there."

"Thanks. It's good to know." Indy gestured to the next street corner. "Let me off just ahead."

Henshaw eased the cab to the curb. Indy waited until no pedestrians were near the cab. Before Henshaw realized what was happening, Indy had slipped away and was just turning the corner.

The burly man wearing a heavy windbreaker, scuffed boots, and a seaman's knitted cap shuffled clumsily toward the entrance to Chicago's jazz and blues club, The Nest. Indy limped badly in a lurching motion as he approached the brightly lit awning and an entrance doorman about the size of a small grizzly bear. Mike Patterson was all show as a doorman. An ex-prizefighter who failed to make the big time, he was big and tough enough to handle his real job as a bouncer, and as an entrance guard to keep out the bums and riffraff like this shuffle-footed geezer trying to get inside.

"Beat it, ya bum," Patterson growled at the figure before him. "Y'know something, Mac, y'stink. I betcha ya ain't had a bath in a year of Mondays."

Not even Henshaw had seen the beard that appeared on Indy's face moments after he left the cab. It was a perfect fit that Gale had prepared for him, using theatrical glue to secure it to his face. Whoever saw this miserable creature would never think of Indiana Jones or anyone who looked like him.

Stooped over, wheezing, the old "seaman" tried to push past Patterson. "I ain't botherin' nobody," he whined. "Just wanna hear the music, y'know?"

A massive fist hung threateningly before the disheveled

bum. "Ya don't get outta here, y'creep, all ya gonna hear is da birdies singing, y'get me? Now beat it before I whack ya into da middle of next week!"

"Don't hurt me," the old man pleaded, cringing.

Patterson guffawed. This was going to be a pleasure. The beefy fist closed around the windbreaker, hauling the other man from his feet until only his toes touched the sidewalk. The other fist drew back to deliver a pulverizing blow.

It never got started. The old man pushed his face close to Patterson's features. With little effort, he blew a cloud of powder from his mouth into Patterson's eyes. Fire seemed to erupt in the vision of the doorman. He howled with sudden agony, reeling backwards, tripping over an awning stanchion, and falling clumsily to the ground. "I'm blind!" he screamed. "I can't see! My eyes . . . *I can't see!*"

Several men rushed from the jazz club. They stopped short at the sight of Patterson groveling on the sidewalk, knuckles rubbing his eyes frantically. Jack Shannon of the Shannon Brothers, club owners and managers, took swift stock of the situation. Immediately he grasped the smelly bum by the arm, as much to hold him upright as to keep him on the scene.

"What happened here, old man?" Shannon demanded an explanation. He gestured to Patterson. "Did you do that?"

"I didn't mean no harm," the seaman whined. "Want to hear the music, that's all. Gotta listen to this guy, Shannon."

"How do you know his name?" Shannon barked. The question came without thinking. Shannon was known through the nightclub life of Chicago. But this creature—

Shannon stopped abruptly as the old man leaned heavily against him. There was no mistaking the muzzle of the heavy pistol pressed beneath Shannon's armpit. The old man placed his mouth almost against Shannon's ear. The smell of fish and garlic nearly overwhelmed Shannon.

"Inside," wheezed the old man, coughing a spray of garlicky spittle across the side of Shannon's face. The pistol nudged just a bit harder. "We go in like we was old buddies, got it? Friend of the family. Then we walk to the back of the club, see? We goes into your office and you close the door and you don't let nobody else come in. You got it?"

Shannon, tall and slender to the point of cadaverous, nodded. This was wildly confusing and he was sure the old man was crazy, but you don't argue with a gun barrel in your armpit. "Okay, okay," Shannon told him quietly. "But take it easy with the hardware, old fellow, all right? You won't have any trouble."

"Button it, mister." The gun prodded again. "Start walking and don't forget to smile."

Another wave of fish and garlic prompted Shannon into obeying this crazy bum. Club waiters stared as Jack Shannon, the immaculate high-society blues club owner, waltzed arm-in-arm with some derelict along the dim recesses of the back of the club, but nobody said a word. Shannon was one of the master blues musicians, and everybody knew how many band members were down on their luck in the depression gripping the country. Shannon was a soft touch for his buddies who were down and out. So you minded your own business. They'd seen sights like this before.

Shannon stopped short of his office door. The gun jabbed against his ribs. "Remember, nobody comes in," came the hoarse whisper of a warning.

"No problem, old-timer," Shannon said gently. The trick was to keep the old guy from getting excited. A good meal and a shot of whiskey would straighten him out.

Shannon looked to a large man who eyed the scene suspiciously. "Hey, Syd, this is an old buddy of mine," Shannon told him. "Do me a favor. This is sort of personal and I don't want anyone to bother us, okay?"

"Yes, sir, I got it," the man said. Something didn't seem right but orders were orders.

Inside the office the old man turned Shannon back to the door. "Lock it." Shannon turned the lock.

"Now, sit down in that easy chair. Over there." The stranger stepped back to place distance between himself and Shannon. Now the weapon was visible. Shannon stared down the barrel of a powerful six-shot Webley .445. That thing could take down even a moose with a single round.

Shannon's brow furrowed. There was something strangely familiar about the weapon he studied. Guns in Chicago were as common as cigarettes. But who carried a *Webley?* A Smith & Wesson, sure. Or a Colt auto. Even a long-barreled Remington, but—

Shannon's eyes widened as the old man tossed aside the knitted cap. A moment later he tugged the false beard from his face, and broke into a huge smile. The windbreaker was tossed aside, and the Webley disappeared beneath a dark blue suede sport jacket.

"Hello, Jack," the no-longer-old man said.

Shannon was halfway out of his chair, eyes wide. "I don't believe this," he whispered. "Good Lord Amighty, I don't believe this. *Indy!*"

"The one and only," Indy grinned at him. Shannon was on his feet, rushing forward, throwing his arms about his closest friend, hugging him fiercely. They pounded one another on their backs.

Shannon pushed Indy back, staring at him. "Man, you're a sight for sore eyes," he said, his delight unquestioned. "But . . . but why the routine?" He held up a hand. "Just hold it a minute, Indy. After what you put me through, I need a drink." He half turned as he took a bottle and two glasses from a wall bar. "And you, old friend, need some mouthwash and a bath!"

"All part of the show, Jack. Let's have that drink. I can hardly stand this garlic and fish smell any more than you can."

Shannon brought the glass to Indy, his friend from long-gone schooldays, the same man who'd been his closest pal for years. They clinked glasses and for the moment drank in silence. Shannon poured again, but this time Indy sipped slowly. "You look great, Jack. Still thin as a rail, but—" He shrugged. "How's your playing?"

"Better than ever. We got a regular crowd now. Some people have the idea I'm setting a new trend with the blues." Shannon finished the second drink, put aside the glass, and dropped back into the easy chair.

"But I still don't believe all this!" he burst out suddenly. "Indy, what *is* all this? You didn't need to go through a routine to come in *here*! We've been pals forever."

Indy swilled a taste of whiskey around his mouth to cut down the fish and garlic and to remove the last of the powder he'd held in a capsule until he needed it to cut down the doorman. He put down the glass, still half full.

"It's simple, Jack," Indy said, his tone suddenly serious. "No one but you is to know that I've—that is, Professor Henry Jones—has been here tonight."

"I don't get it," Jack Shannon answered, as straight as Indy had spoken to him. "In the old days you were a fixture here every now and then. Something wrong, Indy? I mean, you've got to have a good reason for laying low like this." Shannon thought of the past and chuckled. "But then again, you *always* had a good reason for anything you did. So what's the score, pal?"

Indy studied the man with whom he'd grown up in his Chicago days. "Jack, you still with the church?"

"What?"

"I mean, you always stayed with what your family felt was important. I don't remember you ever missed Sunday in church."

"I still *don't* miss it. Just like it always was. Why?"

"It could affect what I have to ask you."

"Only way to find out is to ask, Indy. But first, tell me: What did you do to Patterson?"

"Who?"

"The gorilla we keep at the front door. I've seen him take on a whole bunch of troublemakers and flatten the place. You had him crying like a schoolgirl."

"Oh, that." Indy nodded. "Tiger Tears. It's a powder I had some chemists whip up for me. They put it in a capsule and you release it by biting down. Makes the eyes smart and tear. Your man won't see much before tomorrow, but he'll be fine after that."

"Thanks for telling me. I mean, Patterson's a pretty good guy. He never made it big in the ring and he works hard to protect us in here. Okay, that's all I'm going to ask you, Indy. The way you're talking I guess you're in town for a quick visit and then you're going to split, right?"

"Right."

"Same way you came in? Beard, limp, the old bum routine?"

Indy shook his head. "Uh-uh. When I leave here I'll be a well-dressed society heel, mustache, racing cap, the works. You still have that private exit to the alley for your car?"

"Sure do."

"That's how I'll go, then. Want to give me a ride?"

"You got it. Now, look, Indy, you're not in trouble, are

you? I know I asked you before, but, well, I'd do anything for you. You're the best friend I've got."

"Thanks, Jack. No, I'm not in trouble."

"You sure you've got to cut out? I mean, buddy, I could play you a couple of your favorite numbers, just for old times' sake, and that all-night joint is still open. Ham, cabbage and beans, right, Indy? Just like we used to do."

"Just save those cornet numbers for me, Jack. Look, friend, I'm going to ask you for help. But it's not for me. Would it sound too corny for you if I said it was for your country?"

Shannon's eyes widened. "You a G-man, Indy?"

Indy laughed. "Nothing like that. I'd like to tell you more, but I can't. Maybe later but not now. You'll have to take my word for it."

"Okay; shoot."

"Your partners ran a newspaper delivery business. They still got their fleet of trucks?"

"Sure thing."

"Can you get them working if you call them in the middle of the night?"

"That's when they do most of their work, Indy."

"I need a bunch of them, Jack. Not tonight, so there's plenty of time."

"Where you want them?"

"Milledgeville."

"What's Milledgeville? Sounds like a home for midgets."

Indy smiled. "Not quite. It's a town about ninety miles west of here. Bunch of small towns in that area. Polo, Oregon, Chadwick, and Milledgeville. There's a rail line that runs right down a valley where they're located."

"Maybe you'll tell me why later. How many of my people do you need?"

"Enough to bring a train to a stop and hold it up tomorrow night."

Shannon's jaw dropped. For several moments he could hardly speak. Then he burst out laughing. "I thought this was on the level! What'd you do, Indy? Join up with Jesse James and his gang?"

Indy shared his laughter. "No. But it *is* on the level. It's a special job, Jack. Like I said, it's *for* your country."

"If I was hearing this from anybody else I'd . . ." Shannon shook his head. "Okay, Indy. I trust you. What's in that train?"

"Gold. Artifacts. Some stuff like that."

"What are *you* after?"

"We don't care about the gold."

"Well, *that's* different. What happens with the gold after it's lifted? I got a hunch you'll be picking that up, too."

"You're right. But I want the gold returned."

Shannon's eyes narrowed. "So there's some sort of, uh, well, something you're after. I got to ask you this, Indy. Will you be keeping it?"

"Only for a little while."

"This is crazy. I suppose next you'll tell me nobody gets hurt in this caper."

"That's right."

Shannon sighed. "I got the right people for this. Okay. I guess you're after one car in particular. Will you have it marked for us?"

"I'll leave all the details with you."

"What about guards?"

"A detail. I don't mind noise and shooting, but nobody needs to get hurt. And I want you to use some special equipment."

"Okay. In for a dime, in for a dollar."

An hour later they were through. "Where do you need to go now?" Shannon asked.

"Farmhouse. Isolated. Twenty miles south of Dubuque, maybe a hundred miles from here."

"I know it."

"We'll need to stop at the bus station downtown. My stuff is in a locker there."

"Okay."

"I really appreciate this, Jack."

"I'll appreciate it myself when you tell me what's really going on, Indy." Shannon held up a hand. "Okay, okay. I'll wait."

Indy clapped him on the shoulder. "I'll lay it all out for you one day. In the meantime—" He reached into his pocket and withdrew a leather bag. "Make absolutely sure this is with the take tomorrow night. Put it in the lift sack."

Shannon took the bag. "Do I look?"

"I'd prefer you didn't."

Shannon shrugged. "What's it worth?"

"Oh, a zillion bucks or so."

"When'd you become a comic, Indy?"

Three hours later the team heard the powerful car approaching along the river road leading to the farmhouse. Gale looked out between window drapes. "Looks like a limousine," she told the others.

"How many?" Tarkiz barked.

"I see only one set of headlights," she answered. "Douse the lights in here so I can—"

Rene Foulois had the lights off before she finished her sentence. "It still looks like just one. The car's stopping. One man is out from the passenger side. He's coming around to stand in front of the headlights."

"Good," Rene judged. "He's making sure we know who he is."

"It's Indy!" Gale exclaimed. "I didn't recognize him in

that . . . that dandified outfit he's wearing. He looks like a racetrack tout."

"Never mind that. Is he still alone?" Tarkiz demanded in his heavy accent.

Gale heard the metallic thud of an automatic pistol loading a round into the chamber. She knew without looking that it was Tarkiz. She became aware she hadn't heard a sound from Willard Cromwell. How could so big a man be so silent? She turned to scan the room. He was gone.

Looking again through the window, her eyes now more acclimated to the gloom, she saw the hulking shadow by a tree trunk to the left of the car. No mistaking that portly figure, *or* the Thompson submachine gun in his hands. She knew if anyone from that car made a sudden move towards Indiana Jones it was all over for them. Willard would riddle the car with steel-jacketed rounds that could punch right through a so-called bulletproof limo. But there was no need. Indy gestured a good-bye to the figure behind the wheel, stepped aside, and stood on the roadside as the car made a wide turn in the yard and headed back in the direction from which it had approached.

Indy called out in the darkness. "Nice cover, Willard. I appreciate that."

Cromwell moved forward and became more visible. "And just how did you know where I was and *who* I was, if I may ask?" he said with good-natured joviality.

"Easy," Indy told him as they walked to the farmhouse. "I just put myself in your place and said, now, if I was good old Willard and I was bored out of my mind, sipping warm whiskey in the middle of this godforsaken nowhere, and there's Indy, and maybe he's in a spot of trouble, I would—"

"Enough!" Willard laughed. Even from the house, Gale heard the distinctive click of Willard snapping on the safety to the Thompson.

When they were all gathered in the living room, Indy stopped the rush of questions with a raised hand. "Food, first," he told them. "Time enough for a round table after that, and then a good night's sleep. We'll be up all night tomorrow, and I want everything ready to go by sunset."

"Before we eat I want the dogs in place."

Dinner—steaks and frankfurters grilled across the open fireplace—was almost ready. Preparations for their evening meal had led them into small talk and, as Indy had hoped, they began to take a more relaxed attitude toward each other. He was pleased to see that Gale Parker showed no discomfort at being the only female in the group. Indy smiled to himself. Only he knew of her prowess as a hellion in a fight, that she was expert in the use of a wide spectrum of weapons.

Just as important to Indy was how the men regarded the fiery redheaded woman. He had rarely joined in a fraternity of this close nature, in which every man was a true and dangerous professional in his own right. So far, not one of the men indicated even a mild measure of contempt for the female in their midst. Either they had accepted the opinion of one Indiana Jones regarding Gale Parker, or two, they would judge for themselves just how she performed when the boom came down upon them all.

There was a third possibility that might measure the track of their thoughts: that Indy had his own personal interest in Gale Parker as a woman to be desired. That was true in only one sense. Gale was most definitely one of the most outstanding women he had ever met, but his mind was anything *but* bent on romantic inclinations. There was this assignment, which more and more appealed to his curiosity as well as demanded a complex strategy. And strictly on a personal level, there was still a heavy measure of pain to be washed from his mind and emotions. He still had nightmares of Deirdre dying in that smashup in the Amazon—

He forced himself back to the moment. The dogs. They had four of them in the barn. Mastiffs: big, ugly brutes, all of them attack-trained. But also trained to obey commands instilled in them as younger animals. "You want to feed them now?" Tarkiz asked.

Indy shook his head. "No. We'll clip their cables to the ground posts. Put the biggest one by the plane. The other three will form a wide circle around this house and the barn. And leave them hungry. If we feed them they'll simply go to sleep. Give them water; that's all. Okay, I'll go with you. Tarkiz, Willard, you come with me. Rene, you and Gale finish getting dinner ready."

Everyone complied. That was the value of a great team. No job was too important, no job too small. They moved the animals to their guard positions around the house and barn, then returned to the farmhouse where dinner waited for them all.

Then they burned the wooden plates and forks in the fireplace along with leftovers from dinner. The knives were no problem. Everyone used his own blade weapon as a utensil.

"We take off tomorrow night at precisely ten o'clock. That will give us plenty of time to use that Hollywood paint to cover our company sign and paint a false NC number on the tail. In fact, the more I think about it, we'll cover the Greatest Wines sign with one that reads Department of Public Works. Even if someone sees us they'll see that lettering and pay no attention to the plane."

Indy turned to Willard Cromwell. "Will, you fly this trip. Gale, you'll be up front with him, navigating and helping him in any way you can. We'll talk to each other with the headsets and helmet microphones for intercom.

Rene, I'll need you to work with me and the maps. Tarkiz, you'll work the snatch hook and the cradle reel. Everybody understand?"

They all nodded.

"And after we leave," Rene offered, gesturing to take in the farm, "what happens here? From the beginning you have stressed repeatedly, my friend, we leave nothing behind us, wherever we are, no matter what, that will be useful as personal identification."

"Right," Indy agreed.

"You do not mind elucidating for us?" asked the Frenchman.

"We feed the dogs just before we take off. Arrangements have been made for them to be picked up one hour after we're gone. Whoever retrieves them drives in, puts the dogs in cages in his truck, and leaves. He does nothing else but that."

"He won't come come into the house?" Cromwell asked lazily.

"Not if he knows what's good for him. No shilly-shallying around. In and out. And all trace of us is gone."

"How can you hide our flying machine!" Rene Foulois objected suddenly. "You have magic to do this?"

The group laughed. But Indy didn't want questions lingering. "Sort of," he told Foulois. "You're right, Frenchy. We can't *hide* the airplane. No way to disguise a big machine like the Ford. Not with three engines banging away. So what you can't hide, you disguise. I told you we'll paint that public works sign on the ship. And tonight, in fact, another Ford will be flying nearby. Tomorrow, during daylight, a Department of Public Works trimotor, the real thing, will be cruising around this area. It's on a highway-and-flood-control survey and it will keep right on flying for a few days after we're gone."

Tarkiz Belem had remained silent through the exchange. "What is all this for, Indiana Jones?" he asked, his tone showing some concern about a detailed plan that seemed to have nowhere to go.

"We're going to rob a train," Indy said. He laughed at the reactions about him.

"Rob a train?" echoed Gale Parker.

"That's right."

Tarkiz studied Indy with suspicion. "I know you do many things, but train robbery . . ." He shook his head.

"Well, I see I've got your interest," Indy said lightheartedly.

"For someone who is an archeologist," Foulois broke in with a touch of sudden jocularity, "you seem to be taking on a new *persona.* What will be next, Indy? Holding up a stagecoach?" He held out his hands with extended fingers and upraised thumbs in the manner of holding two six-shooters. "Bang! Bang!" he shouted. "The fearless international wine merchants blaze their way through hostile redheads—"

"Redskins," Indy corrected.

"Of course. We blaze our way through and hold up the stagecoach. Indy, we might as well have stayed in England and become bandits in Sherwood Forest!"

For someone who was connected with the highest levels of this operation, mused Indy, Foulois was doing a wonderful job of expressing doubts he knew were shared by the others.

He spread out maps on the dining room table and motioned for the others to move in closer.

"Tomorrow night," he said, moving his finger to a circled spot on the map, "this is where we make the hit. Figuring everything necessary to be ready, we'll take off precisely one hour before we're over the train. That way we'll have enough time to correct any problems—mechanical, weather, whatever it might be—so we can be right on time. That's necessary. The timing, I mean. There's a schedule we *must* keep."

Gale could hardly contain herself. "Indy, are you saying that we're going to rob a train *from the airplane?*"

He looked up at her, his face showing no sign of his thoughts. "Yes, I am."

She leaned back, bewildered, but obviously ready to wait for more of whatever wild scheme Indy had cooked up.

"May I ask a question before you go further?" Cromwell broke in. Indy nodded and Cromwell continued. "It's really a small matter, I suppose. But I'm a bit new to this wild and woolly America of yours, Indy. What happens, the consequences, I mean, if we're identified?"

"Oh, I have every intention of our being identified," Indy told him casually. "Not under our names, of course, but as a group under a different name. Robbing the train wouldn't be worth the bother if we didn't get the blame that way."

Cromwell nudged Foulois. "You're right, Frenchy. I do believe he's quite mad."

5

"Ladies! Gentlemen! Your attention, please!" Dr. Filipo Castilano, Ph.D., antiquities investment counselor for museums throughout the world, director of the Office of Research and Confirmation for Antiquity Investments, Ltd., rang a delicate glass bell for attention. He faced a noisy crowd of newspapermen, radio reporters, and special correspondents from throughout the world, gathered in the Archeological Lecture Forum of the University of London.

Castilano waited patiently while the crowd settled down. It gave him a moment to gesture to the university guards to open windows to rid the room of thick clouds of cigarette smoke. It seemed you weren't worth a *lira* as a newsman unless you smoked like a fiend. Castilano, immaculate in striped pants, cummerbund, and vest beneath a pure Italian silk jacket, waved his hand before his face to move smoke from before him. He dabbed his upper lip with a silk handkerchief, providing the media crowd with a whispered agreement that he seemed just a bit limp in the wrist. Castilano had perfected this foppish appearance to a finely honed presentation. He was totally, completely *un*threatening.

He wondered how many of these thickheaded news clowns had any idea that he was one of the secret members of the Board of Governors for the American Museum of Natural History in the City of New York. And maintained the same discreet invisibility in his role as Advisor to the Vatican where, in fact, he maintained an elaborate suite of offices with radio and undersea cable communications links to virtually the entire world. For Castilano was the man who was reimbursed an almost indecent sum by the Vatican to search for historical treasures the Church implicitly believed should be in their hands, not bartered for filthy lucre by dusty peasants and ill-mannered louts.

Castilano, public dandy and fop, had long been a member of the secret Six Hundred of the Vatican, a group of which no names were ever placed on paper, about whom no records were ever kept, and who were sworn to serve the Mother Church now and forever. Long before he accepted that role at the personal invitation of the Pope, Filipo Castilano had been one of the top men of the Italian Secret Service, and was as adept in secret operations, assassination, and espionage as he was now in manipulating the press and their avid readers and listeners.

His single greatest asset was his working relationship, a secret he guarded as tightly as his membership with the Six Hundred of the Vatican, with Thomas Treadwell of British Military Intelligence. As strange as that alliance seemed, it made great sense to the top authorities of the British government, as well as those of the Vatican. The latter judged the alliance to be a bulwark against the dangers of evil. If the British chose a more political position, it mattered little. Both had the same goal in mind: cooperation. And Castilano, his true nature as an undercover agent so well concealed by his polished foppish appearance, had no doubts about his ability to control his audience.

With the room hushed finally, Castilano launched into a news conference intended carefully to surprise, shock, and excite his audience—who would then spread the word throughout the world, precisely as had been planned.

"An incredible treasure has been discovered in Iraq," he announced. "From what I have been informed by my government and the research teams of the University of London, as well as the National Museum of Egypt, the find was totally unexpected. As you well know, Iraq stands in the unique position of encompassing the magnificent ancient lands of Mesopotamia. I need not go into the details at this time. You will all be given the full report of the investigation team made up of scientists from the four countries that were involved in this discovery. Suffice to say the area was in the vicinity of Habbaniyah, which stands along the banks of the Euphrates River, and almost in the very epicenter of the country. The find, again I emphasize, was a stroke of incredible fortune. Heavy rains washed away the slopes of a low hill, and local farmers discovered a massive stone structure beneath the soil.

"You will also be provided photographs of the gold statuary that was found in deep tombs. These turned out to be not burial tombs, but a secret cache for the rulers of the time. What makes this find even more significant is that the artifacts are from the length and breadth of the former Ottoman Empire, and were brought to this one area to be concealed until the rulers of the time judged it was safe to retrieve them. In the wars that plagued those lands, records of the trove apparently were lost."

An uproar broke out, but Castilano stood quietly, both hands upraised until the news crowd subsided. "Everything in due time. I will be brief. The statuary is obviously from the artisans of different cultures. I would have you keep in mind this area was the very cradle of modern civilization in terms of technology of the day as well as historical records, including cuneiform and more identifiable languages.

"It is the latter that has caused the greatest excitement. Apparently—and I have yet to confirm this, so you will not find it in your press package—one or more small pyramid-shaped objects with cuneiform markings are among the statuary.

"With the cooperation and agreement of all the governments and scientific institutions involved, the entire find is now en route to the United States—"

Another uproar, another wait; shorter this time. "To the United States," Castilano continued, "and, specifically, to the Archeological Research Center in the University of Chicago. For those of you unfamiliar with the United States, that is in the State of Illinois, on the shore of a very big lake. For more information I suggest you consult a map."

He paused, and the questions again came in a blizzard. The news crowd here didn't know a fig about historical finds. They had been selected most carefully for their *lack* of knowledge, which meant they'd ask many stupid questions and, more important, would write incredibly confused stories. *And that's as it should be,* Castilano thought to himself. He made sure to keep his answers to the point. When he had just what he wanted from this thick-skulled mob, he would turn the press conference over to that wonderfully crusty Doctor William Pencroft.

"Where is the find now?" a German reporter called out.

"En route to the United States," Castilano replied.

"How is it being transported?" came another query. Before he could answer the next question was already being shouted at him. "What is the name of the ship carrying such a treasure?"

Perfect!

"The entire find is safely aboard the American heavy cruiser, the U.S.S. *Boston.* The cruiser is in the company of four destroyers."

"Why did they need a warship, for heaven's sake!" someone shouted.

"To prevent a repetition of the loss of other artifacts discovered in a deep mine in South Africa." Castilano stopped to let that sink in. That was another story all by itself. Rumors had been flying like locusts about some terrible loss from the South African mines.

"Artifacts? From South Africa? What kind, please!"

"I am not certain. Like you, I am much in the dark about details. However, I have heard that an artifact with cuneiform markings was lost in the missing South African shipment."

"Doctor Castilano, what language is cuneiform?"

It was the question he'd been waiting for. "Cuneiform is not, as some people believe, a language by itself," Castilano answered. "Think of it as an alphabet. The characters that make up this alphabet are shaped like wedges impressed in clay or metal. However, I would add that cuneiform actually stands as the foundation for the great ancient languages such as Sumerian, Babylonian, Assyrian, Persian—that sort of group. But I have heard reports that the identification of cuneiform is in error, that we are dealing with a language that predates any known level of civilization in this world."

There; he'd done it.

"Where is that American ship, this cruiser, now?"

"I do not know."

"Can you tell us its port of call?"

"I cannot, because I do not know."

"When will the treasure arrive in Chicago?"

He was tempted sorely to say *When it gets there, you idiot,* but he held his tongue, smiled, and took the exit opportunity. "I'll see what I can find out for you," he told the reporter. "In the meantime," he paused as Dr. William Pencroft was pushed in his wheelchair to the edge of the stage, "this gentleman will attend to your other questions."

At nine P.M. sharp the next night the train with eight boxes of ancient artifacts, plus a pyramid three inches across at its base, four inches in height, began to move from a siding where it had been kept under heavy guard through daylight hours. It rolled slowly onto the main line stretching east from Waterloo and began to pick up speed, and soon thundered steadily toward Dubuque where it would cross the Mississippi River. From the east banks of the river the rail line swung southeast. The train would roll on this track until it reached Savanna and then run east-southeast toward Milledgeville.

Beyond that unimposing railside town lay another community, Polo. Between the two the tracks ran alongside a small river, at the bottom of an appreciable valley nestled between hills.

"X marks the spot," Jack Shannon said to his men. His long thin finger tapped his map. "Right there. Now, we've got to do all this right on the money, y'know? Split the seconds right down their backside, so to speak. When the train stops, Morgan, you and Cappy and Max, you come with me to the third car. Make sure you bring all the stuff, okay?"

"Yah, Jack, okay," came the reply.

They rolled a tank truck across the tracks and shone their headlights on the bright red GASOLINE—DANGER! sign painted on the tank. Then they built a fire beneath the truck. There was no way to tell, of course, that the tank was filled with only water. When the train engineer saw this giant bomb sitting on the tracks there was no doubt he was going to slam on the brakes like there was no tomorrow. That's when they would make their move, and Jack would do just what Indy had given him by way of instruction. On paper, and with drawings, too.

"It's coming!" a lookout called. Far down the tracks they saw the locomotive headlight sweeping back and forth as the train began rounding the curve to the straightaway in the valley. From the engineer's station in that locomotive, the burning tank car and all those headlights would set up the next move.

It came off like clockwork. The locomotive pounded like echoing thunder between the hills. The engineer looked down the tracks, saw light reflecting on the steel rails, and then, as he came close enough to see the blaze beneath the tanker and that magic word GASOLINE, hauled down on the train whistle, locked the brakes, and tossed people in the following cars like tenpins dumped onto the floor.

Shannon's boys used an old trick. At the first car, the doors were thrown open. Armed guards froze when they saw one of their own gripped tightly about the neck, a revolver held to his head. A second man trained a Thompson on the guards. The routine went the same way in each car. Shannon's men used heavy gangster accents.

"Y'make one wrong move, we blow his head off. Y'wanna see his brains splattered all over everywhere? Throw down your guns! Right where we can see 'em! Now, get to the door at the end of the car, get off the train, see? When you get outside I wants you should keep in mind youse is covered with Thompsons and a buncha double-barreled hammers. Everybody does good, nobody gets hurt. When youse is outside, start walking. You'll see a road. Get on it and make pitty-pat with your feet, double time, like the devil hisself is gonna bite y'head off. *Move!*"

The guard, in the meantime, thrashed about as best he could, putting on an excellent show for the others, who had no way of knowing that the "prisoner" in the hands of the holdup crowd was actually one of Shannon's own men. It worked in the cars with the security teams, and the routine worked perfectly in the third car of the train where the priceless artifacts were kept behind doors barred with iron slats.

Shannon had never understood why they would secure the doors and so often forget the windows. A single burst with a Thompson "opened" the windows. Tear gas grenades followed, misty white swirled within the car, and men choking and with eyes burning hurled open the doors and jumped to the ground, stumbling as far as they could get from the train.

Shannon and his crew clambered into the transport car. Not a soul remained. Quickly they identified the containers with the artifacts. Shannon searched for one with a small pyramid stenciled on its sides. Strangely, unlike the others, it lacked the heavy steel bars and hasps for security. He turned to his men, pointing to the other containers. "Get those things out of here, *now*!" He glanced outside. "And put out that dumb fire under the truck! Max, you stay here with me."

They opened the marked container. Gold statuary gleamed in the overhead lights. Shannon removed one statue of some kind of ancient god. It meant nothing to him. "Max, give me my bag. Move some boxes over here so we can open that sliding trapdoor in the ceiling."

"How did you know about—"

"Just do it!"

Shannon opened the zippered bag. Everything had

been prepared for use, including a thick leather case cable-fastened to a line that stretched to a deflated balloon. He removed the small leather bag Indy had given him in Chicago, and placed that item, along with the gold figurine, in the larger bag.

"Max, help me up," he ordered the other man. They climbed the boxes, slid back the trapdoor, and soon were on the railcar roof. Shannon glanced at his watch. Not a moment too soon. He glanced about him. They'd put out the fire by the truck. In the distance he saw the guards running away.

Shannon sat on the roof. He looked about him until he found one of the security rings used atop these cars when security men rode shotgun up here. He snapped a heavy safety hook to the ring, then extended the raglike balloon. "Hang on to this, Max. Whatever you do, don't let it go."

The deflated bag, the lines, and the heavy leather case were stretched out on the car roof. Shannon inserted a thin hose from the pressure container he'd carried with him, turned a valve to full on, and listened to the sharp hiss of gas flowing from the container to the balloon. Quickly the helium inflated, struggling to rise, but was held by Max's weight.

"Okay, Max, let it up slow-like, you got me?"

Max grunted, nodding. He eased off on his grip and the helium balloon, now fully inflated, rose to its maximum reach of thirty feet above the railcar roof. Wires were taped to the restraining line; the wires went from a battery remaining atop the train to two lights on the balloon, one on top, the other on the bottom so that it stood out sharply in the night.

Shannon looked down the tracks to the west. He hadn't had a moment to waste. The light in the sky was brilliant and it was getting bigger and brighter all the time. Thunder boomed down the valley, rebounding from the hills on each side, a roar rasping and howling all at the same time.

"Flatten out!" Shannon yelled to Max. "Hit the deck!"

Both men dropped prone. The light swelled as it rushed at them, the sound pounding against their ears.

Willard Cromwell cinched his seat belt just a tad tighter until he was comfortably snug in the left seat of the Ford Trimotor's cockpit. To his right, Gale Parker kept her finger moving along the map line marking the course of the railroad tracks. As they passed recognizable landmarks she called them out to Cromwell.

"That's Milledgeville. The tracks will swing just a bit northward here," she told him; shouting above the roar of the three Pratt & Whitney engines.

Cromwell clapped a hand to his right ear. "You don't need to shout," he reminded her. "Just use the bloody intercom. We can all hear you quite well. Don't forget that they're listening to you back in the cabin."

She nodded assent. "All right. Just a few miles to go. Can you see where the tracks ease off on that long curve into the valley?"

"Got it," he said brusquely. He was right at home; this was just like another bomb run, although he'd have to be as accurate as he ever was. He eased in left rudder and a touch of left aileron, a gentle bank to stay directly over the tracks. "Give me the searchlight," he directed her. "We're past the town now and it looks like open country from here on in."

Indy called from the cabin. "Can you see the train yet?"

"We should any moment now, and—yes; there it is! I've got the red lights at the back, and there's a bunch of cars there with their headlights on."

"Let me know the instant you see that double light above the train," Indy called back on the intercom. He lay prone on the cabin floor, a gaping hatch open beneath him, the wind howling inches away. Tarkiz Belem had wedged himself against two seats and he had a powerful death grip on Indy's ankles. Indy could see a few hundred yards ahead of the aircraft.

"I've got that double light atop the train!" Gale sang out. "It looks steady."

Indy and Foulois checked the cable snatch system extending beneath and trailing the airplane. It was the same system used for years by mailplanes to snatch-and-grab mail bags hung on a cable between two high poles; the plane would come in at minimum altitude, trailing a hook system and snatch the bag, and then an electric motor would reel it in.

"Airspeed is ninety-five, Indy," Cromwell reported. "We're right on the money at just under fifty feet above ground."

"Hold it there . . . okay, I've got the train in sight, I see the bag. Get ready! Make this run perfect, Will—"

The Ford thundered out of the night, its powerful landing light a cyclopean monster racing through darkness. The landing gear swept over the train. Cromwell held the airplane rock-steady as they rushed over the last cars, and he felt the slight *thud* as the hook snagged the cable beneath the helium balloon.

They'd worked this out with machinelike precision. The moment Indy sang out into the intercom, "Got it!" Cromwell eased back on the yoke in his left hand, held the throttles exactly where they were, and pulled the Ford into a gentle climb, bleeding off airspeed to just above seventy miles an hour. Back in the cabin, Tarkiz held Indy steady while Foulois rotated a large handle that brought up cable on the winch secured to the floor and seat braces.

"Hold it! Okay; right there!" Indy ordered. He held out

his right hand. Foulois handed him his Webley. Indy held the heavy revolver in both hands, aimed carefully, and fired a single shot into the helium balloon. It deflated instantly into a fluttering rag. Moments later the entire assembly was in the airplane. They slid shut the floor hatch and locked it in place. Indy swung around to a sitting position. Foulois spoke into his microphone. "Cromwell, stay in the climb. Follow the flight plan."

Gale held up a chart and printed instructions. "Eight thousand feet," she called off from the checklist. "All running lights and landing lights out."

"Very good," Cromwell said easily, smiling. "Piece of cake, that was."

"You *are* good," Gale told him with honest admiration. She was right. Cromwell had made this run as if he'd done it a hundred times before.

Foulois and Belem watched Indy open the leather case. He withdrew the gold statue and handed it to Belem. The big man's eyes lit up at the sight and heft of the gold. Indy laughed. "It's not what you think," he told Tarkiz.

Dark eyes narrowed. "What do you mean, Indy?"

"Try cutting it with a knife. It's *plated.* Under that plating that thing is lead."

Tarkiz showed his confusion. He snatched a long blade from his boot and sliced into the statue. He stared at the gray lead beneath the thin outer plating of gold.

"Why in the name of three blue devils did we go through all this, then!" he shouted.

"Because we needed to get that pyramid everyone is talking about," Indy told him.

"And we have it?" asked Foulois.

"It's in the bag." Indy tweaked him.

"But . . . how could you know?" They watched Indy retrieve the small leather sack from the larger bag. He opened the sack and held the pyramid with its cuneiform etchings for them to see for themselves.

"But . . . how could you know it was in that little sack?" Belem said, more confused than ever.

Indy moved to a seat and sprawled, his long legs stretched out. "Easy," he said with an air of nonchalance. "I knew where it was because I'm the one who put it there."

He tossed the pyramid to Foulois, who grabbed desperately for what he had until this moment believed was one of the most anxiously sought artifacts in the world. "You hang onto it for now," Indy told him. He secured his seat belt and pushed his hat over his eyes.

"I'm going to take a nap. Wake me when we're ready to start down."

"Mon dieu," Foulois groaned. He looked at Belem. "I am beginning to believe our man Jones is really crazy."

Tarkiz Belem glared at the worthless statue. "Either he is," he grated, "or *we* are."

6

"Wright Tower, this is Crazy Angels with you at eight thousand, estimate two zero miles out, and landing. Over."

Gale Parker and Tarkiz Belem showed their questions in their sudden stares at one another. Cromwell and Foulois were together in the cockpit, this time with the Frenchman at the controls and Cromwell working radio communications. But who was this *Crazy Angels?*

"It fits perfectly," Belem said to Gale Parker. "This whole affair has been crazy, no? From the beginning. Crazy Angels, it is our call sign, I judge."

Gale nodded. "Sounds reasonable. "What I don't get is why we're going into an army field."

"As soon as Indy awakens, little one, I'm sure he will come up with something new that is even crazier than everything that has happened so far."

Behind their seats, Indy slowly pushed back the brim of his well-worn hat. It was an Indiana Jones trademark and had held off broiling sun and howling snow. An old friend. He peered owlishly from beneath it.

"We're landing at Wright Field," he said to both Gale and Tarkiz, "for some magic."

"Magic?" they echoed.

"Uh-huh." Indy stretched and yawned. "We need to, well, disappear."

"They have vanishing cream, I suppose, at a military field," Gale said with easy sarcasm.

"Close to it." He was on his feet. He clapped Tarkiz on a broad shoulder. "Hang in there, friend. The doors will swing wide very soon and from there you will see daylight."

Indy went forward to the cockpit, standing behind the two pilot seats. He stared through the sharply angled windshield, watching the scattered lights of small towns passing below. Isolated twin beams poked along dark stretches of highway, and he could even make out glowing red taillights.

"They call you back from Wright Field?" he asked Cromwell.

"Only to stand by for landing instructions. They— Just a moment. Here they are now," Cromwell replied. "Here, Indy." He handed Indy a headset.

"Crazy Angels, Crazy Angels, Wright Tower. Your clearance is confirmed. You are cleared to begin your descent now. No other traffic reported, and you are cleared for a straight-in approach to runway one six zero. Please read back. Wright Tower over."

Cromwell repeated their instructions and then added, "We'll give you a call when we have the field in sight. Over."

"That is affirmative, Crazy Angels. The follow-me truck will be waiting for you at the midway turnoff from the runway. No further transmissions are necessary but we will monitor this frequency in case you need us. Wright Tower over and out."

"Cheerio." Cromwell signed off. He turned to Indy. "You catch all that?"

"Very good," Indy confirmed. "How long before we land?"

"Twelve, fourteen minutes."

"Okay. When you shut down, take your personal belongings with you. I'll tell the others."

Less than ten minutes later they had the rotating beacon in sight. Foulois had been descending steadily, and with the field lights growing steadily brighter he eased the Ford onto a heading of 160° to settle for the straight-in approach and landing.

"I've got the runway in sight," Cromwell told him.

"Roger that," Rene said; a moment later: "Got it."

Cromwell scanned the sky. "No traffic."

"Ring the bell," Foulois said easily. Cromwell pressed the button that provided a final warning to their passengers to secure their seat belts. Foulois flew the Ford down the approach as if it were on a railway. In the calm and cool night air the Ford seem to float more than fly. The wheels feathered on without even a rubbery squeak. He let her roll, and picked up the truck with the lighted FOLLOW ME sign. They taxied past rows of hangars and shops. Airplanes were lined up in all directions, a mixture of fighters, transports, bombers, trainers, and some civilian craft. The truck stopped, and a man jumped down and signaled the Ford pilot to cut the power.

Moments later the only sounds from the trimotor were those of heated metal cooling off in a cricketlike singsong of snaps and crackles. A small blue bus came from around the side of a hangar and stopped by the Ford. An officer waited until Indy and his group climbed down to the tarmac. He studied them for a moment and clearly identified Indy.

He walked up to him and snapped a salute. "Professor

Jones, good to see you again." They shook hands. "With your permission, my men will bring your equipment and luggage."

Indy nodded and turned to Tarkiz. "Go with them. You know what to bring." The big man nodded and climbed back into the Ford. Soon their belongings and other gear had been shifted to the bus.

Indy's group gathered about him, and he introduced Henshaw. "You have your orders about our plane?" Indy asked the colonel.

"Yes, sir." A smile played briefly across Henshaw's face. "It is to be made invisible."

Tarkiz turned to Gale Parker with a grimace. "So! Like I said, he is crazy, and this colonel, I think he is crazy, too! They are going to make our machine invisible! *Poof!* We will be like the sky. Not even the birds will see us."

Indy nodded with Tarkiz's outburst. "For a while, my friend, at least for a while."

Cromwell moved forward to the colonel. "If you don't mind, I must insist on being with our aeroplane if there is to be any fueling or servicing."

Henshaw studied the British pilot. "Cromwell, right? Don't you think we can take care of your machine properly?" There was just a touch of sarcasm in his reply.

He didn't make a ripple on Cromwell, who moved up to go nose to nose with the American officer. "Quite frankly, Colonel, I do not. *We* fly this machine. If your people mess it up and we discover their hammy hands while we are at ten thousand feet or so, I don't believe it takes much imagination for you to judge who will pay the piper." Cromwell turned to Indy. "I *insist.* I myself, or Foulois, *must* be with the aircraft for any work or servicing."

Indy turned to Henshaw. "They call the shots with the plane, Colonel."

"No offense taken, sir," Henshaw said to Indy, directing his gaze to Cromwell. "I only wish this same attitude prevailed among all *my* men. You have my word Mr.—"

"*Brigadier*, if you don't mind?" Cromwell said icily.

"Of course, sir." He gestured to the group. "The bus please."

As they climbed aboard Tarkiz nudged Indy. "It is maybe a bother, Indiana, but my stomach will no longer keep silent. I must eat soon or perish."

"With that spread of yours, Tarkiz," Foulois quipped, "you could last as long without food as a camel could without water."

"Skinny people always make stupid remarks," Tarkiz answered good-naturedly. "But I do not want to talk. I want to *eat*. One more cold frankfurter and—"

"It's all taken care of, sir. Just a few more minutes," said the bartender.

The bus rolled through the sprawling base, then stopped before a high barricade of concrete posts and triple rolls of barbed wire. Signs reading RESTRICTED AREA and AUTHORIZED PERSONNEL ONLY were all about the place. Guards removed the entry barrier, saluting Henshaw as they went through. Before them was another great hangar. Army guards rolled back huge sliding doors and the bus drove inside. The doors closed behind it, and with the muffled thump of the doors coming together bright lights snapped on above it.

The group looked about them with interest. Within the great hangar was what seemed to be part of a small village: cottages, stone office buildings, even a lawn with trees. "This is home for the next couple of days," Indy told his group. "Colonel, I'll go with your men and make sure everybody's gear goes to their assigned rooms."

He banged Tarkiz on the shoulder. "You and the others

go with that sergeant. Right to the dining room. They'll take your orders there. Anything you want."

"Dining room? In *here?*"

"I thought you were starving to death."

"You are right. My stomach knows my throat has been cut." Tarkiz grasped the nearest sergeant's arm. "You have ancestors? Ah, very good. Feed me, or you may meet your ancestors much sooner than you think."

Indy refused answers to all questions after dinner, steering conversation to small talk about the events of the evening, leaving the others frustrated but respectful of his silence. That night they slept in comfortable beds, each within a fully furnished room. There were books and radio facilities in each room, as well as a telephone, but all calls had to be processed through a military security switchboard.

Gale Parker had already learned that Indy's strange aloofness was his means of waiting for information from the outside world, or for the arrival of key people involved in their sometimes baffling machinations. Gale was learning the man. She was still confused by his methods, but tremendously impressed with the swift execution of plans he had drawn with meticulous attention. She felt more and more drawn to him, and was caught by surprise at her feminine response to a man who fairly exuded masculinity, yet managed to treat her with the respect he felt she deserved as a woman and an equal.

It was a magnetism to the opposite sex she had never known, and this sudden upward boiling of emotions puzzled and even frightened her. She was well out of water in her personal life experience. Indy's seemingly split personality toward her was as baffling as it was welcome. Gale knew she was as stubborn as a mountain goat, but Indy never tested that streak that ran so strongly in her.

She would gladly have welcomed his personal attention, yet she could not shake the reality that Indy was still living with the ghost of his dead wife. A dozen times she had started to ask him about Deirdre—what she was like, what had brought them together into marriage, how they had shared the wonder of exploration and adventure.

She gasped with surprise at herself when she realized she was jealous of a woman who had died several years before this moment! The revelation came that she *wanted* a relationship that would permit herself and Indy to bond closer. *Nigh unto impossible,* she sighed, *in this group of professional killers.*

Put it aside, woman! she railed at herself. She would have to do just that. She *must.* And then, alone with her thoughts, she realized she was smiling, that she would take every attempt to narrow the gulf between them, to bring Indy to regard her as a woman as well as a partner in this strange mission on which they had embarked.

But does he feel that way about me . . . ?

She slammed a fist into her pillow, frustrated, starting to twist inside. Was she falling for Indy? Could that really be the case? Would she ever be willing to give up her incredible sense of freedom, the lustiness of going with the wind if that was what she desired. *I don't need any man!* she shouted to herself in another attack of self-recrimination.

Another voice inside her head spoke quietly, laughingly. *You're a liar, Gale Parker.*

Alone in her room, she buried her face in her pillow. *Oh, shut up, Gale Parker!*

Cromwell finished his third cup of coffee and stubbed out his cigarette. "Dashing great breakfast," he sighed. Tarkiz nodded and let fly with a horrendous belch, beaming at the others. Foulois ignored him, dabbing gently at his lips with his napkin. Indy smiled; Gale kept a straight face.

"I'd like to see our machine," Cromwell said suddenly to Colonel Henshaw, who'd shared breakfast with them.

Before Henshaw could reply, Tarkiz leaned forward and gestured denial with a wave of his hand. "No, no, you cannot do that," he said as if reproving Cromwell.

Henshaw showed surprise; Cromwell responded in his own unique way.

"And why the bloody hell not?" he demanded.

"Ah, the English have such short memories!" Tarkiz said loudly, beaming, turning from one person to another to assure himself of his audience. "Do you already forget what our good colonel here," he pointed to Henshaw, "told us last night? He has orders! And those orders are to make our machine *invisible.*"

Tarkiz leaned forward, a conspiratorial gleam on his face. "And not even the English can see *invisible* machines."

Tarkiz was just a bit too ebullient, judged Indy. He smelled some sort of deliberate confrontation. He knew how much Tarkiz hated being kept in the dark about anything, and that invisibility remark had been chafing under his skin the night through. "Leave it be," he said quietly to Tarkiz.

The big Kurd stared back at him. "Indy! You wound me, my friend. I want very much to see our invisible airplane. The good colonel apparently can work miracles." He turned to Henshaw. "Tell me, Colonel. Does our invisible airplane still fly? Even though we cannot see it?"

If he thought Henshaw would be taken aback by his sudden sarcastic thrust he was greatly mistaken. Indy busied himself with his coffee mug to keep from bursting into laughter. Henshaw, his face as bland as he could make his expression, looked directly at Tarkiz.

"Mr. Belem, the answer is yes. Your airplane is invisible, and it flies, and it matters not one iota if *you* can see it."

"How marvelous," Rene Foulois joined in. "I've never flown an invisible airplane. I look forward to such a unique experience."

Gale Parker studied the men about her. "Does anybody get the feeling there's an enormous amount of leg-pulling going on here?"

They turned, as one, to her. "*Miss* Parker," Cromwell said with heavy civility, "either you have the answer, or I suggest we go see our invisible aeroplane."

"He does not yet understand," Tarkiz jumped in quickly, enjoying the mild furor he'd brought to the table. "It is like the British lion. All the British are proud of the way it rules so much of the world, but no one has yet seen that shaggy beast."

"Everybody up and at 'em," Indy broke in without a moment for the exchange to heat up. "Colonel," he turned to Henshaw, "let's see your magic at work."

The friction evaporated as they went to the bus parked inside the hangar. Henshaw stopped them by the entry door, handing each member of the group a clip-on, glass-sealed identification tag. "You'll need these ID tags anywhere on this base," he explained. "Please have them clipped to your clothing at all times."

Foulois studied his carefully. "Colonel, you fascinate me. This tag has my name, physical characteristics, a photograph of me, *and* the thumbprint of my right hand." He studied the colonel. "I did not have my print *or* my photograph taken, so how could you—"

"Standard procedure, sir, when we prefer not to bother our guests with routine. Photographs, including films, have been taken of you a dozen times. And whatever you touched—a glass, a cup, personal articles—well, you left good prints everywhere. We simply lifted them for each of you. Standard procedure, Mr. Foulois. Can we board now, please?"

The bus stopped a hundred feet before the huge hangar where the Ford Trimotor had been kept for the night. As they walked before the bus, Henshaw motioned for them to stop. "If you would indulge me for the moment, please? Wait here while they open the hangar doors."

He turned and gave a hand signal to the hangar crew. An electric motor hummed loudly and the huge sliding doors began to move right and left until the interior of the entire hangar was exposed to them.

Except for Indy, who had known all along what would happen during the night, the group stared in confusion. Suddenly Gale Parker burst into laughter. "By God, he's done it!" she exclaimed, clapping her hands.

"But . . . but . . . which one is *our* aeroplane?" Cromwell said, squinting to make out details.

Henshaw enjoyed the moment immensely. "You tell me, Col—sorry; Brigadier. Point out *your* airplane."

They stared at six Ford Trimotors in the hangar, every one of them painted in army numbers and markings. With the exception of different identifying serial numbers, every airplane was exactly like the others. It was impossible to distinguish the trimotor in which they landed here the night before.

Tarkiz clapped Henshaw approvingly on the shoulder. "Colonel, I take off my hat to you." He looked to Cromwell and Foulois. "He has done it. We can see our airplane, but we cannot because we do not know which one it is. Wonderful!"

"The news of the train robbery last night," Colonel Henshaw said to the group, "is all over the papers and is being broadcast on every radio station in the country.

What amazes everyone is how it was carried out, and that nobody was killed or even hurt. The missing gold statues, and something about an ancient small pyramid, are headlines everywhere. And there are reports that a large airplane was involved. The crew of a public works department was arrested last night and questioned for hours, but they were all released early this morning. Seems they had an engine being replaced and their machine was unflyable. So," he said with a smile, "it seemed rather inappropriate to have anything with a public works logo splashed on its sides on this field. Anyone who comes here—and we expect questions and likely some visitors from the media—is welcome to stand just about where you are and do all the looking they want."

Henshaw turned and pointed to the east. "In fact, there's a U.S. Marines Ford on a long approach to this field right now. This afternoon, a Navy Ford will also be landing here for some special tests. *Your* airplane, as far as the world knows, simply never existed."

They started walking toward the hangar. "Colonel," Cromwell said quickly, "my request last night about servicing? Did—"

"No one has touched your machine except for the new markings," Henshaw anticipated the query. "When you're ready for servicing and the equipment changes Professor Jones has specified, you, and whoever else works on the machine, will be provided army coveralls and the proper identification so that you will appear just like the other mechanics and technicians who work here."

Not until Cromwell and Foulois were able to run their hands over the different airplanes could they detect the trimotor with the belly hatch. And that didn't help too much, for three other Fords had the same.

"Marvelous," Gale Parker said for them all.

. . .

Gale Parker sat with Indy in the group's private dining room—an army mess facility with extra trimmings—within the sealed hangar. Cromwell, Foulois, and Belem were hard at work on the airplane with a group of army mechanics and technicians. Their work would require several days of special attention, and Indy planned to use that time setting up systems of communication between his team and headquarters.

Gale toyed with her coffee mug. "Mind if I ask some questions, Indy?"

Like the others, he and Gale wore mechanics' coveralls. They were much less likely to draw attention with shapeless, almost baggy outerwear.

"Go ahead," he said. "The others will be along shortly. They won't be needed for the engine changes."

"You're changing engines?" she asked with open surprise. "They sounded fine to me."

"Nothing wrong with the engines. But with what we may be doing and where we'll be flying, I want some specials. Our airplane has standard Pratt and Whitney radials. We get just about thirteen hundred horsepower from them. But the army has some changes hardly anyone knows about. Pratt and Whitney sent a bunch of their modified Wasp engines down here for us. The whole idea is to convert horsepower to thrust. We won't be much faster than we are now, but we'll more than double the rate of climb we can get from the Ford. And we'll be able to accommodate the special long-range tanks that are being installed so we can fly at least fifteen hundred miles without refueling. More, when they finish the installation for tanks we can hang beneath the wings. We'll need all that power when we're fully loaded just to get off the ground."

She sat in silence, caught by surprise with his words. He finished his coffee. "Also, with the new power packages, we'll be able to land and take off from really small fields. Oh, yes, balloon tires also, for rough field operation."

"Indy, you amaze me! I didn't know you were a pilot!"

He rolled the cigar between his fingers. "I'm not. I've always wanted to be, but every time I started taking lessons I either got buried in my teaching classes, or I was off in the hills, or the jungle, or the desert—"

"I know," she broke in.

"Well, I just never had the opportunity." He looked wistful. "One day, perhaps. I really should learn."

"Then how come you know so much? I mean, everything you've just said—"

He smiled at her. "Not being able to fly doesn't mean I don't know how to listen. I've spent many an hour with engineers and pilots. The guys who really know how to take a rugged lady like the Ford and turn her into a ballet stepper. There's a lot more they're doing, but I'd rather you heard that from the others."

They heard a vehicle pull up outside the hangar doors, and soon the rest of their crew came in. Their coveralls were smeared with grease. "They won't need us for a while," Cromwell explained. "They're changing the tires and doing the engines and props. Those are the greatest superchargers I've ever seen. They could take us right to the top of Mt. Everest, the way they suck in air. It's like three tornados working for us."

He fell heavily into a seat. "Frenchy and I were talking about a change in the brake system. It will go especially well with those new tires. You know how the brakes work, right?"

Indy nodded. "That big handle right behind the pilot seats."

Foulois made a sour face. "The Ford is a wonderful machine but that kind of braking system is from the dark ages. Maneuvering on the ground is terrible. And since we have all those people and the right equipment, and it shouldn't take more than one day of extra work, I'd like to change the hydraulics from that handle to foot pedal brakes for both pilot seats."

Indy glanced at Cromwell, who said, "It pains me when a Frenchman is so smart, but he's right. It's a bloody good idea, Indy."

"All right. Do it." Indy looked up. Colonel Henshaw and another man were standing behind the others.

Henshaw gestured to his companion. "Master Sergeant David Korwalski. He's the chief maintenance and modification man in our experimental section."

"Don't let him get away from us," Cromwell added. "The man has magic in his hands, the way he works on aeroplanes."

"This time it is the British gentleman who is correct," Foulois said, winking at Indy.

"If you have a moment, Professor Jones," Henshaw came into the exchange, "we'd like to go over the rest of the work you and your people want done. That way we won't waste any time, and my crews can work right around the clock. Twelve-hour shifts."

"Colonel, I appreciate that, but I don't want to overdo your help to us."

"No problem, sir. The men all volunteered."

Indy nodded to Cromwell and Foulois. "You have the rest of the list?"

Cromwell drew a sheaf of folded papers and specifications from his leg pocket. "Right here." He spread them across the table. Tarkiz squeezed in between the other two men. "You do not mind, Indy? I am learning much."

"You're one of us, Tarkiz. Of course."

"Good! I have ideas, too. But I will wait until these two are done."

"Will, let's do it. Colonel, why don't you and Korwalski sit down here with us."

It went on through two hours of planning and no small number of arguments, two pilots each putting forward his own best ideas. Generally, however, they were in agreement to modify the "gentleman's airplane" into a machine with greatly increased performance parameters and capabilities never planned by the Ford Company.

"Will, put aside that remark you made about climbing as high as Everest. Now, the book numbers show eighteen thousand or so as absolute ceiling," Indy said.

"That is correct, Indy. Service ceiling of seventeen thousand," Foulois replied.

"What's the difference?" asked Gale.

"When the airplane is still climbing at one hundred feet a minute," Rene explained, "that's the service ceiling." He tapped the drawings of the engines. "With those superchargers and new propellers, this machine will fly to thirty thousand or higher. We won't really know until we start getting up there."

"And we'll freeze," Indy commented. "Colonel Henshaw, that series of high-altitude flights that were made from here some years ago. I think McCook Field was the actual base. Didn't they break forty thousand then?"

"That was Lieutenant John Mcready, sir. And it *was* some time ago. September of 1921, in fact. McCready took a LePere up to over forty-one thousand feet. It was a rough flight. His flight gear was still experimental, so he suffered from the cold."

"*How* cold?" asked Gale.

"About sixty below, Fahrenheit. The thermometer busted then," Korwalski answered.

"Great," Gale murmured.

"We'll have high-altitude gear for your airplane. Besides, we can boost the heat output from the engines, and your ship is already set up for direct heat flow into the cockpit, besides the heat registers already in the cabin floor."

Henshaw showed his surprise. "You really intend to go *that* high?"

Indy toyed with a pencil. "Hopefully, no. But I want the altitude capability. Just in case."

"If you do," Henshaw said doubtfully, "you'll be awfully lonely up there."

Down the list they continued. All available types of engine instruments and flight instruments, including the latest gyroscopic devices for navigational headings and the artificial horizon, that would permit them to fly not only safely but with great accuracy even when they were enveloped in clouds or storms. The military had been developing an advanced ADF, an Air Direction Finder that could home in on radio broadcast stations and weather stations from hundreds of miles away. Into the Ford went first-aid kits, fire extinguishers, an electric galley, water tanks, additional booster magnetos and spark plugs and other spares for the engines, fuel funnels, mooring ropes and stakes, tool kits, an emergency starting crank if the electrical system failed. They installed parachute flare holders and firing tubes, able to be activated from either the cockpit or the cabin.

Cromwell, who'd flown to remote locations about the world, insisted on an earth-induction compass that had dead-on accuracy even if all their electrical systems failed. "That's what got that Lindbergh fellow through the worst of his flight," he explained in reference to Lindbergh's nonstop solo Atlantic crossing three years before.

"I'll say one thing," remarked Colonel Henshaw when they completed the list. "You can live out of this machine anywhere in the world."

"Almost," Indy corrected him, to the surprise of the

group. "We've got thirteen seats in the cabin. Remove nine of them. Put in a couple of folding cots against the inside fuselage walls. They'll weigh less than the seats and give us extra room inside the cabin. Also, we can use the additional space for a small gasoline generator and other equipment."

Korwalski scanned the list with Cromwell and Foulois. "I guess that does it," he said, nodding to Henshaw that he was anxious to return to the Ford to resume his work.

"One last thing," Indy said unexpectedly. They waited for him to continue as he spread the cutaway schematics of the wing structure. "Here," he tapped the schematics, "we've got the baggage compartments. They're right between the second and third spars on each side of the cabin. We're not carrying passengers or their baggage, and those swing-down compartments are designed to hold at least four hundred pounds on each side." He glanced up at Cromwell and Foulois. "Everybody still with me?" They nodded.

"That's wasted space, and I need both the space and the weight capacity," Indy went on.

Cromwell looked at Foulois. "Are you thinking what I'm thinking?"

"I am beginning to understand," Foulois said slowly.

"*I* do not understand!" Tarkiz Belem glared at them.

"He bloody well wants to install a machine gun in each wing compartment!" Cromwell burst out.

"Machine guns?" Gale Parker echoed.

"He is correct?" Tarkiz asked Indy.

"One in each wing," Indy confirmed. "And a mount back in the cabin with a sliding top fuselage panel so we can raise or lower the mount for a single weapon.

"Sergeant?" Indy turned to Korwalski. "Think you can mount a fifty-caliber in each of those locations?"

Korwalski nodded. "I can, sir. But I don't recommend it."

"Tell me why."

"Well, it's not just the weight, sir. It's setting up the absorption system for vibration and that means being absolutely certain we don't weaken the wing. You have a heavy piece up in there, and you fire it when you're in a steep bank, you are *really* putting the hammer down on the wing structure. Enough to do some damage. And there's the weight, of course. And if I'm guessing right, sir, you're going to be in some pretty oddball places where getting caliber fifty ammo is going to be a real headache."

"I gather you have an alternate solution?" Indy pressed.

"Yes, sir, I do."

"Let's hear it."

Korwalski turned to Henshaw. "Sir, I need your authorization. About the new weapons, sir. They're still under security."

Henshaw chewed his lower lip and exchanged a look with Indy. Finally he nodded. "Their authorization comes right from the top of the War Department, Sergeant. Spell it out."

"Yes, sir." Korwalski turned back to Indy. "We've developed a new caliber thirty piece, sir. It has a hypervelocity round, about twice the muzzle velocity of anything that's ever been put in an airplane. That about triples its effective range. It's lightweight, and it'll take any kind of round. Incendiary, steel-jacketed for armor piercing. There's also a special round we've developed with an explosive charge within the round. It'll take care of any, ah, well, any problems you may have in mind." He drew himself up straight. "Sir," he finished.

Indy was a bit out of water here. But he had three men, two of them pilots, who were experts with machine guns. "Gentlemen?"

Tarkiz turned to Korwalski. "The rate of fire. You tell me, please?"

"Fourteen hundred rounds a minute. And you can carry a real load with that system."

Tarkiz beamed. "Take it," he told Indy. "It is a dream."

"Will?"

"Wish I'd had something like that when I was mixing it up with Jerry," was Cromwell's answer.

"Rene?"

"With that kind of weapon," the Frenchman said quietly, "I could have doubled, maybe tripled, the Boche I shot down."

Indy looked to Gale. "What do you think?"

"About what?" she exclaimed. "I'm strictly bow and arrow, remember? Or a crossbow. The professionals say go with it. No arguments from me."

Indy laughed, and pushed together the charts and schematics and the lists they had compiled. "Gentlemen, that does it. Colonel Henshaw, the sooner all this is done, the better."

"Yes, sir. Like I said, my men will be working on double shifts, right around the clock."

Sergeant Korwalski hesitated before speaking again, but he couldn't hold back the question that had been growing in his mind. "Sir, this may be out of line, but can I ask you something?"

"Feel free, Sergeant."

"Everything you're doing with this airplane. I mean, we're building some special bombardment models of the Ford."

"You can tell him," Henshaw said. "It's the XB-nine oh six project."

"But this is way ahead of our schedule," Korwalski went on. "Sir, are we going to war?"

Silence hung among the group like a fog. Indy rose slowly to his feet to face Korwalski, and Indy wasn't smiling.

"Unfortunately," he said slowly, "the answer to that is yes."

7

"Change."

"What?"

"I asked you to change," Indy said to Gale Parker. "You know, a different outfit."

Gale studied herself in the mirror. "What's wrong with what I'm wearing?"

"It's great if we're going hunting, or mountain climbing," Indy answered, trying not to show a smile. "But not for dinner."

"Indy, we're inside a hangar at an army base where—" She studied him carefully, her head tilted slightly to one side.

"I had a dog used to do that," he jibed. "Good-looking dog, too."

"You're comparing me with a *dog*?" she exclaimed. A touch of red appeared in her cheeks.

"Well, she didn't dress for dinner, either. But I meant the way you tilted your head to one side. Like you were listening extra carefully."

"Indiana Jones, you've lost your mind," she said

sharply. "I will *not* change my clothes simply to sit with this gang of yours in this hangar and—"

"Who said anything about dining with a gang?"

"You said . . ." She faltered for a moment, trying to get his drift. Try as she could, she couldn't get past the poker face he was holding. "You said, *dining*," she completed her sentence. "Indy, are you asking me for a *date*?"

"You could call it that. You could also call it an order. But, yes," he admitted, "it *is* a date. Not in a hangar, not with our crew. You, me. Downtown. You know, Dayton. There's a great Italian restaurant there. I've made reservations and we leave in ten minutes, so I'd appreciate it if you wouldn't waste any more time playing word games."

She started to answer but only managed an open mouth.

"Oh, yes, one more thing." He reached into his leather jacket and withdrew a strap holster with a .25-caliber automatic snugged tightly within the leather. "Wear a dress. Strap this on just above your knee. I assume you know how to use this if necessary?"

She had recovered quickly. "Are we going to kill something for dinner? A wild lasagna, perhaps?"

"That's pretty good. I'll tell that to the manager at Del Vecchio. We're going to be late if you don't stop asking questions, lady." He started for the door, looking over his shoulder. "Ten minutes." He was gone.

She stood looking at the closed door for a good thirty seconds. She felt bewildered. Indy . . . taking her out to dinner? To a classy restaurant? She rifled through her closet. *I'll kill him. This is an expedition, not a social event. . . .* Quickly she selected a flare skirt, hardly evening dress. But a silk blouse and a kerchief and— *No high heels. The suede boots. They'll do. . . .* She had barely finished dressing and was frantically trying to make something sensible out of her hair when she heard Indy knocking at the door.

She had only once seen him in anything but that beaten-up leather jacket and rumpled trousers. She recognized the suede jacket he'd worn when he went to Chicago, and was amazed to see him in neatly pressed brown trousers. He had a bolo tie. *Naturally, it's got the head of a rattlesnake for that real dressy look*, she thought sarcastically.

He looked her up and down. "You, Miss Parker, are one spiffy lady."

"Spiffy?"

"It's a compliment."

"You have a strange language over here, Indy."

"Okay," he said pleasantly. "You look swell. Dynamite, in fact. Let's go." He turned and started down the corridor, letting her run to catch up. Outside the hangar a black Packard was parked. He opened the door for her. She wondered if he was going crazy. They were partners, everyone equal. She *liked* equal, and being offered the courtesies due a lady for an evening engagement was foreign to her.

They sat in silence for several minutes until they were on the road to Dayton. "Indy?"

"Uh-huh."

"What's the occasion?"

"Great food, great wine, beautiful woman. What more could a man ask?"

"No hidden agenda?"

"Who? Me? You wound me."

"Is that natural or from a script?"

"Will you relax, please?"

"I'll try."

"Good girl."

She tilted her head. "Good doggie. That's me."

He burst into laughter and she couldn't help it; she joined in.

"Indy, dinner was *fabulous,*" Gale said with genuine feeling. It was a meal she had never before encountered. Steamed mussels with wine sauce, Caesar salad, rolls baked right in the kitchen, broiled Maine lobster, and a white wine she had never heard of but that equaled anything she had ever had in England or France. "I've never had better. I'm overwhelmed."

"Dessert?"

She shook her head. "I'll pass. But I will accept a cappuccino."

He leaned back in his chair and motioned for their waiter. "Cappuccino for the lady, and I'll have a brandy."

The waiter wasn't gone a minute, but he returned empty-handed. "Dr. Jones, the manager would like you and your companion to be his guest for after-dinner drinks in his office."

Indy lifted an eyebrow. "Ah, you must mean Dominic Carboni."

"Yes, sir."

"We'd be delighted. Just give us about ten minutes, then come back for us."

The waiter beamed. "Yes, sir," and he was gone.

Gale frowned, leaning forward. "How did he know who you were?" Before he could answer she went on. "Of course. You made reservations."

He nodded, but she was still puzzled. "But how, I mean, why would the manager, this fellow—"

"Carboni."

"Why would he want us for company in his office? And how would he know who you were? I don't mean by name, Indy, but—"

"Let me cut this quickly, Gale. He knows who we are because we were in the newspapers today."

"We were?"

"There's a strange echo in here."

"I can't help it. I don't understand what's going on."

"A newspaper story was set up. Professor Jones and Doctor Parker are visiting the workshop of the Wright Brothers. Research on the beginnings of flight. Remember, the original airplane the Wrights built went to England. They were unhappy with the American government and that was their way of telling everybody off. So," he straightened his napkin, "we came here to see how much influence the Wrights had on aircraft design in the early days of flying in the British Isles."

"But that's no secret!"

"No, but it does well enough for a newspaper blurb."

"And this Carboni fellow has something to do with airplanes?"

"I don't believe he's ever set foot in one."

"Indy, you're toying with me."

"Not really. I had to make sure that certain people would know I'm in Dayton tonight. They could find out easily enough that I made dinner reservations here."

"But *why*?"

"Well, I figured that was the best way for them to find me."

"You *wanted* to be found?"

"You're getting the idea."

"You didn't tell me *why*."

"They want something very badly."

"It couldn't be that strange little pyramid, could it?"

"Brilliant deduction, Miss Parker."

"But—"

"Let it rest, Gale. Here comes our guide." The waiter withdrew Gale's chair, and she and Indy followed the waiter through a curtained doorway and down a long corridor, stopping before a door of massive wooden construction. Indy scanned it carefully. He listened as the waiter knocked on the door, judging that sandwiched between heavy wooden panels was a layer of steel. He knew he was right when he saw the effort it took the waiter to push the door open.

A bulletproof door.

Dominic Carboni rose from a deep leather couch to greet them. Their drinks waited for them on a marble table. Gale looked about the room. "You have exquisite taste," she told Carboni.

"Thank you. The finest there is. I don't hold back nothin' when it comes to the real goods. Real swell, huh?"

A lout in a marble palace, she judged immediately. *He has no more business with Indy than he does with me. He's a front for someone else.*

They went through small talk as they drank. "This your first trip to Dayton, Miss Parker? How does our town hit you?"

"I haven't really seen it," she parried. She remembered Indy's description of the cover story he'd dropped into the papers. "Mostly I've seen the bicycle shop of the Wrights, studied their wind tunnel, gone over their notes. It's really quite fascinating."

"Uh-huh. I guess it's real interesting," Carboni said. "If that's what you like, I mean. Me, I'll take the nightclub scene any time. I ain't never seen an airplane that looks better than a great broad." He guffawed with pleasure at his own remarks.

Gale couldn't miss the change in Indy's demeanor. Even the way he sat had undergone a subtle shift. She had been a huntress long enough to recognize when someone moved from relaxation to being a human coiled spring. He placed his brandy snifter gently on the marble table and again shifted position in the chair.

"Carboni, lay it out."

In that moment, Carboni too seemed to change to a different person. The expensive suit and furnishings couldn't disguise the low-life before them.

"I didn't know you were in a hurry, Jones." *There it is.* Gale spotted it immediately. *No more Professor or Doctor; just Jones.*

"My driver is waiting for us at your back entrance," Indy said. "And he is a very impatient man."

Would Indy ever stop catching her by surprise? *What* driver? They came here in that Packard that Indy drove himself. She forced herself to remain quiet, to watch. She shifted in her own seat so that the .25 automatic nestled against her leg was easier to reach. Somehow she knew the polite chitchat was just about over.

"How'd you know about the back entrance, Jones?" Carboni looked at Indy with suspicion. "You ain't never been here before."

"Cut it," Indy snapped, leaning forward. "You're just the agent for Mr. Big, whoever and wherever he is. What's your pitch?"

Carboni smiled like an eel. "You're real cute, you know that, Jones? Besides, you go out the back door you're going to meet a couple of my yeggs who might not like your leaving here without I say so."

"What does Mr. Big want?" Indy pushed.

"Hey, how do you know *I* ain't Mr. Big?" Carboni sneered.

"Look in the mirror," Indy offered. "What you'll see is a two-bit messenger boy."

Carboni's face flushed. His hands twitched, and Indy knew he was fighting the urge to reach for a gun. Even a messenger boy can be dangerous, when he's a big frog in a small pond.

But the fact of the matter was that as much as Carboni would have liked to put enough holes into Indiana Jones to make him resemble Swiss cheese, he didn't dare to cross or even interfere with the instructions of his overseer. Indy waited as Carboni swallowed both his anger and his pride.

"Hey, just joking, see?" Carboni said quickly. "No need to get upset."

"As a joker, you'd starve to death."

"I don't getcha," Carboni said, brow furrowed.

"Forget it. Cut the games, Carboni. What's the message you were told to deliver to me?"

Gale was amazed at Indy. It was incredible the way he could shift from a stereotypical professor to someone who seemed right at home with cheap gangsters.

Carboni lit a cigarette, watched the cloud of smoke he blew away to collect his thoughts, and then dropped his hammer.

"A cool million, Professor."

"A cool million *what?*" Indy demanded.

"One million dineros. A million of the long green. You know what I'm talking about. One—million—dollars," he emphasized.

"That's nice," Indy replied. "But what's it for? It's not even Christmas time."

"Look, Professor, we don't know how and why you got mixed up with that train caper the other night. We do know that some big-time operators used a plane to snatch the real goods. Not them funny-money dime-store things the papers wrote about."

Carboni took a deep breath. "One million dineros for that pyramid."

"What pyramid?"

"You think you're a hard case, doncha? We know you got it, Jones."

"And you want to make an exchange. I give you the pyramid I'm supposed to have, and you hand over a million dollars."

"Cash."

"When?"

"The sooner the better, Professor. In fact, if it's sooner, you get to live longer."

"What if I told you I don't have it."

"I'd call you a liar."

"And you'd be right," Indy laughed.

Carboni's eyes narrowed. "So you *do* have it." His breathing grew heavier. *They get that pyramid, and it's permanent occupancy in a deep hole in the ground for me and Gale,* Indy knew without any question.

"The problem, Carboni, is that it's not for sale. At *any* price."

"No? We'll see about that." Carboni pressed a call button on his desk. A side door opened and two thugs came in fast, guns in hand. "Cover him," Carboni ordered. The weapons held level at Indy.

Indy paid close attention to his nails, rubbing them against his jacket. "This is so dumb," he said.

Carboni moved with unexpected speed, crossing the room to Gale. In a sweeping motion he gripped her hair and snapped her head back. The room lights glinted off the knife blade he held at her throat.

"You tell me where it is, Professor, or this little lady won't ever need to breathe through her nose again."

Indy scratched his stomach. "Go ahead."

Gale's eyes were huge, and she was in obvious pain from the angle at which Carboni was twisting her neck. "You're bluffing, Jones!" Carboni said wildly. "First she gets it and then you!"

"You won't do it, because if you do I'll have to take on all three of you mugs, and since your two buffoons have the drop on me, I'll probably go down—"

"I guarantee it, Jones!"

"And if I go down your Mr. Big will *never* know where that pyramid is, and that means you and these twinkle-toes, here, are next in line for cement shoes. Get stuffed, Carboni. You're just a big bluff."

"I swear I'll cut her heart out, Jones!"

Indy shifted slightly in his seat. Again he scratched his stomach, a cover for his fingers depressing his belt buckle. Barely a second later the door leading out the back way of the office burst open, a dark figure rolled like a great ball on the floor, and Tarkiz Belem remained in a crouch, firing with deadly aim. The Mauser in his hand, silencer-equipped and modified to full automatic, sprayed a dozen rounds with a lethal hissing sound. Both men holding guns on Indy hurtled backwards, blood spurting.

Carboni had only that moment to see the carnage beginning when a loud *crack!* came to his ears; in the same instant Indy's bullwhip, freed from around his waist, slashed through the air to whip about Carboni's knife hand. Indy jerked down hard, breaking Carboni's wrist with the violent motion and sending him crashing head-first against the marble table.

Gale fell back into her seat, a thin line of red showing along her neck. Indy was by her side immediately. "Barely cut the skin," he said casually, bringing a handkerchief to her neck. "You won't even have a scar for a souvenir."

"Indy, I'll— *you set me up for this!*"

"True," he admitted.

Tarkiz snapped another magazine into the Mauser. "What do we do with this one?" he motioned to Carboni.

"Don't you dare touch him!" Gale hissed. She came out of her seat with catlike speed. She jerked back Carboni's head with a handful of his hair and in another swift move she brought out her .25 automatic and jammed the short barrel as far as it would go into Carboni's left nostril. His eyes rolled like a madman's as he focused on the Beretta. Gale brought back the hammer with an audible click.

"If I cough or sneeze your brains are going to be all over the ceiling," she said quietly. "Any reason why I shouldn't squeeze this trigger?"

Carboni gurgled. "Ease off, Gale," Indy said quietly. "He still has the message to carry, remember?"

For several very long seconds she held her position, then looked Carboni in the eye. "Bye-bye," she said softly, and her finger curled back on the trigger.

A metallic *snap* mixed with a gurgling scream from Carboni. Gale stood slowly, wiping the barrel of the gun on Carboni's jacket. She turned to Indy. "Imagine that," she said with a thin smile. "I must have forgotten to put a round in the chamber."

She looked down at Carboni, sprawled unconscious on the floor. "What's with him?" she asked.

Indy laughed. "Our tough boy has fainted. Let's go."

In moments they were in the back seat of the Packard, Tarkiz at the wheel. "Wonderful!" he shouted. "It is good, *good!* to do something again!"

Gale turned to Indy. "You set this whole thing up, didn't you?" He nodded. "But, how did Tarkiz know when to come in? In fact, *how* did he know to come in?"

"My belt buckle. It's a battery-powered radio transmitter. Tarkiz had an earpiece receiver with the same frequency. I pressed the buckle, he heard the clicks we'd prearranged as a signal, and he knew to come in loaded for bear."

She studied him carefully. "Indy?"

"Name it."

"You made us targets tonight, didn't you?"

He nodded. "I had to get their attention, somehow."

"But . . . why didn't you tell me what was going to happen?"

"What, and let you *worry*?"

Tarkiz guffawed.

8

"I've never seen him quite like this before," Gale said to her group. The four sat together at a corner table in the hangar dining mess. Neither Rene Foulois nor Gale cared to eat at the ungodly hour of six o'clock in the morning. But the clock meant little to either the expansive frame of Tarkiz Belem or the portly figure of Willard Cromwell. The time to eat was whenever something tasty was put before them. Yet they paid full attention to the comments of their two comrades as the four of them studied Indy, seated alone at the opposite corner of the mess.

"He's not eating, you know," Cromwell pointed out as he swallowed a chunk of bacon. "Just sucking up that horrid black muck you people call coffee."

"Fourth cup, the poor fellow," Foulois agreed.

"He certainly seems antsy about something," Cromwell said as he renewed his attack on his meal.

"What is this antsy?" Tarkiz questioned.

"Well, I certainly wouldn't call Indiana Jones *nervous,*" Gale said critically of the others' remarks. "He's well, preoccupied. I'd say something very big was in the air."

"You are all making with the crazy talk," Tarkiz growled through a mouthful of bread soaked in butter and honey.

"You're drooling, old chap," Cromwell noted.

"I know. I eat like starving bush hog. My wives tell me this many times," Tarkiz smiled. He turned back to Gale. "So you tell me, woman. What means this antsy and what else you say about something falling down on us."

His words brought smiles among them. "Antsy means nervous or upset," Gale said.

"You are not talking about Indy," Tarkiz said angrily. "I have followed many men. All over the world, woman. He is a man sure of himself, what he does. Quick, smart. Many good things. But this antsy?" Tarkiz shook his head angrily, spattering the others with food. "That is *dumb.*"

"I'm with you," Gale placated the Kurd glowering at the others.

"And as for what's in the air," Cromwell broke in, "there's the first sign. I *knew* there'd be trouble about last night."

"No trouble was with last night!" Tarkiz growled, a fist slamming against the table, bouncing dishes and cups and silverware noisily. "You do not understand! *Nothing* happened from last night because no one will ever say anything." He sneered at Cromwell and Foulois. "You think that someone would call the police? That is *last* thing that will happen!"

"Then what, if I may be so bold, was that fracas about last night? After all, Tarkiz, all we know is what you and Gale have told us," Cromwell said pointedly.

Gale rested her hand on Tarkiz's arm. He started to jerk away his arm, thought better of the move, and sat quietly. She turned to the two men watching her and Tarkiz. "I'll let Indy tell you himself. But I can tell you this much. Everything he did was worked out to the nth degree. Don't you understand *yet?* He set himself up as a target! He might as well have painted a bull's-eye on his forehead—"

She stopped in midsentence as a man in a severe gray business suit, wearing a bowler hat and carrying a brief-case, joined Indy at his table. Cromwell leaned closer to Foulois. "Frenchy, I never forget a face. I know that chap."

"Who is he?"

"I don't know his name. But I've seen him before at Whitehall and—" Cromwell snapped his fingers. "*And* at the Air Ministry. By Jove, if my memory serves me, he's top echelon with British Intelligence."

Rene Foulois smiled. "It promises to be an interesting day. And here comes our good Colonel Henshaw."

The army officer moved a chair to their table. "Am I interrupting things?"

Rene smiled. "No, no. Our friend Tarkiz was about to start on his third breakfast, that's all."

"Well, I'm here to tell you that at twelve noon today there will be a special meeting. I imagine you know you're expected to be there," Henshaw explained.

"Where? This meeting is where?" Tarkiz said through another huge mouthful of food.

"If you'd be here no later than eleven-thirty, I'll be here to take you to the meeting. Oh, yes, Professor Jones said you're free to do a flight if you'd like."

Foulois showed his surprise. "All the work is com-pleted?"

Henshaw shook his head. "Not yet. But we're held up for a few hours waiting for equipment to arrive. Taking the ship up won't interfere with our program. In fact, we'd appreciate your doing a test flight. Check out the new engines and props, for one."

Cromwell and Foulois looked at one another and both nodded. "Gale, will you be with us?"

"Next time. I have some things to do. Colonel Henshaw, may I have the use of your machine shop until that meeting?"

"Of course. Anything special you need?"

"Grinding machine, polishing lathe, metal forming. Routine."

"You've got it."

"Thank you. Tarkiz, I recommend you go with these two in the Ford. I'd feel better, after last night, if you'd watch *their* backs."

Tarkiz grinned. "Sure, I do! I am good baby-sitter, no?"

She patted his hand. "The best, Tarkiz. The best." Back to Henshaw. "Colonel, I'd like to get right to it."

"Let's go, Miss Parker. I'll take you there myself and make certain you have all the cooperation you need."

That will help, she told herself. *Because after what happened last night, I want some invisible tricks up my sleeves.*

Henshaw gathered them together at precisely eleven-thirty. They had time for a quick coffee and a sandwich each, then Henshaw, clearly on edge and watching the clock, prompted them to board one of the many similar buses on the field. It was half filled with enlisted men in the ubiquitous work coveralls, and they blended in perfectly with the larger group. None of them missed the fact that every man on the bus was carrying a .45 Colt Automatic strapped to his waist. No one spoke to them and they kept their own silence.

They watched with growing interest as the bus went through a guarded gate into an area marked with signs: DANGER! FUEL FARM—EXPLOSIVE! KEEP OUT. AUTHORIZED PERSONNEL ONLY, and other dire warnings against unauthorized entry.

Finally Gale couldn't keep back her questions. "Colonel Henshaw, this fuel farm . . . thousands of gallons of aviation fuel all around us. Why are we *here,* of all places!"

"You'll see in a few moments, miss." He would say no more. Tarkiz, Willard, and Rene answered her looks with don't-ask-me shrugs. Then they drove into another huge hangar. The bus stopped as the hangar doors closed behind them. Military police with submachine guns and leashed attack dogs moved along all entrances to the hangar.

They left the bus, following Henshaw to a guarded door. Two MP's checked his identification, then studied the ID tags of the four people with him and used a telephone to verify names and identification. One MP slid back a heavy steel door. "Go right through here, sir."

They entered a waiting room. Raw concrete, naked light bulbs about them. The door clanged shut. A buzzer sounded and a section of the wall to their left slid open. Henshaw gestured for them to follow. "This way, please." They walked behind him onto a sloping, curved corridor, leading to a lower level. Then another guarded portal, with three MP's and dogs. Once again they went through a security check before the door was opened. Inside, they were kept for several moments in another concrete anteroom. A light glowed above a steel door, it slid to the side slowly, and they looked in surprise at a huge room. "It's a bloody war situation room," Cromwell exclaimed softly. "I've been in them before, but I've never seen the likes of *this.*"

"I can explain now," Henshaw started as they walked with him along a yellow line painted on the floor. "This meeting is of a CFA—"

"CFA?" Cromwell broke in.

"Sorry. I forget we're overheavy with acronyms. It best works out as Committee For Action."

They passed through a final checkpoint, and guards pened a steel door. It was Cromwell who again grasped he situation. "Listen carefully, my friends," he said in a ow tone. "I've only once in my life ever been within what ve call an inner sanctum. That's the nerve center of a arger war room, and that is quite where we are at this moment. Whatever is going on, it is *very* weighty, or ominous might be a better word, but I'll tell you this. *We* are n it right up to our bloody armpits."

"You have such quaint expressions," Gale grimaced.

"However, he is certainly correct," Foulois said with he practiced ease of someone who seems casual about his urroundings, but is actually at hair-trigger alertness. It vas almost as if these two wartime veterans could *smell* rouble. Gale had often had the same feeling in the forests and mountains. If Cromwell and Foulois were that ouchy, the moment deserved all *her* attention. She glanced at Tarkiz. He had bunched up his shoulder muscles and was walking with a catlike tread as if any moment ne might have to spring away from danger.

"This way." Henshaw's voice broke into her thoughts. "That table to the left and slightly behind Professor Jones. Please take those seats."

Indy had watched their entrance, had, indeed, studied them carefully as they approached. He offered the slightest nod to acknowledge their presence and then locked his gaze with Gale's. No changing facial expression, but she swore she could read a message in his eyes. *And his dress! He's wearing his "working clothes." That leather jacket and that sodden hat of his, and he's carrying the whip by the belt loop. Why on earth is he wearing that Webley in such an obvious manner?*

She took her seat and looked about the round table where Indy sat along with a dozen other men. *No women,* Gale confirmed. *This is strictly business for these people, and by their expressions they are confused, angry, or . . . I don't know. But at least now I know why he's dressed deliberately in his own attire. He's setting himself off from the others. Everybody else dressed to the diplomatic and political hilt, starched shirts and squeezing neckties and suits that cost a hundred dollars or more. Everybody but Indy. A beautiful move on his part. Without saying a word he's told them all that he and they exist and live and work in different worlds.*

She felt Tarkiz nudging her elbow. They leaned closer to one another. "Woman," he whispered in her ear, "be ready for what you call, uh, skyrockets?"

"Fireworks," she helped him.

"Yes, yes. I have come to know our Indy. He is on the edge of telling everybody here to, how is it said? To get out of his way. To go away and don't bother him. He is telling them—"

"I get the idea," she broke in. "You're right. Let's hold this for later. Looks like the players are ready to deal."

"Hokay. Just one more thing. Is important." She motioned for him to go ahead. "You see fellow with glasses? Blue tie, green shirt? Looks like dumb farmer? Is big act. Very smart, very dangerous. Head of secret police for Romania."

Gale looked at the small table placards, those that she could see, that were being set down before each man. Tarkiz was right. The placard before the "dumb farmer" held the name PYTOR BUZAU, ROMANIA. She tried to read as many names as she could, then stopped as Colonel Henshaw came by and placed a roster before her. As he passed by he whispered to her, "Read it quickly and then slide it to your lap and *put it away.*" She nodded agreement. At the same time she wondered why Henshaw was acting like something out of a fictional spy book. Good grief; all those people knew who they were, and the nameplates identified everyone else! Well, perhaps there was a reason. She'd look into it later. For the moment she went down the list.

She already knew what lay behind the name of Buzau. Cromwell had already mentioned a face she recognized; he said the face belonged to someone with British Intelligence. Now she connected the name: Thomas Treadwell. She was surprised when she read Filipo Castilano. She not only had seen him, but had spoken with him several times at the University of London, and once or twice at Oxford, on the subject of ancient artifacts. And here he was with his name linked to the Vatican. How *very* interesting. . . . Whatever could have persuaded the Italian government to let themselves be represented by the Church!

She continued down the list. Erick Svensen from Sweden. Sam Chen from China. *Sam?* Well, he probably went to school in the United States or England and wisely adopted a name everyone could pronounce easily. Besides, it lessened the Asiatic imprint enough to make him seem, well, more *acceptable.* That wasn't the case with the imperial, rigid figure of Yoshiro Matsuda from Japan, right down to his frozen, erect figure and his silk top hat.

Jacques Nungesser from France; ah, yes, he was a cousin of their great fighter ace from the war. She would ask Rene about that one later. George Sabbath from the United States? But there was Indy, and he was an American. She put aside her questions and continued with the list. Vladimar Mikoyan from Russia; Antonio Morillo from Venezuela; Tandi Raigarh from India; Rashid Quahirah from Egypt.

At the bottom was Professor Henry Jones . . . and beneath that a company name—Global TransAir.

. . .

They didn't waste any time. A buzzer sounded and the entire room went quiet. Treadwell leaned forward, scanned documents before him, and went directly to the point.

"Gentlemen, you are here because, above all else, you are trustworthy of judging what is best for your government and your country. We are all here for the same purpose. To identify what appears to be the single greatest threat to world peace, on a truly global scale, that we have ever encountered in our lifetimes. You have sufficient background before this meeting, which is the communications nerve center for all of us, to understand that even if we have yet to identify and define our adversary, we are aware of its growing power and danger to us all. Before we reach what is the most contentious aspect of what we have joined together to identify and defeat—which is how it is possible for us to face certain machinery that, by every standard of science and engineering we know, cannot possibly exist—I wish to thank you, one and all, for your support. Not only for financing this operation on an equal per capita basis, but for the magnificient cooperation we have received—"

Filipo Castilano half rose from his seat. Gone was the suave, debonair figure. *"Mister* Treadwell, sir, *please,* do not tell us what we know. I accept on behalf of all of us that we are wonderful people. Get to the heart of the matter!"

Treadwell was unflappable. "Thank you, Signor. I am grateful to dispense with the diplomatic posturing."

"Thank God," someone muttered from the group.

"All right, then." Abruptly, Treadwell was no longer the flawless epitome of diplomacy. The hard professional beneath emerged as suddenly as a light switched on in a dark room. He pushed aside the papers before him.

"An industrial organization, as powerful politically and

financially as it is in trade and industry, has obviously decided that the Great War only twelve years behind us was a warning for the future. They apparently hew to the line that the only way to prevent another global conflict is to have the levels of power—industrial, financial, trade, and military—invested in the hands of only *one* group. That group is to be so powerful that no nation or group of nations could ever resist its pressure or direct attack."

"Your words might come almost directly, I would note," interrupted Japan's Matsudo, "from the proposals for the League of Nations which, I add quickly, has all the power of a tiger without teeth. Very pretty, but no bite."

"Point well taken," Treadwell parried, "except that at its very worst and most confusing, the League did not kill people *en masse,* destroy commercial ships and aircraft, and embark on its own murderous means of achieving its goal."

Matsudo bowed briefly to accept Treadwell's rebuke, leaving the Englishman free to continue. "This group, which has so far kept absolutely secret the identity of its members, believes in what it is doing. That makes them doubly dangerous, for they are zealots with a new brand of fanaticism.

"I will be blunt. Many of us, if not all, are aware of the rise of new power in Germany. That country is on the upsurge of a new militarism, and for a while we believed that this group, or one of several groups, was behind the attacks from South Africa to the inland Sea of China. But that is not so. Even the best of German engineering has been helpless before this group as it continues on its destructive and, regretfully, successful path.

"We have identified the name under which they operate."

That was enough to bring a hornet's nest of shouting from the group. Treadwell stood still while waiting for quiet to resume. Gale watched Indy; he was missing nothing. She hadn't noticed the strap about his neck. Of course! All that paraphernalia he was wearing . . . how beautifully it all but concealed the Leica camera strapped about his neck and suspended just above table level. She watched Indy shifting in his seat, his right hand in the wide pocket of his jacket. *So that's it!* she realized. Every time he looked directly at any one person, he needed only to squeeze the trigger bulb in his pocket, and he had taken a picture of his target. He never touched the camera draped so casually from his neck along with other equipment. And he made sure to use the camera trigger only when there was enough noise among the group to conceal any metallic clicking sound.

Treadwell went on. "They are very sure of themselves, and be advised that it is our opinion the name we have discovered is used deliberately to convince us they are more powerful than all of us put together. That name is Enterprise Ventures International, Limited." He held up both hands. "I know, *I know!* The acronym is EVIL. They apparently like to tweak us, along with committing their very lethal operations. But EVIL also has offices in several countries. You will be given addresses, telephone, and Teletype numbers. They maintain these offices so that any of us, or the group, may contact them and yield to their pressure."

"Never!" shouted Buzau.

"Hopefully, you are correct," Treadwell said quietly, earning an angry glare from the Romanian. He ignored the daggers in Buzau's eyes. "I said I will get right to it and I will. The United States has been selected by us all as the main guiding force to act on our behalf. We had all agreed before never to identify who actually heads our program, even though we also have agreed to supply all the weapons, manpower, and other support this person or group deems necessary. We hope the American group, which for obvious reasons of security shall absolutely remain unknown to us—"

Vladimar Mikoyan was on his feet. "You make sounds, my friend, as if *we* are not to be trusted!"

"A point well taken, Vladimar. Tell me, do *you* absolutely, implicitly, unquestionably, *trust everyone* here, as well as their government contacts, *not* to compromise what I have just outlined?"

"Well, there is always a possibility that—"

"That will do, Vladimar," Treadwell snapped icily. "You've answered my question."

Mikoyan took his seat slowly, obviously smarting from being whipsawed so easily.

"I have had my say," Treadwell concluded. "You will now hear directly from Colonel Harry Henshaw of the American army. So you will understand his position, he is the communications center of this facility. Or I should say, he commands this organization. He does *not* know the identity of the group tracking down the members of EVIL. He is strictly a conduit, but reports from all over the world funnel through this facility. Colonel Henshaw, if you would, please?"

Gale Parker came up stiffly, her nerves taut, as Henshaw began a recital of deadly attacks against ships at sea, commercial airliners, and selected targets such as banks, show galleries, and privately held vaults. (*And trains!* she smiled to herself.) Every few moments she studied Indy. He was surprisingly disinterested in Henshaw's reports, either deliberately so as to mislead the others, or because he really didn't care for the growing mountain of minutiae. She'd find out later when she was alone with him.

"A prime example of what we face, that illustrates the very considerable *military* power this group, EVIL, has brought together, involves the *Empress Kali*," Henshaw related. He paused as the group about the table looked to each other for information.

"If you have heard of what happened to the *Kali*, I assure you much of what was reported was unfounded conjecture. What is reality is that the *Kali* was not any ordinary freighter. In appearance, yes. In performance and cargo, no. The *Kali* left Nacala in Mozambique with a cargo of Zambian wood for a southern French port and then overland shipment to Switzerland. The vessel was built with sealed holds; in brief, to be virtually unsinkable. And, she was *armed.*"

He paused to let eyebrows rise with that last remark. "Two three-inchers on the decks, fore and aft, and three gun tubs with heavy machine guns."

For the first time Indy made himself known. To gain attention he eschewed the accepted raising of the hand. Instead he rapped his knuckles on the table. Heads swiveled. Indy kept his eyes on Henshaw.

"Why?"

His voice was like a shot in the room. Against all the previous verbiage, his single-word query cut to the bone.

Gale watched Henshaw. He too was timing his words for the moment of maximum effect. "Obviously, the cargo was worth a great deal, and with the publicity attached to ships that previously were attacked—"

Again Indy sliced into the presentation. "If the cargo was worth all that firepower it was especially valuable. Obviously it was not *wood.*" Smiles met his statement. "So I will add questions, Colonel. What *other* cargo was that ship carrying? And who attacked that vessel? You would not be presenting us with the lamentable fate of the *Empress Kali* unless disaster befell the ship."

"You are correct, sir," came the response. "However, all I know of the apparently unidentified and presumably valuable cargo, other than wood, is that we cannot identify it. We have confirmed a value in the hundreds of millions of dollars. The cargo was insured by a Swiss carrier, reportedly in concert with Lloyds of London, but they will release no information as to *what* it was.

"To get right to the most important issue, *who* or *what* attacked and destroyed the *Kali,* our information derives from three survivors. Two men were from Mozambique, the third was a Portugese national. We obtained his story because the rescue vessel was a Portugese destroyer." Henshaw paused, tapped his notes on the table before him, then spoke slowly.

"I am not sure if this esteemed group will believe the description of events as provided by that survivor."

"We appreciate your concern," said Tandi Raigarh, "but I suggest you offer fewer apologies and give us specific information. We will then decide what to believe."

Gale began to understand just how Henshaw was playing this group. Rather than trying to sell them on the veracity of the reports, he had, with Indy's perfectly timed interruption, brought the group virtually to demand his information. He took a deep breath and went on.

"Our report states that a strange flying machine appeared over the *Kali,*" he said, making certain he appeared confused by his information.

"What do you mean by strange?" demanded the representative of Egypt. Rashid Quahirah had little patience for long-winded stories. Again it played perfectly into Henshaw's agenda.

"The machine over the *Kali* was shaped like a great scimitar. Like a blade rather than a rounded boomerang. It shone brightly in the sun, its metal highly reflective. There were no engines, no propellers, but it made what the survivor called the shriek of a thousand devils. Its speed was considered fantastic and its noise was terrifying."

"How fast is fantastic, if you please?" That from China's Sam Chen.

"The survivor's report states many times faster than any aircraft he had ever seen."

Erick Svensen of Sweden coughed to cover his amusement. "And what did this sensational machine do?"

"This is the strangest part of all. It made radio contact with the *Kali*. It spoke the native tongue of Mozambique, and quite perfectly. One of our survivors had been in the radio shack and heard the radio call. It ordered the ship to hove to, and to bring its concealed cargo from the safe onto the deck. If there was resistance the ship would be destroyed."

Murmurs ran through the group; Henshaw kept going. "Somehow, this vessel was ready for some sort of interference. The cannon and machine guns opened fire on the scimitar air machine. It accelerated with tremendous speed, swept around to the opposite side of the ship, and as the gunners tracked it a *second* scimitar machine swept in from another angle. It fired rockets at the *Kali*."

"Rockets?" someone echoed.

"Rockets," Henshaw emphasized. "When the rockets struck and exploded, they released a terrible gas that soon had the crew choking. They were falling all about the decks. Some apparently died within seconds or minutes."

Antonio Morillo slammed his hand against the table. "This is ridiculous!"

"Do you wish me to continue?" Henshaw asked smoothly.

"Be quiet! Let the man finish!" shouted Treadwell.

"One of the aerial machines fired rockets into the rudder to disable the steering mechanism. Then one scimitar slowed and hovered just above the foredeck. A gangway extended down, and figures in silver suits and globelike helmets descended. They went directly to the captain's cabin. An explosion was heard, obviously to blow open the safe and take what was held in there. We have heard everything about the contents of the safe from a crystal skull, to diamonds, to a cube or pyramid with unusual markings on it. This is all guesswork—"

"Guesswork, my Aunt Millie," George Sabbath spat. The others turned to the American, who glared at them all. "This is poppycock. Drivel!"

"Perhaps so," Henshaw said, unperturbed. "I will not even attempt to explain what happened next. I presume, and you will judge for yourself, that a submarine was also involved. Two torpedoes struck the *Kali* after the men, or whatever they were, in the silver suits ascended back into the scimitar craft, which had been hovering all this time, continuing to howl like a thousand devils. The hatch closed, the scimitar machine accelerated swiftly, and the ship was torn in two by the torpedo hits. The three survivors clung to some of the cargo of wood and were picked up the next day."

The Romanian delegate, Pytor Buzau, motioned for attention. "I would rather believe the stories of vampires from our old castles than what I am hearing."

"I suggest," Henshaw replied with measured distaste, "you tell that to the Mozambique government, which has lost a ship, its cargo, and fifty-eight men."

Thomas Treadwell stood, waiting until quiet was again at hand. "I will be brief. One of our airliners, six engines, was lost right at our doorstep. The event was seen by several hundred people near Dover. Do you understand? *Several hundred witnesses.* Above the airliner, en route to France, the witnesses saw an incredible torpedolike machine. Very high, no engines, great speed, shining in the sun, and making a sound like a great blowtorch. All these people watched three scimitar-shaped machines fall away from the larger craft, which they estimated was at least fifteen hundred feet long. Then a fourth machine fell from the mother ship. They said it looked like a great flattened dome, but with the body thickest towards the center. This latter machine flew alongside the airliner and put explosive shells into the cabin. It apparently damaged the airliner just enough so the pilots could make a crash landing along a beach. Once again, just as with the *Empress Kali*, a scimitar machine hovered by the wreckage, the figures in silvery suits emerged, released that terrible gas that killed everyone aboard the airliner, and went into the wreckage to apprehend a sealed briefcase. That was all they took. They returned to their devilish machine and sped upwards, apparently to be recovered by the mother ship."

He paused, distressed. "As I say, there are several hundred witnesses."

Jacques Nungesser of France rose by Treadwell's side. "I confirm everything you have just heard."

"What was in that briefcase?" queried Yoshiro Matsuda.

"The plans for a new mutual defense treaty between Great Britain and France, with a most thorough review of the capacity of both countries to produce new armaments. *And*," Treadwell said ominously, "the reports of British Intelligence on the military capacity of every nation in Europe."

Both men resumed their seats. There was no keeping this group quiet anymore, and the gathering soon disintegrated into a shouting match.

9

"Indy, you just cannot keep piling weight onto this machine!" Cromwell became ever more agitated at Indy's seeming indifference. "I'm serious, Indy. We're already well above the permissible gross weight—"

Indy waved Cromwell to silence. "As you would say, Will, bosh and bother." Gale grinned at his choice of words and Indy acknowledged her compliment with a slight bow. "I may not be a pilot, but I know the mathematics of flight," he continued with Cromwell. "*Your* figures are for a commercial model with specific restrictions, right? And they're for the engines without our superchargers or the fat blades, *right?*"

"Well, yes, but—"

"But me no buts, my friend. I've worked out the wing loading, power loading, the shift in center of gravity, all that stuff."

"All that stuff, he calls it," Cromwell complained to Foulois. He studied Indy carefully. "I thought you said you're not a pilot."

"I'm not. *Yet.* But numbers are numbers, Will. We've

still got the power and lift to handle another two or three thousand pounds."

"And she'll fly like a sodding brick!" Cromwell shouted.

"Tish and blather."

"*What?* You sound like a charwoman down on the docks."

"Get ready to fly, both of you," Indy ordered. "We're going down to that restricted area. I want to test out the additional equipment we've added to this thing."

Tarkiz pushed closer, anticipation stamped on his face. "We fire guns?"

"We do," Indy told him. "The works. And I want to test those wing shackles for the tanks, too. We could hang bombs instead of fuel tanks externally, couldn't we?"

"Bombs?" Cromwell groaned, then shook his head in defeat. "Yes, yes, we *could.*"

"Isn't that what you did with those clunker boats you flew in the war?" Indy demanded.

"That was different," Cromwell sniffed.

"Why?"

"Because it was a bloody war, that's why! And you took chances!"

"What do you think we're getting into?" Indy asked quietly. "Tea and crumpets? We may need every piece of hardware this thing can carry. And, by the way, every chance we have, I want you to teach me and Gale how to handle this airplane. There'll be times when we can spell you and Rene on a long flight. All we need to do is hold her steady on course. Shouldn't be too difficult."

"Nothing to it, right?" Cromwell said sarcastically.

"That's the spirit. Load up. Let's go. Henshaw has closed the firing range to everyone but us."

They climbed into the airplane, now painted with new lettering and numbers. Gone were the army stars and tail numbers. Blue and red stripes adorned the upper and lower fuselage, and in between were the large letters reading GLOBAL TRANSAIR. "For the record, we're checking out routes for our airliners."

"How many planes do we have?" Foulois laughed.

"One," Indy replied. "Let's go. I'm going to stand behind you two flyboys and start learning how to handle this thing."

"You want to start from the ground up, right?"

"Right," Indy said.

"Good," Foulois smiled. "So you start with a walk-around inspection. You will learn to look for popped rivets, any twist or malformation of metal—come along, Indy, you learn as we go through the checklist. And you check the fuel by dipstick, because such instruments as fuel gauges are not to be trusted. The same with the oil." They started at the left engine, inspecting fasteners, the wheels and tires, looking for signs of leaking hydraulic fluid. "Check the propeller blades for nicks or damage. Ah, look carefully at the propeller fastenings. And while we walk, you check the external control cables. Look for slack or cable wear. Check the oil coolers to be certain they are clear. And, over here, we drain fuel from each tank to get rid of any water that has collected from condensation."

When they were through, Tarkiz emerged from the cabin with a large fire extinguisher. "He'll stand to the side of each engine when we start," Cromwell said. "We may not always have time to do it this way, but whenever we can, we follow the book. If there's a fire, he can douse it at once. All right, inside we go. Wait. We won't go anywhere with those chocks by the wheels. Remove them. *And don't walk within the radius of those propeller blades!* If one of those things ever kicks in it can slice off your arm or cut you in half."

"Yessir," Indy mumbled.

They climbed aboard. Indy listened to Foulois reading off the checklist. They set instruments before starting, adjusted the altimeter to the field elevation, then nodded to one another. Brakes locked. Controls free. Propellers clear.

"Indy, go back and check door-lock security," Foulois directed.

"Tarkiz closed it. I heard—"

"You want to do more than fly, my friend." Foulois smiled. "You want to *operate* this machine. Check the door."

Indy disappeared, came back with a nod of his head. "Done."

"While we did the walk-around, did you check the security locks on the underwing lockers?"

"Why, I didn't—

"I know. I did," Foulois scolded gently. "You do it by the book, Indy, and you learn to memorize everything. Now, we'll taxi out. I'll work the radios, Will," he told Cromwell, then turned again to Indy. "Notice how he keeps the yoke full back when we taxi. This keeps the tail down and gives us better control on the ground. And while we taxi we'll keep checking the gauges as the engines warm up."

They stopped well short of the active runway. Another checklist, another litany of shouted calls and checks and rechecks. They ran the engines to full power until the Ford rattled and shook as if it had palsy.

Both Cromwell and Foulois turned to grin at Indy. "You remembering everything?"

"Huh? Oh, sure!" Indy said hastily.

"There's a great American saying, my friend." Cromwell laughed. "In a pig's eye, you are. But you'll learn. Now, we'll break a rule. You should be strapped into a seat, but being the magnificient pilot I am," he showed a broad toothy smile, "we'll let you stand where you are. Get a good grip on the seat backs *and don't touch anything that moves.* Got it?"

"Got it!" Indy told him.

"You're clear to the active and for takeoff," Foulois told Cromwell. The Briton worked the outboard engine, tapping the brakes gently, and lined up the airplane on the runway centerline. He moved all the controls again to their limits, held the yoke full back, adjusted the friction knobs for the throttles, and nodded to Foulois. "Ready?"

"Like a French goose," Foulois told him.

Cromwell held full pressure on the brakes, and moved the throttles steadily forward to their stops, the propellers screaming. He scanned the gauges, nodded to himself, and released the brakes. The Ford surged ahead, howling. Almost at once the tail came up and Indy had a clear view of the runway. Cromwell held in right rudder pressure to keep the Ford tracking true, the speed building up swiftly. In less than four hundred feet the main wheels were off the runway, and Indy looked around to see the ground fall away.

It didn't. Engines and props howling, the Ford tore down the runway barely above the concrete, building its speed steadily. The grin on Cromwell's face told Indy more than enough. These guys were going to pull a surprise on him. Unknown to them, he'd read the pilot's operating handbook on this airplane, and he knew that even with a full load it was flying and climbing very well, even as slow as eighty miles an hour. He saw the gauge needle on the airspeed indicator tremble at 100, and it kept right on moving around as the runway end rushed at them.

"And it's upsa-daisy!" Cromwell sang out as he hauled the yoke back suddenly. Indy was already braced, but he was still surprised and delighted as the "old lady" trimotor lunged skyward in a wild climb, and then seemed to hang vertically as Cromwell wracked her over in a steep bank. The three men were laughing and whooping it up together; Indy glanced back into the cabin where Gale had a grin from ear to ear, and Tarkiz showed a face turning green as his stomach tried desperately to flee his body.

I'm going to learn to fly this thing myself, Indy swore.

There wasn't time for anything else but their checkout schedule. Once in the restricted airspace reserved for them, Tarkiz staggered back to the circular container near the cabin rear. He pulled back and locked the sliding hatch atop the fuselage, then turned a crank handle that lifted the machine gun mount and the weapon into the airstream. Lying flat against the fuselage was a panel of curving armor glass. Tarkiz pushed this upward and locked it into place with folding metal braces; now he had a buffer against the powerful winds of flight. He released the securing pins of the machine gun, slid a heavy round canister with two hundred rounds of ammunition, and shouted at the top of his lungs: "Give me something to kill! It makes better my stomach!" Gale went back, tugged at his sleeve, and handed him a leather helmet with earphones and a mike within the helmet so he would be on intercom.

"Just hang in there and enjoy the scenery, old chap," Cromwell instructed him. "You'll get your chance to play with your new toy."

"Hurry up," growled Tarkiz.

Foulois pointed out their objective, a wide plain of several thousand acres. A huge circle had been painted on the ground and in its center was a small cluster of buildings. "That's our target," Indy announced. "Let's see you two mugs tear it up."

Without hesitation, hurling Indy's body against the entrance side to the cockpit, Cromwell slammed the Ford into a wing-high rollover, coming back on the yoke, rolling in full left aileron, stamping left rudder, and shoving the throttles full forward. He kept his controls moving as the trimotor swung up and around to peel off for the ground, and the next moment their speed went right through the gauge's reading of 150 mph. It was a breathless rush earthward at a terrifying angle. Cromwell seemed like a madman intent on reaching the ground in the shortest possible time. Indy noticed what he'd failed to see before; a vertical line with crosshairs marked on the windshield.

"Damn it, Will," Foulois shouted, "what's the redline on this thing!"

Redline, redline, thought Indy furiously. *Of course, that's what they call never-exceed speed. I think it's about one-forty or something. But we're already doing one-sixty and—*

"I don't know and I bloody well don't care!" Cromwell shouted back to the Frenchman. "You can't hurt this thing and you know it. Now shut the devil up and get with the systems! Guns charged?"

"Charged!"

"Tank jettison armed?"

"Armed!"

"What the blazes are you going to do?" Indy shouted. "Drop our fuel tanks?"

Cromwell glanced about for only a moment. "Yahooooo!" he shouted in a very unmannerly British war yell. He brought the nose of the Ford up slightly, eased in right rudder to line up his sight markings, and the next moment depressed the button on his yoke. The airplane vibrated and shook from nose to tail as the two wing machine guns roared. Fountains of dirt leaped up along the ground, and then boards splintered and shattered as Cromwell fired dead center into the target buildings. He pulled out of the dive perilously close to the ground, and with their speed still high, hung the Ford on its wingtip in a screaming vertical turn. "Tarkiz! Your turn! Get the center building!"

They heard the machine gun in back firing in staccato bursts, the wind backdraft bringing acrid gunpowder to their nostrils. Above the screaming wind, howling engines and propellers, and firing gun, they heard a terrible strangling noise. "What's going on back there?" Cromwell called to Gale.

She could hardly speak. She seemed to be choking. Indy rushed back, staggering from side to side of the cabin through the wild ride, the hammering gun, and thundering bedlam. Gale grabbed Indy close, spoke into his ear. "It's our hero! Tarkiz! He's throwing up out there!"

She was convulsed with laughter. Swept up in the rush of emotion, she grabbed Indy's waist to hug him fiercely. Their eyes caught and held. For the instant they might have been alone on a mountaintop. Impulsively Gale's hands swept up, grasped Indy's head, and kissed him fiercely.

He was astonished. He still held her tightly, wide-eyed. "This is *marvelous!*" she shouted. "Let's go forward and see how Tarkiz did!"

Holding onto one another they pushed into the cockpit deck. Foulois pointed to the center building. "He is a superb marksman," Foulois remarked, as calmly as if drinking tea on some quiet veranda. "In America, I suppose you would call him Dead-Eye Dick. He is really very good."

"Rene, I'm going to sling those tanks into the buildings," Cromwell announced to the Frenchman in the right seat. "As soon as I do that, you've got the controls. Bring her around in a climbing turn and then see if you can put those rockets where they'll do the most good!"

"Righto, cheerio, and wot for, eh?" Foulois mimicked his friend. "Have at it."

The Ford came around with diminishing speed; control and accuracy were everything now. Cromwell held the trimotor straight and true as Foulois held his hand on the emergency release cable handle. "On my mark!" shouted Cromwell. A moment later he sang out, "Three! Two! One! *Mark!*"

They felt a jolt as the tanks were ejected by powerful coiled springs. Cromwell brought the Ford up in a high swinging chandelle, close to stalling speed at the top of the curving climb with the left wing down so they could all see the two tanks tumbling as they crashed into the buildings. A white mist leaped into being as the tanks ruptured.

"Bingo!" Indy shouted his congratulations.

"You've got her," Cromwell called to Foulois. The Englishman held aloft both hands and clapped them together in the traditional handing-over of control. There wasn't a nudge to the airplane as Foulois took the controls. He brought down the nose, swept about in a wide turn, and eased into a shallow dive. "I'm going for one-thirty," he announced to Cromwell. "Call out the speeds."

"One-forty, coming down, one-thirty-five, and, that's it, one-thirty on the nose." Foulois nudged the throttles as if stroking a woman's hand, and the airspeed needle pegged on 130.

Foulois's voice was calm and cool as if he might be talking about a soccer game or ordering a drink at a Paris club. "Confirm rocket release doors open." Cromwell looked up at the wings; the covering panels had slid away. "Doors open, electrical primers armed."

"Very good. Thank you."

Indy nudged Gale. "I think he's got ice water in his veins."

Gale was too excited to talk. She clung to Indy's arm, eyes wide, immersed in the moment.

"Just about time, and . . . *fire,*" Foulois said calmly, pressing the button. Two rockets from their rails ejected flame and smoke behind them, racing earthward toward the buildings, squiggling like tadpoles as they arrowed ahead of the trimotor. They struck with spouts of flame, and then the gasoline vapors ignited with a huge fireball leaping upward, a boiling mass of flames and smoke.

Foulois already had gone to full power and wracked the trimotor about on its right wing, climbing away from the rising fireball. Safely out of range he swung back again to the left.

"You're hired," Indy told him, slapping him on the shoulder. The buildings were flattened, burning fiercely. "That's it," Indy added.

Cromwell glanced at Foulois. "Take her up to four thousand. It's time for the school bell to ring."

Foulois leveled off at four thousand feet and set the power to cruise. Behind them Tarkiz had lowered the gun mount and closed the hatch, reducing the howl of wind and engine roar from outside. Cromwell climbed from the left seat. "Who's first?" he asked Indy and Gale.

"Ladies first," Indy said. "I'll watch her, and then I'll give it a try."

Gale climbed into the left seat, fastened the seat belt, and let her fingers run lightly over the yoke. "Now, all I want you to do is hold our present course," Rene said soothingly. "You can follow that road ahead of us. If you pick a point on the horizon, just aim for it. Make all your control inputs gently. And don't worry about a thing. I'll be riding the controls with you. I'm sure you'll do fine."

Gale hadn't said a word. Foulois held up both hands in the time-honored signal. "You've got it," he told Gale.

They all expected wandering, the nose rising and falling, swinging a bit to left or right. *It didn't happen.* Indy stared with growing disbelief as the Ford flew on as though it was on steel rails. Cromwell and Foulois exchanged glances. "I'll be hanged," Cromwell said finally. "She knows *how*!"

Indy leaned forward, watching everything Gale did. His face mirrored disbelief and no small awe at the woman, her red hair flying in the wind from the open side window. Finally he tapped her shoulder. "You really *can* fly," he said with masterful understatement. "Why in thunder didn't you tell me?"

She glanced back at Indy, her eyes gleaming, loving his surprise. "No one ever asked me," she said.

Cromwell pushed next to Indy so he could talk to Gale. "Miss Parker, you're no novice."

"Thank you," she said, exasperating the three men all the more.

"When?" Cromwell barked. "I mean, when did you learn?"

"When I was twelve, I spent a summer in Germany with some cousins. They were all mad about gliding, and I joined them. I had three months of flying gliders almost every day."

"Did you solo?" Foulois asked.

"Second week," she said with a straight face.

"And after that?" Cromwell pressed.

"Scotland. More gliders, then an old training plane. My mother had the money, and I spent another summer at a flying school up there."

"I suppose you flew solo in powered machines?" asked Cromwell.

"Yes."

"Well, will you get to the bleedin' point, Miss Parker! Do you have your certificate?"

She turned again with the smile of a lynx. "Single engine, multiengine, commercial privileges."

"I'll be hanged," Cromwell said quietly.

"Indy, do you want to give it a go now?" Gale asked the perplexed man behind her.

"Let's let it wait until tomorrow," Foulois broke in. "I have the field in sight. Not enough time left for now. All right, Gale, I'll take it from here."

She kept her left hand on the yoke and began easing back the throttles to start their descent toward the airfield. "Why?" she asked.

"Well, it's obvious, I mean, ah," he faltered.

"Why don't you work the radio?" she asked sweetly.

Indy seemed to have a thundercloud over his head. "Sure, you work the radio, Rene," he said in clipped tones. He couldn't believe this. She was going to try to land this thing, her first time on the controls!

She brought the Ford down in a perfect three-point landing. She taxied off the runway onto the long taxiway back to their hangar. "Would you mind taking it from here?" she asked Foulois as she started from her seat.

"Oh. Yes, of course. Thank you," he said, feeling like an idiot.

She squeezed past Indy, close enough to brush his lips with hers as she went by. "Excuse me, Indy. I need to fix my hair."

10

Indy stood before the door to Cromwell's room. He raised a fist, hesitated, then slammed his fist against the door. He heard a startled "Good God! Are the Huns attacking?" as Cromwell burst from a deep sleep. The next moment a loud crash ensued from the room as Cromwell lurched from his bed and fell over his boots. Indy pushed open the door, staring down at Cromwell with his face pushed into the floor. Indy grasped his arm and hauled the portly Britisher to his feet.

"Do you know what time it is, Will? Do you remember what we're supposed to do first thing this morning? Did you arrange for the plane to be ready?" Indy hurled a barrage of questions at the befuddled pilot still trying to shake cobwebs from his brain.

"No. What time is it?" he mumbled.

"It's already five-thirty, man!"

"Five-thirty? What are you doing up at this ungodly hour?"

"You're going to teach me to fly this morning, you nit! Wake up!"

"I'm trying, I'm trying. Maybe this is just a bad dream. Go away, Indy."

Indy shook life into the sagging body. "Ten minutes, *Brigadier*. See you in the mess."

Indy stomped into the dining mess, poured a mug of steaming coffee, and slumped into a chair at the table.

Foulois studied him carefully. "Someone left some hot coals in place of your eyeballs, Indy."

Indy grunted, sipping coffee. "Studied most of the night."

"All fired up to get at the controls, no?"

"Something wrong with that?" Indy challenged.

"Perish the thought. I admire your spirit. Where's Colonel Blimp?"

Cromwell slouched into the room, wobbled before the coffee urn, filled his mug, and dragged himself to the table. He eased into a chair. "I tried your guaranteed, money-refunded, can't-miss wake-up system, *Professor* Jones."

"I would like to hear what that is," Foulois said.

Cromwell looked at the Frenchman. *"He,"* he started, pointing at Indy, "said the way to come awake is to stand bloody naked in the toilet bowl and pour hot coffee over your head. I tried it. My scalp is scalded, the hair is burned off my chest, and not a drop made it down to my feet. The only problem is that while it is somewhat agonizing, it doesn't wake you up. It just sent me rushing into a cold shower."

Indy nodded to Foulois. "See? It works." He turned back to Cromwell. "Drink coffee. Eat if you can. Then we *fly*."

"Ah, but you are to be disappointed," Foulois said with a gesture of defeat. "Not today, *mon ami*. Have you looked upon the world outside?"

Indy stomped into the hangar and headed for a window. Before he reached it he knew the bad news. A hissing roar, a sudden flash of light, and a deafening crack of thunder from the lightning bolt. At the window he stared at a monsoonlike downpour.

He stomped back into the mess. "All right," he said grimly to Cromwell, "we'll do ground school then."

"Not with me, bucko," Cromwell deferred. "I've got a schedule to keep with our iron bird. But *first* I'm going to get some more sleep. Then I'll fill in the missing items we *should* have put on our checklist."

"Like what?" Indy demanded.

"For starters, parachutes," Cromwell said.

"Life jackets," Foulois added.

"Survival rations," Cromwell chipped in. "Never mind. We'll take care of it. I'm sure Miss Parker, now identified as our secret ace flyer, can teach you some of the salient points of aeronautics."

Colonel Henshaw joined them in the midst of their exchange. He held his coffee mug to warm his hands. "No schoolwork for you today, Indy."

"Schoolwork! Is that what you call flight training?"

"Every bird must be dumped from its nest, Professor." Cromwell smiled.

"We all went through it, Indy," Henshaw said to mollify the obviously disgruntled Jones. "I know I did when I was a flight cadet."

Indy glared at the group. "Does *everyone* around here fly except me?"

Tarkiz lifted his head from the next table where he seemed to have been sound asleep. "Indy, my good friend! You, me, we are only two sane people here. We leave flying to the birds and the crazies. Sensible, no? Allah wants us to fly, we would have airline tickets from heaven."

Foulois looked at Belem with surprised respect. "And I always thought the mountain man was a humorless clod."

Indy waved them to silence. "Harry, what's up?"

"Coded message." The quiet hung in the room. A coded message and Henshaw's unexpected appearance meant something heavy had come upon them.

"The prefix is notification of a yet unspecified action," Henshaw continued. "Some travel, it appears. That's simply to alert us. I mean, *you.*"

"And?"

"We're decoding the full message. Finish your coffee. We have at least twenty minutes."

"Who's it from, Harry?"

"First I need to know your handle."

Eyes locked on Henshaw, then turned to Indy. "No offense," Henshaw said quickly. "Those are *your* rules."

Indy smiled. "Very good, Harry." He had set up the system with Treadwell. He wrote the coded "handle" on a slip of paper and handed it to the army officer. Henshaw read, *Lone Ranger.* "Thank you."

Twenty minutes later they were in the message center. A sergeant handed the decoded sheet to Henshaw, who glanced at the name on top and in turn gave it to Indy.

> MUST SEE YOU IN PERSON SOONEST POSSIBLE. FACE-TO-FACE MEETING IMPERATIVE. WE HAVE RECEIVED OFFER FROM THE PAN-ARAB ARCHEOLOGICAL INSTITUTE OF JORDAN TO SELL US AN EXTREMELY RARE ARTIFACT. DESCRIPTION IS CUBE, METALLIC ORIGIN UNKNOWN, UNDECIPHERED CUNEIFORM MARKINGS, THREE BY THREE INCHES. YOUR JUDGMENT REQUIRED. FUTURE ACTION REQUIRES YOUR PRESENCE BEFORE WE RESPOND. ADVISE ASAP WITH TRAVEL PLANS. ST. JOSEPH.

Indy gave the paper to Henshaw. He read it quickly, then looked up with a puzzled expression. "St. Joseph?"

"That's St. Joseph of Copertino. A monk who could levitate. It's the handle for Castilano."

"He's one of *us*?" Henshaw was wide-eyed.

"Sure is. Harry, they want me there *now.* I want Gale along as another set of eyes, with Tarkiz for backup. How long will it take the Ford to make it to New York? That seems like the fastest way."

"No dice, Indy. Even the birds are walking. That weather front, and it's a mean one, has stalled out over this area. I can get you two compartments on the Silver Streak Special. Fastest train in the country. It leaves this afternoon and you'll be in New York tomorrow morning. I can also have private transportation arranged. I'll have the details ready for you in an hour."

Indy nodded. "Thanks. Do it."

"You," Indy said through gritted teeth, "are sleeping with *me.*"

Gale responded with a joke. "Do I take that as an order or an invitation?"

"You know what I mean," Indy snapped back. "I don't want you sleeping *alone.*"

"So I gathered. But your technique is somewhat Stone Age, just in case you're interested."

"Confound it, woman, I'm not asking you to sleep with me!"

Gale studied her nails. "You could have fooled me."

"With me, too," Tarkiz grunted. "Sound like invitation to—"

"Shut *up,*" Indy snarled, stabbing a finger at Tarkiz. He turned back to Gale. "You are not going to sleep alone in a compartment on this train. Take that as an order if you want. You'll sleep in one bunk and I'll sleep in the other. We have a direct telephone connection with Compartment E right next door where Tarkiz will be staying. We can be in touch with each other at any time. Do I make myself clear *now*?"

"You disappoint me, Professor," Gale said lightly, "but, yes, I get your drift."

"We'll stay out here in the passageway while you do whatever you do at night," Indy told her. "When you're ready, open the door. If you don't open it in five minutes, we'll break our way in."

She studied him carefully, the teasing gone from her words and her expression. "You really are concerned," she said softly.

He nodded. By now she could recognize the signs on his face, the slight furrowing of the brow, his heightened tension.

It's more than a sixth sense . . . my God, he knows we're vulnerable. He's expecting something bad tonight.

"All right," she told him quietly. "Whatever you say. I don't need to be in the compartment alone." She swiftly drew a conclusion. "I'm sleeping in my clothes."

Indy seemed relieved. "Good. Tarkiz, you all set?"

The Kurd nodded. He waited until Indy and Gale had closed their door behind them, then switched the name-plates on their door with that from his own. He slipped into his compartment, and tried the telephone line to confirm its working. Then he tied a string about his own door latch, at the end of which was a small prayer bell. Its sound was barely audible, but to the man who had prayed all his life to the sound of that bell, it would serve as an instant alert to any movement of the door latch. He smiled.

Shortly after three in the morning, the train rolling steadily through the stormy night, he heard the whispered sound of his prayer bell. Immediately he moved to one side of the door, just before it opened smoothly. In the gloom he made out two forms. The moment the door closed behind them, Tarkiz flung his net, studded with fishhooks, over their bodies. Shouts and cries of pain answered the hard yank he gave to the net, sending barbs into flesh. Tarkiz moved swiftly with a flexible metal rod, bringing it down with terrible force. He turned for a moment, and shoved open the compartment window.

Above the yelps of pain and cursing from the men struggling within the net, he heard pounding on the door. He shouted, "I be right there! I—"

A knife blade stabbed into his leg, a white fire of pain. Tarkiz ignored the wound as one man freed himself from the net, looming before Tarkiz with the knife stabbing downward. It never reached the maddened Kurd. A single sideswipe with the metal rod smashed the knife into the wall.

Indy kicked open the door, the Webley in his hand, just in time to see Tarkiz heaving his attacker through the opened window space. In an instant he was gone, the train speeding onward. He turned to see the other assassin bringing down a curved blade.

Indy was already there, smashing the barrel of the Webley across the man's wrist. Bone cracked audibly, and the man screamed. Tarkiz spun about, but as he grabbed for the man his wounded leg gave way and he fell to all fours. Indy moved forward, grasped a handful of hair and the belt of the killer, and hurled the man through the window.

Gale slipped past Indy and snapped on the lights. In a moment she took in the bloody leg. "Tear me some bandages from the sheets," she ordered Indy. She helped Tarkiz to his bunk. "Your whiskey. Quickly," she told him.

"Whiskey? I do not—"

"*Shut up* and give me the flask," she snapped.

Silently, he handed her the flask from his pocket. She put it onto the bunk, soaked a towel in the sink, and washed away the blood. Indy had already tied a tourniquet above the wound. Gale opened the flask and poured whiskey into the wound to sterilize the exposed flesh, then wrapped the makeshift bandages about the wound.

"Only woman would waste good whiskey," Tarkiz complained. But his eyes showed his gratitude.

"So you changed the nameplates?"

Tarkiz nodded. "It worked, no?"

"You have any idea who they were?"

"Brown skin. One had turban. That means they were professional assassins. Somebody not like you, Indy."

"Yeah. I must have missed out on the popularity contest. By the way, that's a neat trick with that net of yours."

Tarkiz beamed through his pain. "Old Roman trick. *Very* old. Also popular with Mafia."

"With me, too," Gale added.

"Well, the lock on your door is gone," Indy observed. "You'd better stay with us the rest of the night."

"No need. I sit here on bunk so I can see door." He reached behind his back and withdrew a sleek .32 automatic from a concealed holster. "Besides, Gale is good woman. She does not waste *all* my whiskey. Sometimes I like to drink alone. Good night."

"Gale, take the upper berth."

She climbed up and sat cross-legged. "How did those people know who we were, where we were on this train, when we'd be here?"

He smiled. "You haven't figured there's a big fat leak in our security?"

"I have *now,*" she said angrily. "Any ideas?"

"Some," he shrugged. "I'm working on it."

"But why would they want to *kill* you?"

"*Us,*" he reminded her.

She shuddered.

"They'd have to kill you also," he went on, checking the Webley. "We're a team. If they don't get you, they could be identified later. So, you're also a target."

"You still didn't say *why* they want to kill you. Us," she amended.

"Tomorrow."

"You expect a lot tomorrow."

He nodded.

"Indy, you can't go around New York with that cannon hanging from your belt."

"I know." He was already removing the Webley from the belt holster to slip it into an underarm holster. Abruptly he slammed a fist into his hand. "Sometimes I feel like an idiot. I've been carrying that thing loaded and ready to shoot, and I never took any pictures when I had the chance. Those people in Tarkiz's room, I mean."

"*That's* bothering you? You didn't take *pictures*? Just saving our lives wasn't enough? You're upset because you didn't use your *camera*?"

"That's what cameras are for!"

She sighed. "Good night, Indy." He heard a muttered "Good grief . . ."

They moved through Pennsylvania Station in the midst of the early morning crowd rush. Normally, Indy disliked being shuffled along with cattle herds of people, but this time it served his purpose by swallowing up his group of three. Indy and Gale walked together, Tarkiz several steps behind them, maintaining their pace despite a swollen leg and a painful limp. They departed the station on the north side, where a long line of taxicabs queued up. Indy saw what he wanted across the street: a Yellow Cab with the number 294 on its side. He nodded to Tarkiz. "That one's ours."

"His sign says he's taken," Gale noticed.

"He is. By us," Indy said in clipped tones. The driver leaned back and opened their door. Inside, they took stock of the man in the front seat. He was a huge black fellow with a heavy beard and dark glasses that concealed his eyes, and he spoke with a melodious British accent. "Welcome to New York," he said with a hearty laugh.

Gale nudged Indy and mouthed the word *Jamaica.* He nodded.

The big man before them adjusted his rearview mirror. "You are right, miss. Jamaica it is." Laughter greeted her expression of surprise. "I do not read minds, Miss Parker. I read lips very well."

"And you know my name," Gale said cautiously.

"But of course!" came the reply. "Yours, and that of Professor Jones, and that very ugly fellow with the strange name of Tarkiz Belem. Ugly with a strange name. His mother must not have liked him very much."

Tarkiz started forward. Indy motioned for him to sit quietly. Whoever this man was, he was incredibly cocky and self-confident. "You were sent, no doubt, by the man from Copertino," Indy offered, referring to the coded message Henshaw had given him.

White teeth flashed in a wider smile. "Saint Joseph has assigned me to your good health and needs. My name is Jocko Kilarney. While you are in New York, I am your guide, your friend, your driver, and your protector."

Indy felt *right* about this man. He was big and he was powerful, and even under his shirt musculature rippled across huge shoulders. Indy would have bet a dollar to a dime he also knew his way about the sordid underworld of this city.

"By the way, Professor, your man, this big ugly fellow with you, he is really very good," said the driver. "Sometime this morning two bodies were found along the railroad tracks over which your train brought you here. Before you find the need to ask, Professor, they were both quite dead, and neither body had any identification. The police will simply dispose of the bodies in Potter's Field."

"What's that?" Gale whispered.

"Cemetery for the unknown and unwanted," Indy said to Gale. He directed his attention to the driver. "Any connections of any kind?"

"Nobody knows anything, mon, and you may forget about anyone claiming those two." He turned to look at Indy and Tarkiz. "That was quite a technique. I admire efficiency. A net studded with fishhooks. Very original."

He started the engine and depressed the clutch to shift into first gear.

Indy felt pressure from Tarkiz's hand, a signal. Indy nodded. The big man was still steaming from Kilarney's playful insults, and Indy decided to let him have his head.

"Hey, you fellow, Jocko!" Tarkiz called out.

"What may I do for you, goatkeeper?"

"You listen to me, black Irish, maybe you live longer."

"Do I hear the voodoo drums, llama man?"

"Soon you no more hear. You listen good. There is deadly snake in front of cab with you. Little snake was in my bag, somehow get out. Back home we call snake a two-step. Nice name, huh?" Tarkiz offered a wide toothy grin to Jocko. "Snake bite man, he take one step, feel bad. Take two step, he fall down dead. No antidote. If you do not get out of cab right now, snake going to bite you, and we send home your head in basket."

Jocko looked about warily, then his eyes grew huge as a bright yellow-and-orange snake wriggled toward his foot. In a flash he had his door open and stood in the street several feet from the taxi. "You crazy, mon!" he shouted.

Indy and Gale leaned forward, ready to abandon the cab if necessary. "Good God, it's really there!" Gale said in a hoarse voice. She stared in disbelief as Tarkiz leaned into the front of the cab and snatched up the snake. He petted it gently along its back and dropped it into a side pocket of his jacket. Gale screeched and threw her arms about Indy.

"Get it out of here!" she yelled.

"It's his pet," Indy answered. "I can't do that."

"GET IT OUT!" She buried her head in his chest.

Indy patted her gently on her shoulder. "No need to worry, Gale. Once he has the snake in his pocket, it's harmless." He met Tarkiz's eyes and the two winked at one another.

In his quick glance, Indy had seen what the others missed. The snake was a beautifully articulated wood or metal mechanical device with a real snakeskin covering the body, and nasty fangs for good measure in the gaping mouth. But Indy knew snakes, had dealt with them even though they gave him the creeps, and just the way this "creature" moved heightened his suspicions, all confirmed by the way Tarkiz smiled triumphantly as he dropped the "kill in two-step" snake into his pocket.

Jocko, tense from anger and his open showing of fright, returned to the cab and stabbed a finger at Tarkiz. "You and I, dungheap, we got unfinished business."

Tarkiz guffawed. "I not worry about man who is frightened like little girl by worm."

Indy leaned forward to tap Jocko gently on the shoulder. "Straight to the museum, my Irish muse, and no more detours or stops, got it?"

Jocko turned around, pointed a finger at Indy, and snapped his thumb forward like a firing pin closing on a round. "Gotcha, Boss."

11

The American Museum of Natural History sprawled over several city blocks from its entrance at Central Park West and 79th Street in Manhattan. As impressive as were the museums Indy and Gale had visited elsewhere, this structure and its vast and complex interior stood in a class by itself. It seemed to go on forever. Hundreds of exhibit rooms and huge halls, some thirty to fifty feet in height, accommodated dozens of fauna from throughout the world, including such creatures of monstrous size as the great blue whale. To stand in a room and look upward at the preserved specimen of the largest creature that ever existed on the planet, itself surrounded by dozens of other specimens large and small, was an overwhelming sight. Throughout the museum were literally hundreds of thousands of life forms.

Gale walked with Indy and Tarkiz down long corridors through just a small part of the museum to a private area several stories below ground level. Her eyes moved constantly. "This is incredible," she said with unabashed awe at the exhibits about them. "I could stay in the Egyptian archives for a month!"

"They have a worldwide exchange program," Indy acknowledged. "They trade off with institutions from just about everywhere. And it helps that this museum, or its foundation, is sponsored by some very wealthy people. There's a lot about this country that needs improvement, just like anywhere else in the world, but this place," he spread wide his arms as if to encompass the magnificient structure, "well, it's one of the finest statements ever made about people trying to understand his world."

Jocko Kilarney, leading the way, turned to Indy. "Professor, I've never heard it said better. In fact, you've done field research for the Foundation, haven't you?"

"I have the idea you already know every step I've taken for the Foundation," Indy said wryly.

Jocko shrugged. "I meant the compliment, sir, most sincerely."

"You're a man of many different faces, Jocko," Gale told him.

Jocko replied with a smile and a brief bow. "We will take the elevator at the end of this hallway," he said.

They stopped by elevator doors with a large red sign that said FREIGHT ONLY. NO PASSENGERS.

"I guess we come under the heading of freight," Indy noted.

"Consider yourself valuable cargo," Jocko said lightly. The doors opened, and they were soon on their way to a third-level subbasement. They emerged from a sloping corridor to a surprisingly large domed area. Gale stopped short, looking about her with surprise and wonder.

They seemed to be in the middle of a northern forest, trees looming about them, rocks, slopes and even a brook gurgling unseen within the heavy growth. Gale froze as a tree branch moved aside and a huge brown bear rose to its feet and roared. Immediately Tarkiz shoved her aside, placing himself between her and the bear. His automatic, pitiful as it was against the enormous animal bulk, was in his hand. Then another bear emerged through bushes, this one on all fours. Suddenly it reared high: the deadly Kodiak, largest bear in the world.

"Put away the gun," Indy told Tarkiz.

"But—"

"It's a diorama," Indy told him.

"It is big damned bear!" Tarkiz shouted.

"Ah, but this bear, and all the others," Jocko broke in, "are very dead."

"Dead bears do not walk and roar," Tarkiz grated.

"They're mechanical inside," Indy said to Tarkiz, gently pushing down his arm and the weapon. "Apparently this is where they set up the dioramas—that's a duplicate of the real world—before they move the display upstairs for the public."

"You mean," Tarkiz said, wide-eyed, "these are like big toys?"

"Sure," Jocko told him. "Electricity runs their mechanical systems." He laughed. "Like a player piano."

Indy wanted as little as possible to do with meetings. He felt stifled, hemmed in. Best to get this one over with as quickly as possible. "Jocko, let's keep it moving."

"Yes, sir." Jocko led them down another corridor and through a set of double doors, where a group of people watched their entrance. Filipo Castilano rose from a table to greet them. Gale took note that Indy obviously knew this man well. Her eyes swept the group; she recognized Yoshiro Matsuda from the gathering in Ohio. Rashid Quahirah had been known to her from Egypt, long before the Ohio meeting. She turned to Indy, and saw him studying a striking woman at the table's far end. At the same time she realized Indy was working the concealed wire-lead camera trigger; the Leica was clicking away as Indy turned his body to capture everyone present on film. He stepped aside to let Gale pass him, and from the corner of her eye she saw the deft movement as he replaced the leather cover to the camera.

Indy locked his gaze with that of the woman. Castilano introduced her. "It is my pleasure," he told Indy. "This is Madame Marcia Mason."

Indy greeted her with a murmured, "My pleasure, Madame," and in return he received a nod and a study of himself from the woman. She had a powerful presence. Indy could almost feel her strength, yet he judged her name to be a false identity. He took in her severe yet striking features and dark hair. She was elegant in dress and presentation, and held herself with a confidence that came only with an athletic, hard-muscled background. *Intelligent, tough, and accustomed to giving orders.* Castilano had introduced her as from Denmark. That was so obviously untrue; *my money is on Romania or Russia,* Indy figured. *And a double identity in this closed circle doesn't fit. I'll have to watch this one carefully.*

Indy took his seat, Gale and Tarkiz arraying their chairs behind him. Castilano spoke to the group. "May we get right to the matter at hand?" Murmurs of agreement met his offer, and he looked directly at Indy.

"We know about last night," Castilano said.

Word travels fast, thought Indy, but his face showed no idea of what he was thinking. He'd already made his decision to play this scene as easily and as quickly as he could. He shrugged. "It wasn't the first time," he said in reply.

Ah, that struck a chord. Marcia Mason had leaned forward, an easy movement that brought her the attention of the others. "Perhaps you can tell us why such things are happening to you, Professor Jones. I, for one, fail to understand."

"I'm a thorn in the side of the people we're trying to identify and to locate, Miss Mason. They have the idea that if they dispose of me, well, then they can continue their game unhindered."

"Is your presence so important to them?" the woman came back smoothly. It was as much a put-down as a question.

Filipo Castilano glanced at Merlyn Franck, the real power behind the museum. Castilano spoke quickly to head off what could become an unpleasant exchange between Indy and the woman.

"Mr. Franck, do you have any conclusions on this matter? Any further news as to what we're up against?"

Merlyn Franck didn't smile, which told Indy that he was in at least partial agreement with Marcia Mason. "I confess," he said slowly, "that some people are of the belief that Professor Jones has created a furor about himself in order to give him carte blanche in his, well, his investigative process."

"Doctor Franck, you're mincing words. If there's a criticism of what I'm doing, or how I'm doing it, just come right out with it."

Franck nodded, sighing with some inner regret. He and Indy had worked on projects long before this meeting and he wanted to maintain the excellent relationship between them. Yet, now he felt he had no choice but to be blunt. "We have been told, Professor Jones, that the incidents of personal attacks against you might never have taken place. That you have told us these stories for some reason which, I confess, I myself can't fathom."

Indy resisted a sharp answer. Franck meant well; that was what counted. He was simply in an unpleasant position.

"Sir, I can't be responsible for what people tell you. I don't even care to know who they are, but I will say that whatever you heard it wasn't from those men on the train. The old saying still fits: Dead men tell no tales."

Franck sighed again. "Professor Jones, there are members of our group who have difficulty with this 'evil empire' we've been told about. The consortium supporting your, ah, activities, now has grave doubts about such an organization."

"Fair enough," Indy said. "What *do* they believe?"

"That the evil empire as an entity is simply a front, and that none of us really have hard facts about what's going on."

"Hard facts?" Indy took a tight grip on himself not to offer a sharp retort to Franck. "What happened in South Africa, the train wrecks and slaughter . . . *those* are facts. The flying boat, the *Empress Kali,* those are facts."

Castilano gestured for attention. "There is more, Doctor Franck. We are still trying to sort out the details, but two more ships have been raided and sunk. There was an assault deep within Russia and a collection, priceless, of crown jewels stolen. But the strangest of all is that a member of our group has been contacted by a source that remains, for now at least, nameless. They want to sell *us* that mysterious artifact that was stolen in the flying boat attack."

"A question, please?" Indy said quickly.

"Of course."

"How did this unidentified source *know* that we were a group?" Indy smiled. "Before you answer, would I be wrong in assuming they're asking a very high price for the cube? Letting this group believe that the artifact is not from this world?"

Franck eased into a more personal exchange with Indy by dropping his formal title. "Indy, if this artifact is as described, then it is beyond *any* price."

"Does anyone here have a number?" Indy pressed.

"One billion dollars," Franck said tersely.

"Would you pay it?" Indy asked.

Franck never hesitated. "Absolutely."

Sitting to his right, Gale Parker was more confused than she'd been since this meeting started. She already knew that Indy had set up the mock artifact in the Milledgeville train robbery, and now he was acting as if *he* believed the artifacts were real! *Shut up and listen,* she told herself. *Indy knows what he's doing.*

"All the money this group is amassing," Indy said. "What do they do with it?"

Matsuda motioned to the others that he would reply. "Such funds buy weapons. Tanks, bombers, submarines and so on. But weapons are not enough. With enough money you can buy loyalty. You establish your own power factions within governments. You control the press, you wield great propaganda, and you move into controlling industry. Control the food supply of a country and you control the country. I am of the opinion that this group is determined to wield control over international commerce as well as military power."

"The old benevolent emperor routine," Indy responded.

"Perhaps not so benevolent," Matsuda said.

"Am I right in judging that all the people in the consortium behind us are not necessarily in agreement with each other?" Indy asked.

"That is to be expected," Castilano said stiffly. "We are fighting both great power *and* shadows."

"And you're seriously considering paying as much as a billion dollars for that so-called extraterrestrial artifact?"

"That is my position," Franck confirmed.

Indy's smile almost had the touch of canary feathers. "Let me save you a billion dollars." He reached into a pocket of his jacket. "In fact, make that *two* billion dollars." He tossed a "pyramid artifact" onto the table where it bounced to a stop, and then produced a double of the "cube artifact" that had created such a furor.

They were stunned. They passed the two objects about the table, handling them with unabashed reverence. Finally Merlyn Franck returned to the moment. "How . . . how could you possibly have obtained these? And forgive me, Indy, but you seem cavalier about something for which men have died!"

"There aren't any artifacts from outer space," Indy said quietly. "Well, not these, anyway."

"Could they be from some ancient culture on our world?" Castilano queried.

"Not a chance."

"But . . . but how did you get these!" Marcia Mason burst out.

Indy studied her carefully, but not to any greater extent than the others in the room. Somewhere in this group there was a traitor. He'd been warned long before about that by Treadwell, but up to this moment no one had been able to point a finger with any confidence at anyone else. The woman's surprise as to his possession of the artifacts could be genuine, if she was faithful to the group. *Or it could be surprise as to how I got these if she isn't,* Indy mused. *I'm not getting anywhere fast. . . .*

Castilano was openly agitated. "Indy, tell us. How did you get these?"

"I'm not going to tell you anything that our opponents don't already know," Indy said quickly. "Keep that in mind, please. First, I have a contract with the De Beers diamond mines. It is their custom always to place something in their jewel shipments that is easier to trace than diamonds, which can be recut to any size or shape. In this case, we used the cube artifact. The cuneiform markings simply gave it more authenticity. Or led people to believe that. But the cube, and this pyramid, were manufactured in England. I don't know the alloys involved; that's out of my field. But it's very much a homegrown product. My contribution was the markings. Someone who gets hold of this, and also believes in its rarity and value, must try to use or sell it in some way. So it acts as a beacon."

"Are you telling us that this group, whoever and whatever they are," Marcia Mason asked slowly and deliberately, "are trying to sell us a fake that our own group, yourself, created?"

"Yes, ma'am."

"But how could you . . . I mean, why would you have us believe these things were of such tremendous value!"

"*I* never said they were of any monetary *or* historical value," Indy told the group, but looking at Mason. "Just about everybody else did that. Including the people who have committed the crimes we're trying to solve. The stories about these artifacts were so effective that the people who robbed De Beers and the others figured the artifacts were the most valuable of all."

"But why try to kill *you*?" Franck burst out.

Castilano laughed. "Professor Jones is a better teacher than he is a secret agent. He almost set up his own execution. Once the group we are facing had determined these artifacts were spurious, they *had* to get rid of Jones, and his associates, *before* they could let the rest of us, or other customers in the world, know the things were worthless."

"And they came very close to succeeding," Gale Parker spoke up suddenly.

"There's another reason," Indy told the group. He had their instant attention. "Our opposition has a plant among us."

"A what?"

"We have a traitor in our midst," Indy said calmly. "For money, idealism; whatever. But someone within this group, which includes those people not present at this meeting, works for our enemy."

"That is a grave charge," Franck said, visibly disturbed.

"Yes, sir," Indy agreed. "It is also true."

For several minutes, the conference room resounded to arguments, rising and falling in volume and varying tones of anger and confusion. Indy had hoped this would follow his shocker of there being a traitor in their midst. Now, if Treadwell's own skills could be applied through Indy's next words, he might be able to rattle even more the cage of their unknown adversary. He waited until quiet returned to the group; they obviously hoped he might have more to tell them. Indy did, but his purpose was to pass on a "message" to their opposition.

"There is one other matter that needs clarification," he began. He had already caught them unawares, and knew he had their close attention.

"Those flying machines," Indy said, seemingly confused about the issue. "We haven't said a word about something the best aeronautical engineers in the world really can't explain. Discs, or saucers, or whatever they're called, flying at speeds that seem impossible. The mother ship, if that is really what it is, well, that's much easier to understand. It's sort of a super zeppelin—"

"But we don't know what makes it go, do we?" Dr. Franck broke in.

"No, sir, we don't," Indy admitted. "Let me change that, sir. *I* don't know what makes it go. I'm no pilot and I'm no engineer, but I do listen to the really sharp people in those lines. And they tell me the stories of those discs, or scimitars, coming from outer space, well, as far as they're concerned, that's nonsense."

"In the face of what we've heard," Castilano said, "they still feel they're from right here, from earth?"

"They sure do," Indy said.

"I must beg to differ," Matsuda broke in. "I do not say they are from other worlds, Professor Jones, but there is nothing known on *this* world that flies without wings, at five hundred miles an hour, that can hover, or levitate. What they do is impossible by everything we know."

"I'm not arguing with you, sir," Indy said. "I wouldn't do that. I tell you only what the experts tell me."

"Then your experts, Indy," Castilano followed Matsuda, "seem in need of better information. Our flying machines are helpless before these discs. There must be an explanation beyond the mere statement that they are of local origin."

"I agree. But I am explaining to you that the professionals in this field are convinced we are dealing with terrestrial vehicles, produced in a manner we can't yet explain, operated by a force we can't yet identify. No, I shouldn't say that. I don't get into the technical side of all this. They believe they either have the answers or they're about to get them."

That should do it, Indy concluded to himself. *Whoever is on the side of the opposition is going to get back to them as fast as they can that their plan is starting to come unglued at the seams. I sure hope Henshaw and Treadwell are better at this than I am. . . .*

Indy rose to his feet. "I have a lot to do, much to learn, and I'm racing a clock. I've also got some great help now. We may be closer to answers than any of you realize."

Gale and Tarkiz also were standing. They didn't say a word. But their facial expressions and the manner in which they stood made it abundantly clear they were in full agreement with Indy. In the uncomfortable silence that followed, as one by one everyone else stood, Indy caught a fleeting glimpse of a workman, olive-skinned and in a turban, leaving through a rear side door. Just a glimpse and the man was gone. It should have meant nothing, but who would leave this incredible scene? Because if he were privy to listening to the exchange, he already had been judged as loyal to the group.

"You are really quite disturbing in what you say, Indy," Franck finally broke the ice.

"You have our continued full support," Matsuda assured him.

"And ours," said Castilano.

"I await further word, I must admit," Quahirah smiled, "with great anticipation."

Only Marcia Mason remained silent. Indy ignored her. He knew she would figure in his life soon enough. Without another word or a backward glance, he left the room, followed closely by Gale, Jocko, and Tarkiz.

Waiting for the elevator, Gale turned to Jocko. "Could we go through that diorama again? I'd like another look at that. It gives me ideas for museum presentations."

Indy nodded. He was still thinking about that workman and the manner in which he'd left their conference room.

They retraced their steps to the huge hall with the northern woods diorama. Indy was impressed. They'd even kept a woods scent present in the area. He looked up into the trees, and they were *real* trees, their roots in tubs concealed by brush.

He was impatient to get back to his search. He turned to Gale. "Seen enough?"

"Yes." Her eyes shone with pleasure. Suddenly her eyes widened. *"Indy!"* she gasped. *"The bear—LOOK OUT!"*

He heard the coughing roar from behind him. For just an instant his senses triggered to the presence of danger, even though he realized where they were and that the bears were electromechanical objects.

The next moment he was struck a powerful blow; he felt as if he'd been hit by a charging rhino, and felt his body spinning about as he was hurled from his feet. He had a fleeting glimpse of Tarkiz—the man had dashed full-tilt into Indy to smash him aside. Indy shook his head to make sense of what was happening.

Then he saw the huge Kodiak bear lunging forward and downward from its display position, its front paws with terrible claws unsheathed swinging together as it came down. The great "animal," fully nine feet tall and weighing several hundred pounds, crashed into Tarkiz, one paw slicing across his face with savage force.

The claws laid the side of his head open to white bone. A ghastly gurgle rattled in the big man's throat as he toppled to the floor beneath the immense figure of the bear. Tarkiz died instantly.

Indy had already spun about. There! A flash of white . . . the white coat of the turbaned workman who'd slipped away from the conference room. If anyone would have worked the controls to send the mechanical animal rushing at Indy it *must* have been him, and now he was trying to sneak away.

Jocko was already running full speed to head off the man before he could disappear into the labyrinthine hallways and side rooms of the below-ground sections of the museum. Indy had his hand about the grip of the Webley, but before he, or Jocko, could stop the man, Gale had stepped forward, one arm held stiffly before her. Indy heard the sudden *twang* of metal under strain and a hissing sound. He saw a blur as something snapped across the room toward the flash of white.

A moment later a muffled scream reached them and they heard the crash of a falling body against a floor. Indy turned to look at Gale. She had a strange smile on her face; a look of unexpected triumph.

"Got him," she said quietly.

"With *what*?" he asked.

She pulled back her jacket sleeve. Indy stared at a circular bolt-launcher fitted securely to her forearm. "Remember when I used the machine shop back at the airfield?" she asked.

He nodded. "Notched bolt," she explained. "Fast as a crossbow." She smiled grimly. "Never mind how small it is. It's tipped with curarine. About six times deadlier than curare. He's paralyzed, and he won't live much longer."

Indy was already running about the wide curve of the diorama. He came upon the man in the white jacket and turban on the floor, Jocko standing over him.

"Don't kill him," Indy snapped. "I need some answers from him."

"Too late, Boss. I don't know what hit him, but his lungs and vocal cords are paralyzed. He won't last much—"

There wasn't any need to continue. Eyes bulging, tongue protruding, the man twitched violently, heels drumming on the floor. His head snapped back violently. They heard the crack of his neck breaking.

"Let's get out of here, *now*," Indy ordered.

"You're leaving two dead men behind," Jocko said unnecessarily.

"Castilano will handle it. He's an old pro at getting rid of bodies." Gale had followed them and he grabbed her arm, half dragging her to a stairway.

"Lead the way, Jocko. Right to your cab," Indy snapped. "When we're driving, make sure we're not being followed, and then get us onto Long Island."

They dashed up the stairways. Jocko went into the parking lot first, opened the cab's hood to check for any explosives, slipped beneath the cab to do the same, then signaled Indy and Gale to follow.

Moments later they were driving through Central Park. "I'll work us down to the Fifty-Ninth Street Bridge,"

Jocko said. "I know the back roads, and no one can follow us without my knowing about it. Where to on the island?"

"Roosevelt Field. Our plane is already there," Indy told him.

Gale studied Indy. "Any more surprises in your bag of tricks?"

He nodded. "You'll see."

12

Indy sat in the right seat of the Ford cockpit. Cromwell was at the controls to his left, Foulois standing partially between and behind the seats. Unless both men were required by circumstances to be together in the cockpit, Indy was determined to spend as much time as possible with his hands and feet working the trimotor's systems. What he was learning through hands-on experience might not make him a pilot but it sure was a great leap forward. And it kept his mind off the death of his friend Tarkiz, a scene it would take him years to forget.

He was learning the sensations of engine sounds, the rumble of the airplane over uneven ground, the effects of winds, especially from the side that could blow the airplane off its straight-line takeoff or landing. There were control pressures to learn, the need for pressure on the right rudder pedal during the takeoff roll and climb-out to counteract swirling propeller wash and engine torque. Needs small and large, some constant, others only at certain times, but above all he had already cemented into his thinking that flying *skillfully* demanded much more than simply pushing, pulling and shoving. What seemed so easy to his two pilots (and don't forget Gale! he told himself) was a masterful orchestration that *appeared* to be carried out with the most casual effort.

"You'll learn, way beyond the mechanical," Cromwell told him, "that the smoothest flying is actually a constant correction of errors that only you, the pilot, not only know but can *anticipate*. Any clod can push an aeroplane through the air, but that is *not* flying. You've got to caress the controls as you would a lovely lady—"

"Talk about the *airplane*," Indy growled.

"Touchy, touchy," Cromwell grinned. "All right, bucko, I'll add this to the litany of learning. Never, absolutely *never*, try to fool this machine. I mean that, Indy. You can fool anybody on the ground. You can tell grand stories to your mates. But if you lie to your machine, it will kill you. It will do so in a heartbeat. Learn to love your aeroplane as you might love a true mate. You're bonded to it as closely as you ever will be to a human being, and your life depends on it."

He turned to Foulois. "Frenchy, they all strapped in back there?"

Foulois glanced back at Gale and their newest member, Jocko. "I don't believe our dark friend is all that happy about flying," he said, smiling.

"He'll get used to it quickly enough. All right, Indy, as I begin to get us under way, I'll be talking every move, every step of the way, so you will know what happens and can start to learn that secret of anticipation. You ride the controls with me. *Do it gently.* And if you ever hear me, or Frenchy if he's in this seat, say 'I've got it,' get your bleedin' hands and feet off the controls *at once.* Got it?"

"Shut up and fly," Indy growled.

"Ah, the enthusiasm of the wingless young pup," Cromwell laughed. "All right, here we go. Yoke full back; that's it. Brake pedals depressed to hold us in place. Scan the gauges. *All* of them. The throttles start forward now, keep your eyes scanning, check all the temps and pressures, double-check the wind outside, it can change in a flash, throttles all the way forward, feel her shake, she wants to fly, call out RPM, oil temp, cylinder head temp, pressure, fuel flow, quantity, check the revs, see how close they are, look outside, be quick about it, blast you, look for other traffic! All right, you check the trim, you clod? Forget it, I did; now, last glance across the panel, the windsock, look for any animals or people that may have wandered into our takeoff run, everything's set? You strap in your seat belt, and brakes coming off, there's good acceleration, ease off the yoke back pressure a mite, that's it, *get in steady pressure on the right rudder,* DON'T STOMP LIKE A CLODHOPPER, GENTLY BUT FIRMLY! Feel the tail coming up, the vibration is easing, HOLD HER STRAIGHT, YOU NIT, that's it, KEEP YOUR HAND ON THE THROTTLES SO THEY DON'T BACK OFF! You've got speed coming up, watch it, you're drifting left, blast it, Indy, look at your airspeed, why aren't you FLYING? Indy, did you ever think of becoming a cobbler to earn your living?"

Beads of perspiration appeared on Indy's brow and upper lip as Cromwell lambasted him every foot of the way up to three thousand feet where they leveled off and the noise and vibrations eased. "What were you in your former life, Will, a galley slave master with the Romans?"

Cromwell ignored him. "We took off from Roosevelt Field, we're going to that private grass strip on Block Island just east of Montauk Point, right?"

Indy nodded.

"Well, this isn't by guess and by gosh, *Professor.* Have you noted temperatures, humidity, dewpoint, density altitude? What's our ETD, ETE, ETA? Fuel time aboard, how many gallons do we burn every hour at this setting?

When's the last time you scanned the gauges? If your name wasn't tattooed on your forehead you would by God forget that, too! Would you like to meet George?"

"George?" Indy looked puzzled. "Who the devil is George?"

"George, m'lad, is the latest wonder of the ages. Directly from the development laboratory of Sperry Gyroscope. It's a device that's linked to our directional gyroscope and to our artificial horizon. George is our automatic pilot; consider the name as a shameless sign of affection. When I turn on George, it derives heading and bank information from the gyros. It will keep this machine flying with wings level. Here; watch. And stay *off* the controls."

Cromwell moved several controls and leaned back in his seat. Nobody touched the foot or hand controls. "George" was slaved to the gyro instruments and locked the Ford in level flight on the heading determined by the directional gyro. To Indy, it was magic. *The airplane was flying itself.* It flew as though invisible hands and feet were on the controls, rocking gently in mild turbulence, but flying with dazzling precision.

"Where are we, o ace of the skies?" Cromwell nudged Indy.

"What? Oh. I was watching how this thing flew, I mean—"

"You mean you forgot to keep track of where we were flying, where we were, how long it's been since takeoff, how far we are from Block Island, when we're supposed to start our descent, right? Other than that," Cromwell sneered, "you're doing a splendid job. I always wonder how a slip of a girl like Gale is so good at this game, while the world-famous explorer and adventurer, *the* Professor Henry Jones, can't keep track of where he is over Long Island!"

"I may kill you," Indy glowered.

"Tut, tut, my friend. Today was simply an introduction. Piece of cake. Simple for a ten-year-old child. It shouldn't take you more than ten or twenty years to get the hang of it."

"Ignore him, Indy," Foulois said, leaning forward. "It's just been a long time since he screamed and shouted at any students. He's in his element, that's all."

Indy turned to Cromwell who grinned broadly at him. "All right, mate, we'll be starting a long descent. On the controls, gently, just follow me through for the feel. I don't want you doing any work. You've had enough for one session, so this is cheat time for you."

Fifteen minutes later Cromwell, arrowing downward, feeling the headwind fading away, crossed the controls and nudged the Ford into a forward slip, the wings askew and the airplane descending in an unnerving sideways crab. At the last moment Cromwell straightened out everything, and the big airplane sighed onto the grass strip in a masterful touchdown. "There's a barn over to your left," Indy told him. "Taxi over there. By the time we get there the doors will be open front and back, so you can taxi right inside without blowing down the place."

"How wide?" Cromwell queried.

"One hundred ten feet side to side," Indy told him.

"Piece of cake, mate."

He shut down the engines when they were inside the huge "barn," but the only part of the structure that was farmyard was its external appearance. Cromwell looked about him. "Very neat, Indy. In here we have simply disappeared."

"That, slave driver, is the idea." He left the cockpit to return to the cabin.

"How did it go?" Gale asked.

"My ego is flatter than yesterday morning's pancake,"

he told her. "Jocko, help Gale with our gear. We'll be staying in that farmhouse tonight. And sometime this evening a boat will arrive from Connecticut with the equipment we ordered for you."

"You got it, Boss."

"Why do you keep calling me Boss?"

"Sure sounds better than Whitey."

Gale stifled a laugh. "You two are going to be lots of fun."

"Never mind the chuckles," Indy said. "We've got work to do."

"Mind telling me what's on the agenda, Boss?"

"Why not? We've got to find the Martians, or whatever they are. Or, more to the point, we've got to help them *find us.*"

"You got a death wish, Whitey?"

"Boss, remember?"

Three men and one woman ran the Block Island "farm," a rolling expanse on the island isolated by water from the eastern tip of Long Island. None of the four people were farmers; the coveralls they wore provided a loose and comfortable fit for the powerful .44 Magnum revolvers each carried in holsters.

"It doesn't take a physicist," Gale said slowly to her own group, "to conclude that as a farm, this place is a bust."

"Well, it's also a weather station," Indy noted, pointing to equipment atop a small building. "That attends to any questions about towers and antenna for the radio equipment here."

"And if you try to come here by boat at night you got to be stupid or crazy," Jocko said. He'd already studied the angry waters between Long Island and Block Island. "Now I see why this hayfield is such a great landing strip."

In the "farmhouse," one of the men introduced the

others. "I'm Richard. This is Mike, and the short dumpy character is Ozzie. The lady is Katy. Please introduce yourselves and use first names only. We don't need to know any more." When the introductions were complete they helped carry the bags and equipment to rooms on the second floor. "Indy, you've got two-oh-one. Someone else will share it with you tonight."

"Who?"

"I don't know, but you know each other. Will and Rene, two-oh-two is yours. Gale, two-oh-three, and you'll be on your own. Jocko, you're two-oh-four. Several more rooms will be occupied tonight."

"How are they arriving?" Indy asked.

Richard, if that was his name, pointed a finger at the sky. Answer enough.

"We were asked to have an early meal ready for you," Richard went on. "They wish to get right into the meeting after they land."

"Great," Cromwell boomed. "What is the fare, may I ask? Cold bologna sandwiches, no doubt, on this forsaken real estate?"

"Roast duck, spiced apples, choice of wine, candied carrots, kitchen-fried potatoes, French bread, coffee."

"You're serious?" Cromwell gaped at the man.

"Sir, this is a duck farm. That is the truth. We have six thousand ducks here. Katy and Ozzie are superb chefs. That is their profession. Mike and I prefer to kill the stinking birds."

Ten minutes after the table was cleared, they heard the sound of an approaching aircraft. Cromwell went to the front door to open it wide. He cocked his head better to hear the sound. "Radial engine, single, descending, throttled back, coming in fast," he announced.

"You can tell all that by just sticking your ear into the night air?" Indy queried.

"Everything but the pilot's name," Cromwell said confidently. "In fact, ground lights should be coming on about, um, well, about, *now.*" As if in response to his last word, a double row of lights came on along the grass strip, and a floodlight illuminated the windsock. Moments later a two-seat fighter—radial engine just as Cromwell had said—whistled down the runway on a clearing pass. They heard the engine thunder with increased power for the climb, then ease off as the pilot came around in a tight curving descent, rolled onto final approach, and eased the fighter to the grass. As soon as the pilot cleared the runway the lights winked out, the plane was moved into the hangar, and silence lay across the field again.

Colonel Harry Henshaw and Filipo Castilano emerged from the hangar to greet Indy and the others. They went together into the farmhouse. "Coffee," Henshaw said to Richard. His demeanor left no doubt as to whom Richard and the others worked for. Coffee was placed on the table along with sweet rolls.

"Okay, let's get down to it," Indy said. The long machinations until this moment had been grinding away his patience.

"Indy," Henshaw began, "I've been digging as deeply as I can into every known instance of unexplained flight—unexplained in terms of our present science, engineering, and technology—since the first historical records ever kept. I didn't do it myself, of course. We turned to every college and university and research office with which the government has any kind of contract. We leaned on them and we leaned *real* heavy. We have used everybody from Navajo shamans to long-deceased priests, thanks to the effort of Filipo, here," he nodded to Castilano. "We've gone into Hebraic, Moslem, Akkadian, Sumerian, Babylonian, Chinese, Japanese, voodoo, Hindu, every Christian sect and every ancient sect from people who made the ancient Egyptians look like Johnny-come-latelies."

This was Indiana Jones's home territory. He was enjoying himself in a way he hadn't anticipated. "Witches, too?"

"Witches, too." Henshaw wondered about the sudden smile on the face of Gale Parker.

"Colonel, how deeply did you go into the Mayan, Aztec, Inca, and other cultures?" she put in.

"All the way."

"Your conclusions?" Indy asked.

"I've come to the conclusion—and to the great amusement of my Vatican friend, here—that I feel I have missed ninety-nine percent of history."

"Sounds reasonable," Indy said to settle Henshaw's mood. "Look, Harry, no one man knows it all, or even a small fraction of the past. Once you make a concerted effort, you find out that you've been blind to that past. It's too big, there's too much, and it's all convoluted with the intermixing of fact and fable."

"What the devil are you trying to tell me?" Henshaw demanded.

"Simply that I expected you to run into countless incidents, from reliable sources in our past histories, that tell the stories of machines that fly just like the ones we seem to be encountering now. Huge torpedo vessels. Gleaming gold and bronze and silver discs and wheels. Mother ships that spawn smaller vessels. Great scimitar-shaped craft that hurtle through the skies, that perform impossible maneuvers, that blaze brighter than the sun, that hover above the ground. It's a long and fascinating story."

"Indy, are you telling me that what we've run into is simply a replay of ancient history?" Henshaw couldn't hide his disbelief.

"To some extent, yes," Indy said.

"Aha! I *told* you, Harry!" Castilano was almost gloating. "The history of the Church, the history *before* the Church, the histories before anyone even thought of any kind of temple! It's all there, it has *always* been there! And now we are again—"

"Hold it, Filipo!" Indy said in a half-shout. "Save the absolutions for Easter, or whatever. Let's stick to the historical *records*. Stay away, *all of us*, from subjective conclusions."

"You sound like my old history teacher," Henshaw laughed, easing the tension that had suddenly built up.

"He should," Gale told Henshaw. "Remember? *Professor* Jones is the name."

Henshaw nodded. "Okay. Where do we begin?" He shuffled through a thick stack of notepapers. By his side Castilano was doing the same. Gale looked for Indy to put *something* before him but all that appeared was a brandy snifter. He turned to Gale. "Take notes," he told her. "But about tomorrow, not yesterday."

He winked at their fascinated audience—Cromwell, Foulois, and Kilarney. Only the newcomer to their group was fast enough to offer a slight nod in return. That Jocko, mused Indy, was hiding a very sharp mind beneath that gleaming smile and huge frame. He'd have to do some digging on his background.

Indy changed his mind suddenly. He had planned for the two pilots and Jocko simply to be outsiders, permitted to "listen in" without participating. Then he realized how foolish was that judgment; Cromwell and Foulois were *pilots*. Aces! They could fly anything, and in the information they were about to hear, there might hide a sliver of data that would prove valuable to them.

"Will, Frenchy? Come on closer. If you get a brainstorm about something, break in, all right?"

Indy turned back to Henshaw and Castilano.

"Okay. There are certain rules to follow when you're trying to extract information from what's available. First of all, we must gain access to whatever records there are that contain references to unexplained objects appearing in the sky. But in many of those cases we'll be dealing with emotion, religious experience, and inadequate record-keeping. So what we find may have no basis in fact, or it might hold fragments of truth mixed in with nonsense. The point I'm stressing is that the moment we run up against that kind of historical record, we've got to put it aside. Just plain dump it and go to whatever may be more substantial."

Indy looked directly at Henshaw. "From *any* source." He hoped Henshaw got the message: bring up *anything* that might apply. Something had been stuck in the back of Indy's mind longer than he liked because he still couldn't fit it in with events taking place around them. During the work of arming the Ford TriMotor, Henshaw had mentioned a French scientist, Henri Coanda, who had worked on a rocket gun during the Great War. One of his other experiments had involved some kind of new engine that operated like a giant torch. Indy made a mental note to pursue that issue further with Henshaw.

But for now they were far back in history, and he expected Henshaw to help keep things moving steadily. He was right.

"Example." Henshaw could cut right to the bone.

"The cave wall paintings and carvings in China's Hunan Province," began Indy. "They were dug with very sharp rocks, or flint; they were colored with ochre and pigments of unknown origin; and they show cylindrical vessels moving through the sky. I'd like to use them for reference, but you have whatever value they contain in this brief description. We're not even certain whether they were created by

Homo sapiens or prehumans. On the matter that concerns us, it has no bearing."

"Agreed," Castilano said with a nod.

"Go on," Henshaw directed.

"May I?" They turned to Gale. "I believe you must adopt the same rules for Chih-Chiang-Tsu-Yu."

"Who is?" Henshaw asked.

"Not is. Was," Gale emphasized. "He was the lead engineer in the royal court of China's Emperor Yao. I'd love to be able to question him myself," she sighed. "His records are astonishing. He described an encounter with an alien race come to earth, claimed that their craft shone in the heavens, and stated he actually made a flight to the moon and back with the aliens."

"How long ago was this?" asked Henshaw. He was taken aback as those more familiar with the truly ancient records smiled at his question. "Four thousand three hundred years," Gale answered. "I mentioned this item because Tsu-Yu even described columns of luminous air—"

"A *rocket?*" Henshaw asked, incredulous.

Gale shrugged. "Who knows? Indy warned us against extrapolation, so all I'm doing is establishing a framework of historical reference."

"Look, if we wanted to refer to a catalogue of such moments, we could. And we'd be justified," Indy said patiently. "There are records of visitations from outer space all through man's history, from every culture, and throughout every age. I could make a great case out of the *Surya Sutradhara.* That's an ancient text from India in which astronomical events were recorded with incredible accuracy. And not by dewy-eyed stargazers, but by the *Siddas* and the *Vidyaharas*—"

"What the devil are those?" Cromwell burst out.

"Not what; who," Indy replied. "They were the *scientists* of India. They also described flights in alien spacecraft and then went on to write down how they flew, and this is a quote, "below the moon but above the clouds."

"I will be . . . I mean . . . that is so bloody hard to believe!" Cromwell stammered.

"Your belief, mine, anyone else's," Indy told him, "is not the issue. The accuracy of such reports, and how they may or may not relate to what our own people have come to believe are starships from Mars, or whatever . . . *that's* the issue."

"Then we can hardly ignore the Santander caves of Spain, can we?" They turned to Henshaw, who held up both hands. "Sorry, I'm no archeologist or historian. But when I was in Spain I happened to be in that area, and what I heard sent me there quickly enough. I could hardly believe what I saw. Beautiful paintings in prehistoric caves. Paintings of *discs moving through the sky.*"

"And in more places than Spain," Castilano offered. "In fact, Indy and I ran into each other once on the Tassili Plateau. That's the Saharan region. Cave paintings of discs there as well."

"The point is, we've brought up these places and their times," Indy said to move them along, "and there isn't a blasted thing we can do with this information except say, okay, here it is, here's what it depicts, we can't explain it, although we can debate from now to forever. Let me save all of us some time. Even as early as the fifteenth century B.C., people in North Africa were seeing all sorts of discs in the sky. Historians reported they flew with great precision, whatever that meant in the terms of those days.

"Now, in A.D. 747, the Chinese left records of flaming objects cruising overhead *and climbing.* So we're getting a bit warmer."

"What about the German sightings at Nuremburg in 1561?" asked Castilano. "Thousands of witnesses saw cylinders, discs, spheres—"

"They saw the same thing in 1883 in Zacatecas," Gale broke in.

"Is that in Mexico?" Jocko inquired.

"Give the man a cigar," Indy told him. "You got it, friend. Only this time the sky was busier than Times Square on Saturday night. The locals saw more than four hundred aerial torpedos and discs. But we don't have to go that far back. It was, um, 1896 and 1897, right in the United States. California, Kansas, New Mexico, Texas, and so forth. All of a sudden people—thousands of people who were sober, reliable witnesses—saw strange airships all over the place. Including a bunch of them that landed. They spoke English, German, and some foreign languages nobody could understand. They also took off and then climbed with what people said was terrific speed."

"And bloody well showed up again," Cromwell said. "In England, about twelve years later. They seemed much more advanced than the American visitors, but airships they were, all right."

"Zeppelins, no doubt," Henshaw remarked.

"No way," Indy stepped in. "At that time Germany had but three zeppelins flying, and they had poor performance. The British reports numbered in the hundreds, in thirty to fifty locations distant from one another on the same night. Besides, no matter *what* they were, they had engines, propellers, *and* wings, which is a pretty stupid thing to use on a zeppelin."

"But there are more modern sightings of the discs," said Castilano.

"Of course!" came a startled cry from Foulois. "Back in 1880, by a French scientist, Trecul, a member of the French Academy of Science. Ah! *He* was a master observer, a serious and sober man, and he swore up and down he had seen a golden vessel flying overhead. More to the point," Foulois continued, now standing as for emphasis, "he also saw the big ship release a smaller craft that shot ahead of the golden vessel. Indy, my friend, the exact words he used were 'mother craft,' and *that* certainly fits what you are seeking!"

"Did he ever see it again?"

"Non."

Indy scratched his head. "What else do we have?"

"I was with that expedition to China in 1926," Castilano said in a subdued tone. "I never thought I'd talk about it, but—"

"Let's have it," Indy pushed.

"Well, it simply never registered. I mean, an event in such a remote place. In fact, it was northern China, in the Kukunor district. That's rather close to the Humboldt Chain. To be even more specific, now that I'm rooting about in my memory, it was about nine-thirty the morning of August fifth. Not just myself, but the entire expeditionary group caught sight of something huge in the sky. Let me see, now." He absentmindedly rubbed an elbow and tapped a foot. "Ah, yes, we all agreed it was a large, even a huge, oval-shaped object."

"Color?"

"Gold. Burnished gold."

"Anyone use binoculars?"

"To be sure. At least four men. Had an absolutely clear view."

"Any kind of exhaust trail?"

"None reported. There could have been, but—"

"Sound?"

"None that could be detected. We were in the midst of a pretty good wind, blowing snow, that sort of thing."

Indy wanted to break things with his hands. So close! So close, and yet . . . He studied Castilano. "Filipo, my friend," he said quietly, "did *anyone* among your group, a research group, for God's sake, *take a picture*?"

Castilano looked stricken. He shook his head slowly. "How I have wished that we did. . . . I will tell you this, Indy. Whatever we saw was definitely oval. I have considered changing visual points, apparent shapes because of angle. It was *oval,* and if I had a picture, I believe it would be the only confirmed photograph at the time of an extraterrestrial vehicle."

"What makes you so sure it was off-Earth?" Henshaw broke in.

"We calculated distance and speed. It was moving with a velocity in excess of two thousand miles an hour."

"So that leaves us with a memory," Indy said sourly, "and that's not much to go on."

"Why do you say that?" Castilano protested. "Fourteen eyewitnesses are but a memory?"

"That is *all* it is," Indy said with a no-nonsense tone. "It doesn't pin down anything but a sighting of something you cannot identify. Look, Filipo, if Will and Rene took up the Ford and did wild flying around this island and then flew away, and you had never before seen or heard of an airplane, and you had no pictures for later reference, what would you deduce from that sighting? I know, *I know.* Experienced, reliable observers are at hand. But when it's over, what do you have but a wild story? No matter if it's true."

"Wait a moment," Henshaw said abruptly. "There *is* one thing that hasn't come up before. The *Empress Kali* incident. And that flat craft that hovered? I read in the report of one eyewitness that he said the edges of the ship, or disc, or whatever it was, weren't clearly defined. He didn't use that phrase. He said the edges seemed to waver, shift in and out of focus."

Indy could hardly contain himself. *It was exactly the kind of clue for which he'd been searching.* He decided, at that very moment, to keep what he had just learned—

what Henshaw's words had told him—to himself until later.

"Does that mean something important?" Henshaw asked.

"Sure," Indy said, feigning indifference. "Your witness has watery eyes." He rose to his feet, making eye contact with Henshaw, then spoke to the group. "That's it, everybody. We've gone over the ancient records and what we've come up with is that history is loaded with reports of unexplained things moving through the sky. None of which does us any real good except that we've followed the proper rules—examine everything possible. Be ready for takeoff tomorrow morning, please."

"What time, Indy?" Cromwell asked.

"Dawn."

Cromwell groaned. "You're destroying my beauty sleep," he complained.

Indy laughed. "Try a face-lifting instead." Indy turned to Henshaw.

"Let's go over the equipment list again, if you don't mind?"

Henshaw picked up immediately on Indy's unspoken request. Meet together, just the two of them. "Got it. I'll get the papers and meet you back here in ten minutes."

"Did it hit you about the same time?" Henshaw asked Indy.

"It sure seems like it. I'm still not certain of the connection, but when you started talking about the edges of the disc seeming to waver, well, my first reaction was heat distortion."

"You're picking it up quickly," Henshaw told him. "You're smack on target. Heat distortion; why didn't we put two and two together before!"

"Harry, *you* came up with the clue," Indy said quickly.

"You said this Coanda fellow was describing a blowtorch effect with an engine, right?"

"Exactly. We've got to speak with Coanda directly, Indy. Face to face. You learn more that way than you ever will from any paperwork. So either one of us, or the both of us, must go to France, and keep that trip absolutely quiet. Otherwise we make targets of ourselves."

Indy nodded. "Agreed. We'll work out the details later. Anything else?"

"Yes, and I got the news only this morning. This time it's the paperwork that provides what may be a critical lead for us." Henshaw smiled with satisfaction. "The paperwork was buried in old archives in France. I've had a team there with a cover story about exchanging planes and equipment between our museums and theirs. Know what they found? Sorry. Of course you couldn't. An entry in the patent office back in 1914 in Paris. Someone had applied for a patent that year." Henshaw paused. *"For a jet engine."*

Indy smiled. "A buck gets you ten the man's name was Coanda."

"You win," Henshaw said.

13

At five o'clock the next morning the team gathered by the Ford and pushed the airplane onto the dew-wet grass. Henshaw and Castilano were there for brief final conversations. "Everything you need for your crossing will be waiting for you at Bangor," he told Indy. "And you're in luck. I've been getting the weather reports from Canada and the ocean-crossing navigation ships at sea. There's a terrific high that will keep the skies clear most of the way and give you a dickens of a tailwind."

"Great. Thanks, Harry." They shook hands, and the rest of the team boarded the airplane.

Indy wondered if this whole idea of his was really as crazy as it sounded. Crossing the North Atlantic in an airplane that could cruise steadily at only 115 miles an hour sounded like lunacy when you envisioned the huge ocean area before them.

"It's a duck walk, really," Cromwell had convinced him. "With our extra fuel—and we could even shut down the nose engine and fly on only two to stretch time and fuel—the trip will be a piece of cake. The longest stretch over water is only about eight hundred and fifty miles. Just one thing I don't fathom, Indy."

"Which is?"

"Why are you making a public spectacle of us? From what I've been hearing of this lot that's after you, I'd have thought you'd rather be out of sight as much as possible."

Indy patted Will Cromwell on the back. "Got to flush them out. This is the best way. Doesn't it seem just a bit strange to you? If these people really are gathering so much military might, why has no one come after us with all that firepower?"

"I hadn't thought about it, I confess."

"Confession's good for the soul, Will. You and Rene fly, I'll take care of the fun and games."

"As you say, Guv."

They climbed out into the sun breaking the horizon. Indy slipped on his headset and mike intercom to talk to the cockpit. "Frenchy, before we reach the Connecticut coast, hold an easterly heading until I call you back. You'll feel the upper hatch open for a few moments. I'll call you when it's closed."

"Right."

Indy felt the gentle bank and saw they were headed directly into the fiery disc clearing the horizon. He walked back to a storage locker, withdrew a mahogony box, and returned to the upper hatch where the machine-gun mount could be raised. He pushed open the hatch, picked up the box, and then stood on the gun mount so that his head and shoulders extended into the airstream. For a moment he struggled with the mahogony box.

Gale started from her seat to assist Indy, but Jocko placed his hand on her arm to restrain her. "This is for him alone," he said. The look on his face more than his words brought Gale back into her seat.

Standing in the airblast, facing backwards, Indy brought

the box above the gun mount coaming, opened the lid, and began to scatter the ashes of Tarkiz Belem over the waters of Long Island Sound. In the wild turbulence, the ashes flew about in a swirling cloud against his face and into his nostrils; most of the ash cloud hurtled backward and flashed out of sight. Several banging sounds drifted to them.

"Those are small pieces of bone striking the tail," Jocko told Gale. "Not even cremation turns it all to ashes."

Gale shuddered, remembering the big, crude man who had twice saved her life. She remained silent as Indy completed his task and then hurled the mahogony box from the plane. He slid back into the cabin, closed the hatch, and went to the water basin to soak his handkerchief to wipe the ashes of Tarkiz from his face and hands. He sank into a seat across from Gale and Jocko. "Tell Will to pick up his course," he asked Gale.

The Ford set its nose for Bangor.

Gale took sandwiches and coffee to the cockpit as they flew across New England, the sky spotted with puffy clouds. She returned to her seat to join Indy and Jocko in a conversation she'd wanted for days to hear.

"Let's have it out on the table, Jocko," Indy was saying. "I need to know as much as I can about my people. Otherwise I'm liable to miss opportunities when they arise."

"You mean this isn't a job interview?" Jocko smiled.

"I thought you worked for the museum," Gale said between bites of her sandwich.

"I do. But I'm on this airplane because I was instructed to go along with what the professor needs. Or wants," he added as an afterthought.

"What's your background, Jocko?"

"Tell me what you know already, Boss. It will be easier to fill in the blanks, perhaps."

"For starters, you're a hell of a lot smarter than you show with that Jamaican jingo you present to the world."

"That real kind of you, mon," Jocko mimicked his sing-song tone.

"But why do you do that?" Gale asked.

"You can hide that you are a witch, Miss Parker—"

"Gale, please."

"Thank you. As I say, you easily conceal that you are a witch. You even change your name. There is Arab blood in you. I see it in the bone structure of your face, the small differences in your skin—well, call it shading instead of color." Jocko smiled with tolerance born of severe experience. "How long can you hide your family tree if you are as black as me?"

Gale studied the big man before her, beginning to understand his true depth.

"Not long at all," she admitted.

"Why do you hide yours?"

Gale shrugged. "It unnerves people. Upsets them. Even frightens some. So I changed to a name with which people are more comfortable."

"It is much easier to change your name than it is for me to change my ebony appearance," Jocko offered. "Being black, and being intelligent, is acceptable only under certain conditions. And only with certain people."

"You have that much trouble?" Indy asked.

"Being a smart black man in certain places means a very short lifespan. I *know.*" He leaned back and smiled, but with little humor. "Let me explain. It is not just the black that matters. It is the *difference* in color. It is even the difference in the black. Those blacks of African descent, or from the islands, or anywhere, for that matter, if they are light-skinned, they hate people like me. Because I am so *different* from them. It is foolish. It is even stupid. But it is the real world."

"You have your degree in geology from the university in Caracas," Indy slipped into the exchange.

"Yes," Jocko said, offering no further information.

"And you took marine biology at the University of Miami."

"I did not obtain my degree there."

"How many did you get?" Indy asked.

"You know many things, Professor," Jocko said without smiling.

"You don't need to tell us, Jocko. But the more I know the stronger we all are."

"Four," Jocko said.

"Four white men," Indy answered for him.

Jocko shook his head, but he seemed glad this was in the open. "They had a meeting. I guess it was the Klan. Got all liquored up. My teacher, Veronica Green, she was white. She wanted to talk to me about underwater work in the Caribbean—"

"He's a qualified skin diver and deep-sea diver," Indy interrupted. "Searches for old wrecks for the museum. Their treasures are more than gold and silver. Artifacts from an age long gone."

"That's what this woman wanted to talk about. She taught in a classroom, I lived in the world she dreamed about. But we made a mistake. We had hamburgers together at a beachfront joint in Miami Beach. These whites came in, drunk, angry, filled with hate. They said not one word, but suddenly they were coming at me with knives and brass knuckles. They were no problem for me—"

"Four against one and it's no problem?" Gale couldn't hold back the question.

Again Indy answered for him. "He'd never tell you this himself, but Jocko is a martial arts master. Judo, jujitsu, karate, to say nothing of a year he spent in India with the Ghurkas."

Jocko showed his surprise. "How did you know *that*?"

Indy ignored the question. "Finish what happened in Miami."

Jocko shook his head with sadness. "The woman stood before me, as if she were a barrier they could not cross. The man before her buried his knife in her stomach. I—I never have been certain just what I did."

"He killed that man," Indy said for him. "Not the others, though. Once the woman went down they tried to run. Jocko broke their legs, *and* their arms and I understand he did some heavy damage to livers and spleens and—"

"That's enough, Indy. It's not important."

"All right."

"But what happened after that?" Gale demanded.

"I did what any black man with half a mind would do. I got out of Miami just as fast as I could. I had a deep-sea fishing boat and I took off in that. I knew there would be a search, so I doubled back. That night I painted the hull and changed the name, hid in a small island off the Keys, and went back to Jamaica. It was Dr. Franck who straightened it all out."

"And assigned you to this little jaunt," Indy appended.

"I go wherever Dr. Franck asks. I owe the man my life," Jocko said sternly. "Let me ask you something, Boss Man."

"Shoot."

"Just *where* are we going?"

"Paris. Eventually, that is. It's quite a trip."

"Across the ocean *in this*?"

"Uh-huh."

"Couldn't we just take an ocean liner?"

"We could, but we'd miss the attention I want this way. After that, we'll see. Now you two go talk all you want.

Later I want to brief you on this camera. For now, it's nap time."

They watched as he slumped in his seat, patted his seat belt, shoved his wide-brimmed hat over his eyes, and clasped his hands across his midriff.

"Can he just drop right off like that?" Jocko asked Gale.

"Jocko, he's *already* asleep. I'm going forward to see if they need a break up there."

Jocko looked doubtful. "Drive carefully."

"Just like you in your cab," she smiled.

"The Great One protect us," he murmured.

The flight, expected to be long, battering to the ears, and less than comfortable, kept its promise. Every landing was a blessing as they walked away from three thundering sets of propellers and engines vibrating the corrugated box of the Ford fuselage. "When they named this thing the Tin Goose," complained Foulois, "they were short of their mark. It should have been called the Horrendous Honk."

"Or the Boiler Factory," added Cromwell. He looked at the operations shack on Bangor Field. "Now, if we had just remembered to bring along ear plugs . . . Oh, well, we just might luck out here. I'd stuff a pomengrate in my ears if it would help."

They were in luck; spongy ear protectors to screen out the higher frequencies were plentiful, and they accepted them eagerly. They filled their large insulated cans with hot coffee, loading up on high-energy food bars, fresh sandwiches, and other last-minute items to be carried aboard the airplane. They also spent as much time as possible walking about to improve body circulation.

Another takeoff, another opportunity to monitor closely every gauge and mechanical operation of the airplane systems, and a landing at Moncton in New Brunswick, Canada. They topped off the fuel tanks, filled the oil tanks, and headed north for Goose Bay, a remote Royal Canadian Air Force field in Newfoundland. Will and Rene brought the Ford down through buffeting winds in a mildly exciting night landing. Indy and Gale were fast asleep in their seats, but Jocko was in the cockpit, watching every move the pilots made with awe-widened eyes.

"It looks like flying down a tunnel," he told them. "Except for those pitiful little lights. How can you people see where the devil you are going and when it is time to land?"

Cromwell half turned. "It works this way, laddie," he said with a straight face. "I set the machine on final approach, like we are now, descending like the good fairy coming down a moonbeam. Then I close my eyes real tight and—"

"You fly down to land *with your eyes closed?*"

"Absolutely."

"But how do you know when to level out, to land!"

"That's Frenchy's job, you see. *He* watches the runway coming up at us. Just before we're about to smash into the ground, he always—never fails, believe me—sucks in his breath and sort of screams. More like a strangled gurgle, really. When I hear him do that, why, I chop the power and ease back on the yoke and we land just as smooth as a mug of ale."

Jocko left without saying another word.

Goose Bay was on the edge of nowhere. Before them lay a run of eight hundred and thirty miles, give or take another thirty because of the unreliability of charts. With full tanks and the underwing tanks they could fly sixteen hundred miles in still air. One of those "piece of cake" jaunts to which Cromwell referred so often.

But the two pilots went over the weather reports from the ships at sea and Greenland stations with excruciating detail, checking temperatures and winds aloft, shifting pressure zones, and then listening to the advice of the old-timers who flew this part of the world the year-round.

"You'll never have a better time than right now," Captain T. C. Hampton of the RCAF told them. "You'll want to arrive at Narssarssuaq on the south lip of Greenland in daylight. Going in there at night is suicide. I'd recommend you go airborne at midnight or so. With your speed," he smiled, "you should get there with splendid visibility."

They gathered their notes. Hampton leaned on the counter and studied them. "Hard to believe Lindbergh did this only three years ago."

"Assuredly," Foulois told him with as much dignity as he could muster. "But Lindbergh was mad, you know. He had only one engine and he was making the trip nonstop. He even fell asleep on the way and nearly splashed into the ocean. How he expected to stay awake with tea instead of coffee or good French brandy has never been explained."

"Besides," Cromwell added with a sniff of disdain, "you'll remember he took the easy way home. On a ship with his flying machine neatly tucked away in a large box."

"Have a good flight. Take care," Hampton told them as if they hadn't said a word. Nothing would help matters. *Anyone* flying across the North Atlantic was crazy.

Jocko lay spread-eagled on the cabin floor, legs braced against seats, his head and shoulders over the open space where the floor hatch had been slid aside. He looked downward through powerful binoculars. He wanted to convey the incredible sense of wonder he felt, but trying to talk in the engine thunder and wind howling past the open hatch was impossible.

The whales. Magnificent! He'd never seen so many, and even from three thousand feet he saw clearly as they sent white spray cascading above them when they broke the surface. The plane was well into the northern reaches, and icebergs appeared as floating white sentinels. The flight was pure magic to him. He'd already dismissed his apprehensions; if that woman was completely at home up here he could hardly be less so. He felt a tug on his leg, and glanced about to see Indy motioning to him. Jocko slid the hatch closed and joined Indy and Gale.

"You have the look of a teacher on your face," he remarked to Indy.

"And yours is that of the student. The both of you," Indy told him. "You're right. School's on." Indy removed the camera from about his neck. He opened a leather case and brought forth a duplicate of the Leica he'd been carrying. "I want you both to be able to work these things without delaying a moment when you'll need them. I'll carry one, you two will switch back and forth, but either one of you *must* be ready to shoot at any time we're flying."

Jocko had been studying the Leica. "I've seen many cameras. This is something new, isn't it?"

"Test models. Dr. Franck obtained one for us, the other came from Doctor Pencroft in London. They both have the right contacts with Leica. Now, much of this is going to be completely new to you. It was to me as well, so let me start at the beginning."

He went through his instructions with exacting step-by-step demonstrations. "This model isn't on the market yet. It's a Leica One with a factory model number One-B. We'll set up both cameras so they're identical in film, shutter speeds, everything."

The Leica 1B was virtually a handmade model, a 35mm package that used 35mm film in a roll of twenty-four exposures. "You load from the bottom. Normally each exposure for a camera like this must be wound by hand, using this winding and rewinding knob on top. But they've added a battery-powered autosystem so that as soon as you take one picture, the camera will set the film automatically for the next exposure. That way you can take pictures as rapidly as you work the button, here, and the film rotates into position for your next shot. Still with me? Good. Now, you won't have to set the system. Well, it will be different depending upon lighting conditions, but basically we'll keep things as simple as possible."

He passed them a film roll. "This is Plus X film. Its got an ASA of one hundred—"

"Which means?" Jocko asked.

"That's the film speed rating. Watch what I'm doing with the camera and where I leave the settings. That way you can double-check very quickly the way it's supposed to be with the long lens."

"Long lens?" Gale said.

"You don't need to remember these things," Indy told her. "Besides, you can bone up with the instruction booklet later. What it all means is that with this lens, if something is a long ways off, this thing functions like a telescope and brings it much closer. Something that's a dot with the regular lens will be a closeup shot with this lens. What I want you both to do is to shoot scenes outside—beyond—the airplane. Icebergs, any ships we see, coming down over Greenland. Keep a record of the settings and the conditions. Don't worry about wasting film. Use all you want until you're completely comfortable with the system. The first chance we get we'll have the film processed so you can compare what you've been doing with the results. From that point on I expect you both to be whizzes with this thing."

"Uh-huh," Jocko said.

"You have a lot of faith in us," Gale offered with a touch of sarcasm.

"Shouldn't I?"

Jocko said, "You're hoping we'll find something specific to take pictures of? I'm trying to stay one step ahead of what you're after."

"Good point," Indy said. "And you're right. Something very specific."

Gale couldn't remain out of the exchange. "Which is?"

Indy leaned back in his seat, bracing himself against a sudden lurch from turbulence.

"A disc. A scimitar, or whatever shape those things are. In short, a flying saucer. Call it what you like, but it most likely will be flying and it won't have any engines." He almost added the words "that you can see," but kept that to himself.

Besides, both Gale and Jocko were staring at him in open disbelief.

"But, Indy!" Gale exclaimed. "Everything you've said at the meetings, the way you ridiculed . . . I mean, you've made it clear you don't believe in these things!"

He corrected them. "I believe in them, all right. I just don't believe they're from any other planet than good old Earth. They're real. In fact, I'm counting on them to come after us."

Foulois was walking back from the cockpit to talk to them. "I don't think you want to miss this. We've got visual on Greenland. You can take turns up front."

Gale stared out the cabin windows. "I didn't even notice it was daylight!"

"That Canadian, he was right about the weather. We've had a tailwind of better than sixty miles an hour out of Goose Bay. We're way ahead of schedule. And with the light so low on the horizon, the sight before us is—well—" He smiled. "Ladies first, Gale."

She eased into the right seat. "I . . . I never imagined it could be so beautiful!" she said to Cromwell. She stared in wonder at the gleaming white icebergs drifting off the coast and the huge glaciers gripping the coastline. It was a fairyland of white, peaks and slopes and massive ice walls. "Will, how far out are we?"

"What do you think?"

"Ten, fifteen miles, I guess."

"Well, then, this is likely the clearest and cleanest air you've ever been in. That shoreline is seventy miles away." She remained there several minutes, then left so Indy and Jocko could share the incredible sight before them.

Foulois returned to the cockpit. "Sorry, Indy. I'll need to be up here for this approach. The airport we're looking for, a bare strip, really, isn't on the coastline."

"Bloody well it isn't," Cromwell chimed in. "It's a killer. It lies up one of those fjords," he pointed ahead of them, "about fifty miles inland. We're going to be weaving our way in between mountains five thousand feet high and we don't dare make any wrong turns, because then there's no way out. We *must* have the proper fjord, and then we thread the needle." He chuckled. "It's really simple. You've got only one way to get in and when we leave we have only the same way out. And we *must* make a proper approach the first time."

"What if we don't?" Indy asked.

"Well, then, we go smashing into the mountain that's at the far end of the runway."

"Piece of cake, right?" Indy smiled.

"Certainly. If you do it right, that is."

The approach was a dazzling, exhilarating, terrifying, and engine-thundering series of turns and twists through the narrowing walls of the fjord. Then, abruptly, the airstrip appeared before them, and Cromwell brought the trimotor down as if descending on a slope of glass. He taxied to the small operations building. They were expected, and a small tractor towing a trailer with fuel drums moved immediately to the airplane. Both pilots worked with the ramp workers to fill their tanks as quickly as possible. They filled the oil tanks to capacity, and then Cromwell and Foulois went over the airplane from nose to tail, checking everything they could touch. By the time all work had been completed, it was early afternoon.

Cromwell went to talk to Indy. "We can stay overnight and leave in the morning before first light. Or we can take off right away, take turns sleeping, and go in to Iceland while it's still dark. If this wind keeps up, however, we'll have more than enough fuel to overfly Iceland and the Faeroes and make Scotland by sunrise. Then we can pick wherever you want to set down."

"You're the pilot, Will. What do you say?"

"Press on, mate."

"Do it," Indy said. Twenty minutes later they were flying down the fjord toward the open sea.

Two hours later Gale grasped Indy's arm and shook him madly. "Wake *up*!" she shouted, her mouth close against his ear. If he didn't come out of his sleep fog she swore she'd clamp teeth down on that ear.

Indy fairly shot up from his slouched position. "What's wrong?" he asked immediately. He glanced about him; everything seemed normal.

"The ship!" Gale exclaimed. "You've got to see this ship!"

She half dragged Indy to the opposite side of the cabin. They were at four thousand feet, a mixture of clouds another thousand feet beneath them, partially obscuring the view of the ocean surface. Then there was a break. Indy pressed his face to the window, eyes wide, and turned with a snarl. "The camera! Use that camera *now*!"

In a moment he had his own camera working. Nearly a mile beneath them, plowing the sea with a huge V-wake behind its passage, was the largest oceangoing ship he had ever seen. And he had never seen anything like this incredible tanker. It was at least a thousand to twelve hundred feet in length. Instead of the booms and deck equipment of the average tanker, the entire vessel from stem to stern was a huge flat deck. On each side of the ship, long cross-braced beams extended outward. Thick smoke plumed from the huge stack that curved across the right side of the decking to hang over the vessel, its smoke casting a pall that extended out of sight. Indy shot half the roll in his camera, then grabbed a headset and mike and clamped it on his head.

"Will, this is Indy. You got me?"

"Right. Go on."

"Do you have that ship below us in sight?"

"We have had for quite a while. I've never seen anything like it. It's absolutely gargantuan. And that deck. You could land anything on it. If that's what it's for."

"Never mind that right now. But you're right," Indy said in a rush. "Look, I want you to swing out to the side, use as much cloud cover as you can, and then I want you to make a run on that thing from its right side—"

"Starboard, yes."

"Hang the starboard! Just come up from astern along the right side, got it? And when you do, give us all the speed this bucket's got. As soon as you clear the bow, break away sharply for a mile or two, and then climb as fast as you can."

Will and Rene were already following his orders; as they continued their exchange, the Ford dropped its nose, Indy felt and heard an increase in power, and the wind howled louder as their speed increased. "Take her down as fast as you can, Will. *And be ready for anything, understand?*"

"What in the devil are you expecting down there?"

"We may have company. If we do we'll be getting pictures of it from back here."

"You expecting—" Will Cromwell halted his words for several moments as the Ford slammed into turbulence, shaking the airplane as if it were bouncing over railroad ties. Then they were out of the rough air. "You expecting aircraft this far out in the ocean?"

"No."

"Then *what,* man?"

"You'll know when you see it. I'll stay on the intercom with you all the way through." Indy hung onto a seat brace as the Ford's nose swung violently from side to side, then straightened out again. "Can't you go any faster?"

"Certainly. But we won't have any wings to pull out of the dive. Never fear, we're flying faster than old Mr. Ford ever dreamed."

The trimotor came out of a screaming, curving descent, and as they leveled out Cromwell poured full power to the engines. As fast as they were flying, they seemed to be crawling against the huge structure of the ship plowing through the sea. Indy and Gale snapped pictures as fast as they could. They saw men, tiny stick figures against the backdrop of the massive vessel. They were almost to the bow when Jocko rushed to Indy's side, shouting over the roar of engines and wind.

"Company! Behind us to our right!"

"What is it?"

"You were right, Boss. Them are crazy things out there! They look like discs!"

"Gale! Save your film! Get over to the other side. There'll be something coming past us on our right, moving fast! Go, go!"

He was back on the intercom. "Did you get that up front?"

"What's back there, Indy?"

"Jocko called them discs. They should go ripping right past us. They'll have to go far ahead of us. Will, the moment you see them break in front of us, give me everything you have for a climb. *Get us into some clouds as fast as you can.*"

"Right, Guv." Put on the pressure cooker and Cromwell was Mr. Smooth himself. . . .

Indy scrambled to the opposite side of the cabin.

There they were!

Two of them.

Golden disc shapes coming up behind them at tremendous speed. They'd pass the Ford like it was going backwards. Gale was snapping pictures as fast as she could; Indy had his camera ready and started moving film through it. He couldn't take time to *look* for details. There'd be time for that later when the film was processed and he could study the prints.

He saw a blur of movement from his right, and sunlight splashed off bronzelike metal. The "disc" was more in the shape of an oval with a central circular bubble cockpit, and he'd bet his bottom dollar it was armor glass made specifically for strength. Despite the speed with which it hurtled past them, he had a moment to see that the glass dome *wasn't* glass all around, but sheets of flat-paned glass buttressed with metal stringers. It looked almost archaic against that oval shape.

The oval flashed out of sight. Indy tore off his headset and ran to the cockpit. "Get right behind that thing!" he shouted to Cromwell.

"Hang on!" Cromwell shouted back, working the controls in a wild skidding maneuver to place them directly behind the path the disc had flown. Moments later Indy smiled grimly to himself. It was exactly what he'd expected. But he'd chew all that over later. For now it was important to execute that time-honored maneuver of getting the blazes out of here while the getting was good.

"Will, climb. Climb as fast as you can and get us into some clouds. Head for Scotland, but do whatever you need to do to stay in the clouds."

As he spoke Will was coming back on the yoke, the throttles rammed forward for maximum power to haul the Ford up and around in a climbing turn.

"Indy, the way those things move, they'll be coming around right at us and—"

"No, they won't. Not that fast, I mean. Rene, you keep your eye on them as best you can. They'll have to go way out before they can come back to us, and if I've figured this right, we'll be in the clouds by then."

Both pilots gave him startled looks. "How can you possibly *know*," Foulois asked slowly, "the way those things will fly?"

"Because I was expecting this meeting."

He left the cockpit, two dumbfounded pilots staring at him.

14

Until two years ago this very day, his family, his friends, his country, and much of the industrial, economic, and political world had known him as *Konstantin LeBlanc Cordas*. Each name represented powerful family ancestry and vast financial holdings in Russia, France, and Spain, with branch offices and holdings in a dozen other countries throughout the world.

Konstantin LeBlanc Cordas was a billionaire many times over. Not in terms of currency or stacked ingots of gold and platinum, of which he also had many, but in the real wealth of the world. He owned shipping lines, factories, mines, railroads, huge agricultural holdings on three continents. His closest friends were the power magnates of their homelands: owners of steel mills and ironworks and vast munitions plants. Chemicals, synthetics, trucks, shipyards; they had it all.

Cordas was blessed with a powerful, keen and inquisitive mind. His thoughts probed like cold lances through problems and challenges. His memory was phenomenal, and he made a voracious daily study of global affairs. He was also blessed, although he had come to regard this sense of mood as *possessed,* with a curse that would not let him rest. It was the feeling—no; the absolute certainty—that it had been ordained he assist the world through torturous times to stave off, hopefully to avoid completely, the Ultimate War that he and his closest associates knew was inevitable. It was wildly ironic: the War To End All Wars that ended in a final gory burst in 1918 had simply created the breeding ground for even greater and deadlier conflicts to come.

These were the men—Cordas and his closed circle—who *knew* of the terrible mass-destruction weapons formulating in the minds of soulless scientists and evil, grasping men coveting the ultimate of all pleasures: *power.* The Great War with its submarines, bombers, poison gases, automatic weapons, tanks rumbling like ironclad dinosaurs across the battlefields—all this had been but a portent of what was already boiling in the cauldron of the next war.

It must be stopped now, Cordas had finally concluded two years before. It must be stopped by the only means possible. Overwhelming power exerted along every front: political, military, industrial, economic. The minds of men must be controlled, or they would one day respond to the blaring trumpets and waving banners that had sent millions of them to agony and death, and now promised to repeat that horror.

Cordas and five of his closest friends, five of the most powerful and wealthy people on the planet, agreed with one another. They would sacrifice their families, their friends, their very lives in order to gather unto their control the ultimate power that could manipulate the destiny of their planet.

The preparations were meticulous, exacting, shrouded in the tightest secrecy. They knew of the most advanced systems of the military, of science and engineering and flight, many of which were yet unknown to the public.

And when they were ready, they knew they must be ruthless. Six people were paid handsome sums to assume the personas of Cordas and his group. They underwent surgical changes to their faces. Their dental makeup was altered to match exactly the six for whom they would become doubles. Their families were sent to distant parts of the world, provided with homes and financial security. When they were safely out of the way, a grand trip was arranged for Konstantin LeBlanc Cordas and his five best friends.

For their doubles. A grand trip, indeed. Cordas Mountain Industries chartered a huge four-engined Dornier Super Wal II flying boat. In two expansive cabins, located fore and aft in the hull, were twenty-six people: the industrialists, a few family members, and friends from across Europe. Tremendous publicity was afforded the occasion. The Super Wal would take off from a Swiss lake on a tour from Norwegian fjords southward beyond the Mediterranean to an African safari.

A huge banquet launched the festive event. The most powerful group of industrial leaders in the world entered the Super Wal with family and friends. Newsmen by the hundreds were on hand to record every moment of the final good-byes, the famous men and women waving to the newsreel cameras. Fireworks flared over the launching dock and two bands played furiously to be heard above the barking roar of four Bavarian Motor Works engines. The Super Wal taxied to the far end of the lake so that it could take off directly into the wind. Conditions were perfect, with a mild breeze and an open water run of at least four miles. As the flying boat began its final turn the music stopped, so everyone could hear clearly the growing thunder of engines going to full power. Faster and faster it rushed across the lake, a great winged wonder about to grasp lift from the air. Faster, faster; a breathless rush and then—

The explosion began as a searing point of light from the fuel tanks in the wings. In a moment flame lashed outward, and the great quantity of fuel transformed into a searing fireball that covered the tumbling, disintegrating, exploding airliner, its hapless human cargo being incinerated and ground into bloody pulp. The newsreel cameras ground away, recording the horror, capturing the screams and gasps of the onlookers.

Later, the few scattered parts of flesh and bone either floating on the lake waters, or dredged up from the deep bottom, were identified positively as Konstantin LeBlanc Cordas and his select entourage. Funeral services, speeches, sobbing, and statues rushed to completion slowly wound down the aftereffect. But Cordas was satisfied. Completely. He and his elite group were "dead." Six dead; six alive, but the latter unknown to the world except as Cordas planned the slow leakage of information about their names and their control of staggeringly vast resources. Five men and one woman. The loss of Wilhelmina von Volkman was especially a tragedy to her following. She had sponsored musicians, poets, scientists —young men and women of every walk of life seeking an opportunity to become skilled in their arts and professions. And now she was gone.

Unknown to all, of course, reborn as Marcia Mason.

He stared through the thick plate-glass window in the High Tower of the Chateau of Blanchefort, several miles from a second heavily-defended ancient structure, rebuilt within to provide structural strength and add the most modern scientific and technological devices available for world communications. The second great edifice was

Rennes-le-Chateau, a virtual duplicate, internally, of Blanchefort. Halvar Griffin had made a rule that the Group of Six, as he had named them, must never be all in the same place at the same time. It was simple enough to communicate by telephone cable and wall speakers; watching lips move and faces going through various expressions was superflous.

Halvar Griffin missed his wife and children, and wondered how they fared now that their husband and father, none other than Konstantin LeBlanc Cordas, had been sliced and seared in that awful tragedy of the flying boat. But each day Madelon became less real, more ethereal, as did the children, for that was how it must be. They belonged to another life, another time.

The program to assemble the many elements of international power, despite its success, continued to wind a torturous and at times rocky path. Halvar Griffin had been known in his former life as a financier and industrialist, but at heart, and throughout his days at schools and universities, he had become an extraordinarily gifted evolutionist, a man mixing everything from history and anthropology to the psychological and social sciences into a single frame of reference for what constituted the human race. It was not, despite what the moralists claimed with such shrill vehemence, a single race. It was not true that all men were created equal, or that they thought alike, or yielded to the same desires and dreams, or enjoyed the same opportunities for health and wealth.

Mankind was a polyglot of fierce and demonizing emotions, a great field of reeds able to be bent by the slightest wind, poisoned by greed, avarice, selfishness, and, above all, that eternal and infernal need for the power to dominate as many other men as possible, no matter what the cost in lives and destruction. The very survival of the race was at stake.

It was Griffin—and he was slowly disconnecting the final traces of his former self from even his manner of thinking and speaking—who understood that the key to the success they sought as benevolent masters of the planet's future lay in mastering the workings of the social sciences. They must develop the means, through semantics, lust, reward, fear, and every other emotion available, to bring all men to believe that survival *and* their greatest rewards could come only through this benevolence.

That was their goal. So long as none of the members of the Group of Six sought open recognition as power brokers, their task, attempted so many times by so many great empires in the past, had every opportunity to succeed. And they had planned well, and so far had executed very well indeed their opening moves to command the attention, then the fear and wonder, of the world. Acquiescence and obedience would follow.

There is nothing so deeply believed, accepted, feared, and even revered more than what Griffin knew had been a dominating power through all history. The Great Lie. Calculated disinformation could disintegrate powerful armies, suck the energy from national drive, turn millions of people as easily as a shepherd and his dogs drive a flock of sheep. You did not have to *prove* to the masses what you wished them to believe; you needed only to bring them to a condition of acceptance. Then they would believe in whatever they wished, from sorcerers and witches to gods and goddesses.

And an alien race of vast scientific, technological, and military superiority, come here to Earth.

At first the concept seemed ridiculous. Would people really be brought to accept space aliens as real? Griffin laughed at the idea, but his laughter, soon joined by that of his elite group, was one of belief rather than rejection.

"Think of what people believe," he told the others.

"There are spirits in the water, the air, in wheat and temples and lightning and clouds. There are powerful, full-bosomed women who carry dead heroes on winged horses to Valhalla. There are gods who rise from the waters, gods who dwell in the clouds, spirits of trees and bears. Millions of filthy little cats are demonic messengers and servants of Satan. Men turn into werewolves. Vampires are men by day and winged horrors at night. If you lack the wooden stake or the silver bullet, you cannot kill them. The world is flat and you may fall off its edge; millions of people still absolutely believe this is so.

"Ah, our aliens. Yes, yes; but they will not be imaginary. They will be real—seen, heard, visible, and lethal. They will play with human lives as easily as do the winged messengers from Hades, but they will negotiate with the human race. After all, they will impose only discomforting rules, but to break them is to risk destruction. Fair enough! If the people of the world come to believe this is heaven-sent protection to avert the slaughters of future wars, they may well rally to the cause we set. Of course," Griffin grimaced, "they may do quite the opposite. But I believe if we plan carefully and execute precisely, we shall succeed."

Griffin's disciples, three of them in the chateau with him, the other two listening by radio speaker, yielded more and more to his spellbinding oratory.

John Scruggs—a terrible name for a wily Spaniard who was the dominant dealer in opium and narcotics in global trade—motioned for attention. Griffin nodded. Scruggs, with the cunning of an underworld figure who had amassed enormous power and influence, always cut to the heart of annoyances.

"Several matters, Griffin." He smiled. "How long, my friend, do you believe the governments we deal against will accept the charade of aliens from space blasting their way around the world?"

"The governments? As for the scientists, engineers, military men, leaders—not very long at all. Quite a few do not believe it now. They do not *know* what they face. They are baffled, angry, frustrated, but they have suffered these problems before and before too much time passes they will decide that the rest of this solar system remains uninhabitated." He locked his eyes on Scruggs. "But I tell you this. The masses will believe. They believe now, and we shall sustain that belief."

Scruggs shook his head. "You stretch the truth too far. You offer a fairy tale and—"

"Damn you," Griffin snapped. "Don't you ever observe what people really believe in? Chicken entrails and the tossing of bones to tell the future so they may know what to do, and when to do it. Do you trust your life to tarot cards, John? No? Well, then, how about crystal balls? Or the muttering of a gypsy reading tea leaves or your filthy palms! Do you wonder about the wheeling and juxtaposition of planets and moons that will foretell your ulcers or your love life? Anyone who believes in such things, in luck and charms and amulets and all that idiotic nonsense, can be led to believe in aliens! Especially in aliens, as you put it, blasting their way around the world. So far, I remind you, with spectacular effect and unstoppable fury which, I assure you, we will magnify a thousandfold for those superstitious wretches we must guide to their own future."

"Another question, then, Master Griffin."

Griffin ignored the surly title. "Go on, go on."

"Tell me why you have been unable to rid us of that pestilence in our plans."

"I assume you mean the American, this Jones individual."

"You assume correctly. You have tried, how many times now? Three, maybe four, to eliminate him? And failed?"

"Twice, I remind you, with *your* hand-picked assassins," Griffin snapped.

Scruggs smiled and bowed to acknowledge his own failure. "I submit. Then what keeps this person alive? And *why* are we so determined to kill him?"

"Let me answer," broke in Marcia Mason. She explained the meetings she had attended, across the table from Professor Henry Jones, including her verbal entanglements with that insufferable man. "What bothers me is that I have not found it possible to identify so many of the people with whom he works. Certainly that doddering old fossil, Pencroft, from the London university, is hardly a person to coordinate the investigations under way. So there are others. I am convinced Filipo Castilano will sooner or later have to be eliminated. But the others," she clenched her fists in sudden fury, "we still do not know all of them. I am convinced they communicate by codes which we cannot break, and no one knows for certain the entire list of the top people involved."

They turned as a long sigh came from Griffin. "There is more. I have learned of it only recently. Jones and his group crossed the Atlantic in a Ford airplane. A trimotor with very special modifications for range and performance."

Scruggs was puzzled. "So?"

"Jones and his group encountered our ship on the high seas."

"So they saw the ship." Scruggs shrugged.

"They did more than that. They dove out of the clouds and they flew right alongside our vessel, even lower than its decks, and from what the deck crew could tell, took many photographs. From those I believe they will be able to divine the nature of the vessel."

The shrug had become a frown. "That is not good. Our ship can become a target. Even with the undersea boats for protection, it is vulnerable. This is most upsetting, Griffin." Scruggs thought deeply for a moment. "Why didn't you have the discs take care of them? You said their machine was a Ford? The discs are faster by hundreds of miles an hour. Why wasn't their machine destroyed? You also said it was over the ocean. What a perfect opportunity! They would have gone down at sea and been swallowed up in the vastness of the Atlantic."

"The people flying that machine seemed able to anticipate what the discs would do, how they would fly, and what might be their limitations."

"By the horned toads of my ancestors, how could they know *this*!"

"I do not yet know. But Jones either knows or has deduced far more than what I thought was possible. Remember, he is allied with the keenest technical minds of England and America. But I believe it is his own marvelous grasp of the past and his proven ability to meld many small details into larger facts and conclusions that is so troublesome to us."

"How can you find out what he knows? The woman has already said their most vital communications are in code."

"That is simple enough. We will invite him to visit us *here*," said Griffin. "The time for games is behind us. We have consolidated our position just as we planned originally. So it is time to get rid of Jones, to break apart this group behind him."

"I thought you were inviting him *here*," Scruggs said angrily.

"I did. And we are."

"If you kill him here it would be the worst mistake yet—"

"He will not reach here," Griffin answered. "Jones is

going to be at the university in London. We know that. We also know he plans a visit to Paris."

"Which only means," Mason warned, "that if we know his plans, once again we are being *allowed* to know them."

"Perhaps. Even likely. He will cross the channel by scheduled steamer. He will have some of his people with him. That ship will never reach France, and neither will Jones."

15

The passenger ferry *Barclay* eased from her slip at Portsmouth and moved along the northern coastline of the Isle of Wight, slowly gathering speed for the cross-channel run to Le Havre. The *Barclay* carried two hundred and nine passengers, thirty-eight crew members, and various vehicles as well as baggage, mail, and freight cargo. She was a solid vessel, well known on the run between England and France, and the late afternoon passage promised to be especially comfortable with a mild breeze and a sea surface unusually gentle for the English Channel.

The passenger manifest included the names of Professor Henry Jones of the University of London, his secretary, Frances Smythe, and their servant, Jocko Kilarney, who hovered protectively about Jones and the woman. Anyone catching sight of the trio found it obvious that Jones suffered from a terrible cold, bundled as he was in a heavy overcoat and muffler, a warm hat pulled fully over his head and ears. He sneezed and coughed in a dreadful manner, keeping a large handkerchief by his mouth as he breathed fitfully. Considerate of the other passengers, Jones and his two traveling companions remained by the stern rail, using a protective curving wall to reduce the wind of passage.

The *Barclay* was in midchannel when excited calls and shouts rang out through the ferry. Passengers rushed from the interior to the outside decks, pointing at the sky. In the late afternoon sun, gleaming golden, reflecting light, cruised the mystery airship. The incredible giant seemed utterly silent against the rumble of the *Barclay*'s engines, the wind from her speed, and the sounds of the channel surface against her hull.

Frances Smythe watched with the others. "I do wish we'd sent up fighters to dispose of that thing," she said to the two men. "Rid ourselves once and for all. People are beginning to believe we can't touch it."

Intense light flared beneath the golden machine so high above them. In the same instant, a beam of blinding light snapped into being, a pillar of eye-stabbing radiance from the airship directly to the *Barclay*. The passengers had never seen a light so incredibly bright. It lit up the ferry with the effect of a physical blow, bringing people to cover their eyes, crying out in alarm.

The light was seen by dozens of other vessels, small and large, at that moment moving across the channel. It flared long enough to bring heads turning for many miles around, and then the onlookers stared in disbelief as a huge ball of flame erupted from the *Barclay*. From a distance there was yet no sound. Seconds later the force of an enormous explosion boomed across the channel. Moments later the boilers of the *Barclay* ripped the ferry in two, the secondary blasts claiming most of the people who'd survived the terrible initial explosion.

The light from the airship was gone, as if a switch had been thrown. There was still unexpected light on the surface of the channel as the flaming remnants of the *Bar-*

clay began to slip beneath the water, taking more than two hundred men and women with her.

Pencroft's secretary crossed Dr. Pencroft's office to his private telephone on a side table. On the third ring she picked up the handset. "Yes?"

Then she turned to the group and nodded to Thomas Treadwell. "Sir? It's your office."

Treadwell went quickly to the phone. Watching him, Indy, Gale, and Pencroft remained silent as Treadwell listened to the caller for several minutes, interrupting only with terse questions. Henshaw, who had arrived in England by ocean liner only that morning, paced nervously. Foulois and Cromwell were occupied at the aerodrome nearby.

Finally Treadwell said, "Right. I'll be at this number for a while. Call me immediately with anything new."

He slowly replaced the telephone on its stand. A subdued click was followed by a tired exhalation. "That ruddy well does it," he said, his face reflecting inner anguish. "It's the *Barclay*. She was blown apart by that airship. No ghost that. Sent down some kind of light beam, extraordinarily intense from the initial reports, and the *Barclay* was torn in half. Took most of her people with her."

Sir William Pencroft trembled from age, fatigue, and the blow of the news. He looked from Treadwell to Colonel Harry Henshaw. His eyes traveled to Gale Parker, whose impassive look concealed her own feelings. Her eyes were like deep glass marbles, and she sat like a stone.

Treadwell turned to his side. "You're dead, you know," he said to Professor Henry Jones.

Indy didn't answer for the moment. He knew the minuscule odds of Frances Smythe and Jocko Kilarney surviving the ghastly explosion and swift sinking of the

Barclay. Indy shook off the pall of death hanging in the room.

"Any word? I mean, about our people?" he asked finally.

"Your double is confirmed," Treadwell said, forcing himself to remain distant from personal loss. "He was one of our best men. One of the ships that picked up some of the survivors found his body. With your identification, of course."

"Frances?"

"No word. I'm sorry, Indy. As soon as we hear anything—"

Gale Parker emerged from the self-induced isolation that she used to finally subdue her emotions. "Jocko. Has anybody had any news about Jocko? He'd be impossible to miss, and—"

"Miss Parker, we have every available person and search team out there right now," Treadwell said carefully. "Many of the people aboard the ferry were, well, they were—"

"I'm well acquainted with death, sir," Gale said stiffly. "You're trying to tell us that many of the people were blown apart, or incinerated, or were trapped in the wreckage, and they're at the bottom of the channel."

"Yes," Treadwell said. There was no need to elaborate.

Indy turned to Treadwell. "A great many people died this afternoon because this insane group is after *me*," he said, painfully aware of the grievous loss. "If they didn't believe I was on that ferry, they would never have blown up that ship."

"You're wrong, Professor," Treadwell said quickly.

"How?" Indy demanded. "You know they set me up with that invitation to meet with their top people. Why, I don't know, but we all agreed to go ahead anyway." Deep furrows lined his brow. "But why would they destroy the ferry? They didn't need to kill all those people. And I could just as well be one of the survivors." He looked from Treadwell to Henshaw for answers, then returned his gaze to the British intelligence agent.

"The attack this afternoon had a double purpose," Treadwell said. "We've been aware that this group has been setting up a very public demonstration of their power—"

Pencroft coughed for attention, trying to speak, but his throat emitted only a feeble rattle. Immediately someone held a glass of water to his lips. Gale rested her hand on that of the elderly man. "May I?" she said. Pencroft nodded.

"I've stayed out of most conversations," Gale said stiffly. "But now it's time for a question. I've heard you discussing the how and why and the means these people use when they strike at us. And Indy—Professor Jones—has more than once made it clear that one of the flaws in their operations has been that they use the same weapons we use. *Until now,* that is."

Pencroft had found his voice. "What do you mean by that?"

"Tonight they used some kind of radiation beam!" Gale said with a burst of anger. "I've listened to the reports Mr. Treadwell repeated for us. That airship, whatever it is, still races about the sky without a sign of any engines. But with the ferry, the airship aimed some kind of ray, a beam of energy, I don't *know,*" she said, exasperated, "and it blew up the *Barclay*!" She was pleading for an answer. "We don't have anything even remotely like that!"

"We know what it was, Gale," Henshaw said quietly, bringing surprise to the group. Henshaw turned to Treadwell. "This is your ball game, Tom. Sorry."

Treadwell nodded. "The only energy in that beam, that so-called ray-gun apparatus as some of the press are already describing it," he said, "was ordinary light. Oh, it was boosted to a rather extraordinary intensity, but that was all. Strictly for effect."

Gale was taken aback. She looked to Indy, but he was paying close attention to every word Treadwell was saying. "We had sufficient observation of the event today," the Englishman explained. "The *Barclay* was torn up by a huge amount of explosives that had been placed in the engine compartment. It was rigged to be set off by a discreet radio signal. Today was their big show, so to speak. They picked a time with good visibility, so that what happened would be seen by a great many people. They turned on their beam—consider it an extraordinarily powerful searchlight—and focused as tightly as possible, and when that light attracted enough attention, they transmitted their radio signal to detonate the explosive charges."

He leaned back in his seat. "A ghastly sort of demonstration, I admit, but that is all it was. Forgive me for being seemingly uncaring. I'm not. But my job is to discover just what happened. What I've told you *is* what happened. Oh, we'll have confirmation. We immediately sent an aircraft—we've kept several ready to go at a moment's notice—into the smoke from the blast, and I'm quite sure when we do a particulate study, spectrographic and all that, that we'll find quite ordinary remnants of common explosives. Now," he pulled himself upright in his seat, "do let me go on."

He looked to Indy. "This charade has worked very well, Indy."

Gale couldn't help a bitter interruption. *"Charade?"*

"Let me," Indy told Treadwell. "I don't want even a hint of mistaken credit here." He turned to Gale and Pencroft. "You see, for a great deal of what's been going on, I was way over my head. I'm not a pilot, but," he smiled thinly, "you already know that, Gale. Everything I've done has been calculated to mislead this group we're after. The more we could get them to concentrate on us—you, me, Cromwell, and Foulois, and for a while, Tarkiz—the more they were led to believe I was the kingpin in all this. Figuring out what was going on, confirming that this idea of alien spacecraft was so much baloney—"

"Rubbish, all right," muttered Pencroft.

"Exactly like the artifacts. The cube and the pyramids," Indy stressed. "Actually, we had a bunch of them to be used if we needed them, but the trap worked right from the beginning. In fact, the cube with those South African diamonds had nothing to do with this group flying the zeppelin and those discs, because we didn't even know about them at the time. But Treadwell has also worked with the De Beers outfit and others, just like I have. That, in fact, is how we first got together."

Treadwell nodded affirmation and picked up Indy's thread of explanation. "So we also made certain that the people we were after, even if we could not yet identify them, would know of the existence of one Professor Henry Jones *and* his great skills in deciphering cuneiform inscriptions. That meant they must go after Indy, and, in doing so, might well reveal themselves to us. At first, of course, they would want him alive and cooperative. But once they found out we'd slipped them the old Mickey and were playing a bit on the dirty side, why, then they were sure to try to eliminate our good friend, here."

"You all seemed very fast and easy with *his* life!" Gale said angrily.

"That was my choice, Gale," Indy emphasized. "Nobody went into this wearing a blindfold. Besides," he grinned, "I had you along to protect me, right?"

"The point, Miss Parker," Treadwell followed hastily, "is that Indy's cooperation was really our only quick way to get this crowd to show some cracks in their anonymity."

"Ah," Pencroft said pleasantly, more and more pleased with what he judged to be his own role in the affair. "That's one of the reasons behind our arranging that tri-motor machine. On the record, you see, the university, as well as our museum, accepted the cost for that aircraft. It, too, was bait. You can hardly hide a corrugated clanker like that when it traverses the Atlantic! Pack of fools, too, I say. That's what I told them when they laid bare their schemes."

"But it *has* worked," Treadwell offered.

"Then why haven't we figured out those golden discs!" Gale countered.

"Oh, but we have, miss, we *have,*" Treadwell assured her. "Most of that is attributed, by the by, to Colonel Henshaw. He is a very close and old friend of mine. And our government, I should add. We've worked together for years."

"Do you mean to tell me," Gale said with her eyes wide, *"you know what those discs are?"* She glanced at Indy. His sudden sly smile was infuriating to her.

"Oh, we really had some ideas. Right from the beginning, I mean," said Henshaw. "We have some pretty sharp boys in our technical intelligence programs. Research and development stuff. I was doing that back in the war. I worked with a Frenchman, some fellow named Coanda—um, Henri Coanda—who had developed a rocket gun for aerial combat. A couple of things we'd talked about buzzed around in the back of my head for a while after I heard about the discs. It just took me longer than it should to start putting two and two together. Well, sometimes even the experts miss the obvious, or memories leak away, like mine seemed to do. Then our group, a bunch of us, seemed to come up with the same conclusion at the same time. As if we'd all been thunked on our skulls simultaneously."

"Which was?" Gale asked, wishing Henshaw would hurry.

"The weapons those things were using. They weren't any more advanced than the best we had. Or that were in use by several other countries, for that matter. We contacted old Treadwell, here, and then we really started doing some digging into past experimental programs."

"And that's how they started coming up with answers," Indy picked up the explanations. "They brought me into the picture to look over their shoulders. When they had what they judged were some solid leads, they pounded it into my head. That's how I sometimes seemed to be so knowledgeable on the matter. It wasn't what *I* was figuring out. It was all memorizing what these people taught me, and we figured if I made public statements about the discs, it would simply be more bait added to the effect of the artifacts. It would start to appear as if I was behind stripping away the cover of this group."

"We did some high-speed photography," Treadwell added. "That was an enormous help. It was touch-and-go for a while because we had to stumble across an opportunity to film the discs. We used still pictures and high-speed films. Would you believe that out of some sixty cameras we set up with the Americans, only two produced results?"

"And—" Gale let the query hang.

"Hydrocarbons," Treadwell said with triumph. "That was the clue! I felt like Sherlock Holmes. You see, there *is* an exhaust trail behind those infernal devices. The films, and those pictures you people took while you were waltzing across the Atlantic, proved it. Remember that huge ship you encountered at sea?"

"Hard to forget," Gale murmured.

"Your photographs confirmed what we'd suspected. That monster mother airship, easily fifteen hundred feet from one end to the other, could hardly be concealed in Europe. Population density and all that. The key was that any kind of aerial vessel of that size needs servicing, and a lot of it. Refueling, supply replenishment, engine tune-up, lifting-gas refills. That ship took care of *that.* Those side booms extending out on each flank? When the dirigible came down to the deck of that vessel, a mooring mast and the booms came up to snug down the big zep—well, I see by your expression you've already figured it out yourself."

"Wait; *wait!*" Gale broke in. "All right, you have this evidence of hydrocarbons and all, but I still don't know what that *told* you!"

"That Frenchman I mentioned?" Henshaw said. "That Coanda fellow. I recalled he told me that if you designed an engine that worked like a blowtorch—suck in huge gobs of air at one end and set it aflame so you're compressing it, then blast it out the other end—why, you could power just about anything with it. An aircraft, or that great dirigible. An engine like that would even fit neatly into a disc shape."

"No propellers?" Gale asked, amazed.

"Oh, there's *some* kind of propeller, but it's *inside* the engine," Henshaw answered. "We had our people test different fuels and the chemistry crowd said we were dealing with the exhaust from superrefined kerosene."

"Which blew away the theory that we were dealing with mean-spirited ugly little green fellows from Mars," Treadwell added.

"And which let us force the hand of this group," Indy said.

"And how, Jones, did *that* happen?" Pencroft said testily.

"Well, sir, for starters," Jones spoke gently to his aged friend, "those artifacts are paying off in a way I *hoped* they would. Whoever is running this group, or at least is one of the top people, made a decision that the cube and the pyramids were fakes. But he could do that only by coming to a dead end with the cuneiform inscriptions. They were nonsense, of course, but I made certain they *appeared* to be real. You, of all people, Doctor, know how much time must go into working with unknown cuneiform. And whoever was examining those things came to a conclusion much too fast for your ordinary researcher."

"Which means," Gale said suddenly, "he has archeology experience! Of course!"

"That," Indy went on, "and also deciding that as unknown as was the metal that Treadwell had made in the secret metallurgical lab, it could be fashioned by any really competent people in the metalworking business. In short, they knew too much in too short a time."

"Enter one Filipo Castilano," Treadwell added. "Do you recall, or perhaps you never had the chance to notice, the stories that made all the papers about that place in France? That some biblical historians are claiming was the final resting place of Christ?"

"Do you mean the little French town of Arques?" Pencroft asked.

"Yes. We had detailed maps of the area, of course," Treadwell said, "from Jacques Nungesser. Jacques also placed special agents through the countryside. Farmers, tradesmen, that sort of thing, to keep watch on and record the movement of everything that went into or came out of two places in particular. Rennes-le-Chateau and the Chateau of Blanchefort."

Pencroft grumbled his distaste. "That is all nonsense," he stated emphatically. "That story has been cropping up for years. It's in the same league, you should know, with the tales of Christ living out many of his years right here in England. Having a merry old time with the ghost of King Arthur, or perhaps Arthur in person, with Merlin entertaining the crowd. It's about as reliable as the tales of a Christlike figure appearing among the Maya and the Aztecs, and materializing before amazed people in China. Why is all this even brought up in this matter?"

Treadwell remained patient and understanding. "Because there has been major construction work on Blanchefort *and* Rennes. You can't hide that sort of thing. Nungesser's people took elaborate photographs of both chateaus. They located unusual radio antenna *almost* perfectly concealed among the towers and battlements. The moment they saw those, they began a sweep of all radio frequencies that might be used for long-distance transmissions. Nungesser is very sharp, indeed. He struck paydirt almost immediately and, wisely, made no move to interfere or let it be known the places were under surveillance. It wasn't enough to suspect strongly, or even to *know* that this was, if not the headquarters, at least one of the prime locations of the group behind these attacks. We needed to *get inside.*"

"So that's how you used Castilano," Dr. Pencroft said quietly.

"Yes, sir," Treadwell confirmed. "First we set up all that uproar in the press about Christ's bones in a tomb. The Vatican called for an investigation. Which called for Cardinal Castilano, with the blessings of the French government, to make his pilgrimage to the two chateaus and to Arques. Filipo needed to get inside to talk with as many people as he could, to see if he could recognize a face, a voice; anything."

"It sounds to me as if you sent a lamb into the lion's den," Gale said, her criticism unconcealed.

"Filipo Castilano is a professional intelligence and espionage agent," Treadwell said quickly. "He is no lamb."

"Did he find what he was after?"

"We believe he made a breakthrough. Apparently he

recognized one man's voice. His mannerisms. He managed to get a note out with one of his priests—who became ill and had to return to Rome—with his suspicions."

"Who was it?" Pencroft demanded.

"It's still a bit sticky, sir," Treadwell replied. "The name we received was Cordas. Konstantin LeBlanc Cordas. Extremely powerful. Also, as Professor Jones has indicated, someone in that group is familiar with archeology. We know that Cordas is a dedicated evolutionist, a man who believes in socially-directed control of the masses. He is also quite competent in metallurgy. He owns vast steel plants and machine shops. He fits the pattern perfectly."

"But Cordas . . . he was killed in that terrible accident in Switzerland!" Pencroft protested.

"Not likely," Indy said. "Not if he did just what *we* did with the *Barclay*. Put a double on that flying boat. The difference is that Cordas likely killed many of his own people."

"Charming fellow," Pencroft murmured. "Did we hear any more from Filipo?"

Treadwell's face darkened. "No, sir. And I don't believe we ever will. If there was even a hint of suspicion, they would have done him in." Treadwell sipped water. "But it gave us a lead that we needed desperately. We're following through on it, of course."

"And in the meantime," Indy said with sudden authority and no small impatience, "there's that airship and the discs. *And* that huge ship we saw in the Atlantic."

"That ship is gone," Henshaw came into the exchange.

"Gone?" Pencroft echoed.

"The American and British governments believe the ship, in bad weather, perhaps struck an iceberg and went down without warning," Henshaw said with a straight face.

A smile creased the old man's face. "How ruddy convenient," he chuckled. "Serves the buggers right."

Indy turned to Henshaw. "It couldn't be one of those icebergs that fires torpedoes, could it?"

"Difficult to tell," Henshaw said, still with a straight face. "It appears there were maneuvers in that area. Multinavy, so to speak. American, British, French, even one or two submersibles from Italy, I believe. No one's quite sure. Terrible weather, storms at sea, that sort of thing."

"You know, Indy," Treadwell came into their exchange, "it does seem to me there were reports of a most severe explosion in the area. Now, if a berg did slice into an engine room and cold sea water hit the boilers, the effect could be very much like that of a warhead doing the same thing."

"In the confusion of the maneuvers, there's simply no way to tell which submarine was where at what time," Henshaw added.

Indy's hand suddenly slapped the table. "By God, that's *perfect*!" he exclaimed.

"You *are* demonstrative at times," Pencroft chided him.

"I think we've just boxed them in," Indy said with visible excitement.

Gale smothered a laugh. Even the prospect of getting out of these meeting rooms and interminable conferences was enough to get Indy's blood racing.

"I do believe I get your drift," Treadwell said to Indy.

"Would someone mind telling *me*?" Pencroft said testily.

Indy turned to the impatient man by his side. "It works this way, sir. From what Colonel Henshaw has been able to find out, there's only one of these giant airships in operation. Now, when we confirmed the existence of that floating dirigible carrier, which seems"—he smiled—"to have been caved in by a very fast iceberg, we pretty well confirmed their method of operation. They couldn't hide that ship when it landed for resupply. It's too big, impossible to conceal. So they modified a tanker or some other big ship that could accommodate that airship and refuel it and give it whatever else it needed."

Indy almost banged his fist on the table. "But now it hasn't *got* that floating base any more! It's *got* to come down somewhere, to some kind of a permanent base. Something that's big enough to move the airship *into*, so it isn't visible either on the surface or from the air. Does that make sense to you, Dr. Pencroft?"

"A bit muddled, in your usual way," Pencroft nodded. "But I do begin to sense a loss of options for those buggers. You're right, of course, Jones. Now all you need to do is invoke some magical incantation and come up with *where* they're going to go."

Gale had a hand in the air, almost frantic for attention. "Colonel Henshaw, or Mr. Treadwell, *whoever*," she burst out, "we know where that airship was when it attacked the *Barclay*. And you—I mean, they—can't *hide* something that big. Why didn't you send fighter planes after it when you had the chance!"

"Splendid idea," murmured Pencroft. "Set the buggers ablaze, all right." He studied Treadwell. "It would, you know. Hydrogen loves to burn. *Whoosh!* Just like the sausages over the lines."

Indy blinked. *Sausages?* They were leaving him behind. Henshaw spotted his confusion. "Artillery-spotting balloons over the trenches," he said quickly. "Tethered to the ground, surrounded by heavy Jerry ack-ack so they were dangerous as all get-out to hit. But once you pumped incendiaries into them, they'd go up like Roman candles."

"Well, then, why haven't you filled that filthy machine with incendiaries?" Gale demanded of Treadwell. "That would finish them off!"

Treadwell responded with patience. He understood her feeling that they might have missed the opportunity to destroy the great dirigible. "Miss Parker, perhaps I should have made myself clearer with the details. You're right. Set fighters after that zep. The fact of the matter is that we've kept fighter planes at different aerodromes, at the ready, just in case we had a crack at that airship. And when the *Barclay* was attacked, our fighters were already taking off. Of course, it took them a bit of time to climb to the height where the airship was flying."

Gale's face turned red. "I—I didn't know. Sorry—"

"No apology needed, Miss Parker. We should have taken a crack at this long ago. Waited too long, of course."

"Well, what happened!" Pencroft snapped.

"First off, sir," Treadwell responded, "it was a terrible go. That machine was at twenty-two thousand feet. Our fighters made it up there, but control proved very difficult for them. Bitter cold, and all that. One of our machines had radio-telephone and he kept us in touch."

"Did they get a crack at that thing?" Indy broke in.

"Barely so, I'm afraid."

"What I want to know," Indy said, unusually intense, "is whether or not they fired tracers into the airship. If they did, then I assume those tracers could have reached the gas bags inside the hull?"

"Absolutely," Henshaw said.

"Well?" Indy kept at Treadwell.

"At that height, our machines could hardly maneuver. We didn't have machines ready with oxygen equipment. Two of our men passed out, it seems. They fell off in spins. Both of them recovered in time. Another fighter's guns froze in the cold air. The remaining three blokes flew ahead and just above the airship to make a shallow diving attack. Each pilot knew he would have only one crack at it. I've done that sort of thing myself. It's a wicked moment, I'll tell you. From what the chap with the RT called in, three of our fighters, including his, emptied their ammunition into the airship. It flew on as if it had been bothered with mosquitos. Indeed, the chap on the RT said it even accelerated."

"What was its heading?" Indy said sharply.

"East, from what I could tell." Treadwell studied Indy. "You starting to latch onto something, Professor?"

"Maybe. Just *maybe.* I need a few more facts. Tom, is there anything else, *anything at all,* that we may have missed? Even Castilano's message about that place in Frances, Arques, and the chateaus. Did he say anything in his message about *any other* place these people may be using?"

"Well, not really." Treadwell rubbed his chin as he probed his memory. "There was more, of course, but it was sort of gibberish."

Indy rolled his eyes. "What's gibberish to one man may not be the same to another," he said quickly. "You of all people—"

"Castilano made some reference to a city in the sky. *Something* huge in the sky, other than the airship—"

The pieces began to fall into place in Indy's mind with startling swiftness. It was all coming together like a three-dimensional jigsaw puzzle, and the more pieces that dropped into place the faster came the conclusions and the clearer became the picture.

"*Bingo!*" he shouted jubilantly.

16

"It's going to be a rough flight, Indy."

Harry Henshaw spoke directly to Indiana Jones, but his audience included the rest of the team who would occupy the Ford Trimotor. Cromwell and Foulois sat quietly in the mess dining hall of the British outpost along England's west coast, listening and watching carefully. Henshaw was right.

"Why?" Indy asked. "We're taking the same route we took to get here. Just going the other way."

Henshaw studied Indy and Gale Parker, seated by his side. "Sure, it's the same distance in terms of miles. But that's measuring the miles along the earth's surface. Flying calls for judging and considering the winds as well. And we *could* be going directly into headwinds. That means more flight time and a slower speed."

Indy held Henshaw's gaze. "Harry, you want to get that dirigible or don't you?"

"What kind of question is that?" Henshaw asked, visibly surprised. "Of course we do, you know that as well as—"

Indy cut him off with an abrupt, impatient gesture.

"Then let's stop looking for problems. *Let's do it.*" He looked beyond Henshaw to the two pilots.

"Will, Rene . . . can we do it? Fly back along the same route? Handle the headwinds?"

Cromwell shrugged. "Short of a hard gale, not quite a cakewalk, but with our long-range tanks filled—"

"Yes or no, blast it!"

"Yes." Cromwell said immediately.

"Then get us ready for takeoff as soon as we can."

"Just one thing, Indy," Rene Foulois said quickly. Indy waited. "I recommend strongly we plan all our landings in daylight. We may have some weather and—"

"Just set it up and tell me when you'll be ready to *go*," Indy said brusquely.

"Night takeoff," Cromwell said calmly. "Get us to Iceland with plenty of reserve. Check the weather and timing, and go for Greenland. Like you said, just reverse our course." Cromwell turned to Foulois. "I make that just about seven hours from now."

Foulois nodded. "I agree."

"Then that's it. Harry," Indy said to the colonel, "you've got the contacts. Will you attend to provisions and anything else we may need."

"Yes, just so long as you know that I think you're all crazy," Henshaw said with resignation.

"You still going with us?" Indy pressed.

"Of course," Henshaw answered. "I never made any special claims to be sane."

The flight westward, into the prevailing winds, was every bit as troublesome, even dangerous at times, as Henshaw had warned—and quite often worse. Weather in a variety of forms, all of it bad save for favorable tailwinds most of the time, swept down from the arctic regions. Cold air mixed with moist warm air along their route gave the

Ford a hammering, noisy, jolting ride through sky-high potholes, bumps, and violent turbulence.

The weather proved so rotten the first leg of the trip that Cromwell and Foulois chose to land along the northwest coast of Scotland to sit out a period of horrendous rain and darkness. The field where they'd landed was deserted.

Cromwell and Henshaw went about the buildings trying to find anyone on duty. "Not a living soul," Henshaw mumbled through chattering teeth.

"Bloody mausoleum," Cromwell confirmed. "No lights, no people, no *nothing*."

"Let's tie the Ford down, and we'll break in to get out of this weather," Indy said immediately.

They dragged thick ropes from their equipment containers, lashing the airplane to the ground, throwing a thick canvas tarp over the cockpit. Gathering sleeping bags, they pushed through the storm-lashed night to an operations shack. A heavy padlock secured the door. Indy removed his Webley, firing a single round into the lock.

"Look," he said sourly. "Magic. Make a lot of noise and the door's opened."

"That's quite a key you have there," Henshaw told him. "I didn't know you were the criminal type, but I like your style."

"So do I," shivered Gale, pushing past Indy into the protection of the office. "I'll even buy them a new lock."

Thirty minutes later they had a fire blazing in a large potbellied stove, and soon afterward they were gratefully asleep.

Rain was still falling at the first sign of dawn. No one from the field had appeared. Henshaw returned to the Ford and switched on the batteries for radio power. In moments he was talking with a weather reporting center nearby. He hung up, switched off the batteries, and went to the door to call the others.

"It's still pretty cruddy where we are," he explained, "but I talked to Scottsmoor. They have spoken this morning with the islands along our path, and it's much improved the closer to get to Iceland. I suggest we move on out as fast as we can."

Indy looked at Cromwell, who nodded. Gale spoke up. "Rene, give me a hand with our gear in the office. Indy, I'll leave a note and some money to pay for the lock." She looked at the sky. "I know this weather. It's like two fronts converging. Harry, whoever you spoke to just left out one thing. Either we take off within the hour or we'll be on the ground for a couple of days."

"What makes you so sure?" Henshaw asked, just a touch *too* tolerant in his attitude toward a woman talking pilot language.

"Because I learned to fly in this country," Gale snapped. "Day and night for five months. I know it, *you* don't, so I suggest you get cracking, *Colonel.*"

Indy laughed. "Sounds good to me."

Twenty minutes later they thundered along the grass strip into the air, climbing in a steady turn to take them northwest. At a thousand feet Foulois called Indy on the intercom. "Take a look out the right side," he told Indy. "Looks like our little lady knows the weather here better than anyone else."

In the distance, no more than a few miles distant, a huge wall of fog and rain advanced against the field they'd just left. "We'll be above this in several minutes," Foulois added, "and we ought to stay on top all the way to Iceland."

"Good show," Indy replied.

. . .

They flew at eight thousand feet in brilliant sunshine. Gale opened sandwiches, and brought them along with a thermos of hot tea to the cockpit. Like Indy and Henshaw, she preferred coffee while flying. They gathered near the rear of the cabin; away from the propellers, the noise level was almost comfortable and permitted easy speech.

"Harry," Indy said between huge bites of his sandwich, "let me bounce some ideas off of you."

Henshaw gestured with his own sandwich. "Go on. Let's have 'em."

Indy glanced at Gale. "Anytime you feel I'm missing something, step in," he instructed her.

She nodded. She would wait until she had something worth saying or asking. In the meantime, she knew she was in for an education. She knew *how* to fly an airplane, even one so large as the three-engined Ford. But she knew she was about to step into an area where she was a neophyte. Whatever Indy might advance would be measured and evaluated, and the response given, by Harry Henshaw—who was as much a technical intelligence specialist as he was a highly experienced pilot in everything from small trainers and fighters to huge transports and bombers.

"Let's start with the zep," Indy said. "Harry, I want you to consider any statement I make as much of a question as it is a conclusion. You teach me about wings and things and I'll take you smoothly through tombs and pyramids."

Henshaw laughed. "It's a deal."

"Okay," Indy said, "the zep. Treadwell explained that they got at least three fighters into position to empty their guns into that thing."

"Right," Henshaw said.

"And they fired tracers," Indy went on quickly. "Which means, one, they didn't hit the lifting-gas cells."

"Possibility, yes," Henshaw replied.

"Well, if that thing is lifted by hydrogen, then either it's got heavy shielding about the gas bags, which kept the tracers from hitting them—"

"Dismiss that," Henshaw waved away the suggestion. "You're talking so much weight the thing could hardly get above the treetops."

"Got it," Indy said, nodding. "Or the fighters could have missed completely."

"Nope," Henshaw countered. "I checked. The pilots saw their tracers going into the top of the hull."

"Then either those people aboard the airship were incredibly lucky," Indy said, hesitating before finishing his sandwich, "or they weren't using hydrogen, or any other flammable gas."

"Congratulations," Henshaw told him.

"That means they're using helium," Indy came back. "So where are they getting it?"

"I thought you Yanks had a world monopoly on helium," Gale offered.

"We sure do," Henshaw told her. "The main source is—"

Indy gestured to interrupt. "Let me," he told Henshaw. "I've been doing some homework on this."

Henshaw seemed amused with Indy's intensity. "Have at it, Professor." He smiled.

"Mineral Wells, Texas."

"Congratulations," Henshaw said, clearly impressed. "But there are also helium storage points—"

"Too crowded," Indy said quickly. "Too obvious. They can't move something the size of a small mountain where people would go bananas at the sight of a huge gleaming airship zipping along without engines."

"So they must have a base that completely conceals that airship?" Gale asked.

"Give the lady a cigar," Indy said. "You know," he turned back to Henshaw, "each clue opens the door a bit wider to more answers."

"Always does," Henshaw agreed. "A matter of the picture becoming clearer as you fit each piece into the jigsaw puzzle." He eyed Indy with a quizzical look. "Do I get the idea we've heard only part of your conclusions?"

Indy smiled. "I know this may sound crazy, but it looks as if a mixture of anthropology and archeology has the answer we're after. That, and some old but very powerful superstitions, the latter enough to convince eyewitnesses to the airship to keep it a secret."

"You're way ahead of me," Henshaw said, irritated that he wasn't following Indy fast enough.

"Well, one of the best kicks to open the door came from Filipo Castilano," Indy said. "Remember when Treadwell told us that Filipo had made vague references to a city in the sky? At best it seemed terribly tenuous. For all I knew, Filipo was deliberately disguising his message. Likely he figured I would extrapolate from what he was hinting at and come up with the answer he wanted me to get."

"And did you?" Henshaw pressed.

"Not at first," Indy admitted. "A city in the sky could be Asgard. Home of the gods. It might be Mount Olympus. Every culture has some kind of city, or Eden, or heaven in the sky. But I had to keep in mind that Filipo could have been speaking more literally than I suspected."

"Indy, you're playing games with us," Gale complained.

"No; not really. I'm trying to have you accompany me on the process I was using to come up with the right answer."

He ticked off the items on his fingers. "First, the airship can't possibly be using hydrogen. It would have been blown apart by now with its own jet engines. Plus the fact that it has—it *must* have—a huge open ramp at its stern, so that the discs can come in to be recovered. And *they're* also pouring out very high heat."

"Agreed," Henshaw said. "Even a minor hydrogen leak would be a disaster."

"Okay," Indy went on. "So we need helium. Shipping great quantities of helium out of the U.S. would attract too much attention. The government is paranoid on the stuff. But there's no problem in shipping helium by the tanker load *inside* the States. All you need is enough money and you can buy what you want, so long as no one figures it's going overseas.

"Helium from Mineral Wells in Texas. But where would it go? How did this sky city fit into it? And if there really *is* a sky city, it has to be in name only. We just don't have cities drifting around the sky. What if it was a name an anthropologist or an archeologist, or even a student of history, would recognize? It might not be known as such by the public. It would be in a rare language, rare by virtue of belonging to an isolated group, that is. And if Castilano knew as much of Spanish history as I believe he did, he was pointing straight to the *real* Sky City."

"You've been leading us down the garden path, Indy—"

"Not really. It was only when I began to think along those lines that everything fell into place." He paused, relishing the moment. "You see, it's an Indian name. The Acoma Indians have occupied a massive redoubt for thousands of years. In fact, their history claims they lived in their fortified city three thousand years before the time of Christ."

"*Acoma!* Of course!" Henshaw exclaimed.

"*What* is Acoma?" Gale almost begged for the explanation.

"Acoma is the Indian name for our Sky City," Indy told her. "It lies roughly southwest of Albuquerque, New

Mexico. It's fairly close to the Zuni Indian Reservation, but it stands by itself. It's a huge mesa, in places well over three hundred feet high with sheer cliff walls. More specifically, Sky City in the Acoma language means Old Acoma. They have a language distinctively their own.

"And they have their specific and particular beliefs, myths and traditions. The Acoma believe they all originated from deep within the earth, from a huge underground chamber they called Shipapu. Their race started with two girls created by their gods—Nautsiti and Iatiku. When the gods created these two girls, suddenly the race of Acoma Indians sprang to life. People, animals, dwellings, agriculture; everything. They built their homes hundreds of feet up in the sky—*atop their mesa.* It became known as the Pueblo in the Sky."

"Sky City," Gale said softly.

"And it is a natural, powerful fortification, with huge caverns and cave areas big enough to hold half a dozen of those airships. Throughout their history the Acoma Indians defended their territory with a savagery given special notice by the Spaniards when they were moving through those lands in their early conquests north of Mexico. When they reached Acoma—which in various linguistic derivatives means 'the place that always was'—they ran into some very nasty people defending their sacred mesas."

Indy leaned back and stretched his legs. "I recall reading the reports of a Spanish expedition leader, Captain Hernando de Alvarado. Back in 1540, Coronado sent him to learn the truth about this great place they'd heard about. Alvarado was amazed to see the city hundreds of feet above them, the entrances narrow and so well fortified that an attack seemed impossible. In fact, his official report to Coronado stated flatly that Acoma was the most impregnable stronghold he had ever seen. He called it completely inaccessible, and reported there were more than six to eight thousand Indians living atop the mesa, all of them quite capable of standing off any force the Spaniards might have assembled."

Indy rubbed his chin, searching his memory for details. "That's enough of the history, but it lets you know that Acoma is absolutely the perfect operational base for their airship. The local Indians—and the countryside has at least a dozen different tribes—have always believed they had a special connection to heaven. There was a specific event, um, I believe it was the fall of 1846. By now the Spaniards, of course, were gone, and the American army was doing everything it could to control the Indians. This one moment in their history, well, it certainly reinforced the Indians' beliefs. An American cavalry force was camped about a mile from the sheer cliffs of Acoma, and on this night a tremendous meteor came blasting out of space. In fact, it was so bright it turned the night into day. And it didn't come *down*. It tore across the sky, level with the horizon, lit up the world, and, apparently, rushed back out into space again."

"Atmospheric skip," Henshaw said. "It happens sometimes. It makes a believer out of you."

"Well, it's my bet," Indy said firmly, "and I'll stake my reputation on it, that's where we'll find that airship. And if they have a real handle on what's happening, then they absolutely must realize things are starting to come unglued with their program."

Indy showed his concern. "The way these people have been operating, they've got to make a very serious move. Which means they could well decide to destroy even an entire city if they wanted to."

"Destroy a whole city?" Gale showed confusion, even resistance to Indy's statement. "How could they do that?

One airship, even a dozen, couldn't carry enough bombs to—"

"Indy's right," Henshaw broke in. "They wouldn't bother with bombs, Gale. Too heavy, clumsy. They'd make a lot of noise and fire and kill a few hundred people, perhaps, even wound a few thousand more, but that's nothing on the scale of war." Henshaw shook his head. "We run what we call 'war games' on matters like this. Like, what would *we* do if we were in their place?"

"What *would* you do?" Gale pushed.

"If my intention was terror and killing on a huge scale, any one of several things or, more likely, a combination of them all. First, either from the air or from the ground you can poison the water supply of a major city. If your poison is slow-acting, then enough time passes so that most of the people in your city would have absorbed fatal doses even before the poison starts to kill. Nerve paralysis, respiratory problems; that sort of thing. Then there are biological agents. It's not well known but at least four countries have already developed a mutation of anthrax that devastates people exposed to it. It could be sprayed from either the airship or those devilish saucers they've got. You wouldn't need great amounts, in terms of weight, that is. England, France, Germany, Russia, the United States, we were all getting into the biological agents game. Nasty and brutish, I'll admit—"

"Horrible, you mean," Gale said with heat.

"No worse, young lady, than an incendiary bullet in the gut, let me assure you," Henshaw said coldly. "Or being in the direct line of impact from a flamethrower."

"My God," Gale said, very quietly.

"Harry's right," Indy added. "And then there's poison gas. Back in the Great War they had lewisite, mustard, phosgene. Other types were being developed. Tens of thousands of soldiers died from gas attacks. Maybe they were the lucky ones. Tens of thousands more became blind or went mad or were crippled by gas."

"And an unexpecting city doesn't have *any* protection against *that,*" Henshaw said emphatically. "No, I'm afraid Indy's right on target about these people. We've sent their carrier ship to the bottom, so they know we're ready to make a stand against them. We attacked their airship—rather futilely, I admit—but those British boys certainly went at it with everything they had. Now the hunt is on, and the sooner we find that airship and knock it out, the faster they'll lose the advantages of emotion and fear stirred up by those saucers and the airship itself."

"I haven't heard either one of you say what I've been afraid you might say," Gale told them.

"Spell that out," Indy replied.

"If they can attack *one* city," she said slowly, "why wouldn't they attack several, or even many cities?"

"Oh, they could," Henshaw said quickly. "But mass destruction isn't the name of their game. It's fear. Mind control. Change the way people think and you can control them. If they believe in their gods, there *are* gods. If they believe they're helpless—"

"Then they'll be helpless," Indy finished for him. "So the sooner we find that airship . . ." He let the rest speak for itself.

They felt the Ford lurch from side to side. That brought their attention to the moment, to where they were, flying across the North Atlantic to cross by the Faeroe Islands on their way to Iceland. Turbulence increased with every passing moment, and they saw Foulois working his way back from the cockpit.

"Why we ever bothered to give you people intercom headsets is a mystery," Foulois said. "We've been shouting at you for ten minutes!"

"What's up?" Henshaw asked. From the look on his

face as he felt the trembling and shaking motions of the airplane, he didn't need the Frenchman to tell him anything.

"We've got to work our way through a front," Foulois said. "We're into it now." He nodded to the cabin windows, and they saw the rain streaking the glass.

"It's going to be a bit bumpy," Foulois went on. "Better strap in, put away any loose stuff."

"Frenchy, I'll take your seat for a while, okay?" Henshaw said. "You can have some food and coffee—"

"I realize you meant wine, didn't you, Colonel?"

"Of course, of course. I need to use the radio to talk to Iceland."

"Sorry, my friend. The weather. We lost voice contact with Iceland a while ago. But we're tracking off one of the Faeroes broadcasters and it seems we're right on where we belong. That Cromwell is like a bird dog. I think he can sniff his way to Iceland."

"You really want *wine*?" Gale asked, as Henshaw headed for the cockpit.

Foulois rummaged through his bag, bracing himself between the cabin floor and a seat. He held up a bottle in triumph. "Coffee never won wars, my dear," he said, taking a long swig from the bottle. "But if you drink enough wine, you don't even care *who* wins. A very civilized attitude, I might add."

The next moment he was hanging in midair as the Ford dropped like a stone dumped from a cliff. He slammed into the cabin floor as the downdraft reversed.

"A true Frenchman," Indy laughed. "Never spilled a drop!"

Two hours later, strapped in, hanging grimly to his seat, Indy was ready to swear off flying for the rest of his life. The promise of "a bit bumpy" had become a madhouse of slamming about, yawing and wheeling, and pounding up and down, rivulets of water running into the cabin from the cockpit.

"This is so invigorating!" Gale shouted above the din and boom of engines and thunder and wind.

Indy struggled to keep his stomach where it belonged. Bright spots danced before his eyes. He no longer knew what was right or left or up or down. Then, as abruptly as it started, the uproar and violence ceased, and the sky brightened. Indy's stomach began a slow slide back to where it belonged, and through the cockpit windshield, even from well back in the cabin, he saw the volcanic humps of Iceland waiting for them.

17

A day and a half later they landed in Quebec, bone-weary, muscle-stiff, groggy from lack of proper rest or sleep, and hating sandwiches. Henshaw went to the Canadian authorities, and arranged for American Customs and Immigration to "forget" the usual procedures for entering the United States on the basis that this was an official government aircraft, crew, and flight. Tired as they were and desperate for showers and clean clothes, there was no rest for any of them. Cromwell put everybody to work on the Ford except Henshaw, who was "attending to" the tasks he'd received from Indy. They had flown the aircraft hard and long, and the years of experience told Cromwell and Foulois to pay strict attention to the small complaints they could sense and feel from the aircraft and the engines.

Two hours later they were refueled, oil tanks filled, hydraulics and other requirements met. Henshaw returned to the aircraft. "Will," he asked Cromwell, "are we okay for a straight shot to Dayton? When we get there we'll *have* to take a break, and I can have our top maintenance people go over the bird stem to stern."

"After the flying we've just done, m'boy, from here to Dayton will be a walk in the park."

"Okay," Indy told his team, "saddle up and let's move on out."

Cromwell nudged Foulois with his elbow. "Saddle up, eh? What does he think this bird is? A bleedin' 'orse?"

Indy and Gale strapped into seats near the rear of the cabin. Exhausted, Gale was asleep almost at once. Indy leaned back with his eyes closed, but far from sleep. He was moving himself into the immediate future when the chasing and long-distance flying would be behind them.

Now they'd be in a position to flush out their quarry.

And the quarry, Indy had come to learn so well, might just be ready and waiting for them.

Colonel Harry Henshaw spread out flight charts, road maps, and high-altitude photographs of long-strip areas within Texas and New Mexico. Indy stood to his left, Gale to his right, and at the huge planning table with them were several military intelligence officers. Along the opposite side of the table, waiting to be questioned, were several civilians: drivers of tanker trucks and, almost as if he were an intruder in working clothes, a high member of the Council of the Acoma Indians. While they remained within the inner security building inside the aircraft hangar at Wright Field, Cromwell and Foulois were ministering to the Ford Trimotor.

"These are the latest aerial photos taken by our pilots," Henshaw said to Indy, but speaking as well to the entire group. "Let's review with Mineral Wells as a starter." He moved the maps to place aerial photographs in position so that they could be compared. "The main source of helium, as you know, is here." He tapped the map with a pointer. "The wells are just to the west of the area of Fort Worth. Usually helium is transferred in railway tank cars because of ease of transport, storage, and the bulk involved. However, using tanker trucks is also common.

"Now, what emerges from our surveys is that the road traffic has increased enormously in the past few weeks. These photos were taken above three main highways in the past week. The planes flew high enough not to attract too much attention from the ground, and we used transports, mainly, with camera mounts in belly hatches. Our people have circled positive identification of tanker trucks along these roads, and the circles are along lines heading in two main directions. One group works towards Lubbock, which is a main transport center, and the second main group takes the highway down to Midland and Odessa, and then starts to work their way generally northwest into New Mexico."

"How many go into Albuquerque?" Indy asked.

Henshaw motioned to a truck driver. "Indy, this is Mike Hightower. Mike, you want to field that question?"

The burly man leaned forward. "Sure, Colonel." He looked to Indy. "We hardly ever carry helium to Albuquerque. Not much call for it there. Our biggest customers are the navy, for blimps and those new dirigibles they got, and also some manufacturing outfits. Some of them, they ain't got any rail facilities, so we need the trucks."

Hightower moved a map into a position so he and Indy could share the same area. "Bunch of our trucks, they were dispatched to Santa Fe. That's right here." He stabbed the map with a thick forefinger. "But that's pretty crazy to me. There ain't a thing up there in Santa Fe needs that much helium. Unless, of course," he glanced at Henshaw, "the military got some kind of secret project in the works. The colonel tells me no. Even the delivery is kind of screwy. I mean, we drive the trucks to where the drivers are told to go, and then they're told to leave the shipment there. Trucks and all. I raised hell about that, but then I got told by my boss that some big company bought us out and they're using new drivers in shifts. Our boys come back to Mineral Wells by chartered bus. They ain't complaining none, you understand. They get bonuses for what they're doing, and that kind of lettuce keeps everybody happy."

"Any deliveries into Albuquerque itself?" Indy asked.

Hightower rolled a short cigar stub in his teeth. "Uh-uh. Some other trucks, they go direct from Mineral Wells to Roswell, here," again he tapped the map, "and they drop off the trucks there. A few of our guys, they were told to drive to Las Cruces, that's way south."

Henshaw drew a finger northward on the map. "From Las Cruces it's almost a straight shot north toward Albuquerque. That's pretty desolate country. You go through Truth or Consequences, the road parallels the Rio Grande River, then the trucks keep going through the lava fields by Elephant Butte and on up to Socorro. When they reach Belen, they take a cutoff toward Acoma."

"It's a dumb way to go," Hightower offered. "Lousy roads, I mean. Not too many of them paved. Beats hell out of the trucks. But like I said, whoever's bossing this operation, they're throwing dough around like there's no tomorrow, so our guys ain't kicking none."

Indy studied the maps. "But all roads lead to Acoma, don't they, Harry." It was a statement more than a question.

"Yep," Henshaw acknowledged. "Hightower, the drivers, the ones who take over from your people, didn't you say they bring the trucks all the way back to Mineral Wells?"

"Yeah. It's a tough haul, but that's the way they do it. By the time we get 'em back we got to service them pretty good. They're beat up from that kind of pushing through that country. If we complain the trucks are busted up, they tell us to just junk 'em and give us new trucks. Craziest way to run a business I ever saw."

"Anything else you might add?" Indy asked.

"No, sir. In fact, I shouldn't even be here. I mean, these guys are paying me a bonus to keep my trap shut. Don't answer no questions, they tell me. Then a bunch of guys, Feds, I mean, they visit me and say if I want to keep my license and stay in business, all I got to do is have a little chat. Like I'm having now. I been promised I leave here like I came in."

"And how was that done?"

"I went to Gainesville. That's north of Fort Worth. Just below the Oklahoma border. Some army camp. At night a plane comes in, I climb in, and the next thing I know is that I'm here. Like I said, mister, I go out the same way."

"Mr. Hightower, you've been a big help. You forget about this little visit, we'll drop you off at night at that camp outside Gainesville, and we never saw you."

"Thanks, Colonel. Am I all through here?"

"You're free to go. Anything you need, just let us know."

"Well, yeah. Why don't your people take me up to Lawton in Oklahoma? Ain't much out of the way, and I got folks up there, so I'm covered by seeing family. Never came *here.*" He grinned.

"Have a good trip, Mr. Hightower." Henshaw looked at two other drivers. "You people have anything to add?"

Both men shook their heads. "Nope. It's all just like Mike said."

"Great. Thank you."

A captain led the three men from the room.

Henshaw turned to Indy. "There's a lot more detail, but I think the picture's pretty clear. Heavy shipments of helium directly to Acoma."

"They must have a piping system for the airship," Indy said.

"Yes."

They both turned to the Indian. He had remained stoic and silent through the exchanges. Indy paid special attention to him now. Big man for an Indian; at least six feet two inches and with immense shoulders. He wore a stovepipe western hat that on most men would have been ludicrous, especially with the three golden feathers along the left side of the crown. Indy saw that the buckskin trousers and vest were hand-sewn, as were his belt and hammered silver ornaments. Indy couldn't see his feet through the table, but somehow he knew that for footwear the Indian had yielded to the white man's working field boots. That made sense in the rocky desert country.

Both men held the eyes of the other, both men looked down from faces to the weapon each man carried. Indy had his Webley slung across hip and thigh in its covered holster. The Indian carried his Western style, slung low and thigh-tied for security for riding and a fast draw.

Indy nodded to the man. Ceremony was important here. All he knew of this fellow was what Henshaw had told him; that he was a member of the High Council of the Acoma. Indy swiftly learned the rest by his study of the man, his mannerisms that bespoke a long and royal line. It also said something that he was allowed to wear an open sidearm on a military base.

"Jones," Indy said. "Henry Jones. I prefer Indy."

"Good name. I am Jose Syme Chino." Chino's voice came from deep within his barrel chest. Indy saw warmth in the eyes of the man who, Indy knew, could be a fearsome opponent when the moment demanded. There was still some small talk, a feeling-out. If it went well, Indy would have the final cooperation he sought. And by the way Henshaw had taken a step backwards, Indy knew that the colonel recognized the need for these two to palaver on equal terms. The Indians had been treated anything but fairly by the white man's government.

Indy motioned to Chino's holstered weapon. "May I?" Indy asked.

In a lightning move, the heavy revolver—a long-barreled .44 six-gun—was out of its holster and offered butt first to Indy. Indy hefted the weapon, sighted down the long barrel. "Good range?"

Chino barely nodded. "Heavy load, high velocity. Yes. Good range."

Indy returned the .44 to Chino, unholstered his own weapon and, gripping the Webley by the barrel, offered it across the table to Chino. The same examination took place. Chino smiled. "Much use," he said.

"Yes," Indy replied. Chino had learned all that from the weathered feel of the Webley. Now Chino pointed to the curled whip hanging from Indy's left waist.

"That also has much use," he said.

"Yes."

"I am master with whip. We must test one another," Chino offered.

Indy smiled. "That will be . . . interesting."

A deep laugh boomed from Chino, and in that moment the short-clipped speech of the "backward Indian" was gone. "I imagine that in certain circumstances, Professor Jones, your camera is even more effective than the whip and the gun."

I was right! This guy probably has more degrees than I've got under my belt! But Indy made certain not to show surprise or even to hesitate in response.

"You are very perceptive," he told Chino. "It is more frightening to many people to have their spirit captured with this," he tapped the Leica, "than to kill a man who then travels to the gods in spirit form."

"Careful, Professor." Chino laughed. "You sound like a medicine man."

"And you no longer sound as if you're out in the hills hunting moose with a bowie blade."

A knowing smile this time, but Chino chose to wait for Indy to continue. "Just for the record, Jose Syme Ch—"

"Indy for me, Joe for you."

"Great. But like I was saying, just for the record before we get back to the matter at hand, where did you do your studies?"

"You *are* good. Montana for geology, UCLA for meteorology and atmospherics, Texas A and M for agriculture . . ." Chino shrugged. "Whatever I needed to serve the interests of my people in the best way."

"It had to be a tough go at A and M."

"Why do you say that, Indy?"

"As your ancestors would say, Joe, we can't afford to talk with forked tongues. Being Indian at that place is the same as being black. It's a big no-no."

"In some ways, worse. Careful planning helps."

"Such as?"

"I was the heavyweight boxing champ for four years."

"*That's* good planning."

"Now we've got to get down to the nitty-gritty of *your* problem, my friend," Chino told Indy. "You're running out of time. Those people are getting ready to move. They've already started their diversions."

Indy turned to Henshaw. "You know about this? Diversions, I mean?"

"Chino brought us the news. At least the start of it and what we could expect." Henshaw spread the map to table center. "Look, here's Acoma and the Acoma Indian Reservation. To the west—"

"Colonel, may I?" Chino broke in.

"By all means, please," Henshaw said quickly.

Chino leaned forward. His hand slid along the map, from the reservation area of the Acoma westward. "This is Cibola," he pointed out. "National forest. What's more important is south and west of Cibola. This area," he tapped the map, "is lava flows. Vicious. The stuff is often needle-sharp. Eat a man's boots in one day. Now, just beyond that lava flow area you run into the Ramah Navajo Indian Reservation. The Navajos can be a problem tribe at times. It's the familiar white man and the redskin dancing wildly in the same frying pan. With all that kicking and swinging somebody always takes a shot in the mouth."

Indy laughed. "Best way I've ever heard it said. But you hinted the Navajos weren't a problem."

"Right. It's the Zunis. Normally they're like most of the old tribes out here. Scratching in the sand to eke out a living. The farming is lousy, the soil bleached, the drought endless, and there's not enough livestock, mainly sheep and some cattle, to keep the people from being on the edge of starvation. The commercial outfits that came in have done their best to shaft everybody. For a while the Zunis, like most of the tribes, were building up a fairly decent tourist trade, and it looked like we'd get some irrigation. The drought, well, it tore us limb from limb. Selling wool became the salvation for most of the tribes, and the Cubero Trading Company had a death grip on most tribes. We started to break away from Cubero two years ago, but right now we're being strangled by the same economic depression that's ripping through the entire country."

Chino took a deep breath. "Don't mistake what I've just said as a stock speech on behalf of the poor Indians. That wasn't my intent. You see, the people with that airship you're after understand everything I've just told you, and *they* are playing that scene for everything it's worth."

Henshaw eased back into the issue. "The state marshal

—he's been working with us, his name is Guy Douglas, and he's an old hand out here—has kept us up to the minute. Look again at the map, the Navajo, Cibola, Zuni and other groups. The Zuni are quite some distance from Acoma, and in the past two days all hell has been breaking loose out on the reservations. It's *not* a case of the Indians giving us grief. By us, I mean law enforcement in New Mexico. They've been *bought* by those people running that airship. In fact, two names we've latched onto are Halvar Griffin and a Wilhelmina Volkman."

A memory stirred. The Natural History Museum . . . Gale Parker spoke up. "Indy, you get the feeling that Volkman is really Marcia Mason?"

Indy nodded, but turned right back to the issue at hand. "All you've been telling me, the both of you," he indicated Chino and Henshaw, "comes to a point. What is it?"

"The Navajo went on a rampage two days ago," Chino answered. "But it's been a careful rampage. They stayed within the borders of their own reservation, so there's no doubt in my mind that it's all been staged. It's a farce. They're drunk, they've blocked the main roads going in and out of their area, they're shooting off guns day and night, and they're threatening to shoot anybody who comes into their territory. That's a diversion, of course. And it's working. The local law enforcement people have been trying to calm things down there. When they thought they had the situation under control—never aware it was all a setup—the Zuni broke loose from their grounds, and started out to the north with a few hundred painted warriors on horseback, heading for Gallup. That's another staged breakout. But it *has* succeeded. There's been enough propaganda about these so-called uprisings to send every lawman for a couple of hundred miles around to those areas, especially Gallup. The people there are frightened out of their wits."

"You've told me what you haven't even said yet," Indy said, frowning.

"Tell *me,*" Henshaw responded.

"There's no local law left in the Acoma area," Indy said. "Sheriffs, police, park rangers, state and federal marshals, they're all pouring into the Zuni and Gallup area."

"Which means, my friend, you've got this hornet's nest on your *own* hands. That airship is going to be on its way out of Acoma in the next two days. At the most," Chino stressed. "So whatever it is you're going to do, you have to get cracking just about *now.*"

"Colonel Henshaw?" They turned to Gale. "Why can't you send over a few bombers and put that dirigible out of action right away?"

"Because Griffin, or whoever it is running the show, has prepared for this moment," Henshaw replied, "and *very* carefully. Mr. Chino can tell you why our hands are tied."

Heads turned to the tall Indian. Chino's face was grim. "If the army, or anyone else, attacks the airship while it is concealed, or even close to the deep cavern where it is out of sight from above, you condemn almost all the Acoma. You see, those people came to us as friends. Our people were desperate for food, water, the necessities of life. A team of strangers came in, both on horseback and with trucks. They had all the right paperwork. They were archeologists and they were surveyors. They were digging out rumored caves which Coronado's invaders had filled with precious artifacts of more ancient times. In return for our cooperation, they promised—and they kept their promises—food, water, electricity for all of Acoma, medical facilities—everything our people needed. I said they had the right paperwork. Licenses, permits, company names. They came in with increasing numbers. There is a huge cavern not visible to the passerby. It is big enough to hold their airship.

"I fear I am wasting time talking, so I will get to the point. The white people who came in cut away a section of cliff. They did so with our permission. This gave them enough room to settle their airship by descending vertically. It sounds like all the devils of hell when it comes down. Its fumes are choking, but the winds blow them away. As the airship descends, they tether it to cables and engines which reel it in carefully. When it is down, it is secured to the ground and it is safe. Then they bring in provisions and their helium. In the hill caves atop the mesas they built holding tanks. For helium and their fuel, they told us. What they did *not* tell us is that they filled many concealed tanks with kerosene and gasoline. They have packed high explosives all through Acoma."

He moved his head slowly to meet the eyes of everyone listening to him. "Do you understand now?"

Indy spoke up. "You're booby-trapped."

"Yes. Attack that airship where it is held to the ground, and you will destroy Acoma and kill thousands of our people. Most of them will burn to death in rivers of fire from the fuel tanks which are so set up they will pour their contents into the caverns and caves."

Indy turned to Henshaw. "So we can't go after them where they would otherwise be helpless."

"I have talked with these strangers," Chino said. "I know something of their plans, as I overheard several discussing what they would do. I know little of flying, but I heard clearly that they plan to lift upward from Acoma at night, when they will not be seen and all the law people are occupied with the Zunis and in the Gallup area. They said they will rise to more than six miles into the sky and then they would go." He shrugged. "Where, I do not know. All that mattered to me was that they were leaving. Then Colonel Henshaw, here, asked to see me."

Indy looked carefully at Chino. "Could you tell *when* they planned to leave?"

"Two nights from now. My new friend, you do not have much time to do whatever it is you plan."

"Joe, can we count on you to help us?"

"Yes."

"It would be a great help if you flew with us."

"You want *me* in the sky?"

"Yes. You know that area. We don't."

"I will go. Until this moment I was always convinced it was the white man who was really crazy. Now, so am I."

"Harry, will you check on Will and Rene and see if all the special equipment is loaded on our plane?"

Henshaw nodded to an aide standing nearby. No command was needed. "Yes, sir," the officer said. "I'll take care of it immediately."

Henshaw turned back to Indy. "If they go above thirty thousand feet, we don't have any combat planes—in service, I mean, ready to go—that can handle them. Your Ford has those special superchargers *and* weapons. Indy, it's going to be up to you and your people to stop that zeppelin *now*. Or we're really in for it."

18

They flew most of the night and well into daylight to reach Las Vegas, New Mexico, a sprawling collection of buildings out of an old western novel. The isolation was perfect for them. Several miles east of the town, near the Conchas River, was a huge open desert area the army used for field trials and training exercises. One large hangar stood at the end of the field, surrounded by tents and basic living facilities for the infantry and ground personnel who serviced the fighters and bombers that flew in for exercises. The isolation was better than they expected. An artillery and a bombing range nearby made it clear the area wasn't healthy for uninvited guests. As many bombs tumbled awry as struck their bull's-eyes, marked in the desert with whitewashed stones.

"Everybody get some food," Indy told his group. "Find out where the latrines are because I suggest we all use them just before we take off later tonight. You've got one hour to take this break. Meet by the plane then and we'll go over all our equipment and weapons, and see if anything new has come up."

"What time do you plan for takeoff?" Cromwell asked.

"How long will it take us to climb to thirty-two thousand feet?"

"Good God, Indy, I've never been anywhere near that high!" Cromwell exclaimed.

"Will, *how long?*"

Cromwell worked some figures in his head. "We'll be lighter than usual," he said finally, "and—"

"Just the numbers, Will," Indy pressed.

"No, Indy. It's going to be *very* tricky up there, and I think it's best if you understand what we're up against. Since we've never climbed that high, I can't tell you what our rate of climb will be. We've got a high-lift wing, and those superchargers, well, I've got great faith in them. But the higher we go, the slower will be our rate of ascent. Do you see?"

Indy waited patiently. No use arguing with Cromwell; in this case he was right. At the altitude they were going for, what you didn't know *could* hurt you.

"Judging we may have some problems, and all that," Cromwell went on, "I'd say we ought to give ourselves at least two to three hours just to get to the altitude you want. We'll be on oxygen above twelve thousand and we want to be sure *that* doesn't freeze up on us. I've checked the charts. Figure on a hundred and fifty miles to this Acoma place. That area, anyway. We'll cover the distance while we're climbing."

"Okay," Indy said.

"Maybe not so much okay," Foulois broke in. "Indy, you must consider something I have not heard anyone speak about."

"Which is?"

"Everything we have heard about this airship, no? It is very fast. It may be faster than we are when we reach upstairs."

"It *could* be," Indy admitted. "We'll have to find out when we get there."

"Ah, then consider," Foulois said quickly. "If this is the way it is to be, then I urge you and my corpulent English friend, here, to attempt to reach perhaps another two thousand feet or so. We can gain speed in a shallow dive. At that altitude, we will become *very* fast."

Cromwell laughed, but without a trace of humor. "Don't forget, Indy, we'll likely have company."

Chino listened with amazement to the conversation. He turned to Gale. "Company? What kind of company is higher than even the eagles fly?"

"Discs."

"Discs?"

"Well, more like scimitars in shape. But discs will do. They have jet engines and they're very fast, and they're likely to do everything they can to shoot us down. So we'll be ready to give them the works, of course. That's why we've got those machine guns on the airplane."

"This all sounds, like, well, like the wild tales our ancients tell the children."

"It's a gas, isn't it?" Gale said.

Captain Hans Ulrich Guenther, master of the super airship *Asgard*, listened to the intercom reports as they came in steadily to the control bridge of the great zeppelin. His second in command, Richard Atkins, marked each item on a long checklist. The *Asgard* was half again as long as the greatest oceangoing vessel ever built, and there existed no room for errors. The airship had to be balanced perfectly, the center of gravity always known. The three men who shifted ballast and coordinated airship attitudes in flight functioned like orchestra leaders. So huge was the *Asgard*, and so sensitive in balance and inertia, it took several men to operate the vessel safely and smoothly.

By two o'clock in the morning all prelift requirements had been completed. Guenther, looking straight ahead through the thick glass panels of the bridge gondola, watched the ground crew in position to begin ascent. From this height, even tethered in the tight-fitting canyon of these American savages, the men appeared like toys. Guenther, without turning his head, spoke to Atkins. "All flight crew aboard. Confirm."

Atkins's answer came immediately. "Three to go, sir. They are boarding now. Two minutes."

Soon Atkins approached Guenther. He held the checklist before the captain. Guenther waved it aside. He had absolute confidence in his second. "Mister Burgess!" Guenther announced with raised voice. Andrew Burgess, the most experienced pilot aboard, stepped forward. "Sir!"

"Start all engines, Mister."

"Start all engines, sir," Burgess repeated. He went to the control position. Three banks of instruments were spread out before him. To each side of the position where he would stand were several wheels for raising and lowering the nose, for operating through an elaborate system of hydraulics and cables the elevators and the rudder, and for dumping ballast when necessary. Burgess secured the standing harness about his body; were the vessel to shift to a steep angle of any kind he would be able to remain in the precise position he required to reach and operate the controls.

Standing behind and to his right were three more of his control team, who would relay commands and information from and to the pilot. They would also keep an eye on their own instrument panels. Backup for backup for backup; it was the only proper way to manage the greatest aerial vessel the earth had ever known.

Vibration beneath his feet. Engines starting. A distant

roar as the huge jet engines spun up to proper speed, fuel flow, and temperature, and then ignited for operation. This far forward, the sound was a deep wind roaring through a tunnel, but muted like a faraway bass organ.

"*Asgard* ready for lift-off," Atkins announced.

"Stand by," Guenther ordered. He called out another name. "Miller!"

The answer came from amidships. "Weapons Officer Miller reporting, sir." The voice was tinny as the speaker boxes in the gondola vibrated slightly. Miller was four hundred and seventy feet away in the belly of the *Asgard.*

"Miller, confirm security and safeties of the bombs."

"Yes, sir. I report the gas bombs in their racks, fuses set for arming on your order, sir. All racks primed for release on your command, Captain."

"Very good, Miller. Confirm all gunners at their stations."

"Confirm all gunners secured at their stations, weapons at the ready, sir."

"Flight Leader Moldava! This is the captain."

"Moldava here, sir."

"Status of the discs, Flight Leader."

"Four discs secured, fueled, armed, and in position for launching at your command, sir. The bay doors have been tested and are ready for power opening, manual backup confirmed."

"Thank you, Flight Leader."

"Mister Burgess, order lift to commence," Guenther ordered his Chief Pilot.

"Yes, sir. Commencing liftoff." A klaxon sounded and echoed mournfully through the cavern, booming outside to the canyon walls. That was the signal for the ground crew to start easing tension on the holding cables. The *Asgard* tugged at her lines, seemingly anxious to break free of the earth. Burgess would let her lift vertically, the tension cables keeping her moving smoothly forward. Clear of the cavern, the great vessel would be in the canyon, from where she could begin a vertical ascent, the tension cables keeping her enormous rounded sides from brushing the walls to either side.

The *Asgard* rose slowly, lifted by the buoyancy of her helium cells, her jet engines idling, waiting for the airship to lift above the highest point of the Acoma plateau and its buildings. At that moment she would be at the mercy of the winds unless the engines were brought up to power. She would continue rising.

"What are the winds, Mister Burgess?" Guenther called.

"Direct on the bow, sir. Twelve knots. I am initiating minimum power to assist in holding our position over the canyon until we have cleared the walls. We will at that moment release water ballast and increase power, sir."

"Very good, Mister Burgess." Guenther started to add a comment, then held his silence. Burgess knew as well as any man that the moment of danger would come as they cleared the Acoma canyon, when a sudden side wind could swing the huge bulk of the airship to one side or the other, and even raise or lower the nose in an awkward yawing motion that might bring contact with the upper reaches of the vertical cliffs. He would have to lift her steadily, straight up, and as soon as they cleared the cliffs and buildings, he would bring in power and at the same time lighten the airship by ballast drop. They would then rise away from the surface in a climbing turn. With the ground safely beneath them, Burgess would bring in climb power for full control of the *Asgard*, starting the steady ascent to their cruising altitude.

They would rise slowly, much slower than the speed and climb rate of which the *Asgard* was capable. Too swift an ascent would bring the helium cells expanding at a dangerous rate, especially if any cells developed a double fold in their holding girders that could tear open a cell. The slower ascent would also give the crew time to become accustomed to the thin air at the lower edge of the stratosphere. They would don their cold-weather clothing —heavy fleece-lined flight suits, boots and gloves—and their oxygen masks. Once at cruising altitude and beyond the borders of the United States, the crew would take turns in the pressurized compartment within the belly of the *Asgard.* They would be warm there; they could doff their heavy gear and masks, and partake of hot meals.

The remainder of the flight would be six miles above the Atlantic Ocean, and a straight course for London. There the first load of gas bombs would be dropped. The second load would fall on Paris, and the last of the deadly bombs would hurtle down against Berlin.

And nothing could stop them once they reached cruise altitude. Captain Hans Ulrich Guenther was quite satisfied.

Jose Syme Chino came running to the tent where Indy and his team were drinking hot chocolate and finishing off army iron rations for fast energy. Chino wasted no time. "That thing is in the air!" he burst out.

Everyone sprang to their feet. Before Chino could add another word, the question was on Indy's lips. "When?"

"An hour ago."

"How do you know?" demanded Cromwell.

"Telephone. It would have been sooner but the connections from here are crazy and it took forever," Chino explained. "I spoke with one of our offices at Acomita. That's on the highway north of the great pueblo. He had several people ready to call him the moment that airship came into view over the cliffs. It's in the air, all right."

"This makes it a tight go, Indy," Cromwell said immediately. "We've just lost anywhere from one to three hours, and when that bloody machine gets going it's leaving us in its wake."

"I know—" Indy didn't finish his sentence.

"No! Wait a moment," Chino broke in. "Remember you said before, when you were trying to figure what route that thing would take to the east? You all figured they'd skirt around Albuquerque to stay away from the heavily populated areas. Well, they're going to have to do a pretty major diversion down Socorro way."

"Why?" Foulois said quickly.

"Thunderstorms. There's a line of really big storms running north of the Acoma and Laguna reservations. It stretches way up north of Los Alamos, into the Santa Fe National Forest, and that's nasty country. If they try a curving line out of the Santa Fe forestlands, that would take them into the area of Wheeler Peak and Brazos Peak—"

"You're trying to tell us something," Cromwell said impatiently.

"Joe, you're telling us they *won't* go north?" Indy queried.

"Yes! That's right! Not unless they're crazy," Chino responded immediately. "Brazos Peak is due north of Albuquerque, and it's well over eleven thousand feet high. If they cut northwest after skirting Albuquerque, they've got to work through the area of Wheeler Peak, around the Carson forests, and *that* mountain is over thirteen thousand feet high. I'm no flyer, my friends, but I'll tell you thunderstorms in that area, over those mountains, would keep even the great spirits hugging the ground. It is really mean up there when those storms build up."

"Let's cut to it, Joe," Indy said impatiently. "You know the area. Which way, man? What's your best bet?"

"South, at first. Down along the Rio Grande past

Socorro, then cut east along the lava fields of the Valley of Fire. Beyond that there's a world of nothing, and the mountains all hang at five thousand feet and most of them less than that. From there they can break toward Portales or Clovis. Much the same thing. Open spaces and more lava fields, and beyond that sand dunes and open desert."

"And by then," Foulois said, holding up a chart on which he'd followed Chino's descriptions, "they ought to be at the ceiling they want. So we'd better—"

"Let's go!" Indy yelled. He pointed to an army lieutenant. "Get that plane out of the hangar—*now!*" he shouted. "Will, Rene, fire her up as fast as you can. Gale, you and Joe do a last check to be sure all our gear is in the airplane. I want to check a few last things. The moment I get on board, you signal to Will to take off, straight ahead."

He turned to another officer he recognized as the chief of communications for the local military force. "You the one who keeps contact with Colonel Henshaw?"

"Uh, yes, sir."

"Well, I'm getting on that plane in a moment. You call the colonel immediately and tell him you saw us taking off. Keep him on the phone until you see our wheels leave the ground, got it?"

"Sir, it's the middle of the night—"

"Captain, you want to live to a ripe old age?"

"Why, of course, but I—"

"Call him! Besides, he's an early riser. *Move!*"

Indy didn't wait to see what the captain did. He took off on a dead run for the Ford where Gale was holding open the rear cabin door. The moment Indy was inside the cabin Gale slammed it shut and threw the lock. Will was looking back into the cabin from the cockpit, and Indy made a fist and pumped his hand up and down in the air. Cromwell nodded and a moment later his hand was shoving three throttles forward to their stops. The three Pratt & Whitney engines howled their now-familiar song, and in less than ten seconds the earth began falling away beneath them.

19

They climbed slowly and steadily, in darkness broken only by isolated points of light from a ranch or small town far below. Those began to disappear beneath thickening clouds they estimated at four thousand feet. Cromwell and Foulois kept the Ford in its climb toward Puerto de Luna to the southeast. The town stood along the banks of the Pecos River. More important, it lay between Las Vegas and Roswell, and their course would take them along a line just west of Clovis and Portales on the New Mexico-Texas border. Puerto de Luna also had a radio station that broadcast through the night and this gave the pilots a navigational backup. They were able to tune to the station frequency at Puerto de Luna to the south, switch to an all-night station broadcast from Albuquerque to the west, and by drawing lines on their charts with headings and positions from the stations, maintain a running check on their progress. If Chino had figured the terrain and the weather as well as they hoped, the airship, which must stay away from towering thunderstorms, would follow the best route to get into position for its long flight eastward. And that would be over the Valley of Fire, on to Bitter

Lake just north of Roswell and then, at extreme altitude, they needed only to maintain an east-northeast heading. By now Indy knew enough of homing in to commercial broadcast stations to understand that at the great height the airship would fly, they would be able to use the homing signals from one town to the next on a crude but effective radio highway in the sky.

Then he put that all aside. Cromwell called on the intercom. "Better suit up, chaps. It's going to get dreadfully cold a lot faster than you think. When you're into your cold-weather gear, each of you check the other. And make absolutely certain that when the temperature gets down below zero, which it will do distressingly soon, never touch any metal with your bare hands. If you do, you'll leave your skin behind."

"Got it, Will. What about you two?"

"I'll stay on the controls. As soon as the young lady is in her gear, send her forward. Frenchy can leave his seat then to get suited up while Gale takes right seat. When Frenchy comes back he'll take his seat, Gale will take mine, and I'll suit up. Be sure you people check *us* out. One mistake where we're going can be very costly."

"Got it," Indy confirmed. He turned to Gale. "You hear all that?"

"Yes. Let's do it." She chuckled. "It's nice having two gentlemen at the same time helping me get dressed. I feel positively risqué."

"For a grizzly, maybe," Chino told her. Ten minutes later she was ready to agree with him. In a heavy full-body flight suit of fleece-lined leather, thick boots, leather helmet and goggles, and heavy gloves, she felt like an overstuffed bear.

"I can barely walk in all this stuff," she complained.

"So waddle," Indy told her.

She shuffled forward. Moments later Foulois came

back into the cabin, and the three men assisted one another into their thick and clumsy altitude gear. Each checked the equipment of the others, and Foulois returned to the cockpit, sending Cromwell back. When Gale returned, they donned oxygen masks, the life-giving oxygen fed from portable bottles slung about their shoulder to their waist, the straps modified Sam Browne dress belts.

"Each tank is good for two hours," Indy told Gale and Chino. "You've got to be ready to switch tanks at least ten minutes before that time. Will insists that whenever you switch tanks, one other person *must* be with you. If any one of us messes up with the tank valves or fastenings and we don't get oxygen from the tanks, at our top altitude we won't have thirty seconds of consciousness to correct any mistakes. But if you have somebody with you, they can get the air flowing right away."

Chino nodded. "With all this noise, engines and the wind, how do we talk to each other?"

"These masks are the latest army issue. They've got radio intercom. Since it's real short range, like just inside the plane," Indy related what he'd been taught by Henshaw, "the system ought to work real well. However," he warned, "if one of us calls someone else and there's no answer, get to that person immediately. They may be out of air or a valve has backed off. Five minutes without air up high is a death sentence."

Everything worked perfectly, although physical movement was clumsy and slow in their heavy gear and the increasing cold. They looked back and to the northwest. What had been darkness was now a sky split with almost constant lightning exploding from cloud to cloud in the still-building thunderstorms. Huge thunderheads flashed like beacons from within.

"God, I'm glad we're not in *that,*" Gale remarked. "It could tear us to pieces."

"Thanks," Chino said with obvious sarcasm.

Indy clapped him on the shoulder. "We won't get anywhere near that," he reassured the big Indian. "Joe, it's going to be daylight soon. We'd better check out the guns."

The Ford had been well prepared for the planned encounter with the airship. The inner-wing baggage compartments, modified to hold one machine gun each, with a heavy load of ammunition, gave Cromwell and Foulois powerful forward-firing effect. Both men were experienced combat pilots, and that experience was invaluable now.

Beneath the wings, in place of the external fuel tanks, the army had installed rocket-launching pods. The outer casing was the same size and connections as the fuel tanks, but the fuel lines had been replaced with electrical connections to fire the rockets. At the front end of each tank, the metal structure had been replaced with multilayered thick canvas, heavily doped for stiffness. Before the solid-fuel rocket motors would ignite, a small charge would blow apart both the frangible nose cone and the aft covering of the pod, so that the rockets would be free to fire forward without interference, and the rocket flame would shoot rearwards from the pod without any backlash from the rear covers. Each pod held three rockets, much advanced from those Foulois and Cromwell had fired in combat in the war twelve years earlier, Foulois from his fighter plane with which he attacked German observation balloons, and Cromwell in his diving attacks against German submarines.

But the warhead of each rocket was the hoped-for key to the success they sought against their huge adversary. The full explosive charge had been removed from each warhead, replaced with a smaller charge about which white phosphorous incendiary material had been packed. To add to the incendiary effect, the metal casing of the warhead was of magnesium. Both materials, white phosphorous and magnesium, would burn through fabric and metal with equal ease, and the magnesium particles, once ignited, would continue to burn even under water.

These were the keys with which Indy hoped his team in the Ford would unlock the security of the airship, opening up the huge structure like a hot knife slicing through soft butter.

It wouldn't be quite *that* simple. They would be fighting the cold, and the absolutely-no-mistakes procedures with their oxygen systems. Hopefully, they'd get a visual on the airship that was their prey.

There were so many unknowns! Indy had made certain to keep his serious reservations to himself. He'd listened enough times to the pilots to realize they were sailing into largely uncharted waters with the Ford Trimotor. At this altitude there simply was no way to *know* how the thick-winged machine would handle. Rarefied air brought on strange characteristics to aircraft. Despite the superb ability of Cromwell and Foulois, the three people in the cabin who would be fending off a possible attack from those superfast jet-powered discs had all the experience with machine guns that a dog might have riding a motorcycle.

Their one real advantage was that Indy, Gale, and Chino were all highly experienced at shooting and hunting. The basics wouldn't change. You always led your target with your aim to bring your bullet into a block of space at the same time your target got there.

Foulois had spent time with Indy on the matter of firing the machine guns. "In the air, you have tremendous wind. That affects your fire, no? Of course, yes. The path of your bullets is affected by the wind. They will curve away, flying with the wind. Even a machine gun can waste all its ammunition because of the wind. But you will have incendiary rounds, my friend. Every fourth round will be incendiary, so it will be a bright, bright glow in the air as the bullets fly away from you."

"I know," Indy said quietly.

"Aha! Perhaps you have experience with such matters?"

"Belgian Army. Africa, France," Indy said tightly. "Yes, some experience."

"*Voilà!* Then I do not need to tell you to fire in short bursts." Foulois grasped an imaginary weapon and his arms shook as if he were feeling the recoil of a machine gun. "No firing like you are watering your lawn. No hosing away your ammunition, for it is limited. And even the Belgians knew not to fire too steadily for too long so they would not burn out the barrels of their weapons, no?"

"Yes."

"One more thing, my fine professor. Never forget your ammunition supply is limited. Once it is gone," Foulois shrugged, "it gets very quiet when you squeeze the trigger."

"My God, it's *cold*. . . ." Gale Parker shivered beneath her heavy flight garments. "It's already well below zero. . . . How much worse can this get?"

Indy shrugged, a movement barely visible in his own heavy outfit. "Count on forty or fifty below zero. That's what Henshaw told me. That's why they used special lubricants on our equipment. Regular grease or oil becomes sludge."

Cromwell broke in through the intercom. "Move around back there, you three," he told them. "*Keep* moving as much as you can. Flex your toes in your boots. Beat your hands together. Do whatever you need to keep your blood flowing. Now you know why the Eskimo has so much blubber on his body. Miss Parker, don't you wish you were fat and blubbery?"

"If . . . if it would make me warmer," she said, shivering, *"yes!"*

Indy looked at Gale and Chino. "We're getting up there. We could find our friends at any moment now." He glanced through a cabin window. "We're so high it already seems like we've almost left the world." He shook off the sudden introspection. "Let's check the weapons."

"Wait a moment." Indy turned. Chino continued, "Look, I've been checking the gun positions. You're working the single gun in the belly hatch, right?"

Indy nodded. "That was a last-minute decision. Henshaw's people installed a ball socket mount and cross-bracing. If one of those discs comes up at us, or we're right over the airship, that position could be critical."

"I agree, Indy. But the flooring isn't the strongest. You figure my weight, or even yours. I've been pushing down on the flooring," Chino explained. "It *yields.* And the cold is going to make things brittle. I suggest we put Gale in that position. Secure her with webbing clips to the seat legs so that if anything goes wrong, she'll still be safe."

Indy accepted Chino's observations. Valid, realistic. "Anything else?"

"Yes, there is. You told me to use that open hatch just behind the cockpit. The same ball socket system as we have with the belly gun. But, Indy, I think it would be better if you were closer to the cockpit. We could lose intercom or have some other problems and the pilots would be right next to you if they needed you. I can take the main position in the back, and—"

"If you ladies would like to interrupt your sewing bee for a moment," Cromwell's voice broke in, impatient with all the talking, "you're five minutes past your oxygen checks. Get with it, mates!"

Indy and Chino nodded to one another, went through their systems, exchanged near-empty bottles for full tanks, and did the same for Gale.

"Gentlemen, I thought you'd like to know we're at twenty-three thousand," Cromwell said to them by intercom. "And, blimey, it's already twenty below zero and going down."

Chino shook his head in mock disbelief. "If the old chiefs could see me now," he said in wonder. "The closer we get to the sun, the colder it gets. They would believe the world was mad."

They were near the end of lighthearted exchanges. It was too cold, and getting colder all the time as the Ford pounded upward, the three engines hammering out full power in the steady climb. Even the slightest flaw in the cabin that permitted an inflow of air was like a knife striking a body. The moment belied their senses. The thunderstorms were now distant battlements, first red, then orange, and now blinding white as the sun rose higher. The sky directly above them was darkening strangely to a deeper and deeper purple, and the view all around them was of a steel blue sky, startlingly clear, extending to a horizon that seemed a thousand miles away.

They were shockingly alone, a tiny metal creature throbbing painfully upward. Indy checked the forward machine gun for the fourth time, looking for parts that may have frozen solid. He turned to see Chino weaving on the cabin floor, legs spread apart, one hand gripping a seat back.

"Chino!" Indy called sharply.

"Uh, hear you. Who . . . what . . . world shaking . . . can see bright stars . . ." Chino's voice came over faltering and wavering.

"Get to that bleedin' Indian *now*!" Cromwell shouted,

his voice crackling in their earphones. "He's losing oxygen! Do it *quick*!" Indy moved backward, and bent down to check Chino's oxygen gauge. He had almost a full tank. Then Indy saw the problem just as Chino began to sag. He had unknowingly brushed against the valve wheel and reduced his oxygen flow. He was already into the first stages of hypoxia. Oxygen starvation was insidious. Indy turned the valve to full on and grasped Chino.

"Speak to me," Indy snapped. "Count to ten, *now.*"

"Uh, I do, two, four, no . . ." He shook his head. Indy looked into his eyes. The dim glaze was disappearing. That quickly, he was out of it. "Uh, all right, thanks, Indy—"

"Count!"

Chino rattled off the numbers perfectly. Indy patted him on the arm. "Check your gun. I want a call every five minutes. That goes for you too, Gale."

"I'm having trouble seeing, Indy," she said, pain in her voice.

He checked her oxygen. Everything was fine, including the mask fit. Then he saw what he'd missed. "Your goggles. You've *got* to keep them on. Your eyes are tearing, and the tears are freezing as fast as they come out on your cheeks. Gale, here—" He pulled her goggles over her eyes. "Keep these in place. You can freeze your eyeballs up here."

"God, it hurts. It's all right." She fended off his arm. "I'll be fine."

Cromwell and Foulois were better protected against the cold in the cockpit, where heated air was blasting from bleed manifolds off the nose engine, blowing the hot air across their feet. They could have had more heat within the airplane from wing engine manifolds, but both pilots had insisted the heat from those sources must go to the rocket canisters and the wing guns.

"Twenty-eight thousand," Foulois called back from the cockpit. "We're picking up ice."

He wasn't wasting words. It took only a glance to see frost collecting on the engine-mount struts, icing up the cabin windows and external control cables, all blasted by the equal of a screaming Antarctic storm.

In the cabin Indy, Gale, and Chino worked desperately to keep their bodies warm, beating their hands together, swinging their arms, working toes in their boots. Each time they checked their weapons they had to expose parts of their bodies to the howling gale. The outside temperature was down to fifty-four degrees below zero. The Ford was a block of ice still pushing its way upward.

"Twenty-nine thousand," Cromwell announced. His voice seemed pained. "Check your oxygen, everybody. Call in when you've done that with your gauge readings."

They stumbled over the words but followed Cromwell's orders.

"Controls stiffening," Foulois said.

"Amazing how these engines keep running," Cromwell murmured. "The temps are down in the basement."

Chino's voice came into their reports. "We do not need to fly higher," he said.

"W-why n-not?" stammered Gale.

"Pilots, to our left, a few, maybe two or three thousand feet lower," Chino said carefully. "There it is."

They all looked to their left and slightly below. There was the huge dirigible, reflecting sunlight like a great beacon in the sky.

"Thank the saints they're below us," Cromwell said stiffly. "I don't think the old girl had much left in her. Leveling off, Rene. Gently, gently . . . No, no, keep full power on. We'll need everything we can get. Indy, you with me?"

"Y-yes. Go ahead."

"We've got company, laddie. Look behind and just below the zep. You see what I mean?"

"Uh . . . I don't . . . Got them, Will." Indy had seen sudden bright reflections.

"There's three of them," Cromwell said. "Count on them coming in for a visit."

"Agreed. Gale, Joe . . . your guns. Confirm."

"In position. Strapped and hooked up. Oxygen content seventy percent. Valve full on." Gale was wisely talking in staccato bursts.

"I am with you," Chino called.

"What's your tank showing?" Indy demanded.

"Sixty-five percent. Indy?"

"Go."

"It is *cold* out here." Chino's head and shoulders were exposed to the wind blast down the fuselage.

"It'll be warmer in a few moments, bucko," Cromwell told Chino. Then: "Indy, you still have them in sight?"

"Yeah, Will."

The pilots were banking the Ford gently toward the slowly rising airship. "This is important, Indy," Cromwell continued. "Watch those discs coming in. They're sliding about. Wobbling. They're slick in shape, Indy. That means they haven't much lift up here."

"Indy, Rene here. The Britisher is right. They cannot make any real banks for maneuvering. Watch how they turn, like on a flat table. Do you see?"

Indy watched the discs as they approached in wide, very shallow turns. *They were right.* Those things were devastating down low in thick air, but in this rarefied atmosphere they were barely capable of flight.

"Will, what do you think they'll do?"

"They can't come up sharply from below us," Cromwell answered immediately. "If they try that, leading edge up, they'll stall out. And no pursuit curves, either. Not the way they're flying, like fish out of water. This is a break for us."

"Indy, Rene here. I think they will make a shallow approach from behind. Two of them. Slightly above and behind. They must travel at full speed or they will fall."

"You said two. What about the third?"

"He will attack us from the front."

"Joe, you hear me?" Cromwell called.

"Yes."

"When they come after us from behind I'm going to swing the nose to the right. That will give you a clear shot at the blighters."

"A-all right."

"Not so fast. There's no interruptor mechanism in your weapon. You understand?"

"No."

"It means you've got to be careful you don't shoot our bloody tail right off this machine! Have you got *that*?"

"I have it. Tell them to hurry up. I'm freezing."

"I'll send them a telegram, Joe."

"Indy, right after that pass, the ones from behind," Foulois called, "we must continue our turn, but put the nose down. You understand? That will let you fire at the disc that comes on us from the front. Gale Parker, the one from the front *must* pass beneath us. You will have only a moment to shoot as he goes below you. He cannot climb, so that is how he will fly."

"This ends the sewing circle, ladies!" Cromwell said loudly. "Here they come!"

The discs spewed black smoke behind them as they continued their painful slow turn in toward the Ford. "Get ready . . ." Cromwell said. "Watch those two from behind!"

Chino saw a flashing light at the leading edge of the discs. "They are firing!" he shouted.

Instantly Cromwell shoved in right rudder, swinging the nose to the right, bringing the tail to the left and giving Chino a brief but perfect opportunity. Everything they'd told Chino about short bursts was forgotten as he aimed at a point in space ahead of the discs and squeezed his trigger. Glowing tracers curved out and away in a steady stream.

"Short bursts!" Indy yelled.

His voice went unheard as Chino kept firing. Bullets tore into the Ford's right wingtip, shredding metal, throwing pieces of debris back to vanish from sight. "Hit! Hit!" Chino yelled. "Got him! I see fire! *Eeyah!*"

His tracers had smashed the glass canopy of the disc, and had apparently gone through the cockpit area into a fuel tank. An explosion wracked the disc. The pilot was trying desperately to climb up and away, knowing another disc was about to hit the Ford from the opposite direction. But with the wind screaming into the cockpit and flames tearing at the structure, he was still descending—*straight at the trimotor.*

"Turn left! Turn left!" Indy yelled. "Dive! He's out of control coming straight at us!"

It was a perilous maneuver at this altitude, but they had no choice. Immediately the nose swung left and the right wing went up, as Cromwell brought the Ford around in a sudden diving left turn. Over the roar of their engines a tremendous hollow torching sound burst through the airplane. The disc was out of control, flip-flopping crazily, spewing flames and debris. It passed just under the raised right wing of the Ford, scant feet beneath the plane. The shock wave from its passing smacked the Ford like a giant hand. Cromwell and Foulois fought desperately to keep control. A steep bank at this height could stall them out in a split second. Slowly they brought the Ford from its brief descent, wings level.

A machine-gun burst vibrated through the airplane. "He's below us!" Gale shouted into her microphone. Lying prone, looking down, she'd had a glimpse of the second disc coming into sight. Her reaction was to open fire immediately, shooting wildly in the all-too-brief opportunity. The disc raced ahead of the Ford, easing to the left to remain clear of the third disc, now a gleaming sliver of reflected sunlight racing head-on at them.

"Open fire!" Cromwell shouted to Foulois. "If nothing else you'll give him something to worry about!"

Two machine guns blazed from the wings of the Ford, tracers flashing ahead, sparkling all about the disc. At the same moment they saw the flashing light of the disc's machine gun, firing at the airplane. It came in with tremendous speed. Before they could maneuver, a spray of bullets hammered into the right wing, walking toward the cockpit.

The Ford shuddered as if hit with a truck. "The rocket pack! Right wing!" Indy shouted. "It's gone!" The attack had smashed into the big rocket canister beneath the right wing, mangling the hard-point connections and blowing away the entire system. They were more than lucky. The force of their speed had ripped the rocket pack free before one of the warheads ignited. Well behind and below them, the rocket canister exploded in a searing burst of flame. The wreckage fell away like confetti in a hurricane.

"Will, go for the airship," Indy ordered. "We've got just those three rockets left."

"Don't I know it," Cromwell answered, already easing the trimotor toward the airship. "We'll make it before he can climb much higher," Cromwell went on. "We've still got about fifteen hundred feet on him—good God . . ." They heard the strain in Cromwell's voice. "It's Frenchy. He's hit. Bad. Blood all over the place here. Better get him in the back to stop the bleeding and check his oxygen!"

"Disc is coming in!" they heard Chino shouting. "Behind us and lower. I cannot get aim at him!"

"Gale!" Indy called. "I can see him. When I tell you to, aim your weapon behind you in direct line with the fuselage. He may just fly into your tracers."

"But I'll be shooting blind!"

"You have a better idea? Just shut up and get ready to fire! Okay, he's committed . . . coming in just below us, and he's firing. . . ."

They felt bullets striking the tail. Cromwell shoved hard right rudder, then left, moving the plane from side to side to throw off their attacker's aim. Gale screamed; she was being rolled from side to side herself.

The ball-socket gun mount was a rushed affair. In the bitter cold, the metal had shrunk and become brittle. Indy yelled to her, "Fire now!" and she squeezed the trigger. The sudden movements of the plane, Gale's trying to keep from bouncing around even in her harness, and the bucking recoil of the machine gun were too much for the makeshift system. Metal tore, the cross-mounts snapped like sticks, and the machine gun fell away from the airplane.

Gale had a glimpse of a brilliant disc flashing into view, in line with falling wreckage. She stared in disbelief as the machine gun slammed into the canopy of the disc, shattering the glass and smashing against the pilot. A convulsive jerk at the controls of the disc sent it whirling crazily, all lift gone, the machine in a killer high-speed stall. It spun away like a whirling dervish, spewing forth wreckage and fuel. Far below them, flame blossomed and the disintegrating disc fell toward final destruction.

"Someone help me! HELP!"

Gale's voice . . . in his headset. Indy looked back to

the belly gun position. *Gale was gone!* He saw her legs snagged in her safety harness. From the knees down she was still in the cabin, but the rest of her body was outside in that punishing frigid air. The air blast buffeted her madly, several times slamming her against the belly of the airplane. Indy started toward her, and saw Chino scrambling forward from the rear of the cabin. The Ford rolled wildly to one side. In their clumsy garments and oxygen tanks, they were helpless to get to Gale. She screamed again for someone to help her.

Indy reacted without time for deliberate thought. There was one chance. He grabbed the zipper toggle of his flight suit and yanked it full down, giving him access within the suit. In a moment he pulled his whip free from its snap-lock by his waist. He knew this would be the single most important throw he had ever done. He aimed carefully, bracing himself, and snapped the whip forward. The far end struck Gale's right leg and wrapped about her ankle. Indy braced himself against a seat, holding on with all his strength.

"Joe! I can hold her a while! Get to her!" In the same breath: "Hang on, Gale. . . ."

She screamed something unintelligible. Indy didn't blame her if she was calling him every rotten name under the sun. *Hang on?* With her hands flailing empty air?

Chino was on his hands and knees, moving as fast as he could along the cabin floor to reach Gale. Her body swung wildly as one of the two last restraining straps gave way. Her life now hung by one strap and Indy's bullwhip. Time was rushing away from them. Chino braced himself, grasped her left leg, and pulled her up like a child as Indy also pulled with the whip. Then she was partially back in the cabin. Chino's right arm shot out to circle her waist. Holding grimly to her body, he rolled flat on the cabin floor as far from the gaping hole as he could move.

Indy stumbled forward, fell to his knees, and grabbed a fistful of flight suit. Together they pulled her back into the airplane, dragging her forward toward the cockpit.

Her face was bloody. Beneath the red smears and splotches, her skin was dead-white from the blasting wind and cold. "Oxygen," Indy said to Chino. "Quickly! She's lost her bottle. Get another one."

Chino was gone. Immediately Indy took a deep breath, held it, and hooked Gale's oxygen line to his own bottle. Almost at once he started feeling dizzy. Fighting to retain his senses, he hooked his bottle to Gale's waist. Darkness began closing in as peripheral vision faded. The next moment the bright lights dancing before his eyes dimmed; then Chino was there by his side with a full bottle, hooking him up.

"Joe, get up front. Try to bring Rene back here from the cockpit. Gale will be okay in a moment. But whatever happens, make sure Rene has oxygen. Stop any bleeding. Gale will help; she knows what to do."

Joe went forward. Indy put his hand to Gale's face. She gripped it tightly. "It's all right. I'll be okay. Just help me up so I can help Rene."

"Indy! Will here. Come forward. Joe's got Rene. He's shot up. I need you with me."

Indy worked his way past Chino as he moved Rene to a sitting position against the cabin wall. He slipped into Rene's seat. "Tell me what to do," he said to Cromwell.

"They've decided to run for it," Cromwell told him. "You can just make out that third disc that was after us. He's behind the airship and trying to get back on board. It's a bloody stupid move, I'll tell you that."

Cromwell was shoving as hard on the throttles as he could, trying to squeeze every ounce of speed from the Ford. "Why . . . I mean, what you said," Indy asked.

"Why, that pancake can't slow down this high," Cromwell said quickly. "We've just seen that. The way he's going he'll be three hundred miles an hour faster than that gasbag. Go right on through that thing like a nightmare on the loose. If I don't miss my guess, whoever's flying that airship will have to tell that disc to bug off. Otherwise they'll be shooting at their own man."

"All right. What do you want me to do?"

"Indy, m'boy, it pains me to say this, but we're going to get only one whack at that bloated ugly out there. Take a look at the gauges for the right engine."

"Which—"

"The ones marked number three. The oil pressure, laddie. It's going downhill. And so will we the moment that engine seizes up. I've got to stop that before it does, or we may have a fire on our hands. Look under the right wing, Indy."

"I see what you mean." Indy stared at the huge black stain covering the underside of the wing above and behind the engine. "We took some hits. Same time they blew away the rocket canister. Okay, let's get that zep, Will. *Now.*"

"It's in the cards, m'boy. Now, see that red T-handle in the center of the panel?"

Indy leaned forward, pointing, then reaching for the handle.

"Don't!"

"What—"

"Not yet, not yet. When you pull that handle, it ignites the rockets in the canister under the left wing. All three rockets will fire off at the same time. I'll tell you when, and it will be soon, and—Look at that bloody fool!"

They watched the disc approaching the zeppelin from the rear. It was like a speeding bullet racing after a sluggish huge animal trying desperately to get out of the way. "See the landing platform? That works fine at low altitude, but up here that thing simply cannot hover."

"Or even fly slow," Indy observed.

"Right you are. Now, if I'm right, they'll swing the tail of that blimp up and to the left and—there it goes!"

Much closer now to the great airship, they could see in greater detail. The disc pilot was obviously desperate to return safely to the zeppelin. Indy watched a spume of dark smoke whirling about the disc as it slowed for its approach and landing on the zeppelin ramp.

"Unless I miss my guess, off he goes," Cromwell said.

They watched the disc wobble from side to side, a skittering crablike motion. "He's losing it!" Indy called.

"That he is . . ." Cromwell murmured. "Ah, the bottom is falling out."

The disc slewed wildly, trying to match the sudden motion of the airship as Cromwell had predicted. It was a mistake on the part of both craft. Unable to maintain altitude and control, the disc swept to one side, brushing the lower great vertical rudder of the airship. It tore through, and began a long plunge to the earth more than five miles below.

"We'll never have a better chance," Cromwell said. "We've got to attack before that engine quits on us."

"How long . . . how much longer?" Indy asked.

"I'm getting into position now. We've got to come around for a frontal attack. That will give us only one shot at them. We'll dive toward the blighter, and I'll hold the dive angle so you can yank on that handle. Starting to turn now."

The airship loomed impossibly huge. Whoever was commanding the monster realized what the Ford pilot was attempting, for dark smoke suddenly increased behind the zeppelin. "He's gone to full power, Indy. Get ready. It's now or never."

All thoughts of the bitter cold, the dying engine, the damage they had taken—were gone. Nothing existed but that airship. It swelled swiftly in size as Cromwell began his dive, straight at the tremendous form. The scream of the wind increased, and suddenly the cold was back again as icy fingers stabbed through bullet holes in the windshield. The cold was physical, like being struck viciously.

Faster and faster dove the Ford, unable to slow its descent in the thin air at their height. "They're shooting at us!" Indy called out. He'd just seen the dark areas atop the dirigible becoming large enough to make out what they were. Machine-gun nests atop the airship! Tracers sparkled and danced in the sky as they seemed to float upward against the Ford. They felt bullets striking the airplane. The Ford shuddered and yawed to one side; Cromwell fought her back.

He squeezed a button on his control yoke. The Ford shook and rattled as the two forward-firing machine guns hurled tracers at the airship. "That should throw them off!" Cromwell shouted.

The right engine exploded. The sudden violence hurled the propeller away from the engine, flinging it well off to the side. Cromwell shouted to Indy. "The left rudder pedal! Stand on it, laddie, *stand on it!*"

Indy pressed down with all his strength, both men pushing left rudder as hard as they could to keep the airplane diving straight. The top of the zeppelin filled the entire world, a monstrous thing beyond belief, machine guns sparkling as they continued to fire.

"The handle! Get ready!" Cromwell shouted.

Indy reached forward, ready for the call.

"NOW! PULL THE HANDLE!"

Indy yanked back, a sharp sudden motion. He looked past Cromwell at the left wing. In a sudden fury of activity, the nose cone blew away from the underwing canister, flame speared backwards as the rockets ignited, and three long tubes rushed forward from the airplane, trailing flame and smoke as they arrowed downward into the spine of the great ship before them.

Dark spots appeared on the shiny fabric, then the rockets were gone. "What the devil happened?" Indy shouted to Cromwell. "There wasn't any explosion!"

"There will be—" Cromwell cut himself short as he pulled back on the yoke. "Ease off on that rudder pedal," he ordered. The Ford rolled to the right and the nose came around. They sped past the airship, a toy against a giant. As they flashed by, Indy saw a stab of flame appear along the flank of the zeppelin.

To his left, Cromwell was frantically moving controls and switches, to cut off fuel and power to the shattered right engine. "We've got a fire of our own," he said grimly. He reached to the panel and pulled another handle. "Watch the right engine," he ordered.

White mist engulfed the engine briefly, streaming back through the wreckage, and was flung away by the wind. "Fire extinguisher," Cromwell said. "Did it work?"

"No more fire," Indy told him. The shriek of wind was overwhelming. Cromwell was pulling back on the yoke, easing the Ford from its crazy dive. He maintained their descent, but under control this time, able to bank the airplane better, to see the airship.

"Take a look, lad," he said, quietly this time.

Flame billowed from the flanks of the airship. "What's happening?" Indy asked. "That thing is filled with helium and helium doesn't burn—"

"Right," Cromwell told him. "But it's also got a devil of

a load of fuel for those jet engines. That magnesium, once it's ignited, will keep right on burning through the metal structure, and that means the fire worked its way down to the fuel tanks and ate right through the metal. That fire is their fuel. I'd say we've done a day's good work, because—"

There was no need to say more. A savage glare appeared along the sides and belly of the airship. Indy understood now that blazing magnesium had breached the fuel tanks. Fuel spilled outward, ignited violently, and sent flames hurtling through the fuel storage area. The huge airship wallowed like a stricken whale, dying before their eyes as explosions wracked the structure. Debris and bodies spilled outward. Indy stared as crewmen, arms and legs flailing helplessly, began the long fall toward the earth.

Another blast, a great gout of flame, and the zeppelin buckled amidships, its back broken. The flames continued to spread, and two huge masses tumbled downward, twisting and turning in seeming agony as they dropped to final destruction.

"You need me up here right now?" Indy asked Cromwell.

"Not now. We're below twenty thousand, and I'll keep her going down like an elevator until we're at fourteen. Then we can all take off these miserable oxy systems and breathe like normal people again."

Indy climbed from the cockpit. Back in the cabin he moved immediately to the side of Foulois. Chino was cradling the unmoving Frenchman in his huge arms. Foulois's oxygen mask was gone from his face, telling Indy what he feared most of all.

Indy met Chino's eyes. They didn't need words to say that Rene Foulois was dead.

Gale sat to one side, quietly. Indy saw she had been

crying. Now she was numb, inside and out. Rene Foulois was gone, and they had been on the thin edge of death themselves. Gale had frostbite on her face; she suffered her own pain. Finally she looked up.

"Did we . . ." Her voice faltered.

"We did," Indy said quietly as he could and still be heard over the roar of engines and wind.

"Masks off now," Cromwell announced from the cockpit. They turned their valves to the off position and removed masks and goggles. Indy unsnapped the heavy mouth cover. It was already much warmer at their lower altitude. He helped Gale with her face protection and goggles and removed her oxygen mask. Her lips were still trembling. He looked sternly at her.

"Put your goggles back on," he ordered. "The wind is wild through the bullet holes in the cockpit. Now, get up there."

Her eyes went wide. "I . . . I can't. I—"

"Yes, you *can.* And you will. *You're a pilot!* Will needs help up front. We're coming down with two engines and the right wing chewed up, and we've got a busted airplane on our hands. So get up there and *fly.*"

For a long moment she stared at Indy. She rose slowly, stood before him. "You know something, Professor Jones? I think I love you."

She brushed her lips against his, and was gone.

Indy leaned against the cabin wall. He looked sadly at Foulois.

"He was a very good man," Indy said. "An ace in the war against the Germans. Strange for him to die here, like this."

"Not so strange," said Jose Syme Chino. "All things have their special time. *This* also was a war. A battle between good and evil. As are all great struggles. This man, who had wings, there is a special place for his kind with the Great Spirits."

Indy nodded slowly as they continued their return to earth.

"Amen," he said.

THE END

Afterword

OF COURSE IT'S REAL!

Recently—the summer of 1991—I was a guest speaker at the Institute of Advanced Learning in Lincoln, Nebraska, and the subject that raised the greatest interest and brought in a standing-room-only crowd was, not unexpectedly, a serious study of UFO's. During the question-and-answer period which gave the audience free rein to ask anything they wanted to ask, and likely never before had the opportunity to get an answer, I was asked the inevitable question. Had *I* ever seen a UFO? And if I had, what did it look like and what did it do?

I admit to tweaking my audience. Like most people I've seen UFO's through a lifetime, but in this instance I am being *very* specific. In other words, I had seen at different times *something* in the sky I could not identify: a flash of light, a colorful ray, a physical object too distant to make out any details. The object I saw was simply impossible to identify. Hardly very exciting.

So I told my audience about an absolutely incredible sighting of many years past, a sighting in broad daylight, under perfect visual conditions, with thunder rolling like the end of the world from the heavens.

"It was a vessel utterly alien to me," I related. "It was absolutely incredible. Nearly a thousand feet long! It sailed across the earth maybe fifteen hundred, perhaps two thousand feet high. It was so huge it partially blocked out the sun. Its deep groaning roar sent birds fleeing and animals dashing for safety. It was silvery, splendid, magnificent as it passed over, and I watched it until it vanished beyond the horizon."

Well, not many people believed me. In fact, I doubt if anybody in that crowd believed a word of what I'd told them. I asked for a show of hands from anyone who believed that what I'd told them was absolutely, unquestionably real.

Not one hand went up. I'd struck out. Zero belief. Then I dropped my "belief bomb."

"I don't know why you find what I just described to you as too fantastic to believe. What I was seeing was also witnessed by millions of other people. I was standing beneath the USS *Akron,* sister ship to the equally huge USS *Macon,* the two enormous dirigibles of the United States Navy that were in service in the early 1930's. And, of course, never having seen such a sight before, or having known of these two massive sky vessels, the ship blocking out the sun *was* alien to me!"

Even if it was some sixty years ago.

It was another wonderful moment of fact being stranger than fiction. And remembering that moment, and others like it—such as those times when I flew a jet fighter in pursuit of other objects in the sky that I never caught up with and never did identify—helped me decide that in *INDIANA JONES AND THE SKY PIRATES,* everything that seems exotic, wonderful, marvelous—*and impossible*—is all based on hard, provable, reality.

· · ·

Airships, the bloated, clumsy cigar-shapes put together from bedsheets, ropes, and clumsy rigging first carried men into the air more than a hundred years ago. Some maneuvered through the skies by men pedaling madly on bicycles that turned propellers instead of wheels. Others used dangerous engines powered with benzine, dangerous because they often burned and exploded in flight, ending promising careers with a fiery finality. Huge dirigibles, notably those from the Zeppelin works in Germany, performed from 1914 to 1918 with astonishing success. They bombed British cities, and in turn they were blasted from the skies by antiaircraft fire and fighter planes. The German L-35 began a new era by carrying aloft an Albatross D-111 fighter plane, and releasing it for protection, like a swift hawk covering a giant plump chicken in the sky. Soon British dirigibles were carrying fighter planes, releasing them in flight and recovering them as well—the predecessors to the huge dirigible in our own story in this book. And nearly seventy-five years ago, Germany's L-53 had already climbed to more than 21,000 feet above the earth.

After that war ended in 1918, dirigibles became ever larger, faster, more powerful, and amazingly *reliable*—again setting the stage for the mighty airship in our story. Even today, it is difficult to believe the splendid record of certain airships of past times, such as Germany's *Graf Zeppelin,* which in the time span of nine years flew a total of 17,179 hours in 590 separate flights! The famed *Graf* flew from Europe to America, to South America and the Middle East, crossed the Arctic on an exciting adventure for its passengers, and then flew around the world on a leisurely tour that even today seems like a dream. Before the *Graf Zeppelin* was retired after its nine years of service, it had taken aloft, in luxury and perfect safety, more than 34,000 people.

So what you have read in these pages about a great airship and the flying machines it carried, releasing and recovering them in flight, has a great "reality foundation" in aviation history.

BUT—JET ENGINES IN 1930?

If you search through your history books on aviation, or study thick encyclopedias, or wander through jet aviation exhibits in museums, you are certain to be informed that the first jet airplane took to the skies in August of 1939. This was a Heinkel He-178 of Germany, and it represented a highwater mark in aviation progress.

But it wasn't the first jet flight—which established another foundation for our story. In fact, the He-178 made its first flight *nearly thirty years* after the Frenchman, Henri Coanda, lunged into the skies from the airfield at Issy-les-Moulineaux in France. The year was 1910, and not only did Coanda make the first jet flight (short and disastrous though it was), but he also designed the jet engine for his own sleek biplane jet. Today, the second biplane jet Coanda built is still on display at a French aviation museum. The first machine of its type was publicly displayed in 1910 at the Salon Aeronautique in Paris.

This writer interviewed Henri Coanda at great length, and a marvelous time it was, being with one of the greatest aviation pioneers of history. Coanda began to develop his ideas for a jet engine in 1904, when he attended the French School of Advanced Aeronautic Study. From this learning period he designed and continued to improve on a jet engine he called the turbo-propulsor. His friend, Clerget, built the engine from Coanda's design drawings, and it was installed in the sleek biplane, also of Coanda's design.

Since Coanda flew his jet in 1910, some twenty years before our story takes place, there was certainly plenty of time to develop the original crude jet engine into a powerful and reliable system for the flying discs that Indiana Jones had to face.

But why haven't we heard more of Coanda? Because while he managed to take off in his jet, his landing was a thundering crash. He was performing taxi tests. That is, running the Coanda Jet along the airport to test its power and its brakes, so the pilot would know what to expect before his first attempt to fly. To Coanda's surprise, his jet engine was far more powerful than he'd anticipated, and when he pushed his throttle forward, jet flames burst back from the engine, and it howled like a huge dragon. Before Coanda could stop his machine, it leaped into the sky. When Coanda looked up there was a wall in front of him. Desperately, he yanked off power and hauled back on the control stick, and the Coanda Jet fell off to one side and smashed into the ground. Coanda was thrown clear and was only bruised, but the airplane burned to a skeleton.

In our story we encountered Coanda developing his first jet engine and airplane in 1910, and we ran into him again during World War I when he developed a rocket gun for the French Army. He also applied for a patent (in 1914) for his jet engine. All this is factual history, and it establishes the basis for the jet engines in the flying discs.

In fact, Coanda was also responsible for several flying saucer designs which, when they were made public many years after he worked on those astonishing machines, were known as Lenticular Aerodynes. *And they worked.* So that if the reader assumes that even the flying saucers in our story are, or can be, real—*you're right!*

. . .

The jet engines in this book are based on Coanda's designs built and tested in 1910, and patented in France in 1914. Had the French government, or individual investors, supported Coanda's work, then World War I, from 1914 to 1918, might well have been fought with jet fighters and bombers. But the *immediate* need for planes overshadowed what most Frenchmen had never even heard of, and government authorities looked with suspicion upon anything that revolutionary.

The Coanda engine, as it developed, would have been perfect for the giant dirigible and the flying discs in our story. It fired up like an ordinary combustion engine, but its power came from a rotary system operating at great speed within the engine. The spinning motion created a partial vacuum that drew in huge amounts of air. Then the engine compressed that air, mixed it with fuel, and lit the entire affair in the manner of a continuous explosion. This spun even more blades to increase the flow of air, the density of the fuel-air mixture, the temperature within the engine, and the speed of hot gases hurled back from the engine. There you have it—not merely a workable jet engine, but one that increased its power and compression the faster it moved. And the faster it flew, the greater was its power, so that continuing to develop the Coanda engine gave us the perfect propulsion for the discs and the dirigible that so astonished everyone.

Of course there were still problems to overcome in balancing and controlling the flight direction of the discs, but from the same fertile mind of Henri Coanda came that solution. In his Coanda Effect, the Frenchman proved that by blowing a powerful jet along a flat surface (or engine vane), the flow of the jet will follow the flat surface, and even hug that surface as it begins to move into a circular shape. Coanda designed an Aerodyne machine that created through this effect a partial vacuum above a wing (or a disc in the form of an airfoil) shape. With normal pressure beneath the disc, there was then created a tremendous lifting force. Coanda then designed his jet system into a perfect disc which gave him what he called Three-Dimensional Propulsion. As to balance, the air whirling at tremendous speed in circular motion around the rim of his disc turned the entire disc into a wonderful gyroscope. It always pointed, when flying, to true north. So when the disc maneuvered, it didn't bank and turn like an airplane, but moved in a "skidding motion" through the air. The pilot cockpit swiveled to keep the pilot pointed in whatever direction he desired, and by changing pressure along different parts of the edge of the flying disc, he was able to turn in whatever direction he chose.

Result: a flying saucer. It took years for the Coanda Effect, and Coanda's unique jet engine design, to actually be built and test flown, but the Canadian government finally assembled the Aerodyne shape—and many years ago actually flew its own flying saucer.

Let's return, even if briefly, to the subject of UFO's as they have been reported for thousands of years. As we pointed out in the story—and every reference to historical sightings of strange and unidentified objects in the skies is absolutely true—the entire subject of the UFO has been an area of great controversy. The truth is that there's no question that strange objects hurtle through our skies. There have been many sightings by highly experienced observers, and, since 1947, UFO's have been captured on film, tracked by telescopes, followed on radar, and had close encounters with manned aircraft.

It may seem strange that the most reliable reports and sightings do *not* become available to the public. Many UFO sightings by military forces are immediately classified. They cannot be explained, and our government dislikes intensely being on the "hot spot" as unable to verify what's streaking through our skies faster and higher than any airplanes we have in the air.

Because so many reports have been subjected to ridicule, airline captains and top pilots almost to a man refuse to comment publicly on discs and other craft—which are *not* known to be the property of any country on this planet—they have encountered in flight. This writer has hundreds of such reports from pilots who provided amazing details of the startling objects they have encountered in flight.

Also, when I was in the U.S. Air Force, I participated in UFO-sightings investigations, talking to hundreds of witnesses who had encountered, on the ground and in the air, objects they could not identify. Many reports turned out to be dead ends. Others were exactly the opposite. As a pilot, I have also pursued UFO's while flying high-speed jets. I have chased a startlingly huge disc at low altitude when flying a B-25 bomber; it easily outmaneuvered us and then flew away as if we were standing still in the air. What was it?

I do not know for certain, and I will not draw a firm conclusion when so much hard information is lacking. What we are facing is a mystery that, at least publicly, has yet to be explained in acceptable terms. But the mystery is real; there *are* strange and unidentified objects in our skies, and we'll just have to live with that reality until we learn enough to, hopefully, understand what's been tearing through our skies for so many thousands of years.

HOW ABOUT THAT TRIMOTOR?

There's an enormous difference between *writing* about the way an airplane flies and how it will perform, and the way it feels to the pilot flying the airplane. Writing is one thing, and actually flying what is now an ancient trimotor like the Ford in this book is quite something else. So it's a great pleasure to be able to relate to the reader that the feel, the sense, and the handling of the trimotor in this book comes from the actual flying.

This writer owned and flew a Junkers Ju-52/3m German trimotor that was both a transport and a bomber. It was much bigger and heavier than the Ford, but they were remarkably alike in many respects. In addition to flying the Ju-52 and the Ford, there was yet another old trimotor in which I had the chance to get to know and feel the airplane at the controls, a high-wing Stinson. By the time I'd put in a great many hours in the left seat of these grand old machines, I knew for certain that they were capable of incredible performance and versatility that still astounds today's pilots. Relating specifically to the Ford Trimotor in this book, the reader will no doubt be surprised to find that the barnstormers of old—the daredevil pilots who would fly as an "air circus" from town to town—actually used the Ford as an aerobatic airplane in dangerous maneuvers at extremely low heights! They would loop the airplane "right on the deck," take it up higher, and spin earthward, fascinating and amazing the awed crowds watching these remarkable flights.

But there's another level of accuracy, as well. Ford Trimotors *were* flown by the U.S. Army. Some Fords *were* loaded with machine-gun positions, bomb racks, and other armament, and used in combat in different parts of the world. Everything the Ford does in these pages it did in real life. It's another case of reality outperforming fiction.

SKY CITY

Can there really be such a place as Sky City—*Acoma*—that seems more like a work of imagination than reality? An entire city atop a great mesa in a harsh desert land so vast that the city seems isolated and unknown—yet is really the oldest continuously inhabited community in all the Americas?

Again we are in a land where fact is stranger than fiction, for the ancient sky pueblo called *Acoma* is still inhabited today, and supports the Acoma Indians with ever-growing vitality. Acoma lies to the southwest of the New Mexico city of Albuquerque, and, as described in this book, it is surrounded by such fascinating lands as the Laguna Indian Reservation, with Elephant Butte Reservoir and its great lava fields to the south, as is the community with the improbable name of Truth or Consequences. Further south are the ramparts and scars of the modern age—the great dunes of White Sands where huge rockets and missiles flew in the experiments to open the space age, and near Alamagordo, the town of Trinity, host to the first atomic bomb ever exploded.

Were it not for the National Endowment for the Humanities which in 1973 made a grant to establish accurate histories of four great Indian tribes, including the Acoma, much of the past might well have been lost forever. The Acoma have believed, as far back into the mists and dust of history will reveal, that their people and their lands all were created beneath the earth, in a huge underground world they called Shipapu. When two sisters, Nautsiti and Iatiku, emerged from the subterranean holdings and were exposed to the sun, the first people and everything of Acoma sprang into existence at that moment. The spirits that protected Acoma produced husbands for the sisters, and in time their descendants became the Indians that populated the land, cared for flocks of animals, and farmed the grounds.

It seems strange when reviewing the history of what is now the heartland of the United States of America to discover that the "old times" of several hundred years ago were dominated by Spanish explorers and conquerers. Yet, the old records show that in the year 1629 Juan Ramirez, a priest with a Spanish expedition, was sent from that expedition (on its way to explore the Pueblo of Zuni) to see what might be the needs of the Acoma. For the Spaniards had been unduly harsh in their first encounters with the Acoma, and in 1599, a marauding expedition under Vicente de Zaldivar had wrecked the Acoma communities. The records show that what the Spanish had once destroyed, they then worked closely with the Acoma Indians to rebuild. Their city became stronger and more prosperous than ever, and on the great flatland mesa hundreds of feet above the desert floor, the Indians created a new Acoma with houses three stories high, and accepted Spanish design and religion as their own.

Yet long before the Spaniards, the great community on Acoma Mesa had thrived for multiple generations. When twenty years ago the effort was begun to record the ancient histories, it was learned that Acoma was but one name by which these people were known; others included Acu, Akome, Acuo, Acuco and Ako. All these names make a direct reference that, translated, means that this community of Acoma, atop the great mesa, is the "place that always was."

The first time I saw Acoma came as a surprise so great I wasn't certain that what I saw was real. At the time I was flying a single-engine plane, a Beech Debonair (N935T) on a tour of America from the air, and my friend and photographer, Jim Yarnell, was shooting with a Leica camera marvelous pictures of a country few Americans had ever seen. We crossed the great target areas in the desert where atomic bombs had been tested and huge mushrooms had grown into the sky, then passed over lava fields, empty desert and, suddenly, before us, a huge mesa with a city sprawled across its top! We circled what I came to learn was *Acoma Pueblo*—meaning *Sky City*. The huge vertical cliffs were imposing, like great battlements rearing vertically from a vast and dry ocean. It was easy to see why the Spanish expeditions had judged Acoma Pueblo a fortress that was "the strongest ever seen" and "an inaccessible stronghold."

Soon after my first sighting of Sky City from the air, I had the chance to visit Acoma from the ground. With that airplane available, we also gained permission to visit the Indian lands in the great desert country, landing on dirt roads and visiting a people who not too long ago in history were mighty warriors defending their homeland.

The wars are behind us. Acoma Pueblo flourishes again as it has not done for a long time. Its history has been preserved, its traditions saved for all of us.

But make no mistake—it is as imposing and mighty as it was when the Spaniards first saw this ancient city battlement rising high above the rest of the world.

About the Author

The author of nearly 200 published books, several dozen technical and flight manuals and several thousand magazine and newspaper articles and series, Martin Caidin is one of the outstanding aeronautics and aviation authorities in the world. He has several times won the Aviation/Space Writers Association top awards as the outstanding author in the field of aviation and has also been honored as a "master storyteller" by aviation and science organizations throughout the world. He is the only civilian to have lived and flown with the USAF Thunderbirds jet aerobatic team (and won high honors for his book on that experience). He is also a member of the Ten-Ton Club of England for his supersonic flying in the earlier days of "Mach-busting," and is as well known for his stunt flying and airshow performances as he is for his writing. He has flown dozens of types of military and civilian planes throughout the U.S. as a movie stunt pilot and airshow performer. Caidin is the former Consultant to the Commander of the Air Force Missile Test Center and was involved in rocket, missile and spacecraft development from its earliest days. Of his more than 40 novels, *Cyborg* became his best known work when it was developed into the "Six Million Dollar Man" and "Bionic Woman" television series. Caidin lives with his wife, Dee Dee M. Caidin, in Cocoa Beach, Florida.

STAR WARS®

A three book cycle by Timothy Zahn

[] **Heir to the Empire** (29612-4 * $5.99/$6.99 Canada)
Five years after the events of *Return of the Jedi* Leia Organa and Han Solo have shouldered the burdens of creating the new Republic. Luke Skywalker is the first in a hoped-for new line of Jedi Knights. But many light years away, the last of the Emperor's warlords has taken command of the remains of the Imperial fleet to launch a campaign to destroy the Republic.

[] **Dark Force Rising** (56071-9 * $5.99/$6.99 Canada)
Dissention and personal ambition threaten to tear the Republic apart. As the pregnant Princess Leia risks her life to ally a proud, lethal alien race with the Republic, Han and Lando race against time to find proof of treason inside the Republic Council. But most dangerous of all is a new Dark Jedi, consumed by bitterness...and throughly insane.

[] **The Last Command** (hardcover * 09186-7 * $21.95/ $26.95 Canada) While Han and Chewbacca struggle to form an uneasy alliance of smugglers for a last-ditch attack against the Empire, Leia fights to keep the Alliance together and prepares for the birth of her twins. But the odds are against them: Admiral Thrawn's resources are huge, and only a small force led by Luke to infiltrate Thrawn's power base has any hope of toppling the last remnants of the Empire or of challenging C'baoth, the Dark Jedi.

Available at your local bookstore or use this page to order.

Send to: Bantam Books, Dept. SF 128
2451 S. Wolf Road
Des Plaines, IL 60018

Please send me the items I have checked above. I am enclosing $____________ (please add $2.50 to cover postage and handling). Send check or money order, no cash or C.O.D.'s, please.

Mr./Ms.____

Address____

City/State_____________________________Zip__________
Please allow four to six weeks for delivery.
Prices and availability subject to change without notice. SF128--11/93